Son

Carol Birch is a writer with an extraordinary imagination. She has published two novels in Britain, both of which were prize-winners: *Life in the Palace* secured the 1988 David Higham Award for the Best First Novel of the Year and *The Fog Line* won the prestigious Geoffrey Faber Memorial Prize in 1991. Her novella, *The Unmaking,* was published in America in 1992.

Carol Birch was born in 1951 in Manchester, and educated at Manchester Central Grammar School and Keele University, where she read English and American Studies. After university she worked in London at a variety of jobs, and from 1980 to 1987 lived in south-west Ireland. Returning to London, she taught students with severe and moderate learning difficulties at South Thames College in Putney.

She now lives in Lancaster with her husband and two small sons.

Also by Carol Birch

Life in the Palace
The Fog Line
The Unmaking

CAROL BIRCH

Songs of the West

Mandarin

A Mandarin Paperback
SONGS OF THE WEST

First published in Great Britain 1994
by William Heinemann Ltd
This edition published 1995
by Mandarin Paperbacks
an imprint of Reed Consumer Books Limited
Michelin House, 81 Fulham Road, London SW3 6RB
and Auckland, Melbourne, Singapore and Toronto

Copyright © Carol Birch 1994
The Author has asserted her moral rights

A CIP catalogue record for this title
is available from the British Library
ISBN 0 7493 1828 7

Printed and bound in Great Britain by
BPC Paperbacks Ltd
A member of
The British Printing Company Ltd

For Martin

For Martin

Part One

Part One

1

Con drank his tea standing in the doorway, gazing at the yard in a kind of trance. His belly bulged over his belt, thick golden hair gleamed on his arms. He revived after a while and turned to her, smiling. His face was boyish with a thickening jaw and incipient jowls not quite hidden by a small rough beard. 'Will I go into town?' he said, and answered himself. 'Why not? And just drop in and get the fence posts from the Creamery and see if there's any sign around of the idiot son, while I'm about it. Do you want anything?'

Marie came and stood at the open door and poured a lumpy grey glue of porridge into the big metal bowl for the dogs. They had their faces in it before she'd finished, snorting and wolfing, the sides of their red mouths dripping a gummy excess which they lapped back up immediately. The cats came running across the wrinkled flagstones. Con was getting into the old dogstooth jacket. 'Shoo!' she said. 'Shoo! You'll get yours.' Then, 'No, you go, Connie, I have things to do.'

When he'd gone and the house was quiet she washed her face and combed her thick, slightly flossy fair hair, put on her jacket and went out for her walk. The mist had lifted and the mountains were clear. The sky was white, the grasses on top of the wall completely still. A few brown hens idled round the sheds, crooning, and a small white and mottled cat walked through the field. Marie closed the gate and crossed a narrow grey ribbon of lane, then followed a track that trickled over the mountain through rocks and gorse and heather, throwing out tributaries here and there. She saw no one, pushing on higher to where mangy grey sheep with black legs occasionally lifted their heads to watch her pass. At a certain point she turned from the path. A hare-track dipped down among the gorse and steeply up and over rocks to a little grassy place from where she could see the entire valley. Here she

3

sat down.

A mile away the sea and sky were just a pale enormity. She could see her own house and the other little scattered houses, the grey smudge of Ballinaphuca village, the ragged patterned fields, the twisting lanes, a car going over Miley's Gap towards Strangarvan, and Tim Pat Malachi fixing a fence in his big field below the plantation. But she wasn't looking at any of this, she'd come to spy on Bob Sawle's wagon, distant below at the end of a vertical ravine with gnarly offshoots, a plucked grapestalk full of rocks and bracken. The wagon was picturesque, wooden with yellow wheels and shutters and a little tin-pot crooked chimney on a curved roof. It stood on a patch of rough scrubland owned by a Dutch fellow who'd come and gone and rented it out now to these types who came, these hippies or artists or what have you. There was a brown-brackened gully beyond, an iron gate, the remains of a house like the stump of a tooth, and a track down to the road into the village.

The top half of the door was open but there was no sign of life. A car was parked nearby, a big old bottle-green thing with a fat outline. She was smitten; it was awful, unbecoming, there wasn't an ounce of pleasure in it. She'd been coming to this spot since early summer when he'd first arrived; she'd seen the hay-making, the tourist tents come and go, the carts laden with turf coming down from Rossa. And after all, she said to herself, what harm is there in it? It's a nice spot to sit and if anyone sees me, and they might, I'm just having a rest on my walk and looking at the view. But it was a ridiculous way to behave, this schoolgirl mooning; ridiculous to be in thrall to this awesome draining thing that had somehow crept up on her. She had a girl of fourteen and a boy of twelve. She was sensible. She sold him his milk and eggs, they always got orders from the wagon.

It was November. Marie shivered on the cold hillside, sitting with her coat collar turned up, a woolly hood standing out about her face. She lit a cigarette and smoked peacefully, slitting her eyes at the glare on the sea. I'll give him ten minutes, she thought, I'll not wait all day. She smoked with great pleasure, smiling and relaxing. Sharp little breezes sprang up and nipped at her hair. The sea had a choppy look. It dawned on her that someone was

4

approaching from the main track. 'Ah shit!' she whispered. A stupid female voice hummed. Marie sat very still, her face burning, pleading, please, please, go on past, don't find me.

'Aha, it's you! Found you out!'

Marie composed her face into a welcoming smile. Not her, she was thinking, anyone but Big Mouth.

A thin woman in her forties in a big dirty camel-hair coat, probably a man's, stood over her. A flat cap was on her head, a delicate lilac scarf around her neck hanging down past her waist. She was wearing impenetrable sunglasses and the reddish hair sprouting from under the hat had a dry, dark, dusty quality like the fur of an animal.

'Hello, Rosanna,' said Marie.

'I keep seeing this track and thinking, ah, where does that go to, and now I follow it –' Rosanna sat down cheerily and rambled with drunken expressiveness, her voice gruff and nasal, accentlessly English '– and I thought you were a leprechaun, I did, this little dark hood behind the rock. Cor,' she leaned over dangerously, 'look, I wonder if he realises how overlooked he is? Then I thought, no, leprechauns don't smoke. Or perhaps they do. It's the same wherever you are round here really, isn't it? There's always someone behind the hedge when you're having a pee. Sorry, were you in contemplation?'

Marie laughed but could have screamed. 'Ah no,' she said, friendly as could be, 'just having a little rest and a smoke on my walk. It's nice up here.'

'Ha ha! Dirty dog! Trying to catch him having a slash, were you?'

'Oh, I am of course,' said Marie and laughed again. For God's sake, her of all people, she was thinking.

Rosanna sat down and took a little Martell Cognac bottle out of her bag and drank from it reflectively, sprawling back against the rock. She had a hollow face, a narrow mouth, a large bony nose and a messily healed scar coming out from under the black glasses.

'I've just come up from Kish, came right over the top,' she said. 'My God, it's bracing up top. Look, white lines on the sea, it's going to be wild down there tonight. Clyde's been fixing the roof.' She sniggered. 'Idiot! That means he'll have made it worse, of course. Pillock!' She spoke with exaggerated scorn. 'S'pose we'll be listening to the saucepans tinkle again tonight.' She indicated the wagon. 'Not in, is he? No action? Pity, we could've made scary noises at him and he wouldn't have known where they were coming from. Hey, you could get down here, couldn't you? Reckon? Bet I could. Bet I could get down this ravine.' Her legs stuck out in front in filthy jeans and wellies, the feet waggling rhythmically. 'What you think of old Sawley Bean, then? Bit of a wimp, isn't he?'

'Do you think so?' said Marie. 'I think he's nice. He's better looking than the last one.' She drew on her cigarette and messed with her hair, making it fluff up like wool.

'Keeps to himself, doesn't he?' Rosanna offered the bottle.

'I will,' said Marie.

'He's round your place a lot. Con likes him, does he?'

'Oh yeah, he comes in and has a glass of wine with Connie sometimes.' It wasn't brandy, it was whiskey, and burnt her chest pleasantly.

'What do they talk about?'

'Damp mainly. Yes, damp, stuff like that.' She liked and disliked Rosanna at the same time. Poor woman, she thought, and said: 'So, how's things, Rosanna? What were you doing at Kish?'

Rosanna rolled a cigarette, turning away from the wind. She moved like a man and her hands were all wizened and flaky with eczema. 'Oh, Iko and his lot are camped up there. Bit of a hooley last night and I didn't wake up till three.'

Hippies, thought Marie.

'Told them me and Clyde are getting married next spring and we want them to lay on the music.'

Marie laughed outright, so did Rosanna. Clyde was the squinty little streak of nothing Rosanna lived with on and off and they were never going to get married. It was a standard joke. Could be worse, Marie thought, looking at Rosanna, could be living in a pigsty with a ratty little runt and everybody laughing at me. Rosanna's teeth were dingy with brown tops. Sometimes she smelt. She had perhaps been rather handsome once, but it had all gone. Marie felt better in her own skin for sitting next to her. *She* would never let herself go like that.

'Saw Father Leahy the other day.' Rosanna coughed and chuckled, leaning on an arm and lounging so closely against Marie that she wanted to pull back, but was too polite. 'Told him we wanted a church wedding.' Rosanna was English, but a Catholic who went to Mass every Sunday.

'Shoulda seen his face.' Rosanna chuckled. 'Tried to pass it off as a joke. He's frightened of Clyde,' she said proudly, slumping down further till she was lying on her back with one foot cocked across a raised knee. 'I said Clyde was going to take instruction. Teaching him his creed already, dear little bugger, head bowed over his little book, hee hee hee, anyway, I just love to see the look on the old boy's face. Me and Clyde! Wedding of the year! Walking down the aisle, standing at the altar!' She broke into song, something she often did:

> *You by my side, that's how I see us,*
> *Your folks and mine happy and smiling ...*

Telegram from the father. Good luck, son, to you and your lovely bride. Your loving father, Wormwood Scrubs. And bridesmaids! You could be maid of honour, Marie. And all of Ballinaphuca there!'

She sings nicely too, Marie thought. Such a shame she's like she is.

'He's going to teach me to drive, you know.'

'Who?' asked Marie. 'Father Leahy?'

They both laughed. 'Clyde,' Rosanna said.

And then Bob appeared below, climbing out of the gully with his hands in the pockets of his jacket, a small sack over one shoulder.

'Oh, look,' Rosanna said, 'there's your man.'

'I don't know how you can see through those things.'

Marie looked at his long thighs. She couldn't decide whether he was very handsome or very ugly.

At that moment Rosanna took off her sunglasses and looked round. Her eyes were piggy red slits in a mess of fat lurid bruising. She was smiling and obscurely challenging, and the effect was shocking. 'Oh, Rosanna,' Marie said, disturbed, 'why don't you

7

just get out of it?'

Rosanna put the glasses back on, still smiling. 'Well,' she said cheerfully, 'that's how it goes.'

They watched Bob Sawle jump down the last bit of rock and walk over to the back of his wagon. Rosanna drank and passed the bottle, but this time Marie refused it. She felt a little sick. 'You are mad, you know,' she told Rosanna. 'You're a silly girl. You want to keep away from him and get yourself a council house.'

Rosanna laughed. 'He's not seen us,' she said. 'Look at him, washing his hands. Oh, go on, take your willy out, let's have a look!'

Any minute now, Marie thought, burning, Rosanna would start shouting like a man on a building site, and he would look up and see them there and think they were together and ... Trust her to ruin everything. Bloody Rosanna.

He went up the steps into the wagon. The wind was getting up. Pointless sitting here.

She looked at her watch, stubbed out her cigarette and said, 'Oh, well, I suppose I should be on my way. See you, Rosanna,' then got up slowly and strolled away, heading home with a peculiar feeling of mortification.

2

Rosanna watched Bob Sawle hauling around a gas bottle down below. Can't see the attraction, she thought. Walks as if he's got a pole stuck up his arse. Clyde couldn't stand him. People Clyde couldn't stand usually ended up thumped. So did some he could stand, come to think of it. But God knows what it was about this one, he really hated him, said he was a flash bastard and a ponce, said he thought he was good, thought he was better than the rest of them and who did he think he was? Well, he wasn't that bad, bit of a po-faced sod, but live and let live. Clyde just got bees in his bonnet. Poor bugger down there struggling with that. Weak. First night in Tommy Davy's she'd said, 'Welcome to the Raj,' and tried to sit on his knee. He'd hated it. Froze all up. He wasn't the sort that loosened up and joined in, and his mouth was always self-conscious. She didn't like that type. Boring. And he had this way of making you feel he thought you were stupid when he talked to you, did it with everyone. Got right up Clyde's nostrils, that did. She saw them on stools at opposite ends of the bar, Clyde in his battered black oilskin, Bob looking superior. Music from *High Noon*. The air crackles. Clyde's been telling stories about what a bastard the skipper of the *Mary Ellen* was, docking fifteen pounds off his pay for spending too much time ashore in Vigo. Clyde says the other lads had been on his side. He says it was like Captain Bligh and Fletcher Christian in *Mutiny on the Bounty*. Rosanna says she'd seen the Marlon Brando film, Ger Sheehan says forget that, Charles Laughton's the man. Then this colossal nerd, this Bob Sawle, speaks up.

'Actually,' says he, like that, you know that posh voice, 'Bligh wasn't so bad, by all accounts. Just another of those mythical baddies, straight out of the pantomime.' Then it had gone all quiet and he'd looked stupid.

Rosanna drank peacefully, warmed through and through, looking at the waves rolling in on Caheradown Strand a mile away. The spray would be over the sheep fields tonight. Marie Mullen fancies him, Rosanna thought. She went all funny when I came up. He'd got an axe now and was about to start splitting logs. He's got no grace, she thought, not like Clyde. Clyde can handle things. She thought she'd go down there and irritate him for a while, so she set off recklessly down the ravine, moving with the supreme confidence of the hardened drunk, holding her bottle close to her chest, sometimes sitting down and edging forward to drop to the rock below. Water gurgled and sighed over stones close by. He whacked away at the logs and the sound echoed. Long before she reached the bottom, ten or fifteen minutes later, he noticed her but gave no sign of it.

She approached across the sloping springy scrub, stowing the bottle in her voluminous coat. 'I've just walked over the mountain,' she said cheerfully, 'how about a cup of coffee?'

He went on chopping, raising the axe aloft with a fractured lump of wood cleaving to its sides. 'Quite an unorthodox way to drop in,' he said with the merest trace of a smile. His face was long and ugly, his shirt very rumpled.

'Didn't you know I was Superwoman?' she said.

He worked on, ignoring her, so she went into the wagon and put the kettle on the two ring cooker. The place was dim but she could see that it was a tip, the narrow bed and the table covered in debris: papers, orange peel, cassette tapes, tools and bottles and toilet rolls and the like. It was like being in a boat, except that it was much too hot. A green pot-bellied stove glowed red at the top. A black box file stood open in all the mess on the desk, some kind of typed manuscript half in and half out of it. She was going to have a look at it but he came in, annoyed at her familiarity, and cleared it all away. Then he went to the fridge and squatted down, clumsy-footed, took out a jug of milk and sniffed at it.

He looked perhaps thirty-five, maybe older, with a fading tan and wrinkles in the corners of his eyes. His mousy hair was receding a bit, or maybe he just had a very high forehead.

'There you are,' he said, standing and giving her the jug of milk. 'Milk's on, it seems.' His manner was stiff, distracted.

Rosanna made coffee, for him as well as herself. The way he stood about with folded arms obviously waiting for her to drink up and go was really quite rude. 'Is that the great work?' she asked, nodding at the box file.

It was known that he was writing a mysterious tome about some obscure Dutch painter nobody had ever heard of. He gazed at the file blankly for a moment, as if not sure of the answer. He had a pissed-off, dissolute look, but his eyes, when he raised them, were shy.

'Do you know,' she said before he could speak, 'this place is full of bullshit. Just a lot of mediocre talents playing Gauguin really. Pathetic. Big fish in a little pool, see, that's why they all come here. Most of it's crap of course.'

He laughed. 'After that,' he said, 'there's not very much I can say, really.' He smiled to himself as he lit a tilley lamp, pumping hard till the mantle burst into brilliant white light. 'That's good,' he said, hanging the lamp from a hook in the ceiling, 'actually, I do agree with you.' Then he went outside and she heard him resume his wood-chopping.

Can't even take an insult, she thought, sauntering about the wagon looking at all the stuff revealed by the sudden bright lamp-light, taking off her dark glasses to do so. Her eyes watered in their bed of bruising. There was a cork noticeboard bearing a long overdue invitation to a private view at a gallery in Dublin and a small black-and-white postcard of what turned out to be a view of Warsaw by Bellotto. There was a picture of the Raising of Lazarus, the head of a man with flat-topped dark hair, millions of books about art and hardly anything else. The cassettes were jazz and classical, predictable, fairly obscure. 'Crap, crap, crap,' she whispered. Rosanna loved fifties pop, rock'n'roll, sentimental folk music. Stuff with heart, *real* stuff.

Her eyes hurt and she put the dark glasses back on, yawned, growing tired in this hot, tight little drum of a wagon. The sounds of chopping wood and the hissing of the tilley lamp were mesmeric. She shifted a load of stuff from the bed and lay down on top of its rumpled coverlet. Let him try and throw her out, just let him. She could get nasty.

When she woke up there was darkness at the windows and rain was drumming on the roof. The tilley lamp had dimmed considerably. Bob Sawle was sitting at his desk in the shadows, writing something in a big notebook. His hair had fallen down at the front and a few limp strands stuck out over his forehead. His mouth was open and there was a small pouch of flesh under his chin. He had no clothes sense at all: he'd put on a peculiar girlish pink jumper that was much too small. Marie Mullen had no taste.

She felt nauseous when she sat up, straightening the sunglasses which had managed to stay on her face, and reaching for the bottle. She drank a little whisky to quell the pang.

Bob looked up. 'Hello,' he said, carefully blank, slightly super-cilious, she thought.

There didn't seem much point in hanging around here any more, but as she moved to the door she was taken with the sudden urge to show him her eyes. So she whipped off the glasses as she passed his chair and, smiling, stuck her face close to his, show-ing off her bruises.

He showed no sign of shock and did not draw back.

'Did Clyde do it?' he asked.

11

But she just put the glasses back on her face and said: 'Guess what? Marie Mullen fancies you.'

3

It was dark but the streetlight shone brightly along the wet street. Ballinaphuca had one church, one shop, one Post Office and six bars: Tommy Davy's, Sylvester's, Mrs Costello's and The Rock all in a row, then Sheila's up by the shop and Michael Ruagh's a bit further down. Each was just a front room with a bar in it, apart from Tommy Davy's, which had swish inside toilets and a back room where you could play snooker or watch a video. Most of the blow-ins went in Tommy Davy's and Sylvester's which stood next door to each other. At election times they plastered their fronts with posters for the two main parties. The peeling rags of the last lot still clung to the red front of Sylvester's, the longer ones whipping in the wind.

Rosanna scurried in out of the cold and rain, greeting everyone cheerily. The small room was warm and brown, a single big turf smouldering in the fireplace. Clyde was there with Ger Sheehan, and Con Mullen was behind the bar.

Con began pulling a pint of Guinness as soon as he saw her, then leaned on the bar while it settled. His wide, smiling face was all ruddy in the light. 'You'll never guess what,' he said. 'He's only gone and got a chipper machine. Hey, what's with the glasses, Rosanna?'

'A what?'

'You know, a chipper machine, one of those things that cuts potatoes into chips. He's going to have a sign behind the bar, "Chips, 40p a bag".'

Rosanna burst out laughing. 'What? Too much! Hey, Sylvester!'

A tall shaggy-haired man in a grimy striped shirt appeared from the back, looking as if he'd just woken up. 'They'll all be in for the chips,' he said, standing very straight with both fists on the bar and speaking with great precision because he was extremely drunk. 'See, in summer they're all at the van over there and here they can sit down and have a pint with their chips.' His nose was long and red and pitted like an orange, his eyes danced. He was forty-two and looked sixty. He smiled fondly at Rosanna. More than once they'd been in the Skibberreen drying-out unit at the same time.

'Where've you been?' asked Clyde, not looking at her.

'Partying!' she cried, taking the drink Con set before her. 'Over Kish way. Iko and that bunch. Shoulda come. Just come back over the top so I popped in on whatsisname, James Sawle's brother in his little toy caravan. Gets right up my nose, he does.'

'Oh, the man's all right,' Con said, smiling, wiping sweat from his long upper lip. 'Hey, what's with the glasses, Rosanna?'

'He's stuck up.' Rosanna drank.

'You can't talk,' Clyde said. 'You're a posh, stuck up bitch yourself.' He adjusted the peak of his cap.

'Well, true,' she said, smiling. 'I'm stuck right up your arse.'

Ger and a few of the boys laughed. Clyde ordered another drink for himself and Ger, then turned his back on Rosanna and continued some story he'd been telling in his bored, throwaway manner, his low Cockney voice monotonous, about a fight he'd got into in Bantry a few days ago.

Clyde was a small, thin, tough man, with a pale hawkish face, acne-pocked and so bony that from any angle its outline was a series of knobs and hollows. His hair was sparse and his eyes, one of which looked constantly away to the side, were very pale and strangely goatish. He was seven years younger than Rosanna and she called him her toyboy. It'd been him against two at first, he said, then it got heavy. It had ended up with bottles being broken and brandished like knives, and he'd had to think quick and distract them, then leg it out of town and hole up at Mick Madden's place for a while.

'Ah, the dirty bastards, the dirty bastards,' Ger shook his head at the two pints of Guinness that stood settling slowly on the rumpled bar mat before him. He had a little pleasant pinched face with heavy lips and his hair was black. He said you could count him in. Some sort of posse was being discussed.

Sylvester clicked his tongue.

'You'll come to a bad end now, Clyde,' said Con, filling up the settled pints.

A drink or so further on, Rosanna began to sing. Her repertoire was eclectic. She worked her way through 'New York, New York', 'Little Red Rooster' and 'The Girl From Ipanema' to 'Whisky in the Jar' and 'Ireland, Boys, Hurrah!' at which Ger Sheehan cheered, a line of cream standing on his shapely red lip. Rosanna got up and walked about, passing the table where an old farmer called Padraic South sat drinking his Smithwick's and scowling at the notes from the courts in the *Southern Star*, his cheekbones fiercely jutting, shining as if polished. His sour old lips stretched wide, as if at an evil taste.

'Well, Padraic!' she cried jovially, sitting down too close beside him and poking her chin over his shoulder. 'Any more of those lovely poteen stories in there?'

He recoiled. His face, always florid, turned some impossible shade and he left his paper and went to stand at the bar to get away from her.

Clyde swivelled slowly on his stool and looked at her. 'Watch yourself,' he said coldly.

She danced around, clicking her fingers, stopping from time to time to berate them all for their boringness and telling Sylvester he ought to get a piano so they could have some really good singsongs, nothing like a good sing-song, and launched into 'The Red-Haired Man's Wife', a bitter, pining lament that ended with a stanza of such utter gloom that she collapsed at a corner table with bowed head, unable quite to finish it. A silence had fallen upon them all and she thought it must be because of the beauty and sincerity of her singing.

'Same again, Padraic?'

'The same.'

'You know what they say about red-haired women,' she rallied, getting up again and parading the bar, fluffing out her dry red hair theatrically.

'Shut up,' said Clyde quietly.

'What do they say, Rosanna?' asked Ger, smiling.

'Say that they're randy as hell.' She laughed and began on her stock of dirty songs, 'The Fly', 'Nine Inches', and her favourite one by Robert Burns about a girl whose pubic hair grew into her fanny and ruined her sex life.

'Where does she get them from?' Sylvester asked wonderingly.

Clyde came and gripped Rosanna just above the elbow and walked her behind the bar and into the passage at the back that smelt slightly of sweat and pee. 'Now, I'm telling you,' he said evenly, 'I'll kill you if you don't shut your stupid fucking mouth. Do you understand?'

She loved Clyde when he was mad, the hard eyes and mouth, the little-boy-hurt neck thrust forward, the burnt-out, sharpened match swivelling round the teeth, slick-slack, a characteristic of several celluloid bad men, brilliantly observed and mimicked to serious perfection. Terrifying. She kissed him eagerly on the lips, laughing and nearly getting skewered on the match. 'You'll never guess what,' she whispered. 'Marie Mullen's got a thing about Bob Sawle! Don't tell Con! Honestly, I was coming over the top and ...'

'Keep your voice down,' he said in the same even tone, unblinking.

'Con ought to watch himself. Could be there bonking his missis right this minute. And Julia too. State of *her*, sashaying about like that, ho ho. Oh, I do love a bit of mischief!'

'Shit.' The dead match stood still for a second between Clyde's thin pink lips.

'You're so pathetic,' she said affectionately, gazing into his eyes. 'Oh, I do love you, you're so sweet.'

'Come on, you silly bitch.' He turned abruptly and walked back out.

She followed, watching fondly as he finished his pint. 'Adieu! Adieu!' she said wearily, smiling and waving as she followed him to the door. 'I am summoned!'

'You have a lovely voice there,' said Con sincerely. 'You'll ruin it, you know,' like someone telling a child not to scuff its shoes.

'Pint of Guinness, please, Connie,' said Ger.

4

'It's a lovely night,' Rosanna said, standing outside and looking across the road, out across the fields to the great shrilling darkness that was the sea, where the light from the Puck Rock appeared, swelling and ebbing like a slow pulse, then was gone. It came and went at intervals, always did and always would, reassuring as a heartbeat on a dark night. Its foghorn voice bayed as she and Clyde walked through the village, a single, hump-backed, bent pin of a street with Davy Scanlon's shop at the bend of the pin. A lone petrol pump stood out front, its heavy oval sign blowing furiously in the wind.

Where the little varicoloured terrace came to an end they set their faces away from the light and into the wind, towards the sea, always sounding wherever you were in this valley. In the village you could smell brine. In wild weather the street was flecked with foam. A mist sprang up. The long lane was all damp and breathing. Dim shoulders of land loomed in the darkness all around, like the backs of extinct beasts. They were freezing when they reached the turning down to the beach. Clyde had on only his denim jacket. 'I'm getting a car,' he said sternly, shivering, 'that fucking does it, I'm getting a car.'

Cars rusted fast here. On shingles, in underused fields and on bits of scrub throughout the region, their corpses slowly decomposed into the earth, passing through every shade and shape of rust, some lovely and delicate. For years Clyde had had a plan to get a really good camera and learn how to use it and go around West Cork photographing all the car wrecks. He saw the pictures in his mind, black and white, stark, magnificent. He would have an exhibition somewhere, Cork, Dublin, London. It would be called, 'Car Wrecks of West Cork', and it would be an immediate and startling success. He saw it: the posey gallery, the nobs and the pseuds turning out, fêting him, and he there in the middle of it all, Clyde the Kid. He'd wait until just the right moment before making his gesture, like he'd just look a certain way and say ... he wasn't sure yet.

16

Bob Sawle had been out with a camera — nice camera, all the trimmings — round the head, out where one of Clyde's favourite wrecks sank shoulder first into the heather. Bastard. Clyde spat. Probably too stupid even to see the possibilities.

They moved together and held each other from the cold. A sombre herd of dripping cows peered at them through the vapour on the little pasture above the beach, and a sandy track led them down through one or two tough little dunes covered in samphire and the dead heads of thrift, to a low stone-built house that huddled beneath the edge. Only a little gravel separated it from the hard flat sand of Caheradown Strand stretching away in the darkness towards the sea that grumbled threateningly beyond a bend in the land. The house was derelict and lacked one corner, which had been sliced off and reshaped when it was found that a fairy path crossed the spot. Its ownership was in dispute. Mice had eaten the putty from around the windows.

Clyde kicked the door and it opened and they went in. Some creature whined in the darkness. Clyde lit the lamp and his miserable dog came shivering from the corner where it had been lying on a bit of sack. Keening, it crept towards them on its belly, waving its bony tail and wrinkling its nose.

'Hey, Molly!' he said and fondled its head.

Rosanna barred the door with a great wedge of sea wood and ran over to light the paraffin heater, an old green battered thing with a Gothic crown of wax and candles.

They lived in one end of the single empty room. The floor was bare concrete, the ceiling low and dark and vaulted. Two small windows were set like deep eyes in one damp-patterned wall. She closed the curtains, frayed squares of faded Indian cotton that still smelt a little of patchouli. On the seaward wall some previous occupant had roughly painted a fireplace with a mantel shelf and a vase of flowers. A double mattress covered with blankets lay before it, and some boxes full of books and clothes, and a freestanding range, shedding ashes and completely cold. Clyde walked over and kicked it. He'd been known to tinker with it from time to time, but it never worked.

'Any tea?' he asked.

Rosanna threw herself down across the mattress with a sigh,

ignoring him.

He poured water from a blue plastic fish barrel into the kettle and set it on a Baby Belling under one of the windows. Then he went across and lay beside her, slowly and carefully as if getting into a very hot bath, taking care that their bodies did not touch. The wind whistled naggingly about the walls. After a moment he sat up and drew from beneath the mattress a long Remington shotgun and played it as if it were a guitar. Clyde couldn't play an instrument but his fingers moved nimbly upon the barrel, forming imaginary chords. His eyes closed. He remembered sitting on the steps of a bus with this American traveller called Chico who'd looked like a Mexican revolutionary and spoken like a Cheech and Chong skit. Chico's long brown toes had curled round the step. 'See this,' he'd wheezed amiably, running through his sales patter, 'pretty good, shoot you a rabbit. Nothing nicer than a rabbit. Pretty good model. Pump-action. Twenty bore. Takes *eight* cartridges, man. Strictly a no-no. How'd I get it in here? Don't ask.' A naked woman had washed herself in a tub out there in the open for all to see. It was cool to take no notice. Really, though, Clyde had been thinking: wow, I'm here watching this naked girl, look at her tits. God, her arse, wow, and this guy, what an accent, straight out of an American film, wow, America, where it's all at, a million road movies speeding through his dope-addled brain — on the road with the Maga Dogs in Mayo, Clare, Limerick, hanging round in the big tent at nights watching the band play and helping the girls out with the grub. Good old days.

The kettle crooned a low worrying tune, got into its stride, higher and higher till it was screaming along with the wind, which had finally cracked like a maniac and set up a thin, feral howling just under the window. They heard the sea charging up the beach towards them. Living here was like being run at by a rhinoceros, hoping that if you stood your ground it might skid to a halt at the last minute, grunt a bit and go away. The dark end of the house was like a mouth.

'Kettle's boiling,' Rosanna said, but neither moved. The kettle screamed on. Clyde went on playing his gun, lightly stroking the well polished wood with small, rather graceful hands, cut and well-used, the nails bitten so far down that the domes above them were bulbous and ugly. His loose cuffs fell back, revealing thin brown arms, strong and smooth. He pursed his lips and raised his thin, mobile eyebrows, picturing himself like Bob Dylan on the cover of 'The Times They Are A-Changing'.

'You go,' he said.

Rosanna yawned, got up and made the tea, brought two mugs over to the bed and sat down cross-legged to drink.

'Take your glasses off,' he said. 'You don't have to wear them in here.'

But she ignored him and went to crouch beside a wide floppy basket spilling clothes. She was an excellent seamstress and got a little money from taking in sewing and mending. 'He's awfully fussy,' she said, taking out some old cord trousers belonging to Sylvester and looking at a worn bit on one knee. 'These could have gone a long way before giving out.'

Clyde squinted along the barrel, aiming at Rosanna's face. The glasses suited her, he thought, hiding half her face and giving what was left quite a striking quality. The gun was loaded and she knew it but showed no fear as she got up, cleaned perfunctorily about the range, turned on the radio and found 'The Rock Show' before returning with her sewing to sit on the other end of the bed. She made sure he got a nice clear aim. Throughout all this he'd kept her in his sights, sometimes her face, sometimes her heart, sometimes her sex organs. She looked up and smiled at the tip of the barrel, making a kissy mouth. It was a game they sometimes played. He aimed at the window, then at his dog, then sitting forward nosed the gun into Rosanna's ear.

'Ooh,' she said with a little wriggle and a laugh, 'it tickles, stop it.'

Like a secret, the possibility of pulling the trigger was always there. He took the gun out of her ear, moved round and put it in her mouth. She lay back, spreading her legs. She would die, almost for certain. What kind of a mess would there be? She was mad. He withdrew the gun and stood up, aimed it at the ceiling and cocked the trigger. 'Da-da-da-da-da-da-da-da-da-da-da-da-da,' he whispered.

She was sewing again. 'This bloody light,' she said.

'Oh, take your glasses off!' He laid the gun down and took

them off her gently. 'Stupid bitch,' he said when he saw the state of her eyes. Then he kissed her violently. He was acting and she saw right through him and laughed. Clyde lay down and put his head upon her knee. 'Don't touch me,' he said.

5

Marie sat up in bed reading yesterday's *Sunday World*. Oh well, I'm not as bad as some, she thought. People had terrible problems. She read 'A Little Bit of Religion', looked at the fashions. Sometimes she wrote an imaginary letter in her mind about her problem. Why did she get these terrible crushes on people? Bad enough when it was someone up there on the screen or in a picture, but now it was someone real. She really should have grown out of all that by now. It was terrible. Well, they pass, she thought, they always do pass in the end, don't they, even if it takes years — mother of God, let this pass too, quickly. I'd never write a letter like that, she thought, reading the problem page, I'm not the type, and certainly not to these Irish columns, oh no. She knew exactly what those women would say. That one on the radio, giving out her advice with the deep, tough, sensible voice. God, she was a heartless woman!

She put the paper aside. A cheap lurid semi-nude tart grinned complacently on the front. Marie got out of bed and went and looked at herself in the mirror. Her face was wide, with a big mouth and a shiny nose that swept up at the tip. There was a gap between her two front teeth. I'm getting some little lines, she thought. Need a decent cut, she thought, hair's like hay. That place in town's no good. I must get into Cork some time. Go in with Tom Davy some Tuesday. Then she turned and stood sideways, holding in her stomach, looking at her body in the long white nightie with the little blue rose sprigs. This nightie hid everything, kept her from Con. She looked around her bedroom. The corner light and soft orange duvet, the goatskin, the peacock-shaped wicker chair and the old pictures that Con's mother had left when she finally moved down to the village. They were of country cottages and flowers and golden-haired children, and Marie had kept them because she liked them. Most of the holy pictures she'd put away, apart from one or two that touched a soft spot.

The sound of soft pop music filtered through the wall from Simon's room next door. She looked at the clock on top of the chest of drawers. Ought to go and tell him to turn it off and go to bed, she thought, but then it stopped anyway and she turned off the light and went back to bed. The paper fell to the floor.

The glow from the Puck Rock came and went on the wall. When she'd first come here she'd lain awake, gazing at it, thinking how it must have shone, just so, just there, when this was Con's own boyhood room. It had made her feel strangely redundant. She stared at it, putting herself through a certain exercise every night before she allowed herself to go on to the next thing: she made herself think very deliberately of all the nice things about Con, that he was funny, that he was kind, that he'd made her those nice little steps to stand on when she was hanging out the wash. Dear old Connie, she thought, he deserves better. And she remembered him when young, when first they had the house to themselves and he'd be grabbing her in the kitchen all the time when the radio was on, and they'd dance a ridiculous dance, falling about with laughter, him with his big boots scraping the floor. He used to shout: Hi-yo, Silver, Away! going off on his tractor. He was only a kid. What? About twenty-four. So she'd been twenty-one. They had fun then.

He was nineteen when she first saw him, she thought he was lovely, his fair hair, his shoulders, his look of common-sense and sweetness and fun. And summer, and the lovely skies and the crowds in Galway. Her brother Patrick had brought her to the races. Con was with a bunch of lads from Strangarvan. She went walking with him down by the Spanish Arch and he gave her tips for the horses. 'You have lovely hair,' he said, 'lovely, lovely hair.' And he touched it with his fingertips and made the nape of her neck prickle.

Then she remembered a day out in Derryvrack Gardens five or six years ago, when Julia and Simon, little kids then, had run on round the bend and vanished and she'd found herself walking with Con through an empty meadow of long grass and ragged robin, those tattered pink flowers that died so quickly. A feeling came all over her that she wanted to lie down with a lover in the grass and see the flowers nodding above against the sky. She wanted someone to touch her, but not Con, whose mouth was turning in, whose flesh was changing in some subtle way, coarsening, rising a little like dough. The fear that had come upon her then was so terrible that the scene still haunted her at nights, and she remembered her mother saying to her once, 'Sure, it makes no difference, you go off them all in the end anyway whatever.' Was that true?

There. She shook herself. Duty done. Now she could get down to the real thing, thinking about Bob. She let herself go. Sometimes she tried to run through in her head all the times she'd seen him or spoken to him, but she was starting to lose track. He had a brother at Dundreen. She'd probably stood beside him in the shop years ago and thought he was just another tourist. After all, he was nothing special. Funny how you just suddenly got a thing for someone. Now she thought that when she first heard his name there'd been something, a little kick, nothing. Then a faint ghostly glow up the mountain late at night, someone in the Dutch wagon. Con had come up to bed and said in the dark: 'The new one up beyond, he's James Sawle's brother.' And the thought had popped out at her, like a sudden face when you're falling asleep: perhaps I'll have an affair with him. Then she'd met him on the old pig run, she and Julia going down and he coming up with a plastic container full of water. He looked away to one side then down at the ground the way people do on a long approach, feeling themselves watched. They all smiled and introduced themselves and he put the container down to shake hands. Some water had slopped on his shirt. One of the buttons was gone and she could see a little pale flesh. He was shy and very polite and looked at Julia the way they all did, once quickly getting an eyeful then hardly at all.

His girlfriend had ditched him for someone else. He was writing a book about a painter. He was clever. She knew all this. His girlfriend's name was Nola, she was a dancer, American. Couldn't have been a girl in a shop, could it? Or a hairdresser or a nurse or a secretary? A dancer, my God, and American. Even the name was fancy.

Some evenings he came in and drank a glass of wine and sat beside her while he talked with Con, about damp and mould and his problems about water. Con liked him. And one evening what if ... oh, yes, wouldn't it be lovely? She had imagined him, minutely. She knew what it felt like to have a prick. She'd felt it with him, in those places. Like dreams they were, only not dreams. So intensely she met him there that it was impossible he should not feel the pangs wherever he might be. And now it was coming over her again, the queer sexy feeling. Sometimes she could get it just by thinking, other times it just came, unwilled – sitting at the kitchen table, standing in the yard, lying in the bath – going through and through her, wearing her out, like having it done to you by the very air and nothing you could do. She blushed. A slow blooming thing came over her, dark and hot, spreading like a bloodstain or a desperation of the bowels. It kept happening lately. God help me, it's awful, she thought, like when the dog's on heat, or the cat sticking her rump in the air the way she does. This is what it feels like. You'd think it would put out a smell. She considered her tongue, tasted it in her mouth, the juicy prong, thought of it as a snake's head gliding here and there, stealing, what it could do to another of its kind if you let it go. Adulterers got the deepest pit in Hell.

She drifted off, waking in the early hours when Con came in. He was happily drunk, singing in the kitchen as he poked about looking for something to eat. 'Rock'n'roll, I gave you all the best years of my life ...' he sang in a fine, deep, lilting voice. Then he turned off all the lights and came upstairs, not bothering to soften the sound of his shoes on the treads. He belched loudly, went to the bathroom and took a pee but did not clean his teeth. In the dark of the bedroom he undressed quickly, pulling off his shoes and dropping them to the floor with two familiar thuds, breathing noisily and sighing with relish for the sleep to come. Marie, a hump under the covers, kept still. He climbed in beside her, then tentatively caressed her hip through the cotton nightie. On the wall the Puck light glowed eerily, silent, on, off.

She kept still, so he settled deeper into the bed, withdrawing his hand and putting it under his pillow where it felt safe.

6

Bob lay on the bed listening to plaintive Gaelic singing on the
radio, smoking and smiling sardonically. In his own quiet way
he was desperate, often. It was the week before Christmas. He
hated Christmas, the fuss, the kitsch, the slop, the Christianity,
desperate and whorish, touting half-heartedly for business on
the edge of it all. Stick it. Oh well, it wasn't so bad here, no
shops, no carol singers, no snow; it never snowed here except
maybe a little bit on the tops of the mountains. The music
ended and the voice of the presenter spoke at length in Irish.
He caught the occasional *agus*, which he knew meant and. That
was nice, total unintelligibility, made him feel foreign. But after
a while he grew bored and turned the radio off. Disco music
pounded distantly from the Christmas dance in the village.
They would all be there; it would be hellish. He sat up and
looked at his desk, the wretched stacks of paper, the old cold
mugs of tea taking over, the typewriter, a natty little Brother.
The book.

Get on with it.

His soul rebelled. He hated it. The whole thing was stupid and
boring and he couldn't be bothered with it any more. It was
beyond him. He'd go down and get a drink at least and try not to
get in any arguments. Keep away from the Holy Joes. Might see
Marie. 'Ah, go on,' she'd said, 'you wanna go, it'll be fine. Sure,
I'll dance with you.' She flirted with him when he got the milk.
Might as well go and get a look at her. She was nice. He liked to
see her in her garden when he drove down to the village, nice
body she had, shapely, firm, substantial.

He found himself getting ready. When he was alone, and this
was for much of the time, he talked to himself. Not just the odd
sentence, the modest 'Hm, now where did I put that?' but a con-
tinual whispering, gesturing mime like the signing of the deaf,
oddly twitchy and disjointed. He made speeches, argued and

laughed while washing his armpits, putting on a clean shirt, boots, a decent jacket, combing his hair at the little mirror high over the sink, and finally stepping out into the clear, cold night.

As soon as he hit the air his dumb show stopped. He locked the wagon and stood looking at it for a moment. In its own way, he thought, it was as bad as the pink hacienda over near Kish, appallingly cute.

It was a beautiful winter's night. He walked down to the village towards the music that pounded up the lane under the crisp sky.

The community centre was on the edge of the village and looked like an abattoir. 'Billie Jean' by Michael Jackson was playing inside as he approached. On the door was Paddy Bawn, entertainments manager, hair snow-white, face rose-red. Paddy was round and perpetually angry and couldn't get along with anyone. He hated blow-ins and scowled at Bob as he took his money, waving him through officiously as if he was holding up a queue, though there was no one behind.

Bob went in and walked straight to the bar that had been set up along one wall. Little Siobhan from the shop served him with a drink and he downed a third of it before looking around. The community centre was bathed in a holy blue light, decked with boughs of holly and Christmas streamers. The stage had been set up for a band to play later. Tommy Davy, young and solemn, was doing the disco. Everyone was there, the young and the old dancing together in a way they only did in England at weddings, so that the place had the appearance of a massive family gathering. Big farmers danced with little girls in party dresses, mothers with their teenage sons. Fat Mrs Shanahan from the Post Office was there, Father Leahy in his soutane, the young bloods and the young girls, and the blow-ins, who drove him up the wall, though he was one himself. They came from all over the place, Dublin, England, Europe, America. They made yoghurt and wove and spun and dug and delved and practised homeopathy and meditation and painted and wrote and sculpted and all that kind of thing. Most of them them were signing on, even the rich ones. And some of them were so rich that they really didn't have to do anything at all if they didn't want to. And in fact, why should he, why should he have to write this stupid book anyway? He'd give it up, go back to Dublin, no London, no ...

The trouble with a place like Ballinaphuca was that you couldn't be a stranger. A man could not stand and brood and get drunk in peace and just watch the balloons flying about and listen to the music – Heard It Through The Grapevine – without some fool coming up and talking to him. First he had to discuss poetry with Feargal Breen, a Dubliner with a wild, foam-flecked appearance. Feargal was the only one who'd heard of Carel Fabritius, but then he probably wouldn't have admitted it if he hadn't.

Ben Bowden, an Armaggedon escapee from the Home Counties barged in. 'Paddy was at the back door again!' he cried.

'Who?'

'Paddy!' Ben, in all this space, was unfortunate enough to live next door to Paddy Bawn. 'Going on about the dogs again.' Ben was little and dark and anxious and lived with a big German woman called Ulrica and kept six dogs which were treated like children.

'Ah, tell him to fuck off,' said Feargal.

'I don't know what to do,' said Ben, nearly in tears. 'The man's mad. You shoulda heard him screaming.' His face distorted and he mimicked: '"You should get the fucking things destroyed! Now! Now!" And I keep telling him, it was not my dogs, it was not my dogs!'

The bar was three deep. Bob just kept drinking. No sign of Marie, though Con was all over the place being the life and soul. Bob wasn't a good drinker, he'd have to watch it. But he had another anyway. He insulted a woman called Felicity who ran a craft shop, argued with someone else about the notion of rights. Then he saw her, wearing a yellow dress he'd never seen before and little heeled grey boots. Usually she was in jeans and things, or a grey skirt she had, or an old-fashioned flowered shirtwaister that really did things to him. He'd never seen her dressed up before. She was half waltzing, half jiving with Con and looking as though she was enjoying it, smiling and looking all around. When she caught his eye she wiggled her fingers at him and he grinned. Fancies me, he thought. Marie had a wide, unusual face, highly animated. He found her beautiful, particularly when she opened her lips and you saw the big shiny front teeth with the gap between. Her hair was loose and stuck out all round her face. The crowd closed up and she vanished.

He mooched about vaguely, suddenly a little depressed, wondered about buying a place somewhere this side of Strangarvan, remembered fragments of useless conversations with Nola. Dan Hogan, a fierce tiny man in an ancient black suit who hung about doors and looked in windows was hovering about on the edges of the crowd getting an eyeful of the young girls. I'm like him, Bob thought. The beautiful Julia, thin, black-clad, danced among the other young girls. He tried to get near the bar. Barney Mac the cobbler, a hale and dapper man in his seventies, was in front of him and got his order for him. Good man. Barney asked if he was enjoying himself and Bob said he was. They talked about building. Everyone here talked about building. Bob had had a few drinks with Barney in Mrs Costello's in the past and Barney had told him about old Quigs who used to live on the bit of land where his wagon now stood, a big man built like a barn, he said, dead now thirty years and his sons in America. He said there were once fifteen people living up there, and that the big rock at the back had been known as the shadow because the shadow of a man had been seen on it once when there was no one to throw it. He said that every rock and tree and field had a name but that most of them were forgotten now. Sometimes, late at night, Bob stopped work in his wagon and just listened to the silence up there and thought about the fifteen people living in that old ruin where the toadstools sprouted and the moss had taken over. Sometimes they kept him awake.

'Hello, Bob,' Marie said. She was with Con.

'Now taste this,' Con said, 'this is lovely stuff.' He had a bottle of whiskey and he poured a capful for Bob, careful as a nurse, and offered it. Bob took it, drank it down, handed back the cap. Jesus, that hit the spot. Bob smiled at Marie, his throat burning. Con poured a whiskey for Barney, then passed on, stopping here and there, dispensing the whiskey to certain chosen ones.

'Are y'all right?' Marie asked him.

'Fine,' he said.

She walked away. Later he saw her dancing with Dan Hogan and thought how nice it was of her to dance with the old bugger, who stank to high heaven. Why not me? he thought. Get a hold of her. But he was swept away by a group of blow-ins. A band was climbing onto the stage, middle-aged men in casual clothes, one wearing a cowboy hat. He sat down, his head reeled. The whiskey on top of all the ... They sat upon two long tables with blow-in kids rattling about obliviously underneath, he and his nearest neighbours, Essie and George, a couple in their mid years who'd been here for ever. Essie was one of those tough crop-haired women with nose-stud and multiple earrings, high-hipped in denim. George was American and looked like Rasputin. They talked about a personal growth weekend at Montsalvat – Montsalvat, for Christ's sake – his brother's place up at Dundreen.

Bob sneered.

'Cleverdick,' said Essie.

Guitars talked flatly to one another, tuning up. A few more fools gathered round and there was all this blather, all this spiritual claptrap. He hated it, hated it, they were fools, all of them. Just fools. The band played a kind of rough and ready folky rock-'n'roll. Someone said maybe they could get Swan Mary to come and speak.

'Oh, they'd never get *her*,' someone else said and they all laughed, as if they were talking about a superstar who only did stadium gigs.

'Oh, bollocks!' Bob laughed. 'Give me all your money and I'll tell you what it's all about. Want to find the meaning of life? Stick your finger up your arse!' He went and got another drink.

Young boys and girls fooled about. Tired children drooped on chairs about the walls. Jackie Bat, huge and blobby-faced, greeted him and they talked for a while about building. Jackie was the one the tourists took pictures of as he walked the lanes with a scythe and a wall-eyed dog. The blow-ins loved him. His bashful great shoulders were uneasy in a suit, his big red fist cradled a cigarette, clumsily protective. Jackie said he was working on Ben Bowden's extension, lisping excitedly, voice full of catarrh. Then he asked after the book.

'What name has it?' he asked.

Bob couldn't voice the title, *A View In Delft*. How stupid it sounded. He blushed. 'I don't know yet,' he said.

'Is it a thriller?' Jackie asked.

Bob felt embarrassed and rather apologetic, as he always did when he talked about the book. He said it was a novel about a painter called Carel Fabritius.

'Ah,' said Jackie, as if he'd heard of him. 'Vincent has his pictures in Killarney now,' and drank his Lucozade.

Bob sucked the froth off another drink. The place frothed about him, people greeted him, he lost track of all their names, what did it matter? He lost track of time, which rolled on, and the children had gone so it must be late and he was so far past his limit anyway that it didn't really matter. Father Leahy went by with a paw print on the back of his black soutane. The crowd was full of shining gums, babbling voices, shrieks, giggles. And then his head cleared wonderfully, as if a mist had suddenly lifted, and he looked about and thought happily: I will stay here for ever and live alone and work. Marie passed, going in the opposite direction, smiling at him as she went.

'Marie,' he said, 'you're beautiful.' She stood still and laughed at him. 'Happy Christmas,' he said.

They waltzed, very proper, her shiny smiling face a long way from his. It was comforting to hold a woman again. She stood on tiptoe and said into his ear, 'Don't be taking it all too seriously,' and he felt confused and wondered what she was talking about, and if he'd said anything and if so what. He wanted to talk to her. She squeezed him a little.

'When I was young ...' he began.

She laughed: 'Oh, of course, you're very old!'

'When I was young I would've loved to have painted you ...' She laughed. 'You look Dutch. I can see you in a seventeenth century painting, sitting at the virginals, carrying in the milk, chopping onions ...'

'What are you on about?'

They didn't speak after that. The music ended and they moved apart and went their separate ways. He did not see her again till much later when people were leaving. The side door was open and cold air came into the hot red cave of the community centre. The music was over but a group of very drunk young men sang 'Spancilhill'. Miserable Paddy Bawn, his red face furious, was clearing up officiously behind the bar. The song was unbearably sad and made Bob yearn, rooted to the spot, afraid he'd stagger if he moved. Marie passed in front of him in a shapeless red coat, the collar up.

A nice woman, he thought.

> *The cock crew in the morning,*
> *It crew both loud and shrill.*
> *I awoke in California*
> *Many miles from Spancilhill.*

'Will you look at the cut of that one there watching Marie,' said Tim Pat Malachi to Clyde and Ger Sheehan, who sat upon a table, smoking and watching the people who filtered out at the side door.

'I love it,' said Rosanna to Ger.

'What?'

'Mischief.'

Clyde had scarcely moved all night. He never danced. People nearly always looked ridiculous when they danced and he couldn't risk that. He'd drunk a prodigious amount, but did not seem drunk. With him it never showed. People drifted by on their way out of the door and his eyes flickered over them like the eyes of someone watching the telegraph poles out of a train window. He saw Bob Sawle amongst them, pissed as a fart. What was it about that creep? One of these days ... There was Julia, jailbait since she was eleven. His eyes stuck on her.

'OK, come on, now, Julia,' Marie called, 'we'll walk on home. He'll be ages.' They were all walking back together, Marie and Essie and Con's sister, Therese. Julia ran after them. Her head was big with a full white face and short dark hair falling in fat, petal-like segments above her brows. Her legs were long and athletic, all her movements quick.

'I've had a lovely time!' she cried.

Rosanna, of course, had started singing. She sang 'The Rocks of Bawn', leaning against the wall with her eyes shut, dawdling through it drunkenly. The women left. Padraic South stood listening to the song, an inch of beer in his glass, shiny red hands clawlike on the handle, his face all smooth red planes, crags, cracks.

'Want a lift, Padraic?' Con asked.

The lights went on.

'Come on, now, come on, now. I need to get under your feet,' grumbled Paddy Bawn with the broom.

'Ah well,' said Barney Mac, jerking up his collar, 'there'll be a fine frost.'

The doors flew open and the cold came in and covered everything.

Bob was just nearing the end of the village, stepping out for home and reeling only a very little from time to time when he tilted his head back to take in the terrifying sky. Orion ramped victorious over Rossa. You could just about see galaxies spinning in the hunter's belt. A satellite passed overhead on its straight and dizzying journey through it all. He was in a state of inebriated joy, slapped so hard by the cold sharp air that he kept thinking his nose was bleeding.

A car came up behind him, dazzling, slowed down and stopped. Con put his head out of the window. 'You've had your fill all right, man. You OK? Come on, so. I'll run you home.'

He found himself in the back of Con's car, the squared ramrod back of Padraic South before him in the passenger seat. Padraic did not turn to greet him.

'We go to Rathmeelabo first and drop Padraic off,' Con said. 'Padraic, wind down your window there.'

Padraic's face in profile was stern and rocky. Bob remembered seeing him on his first day, an old man looking at him over the fuchsia hedge lining the track that ran above Quigs's up to the Mass Rock: fierce cheekbones, wide lips, a steady blue stare under a flat cap, seen and then gone.

The car jumped forward, roaring, towards the darkness. The tyres screeched as they passed the signpost for Strangarvan. Hold it, Bob thought, how much has this man had to drink? The sky flattened itself, pale and star-strewn, across the West; the cold was intense; Con whistled something schmaltzy and jazzy. When the darkness hit, the car seemed to speed up and there was the illusion of flying off the edge of the world. From the darkness, images flashed: rocks rearing up in the headlights, savage-headed trees, the gable end of a house. So what if I end up splattered all over a rock? he thought, too drunk to care, relaxing, invulnerable, consciously enjoying the swing of the headlamps over the heath, the dimly shining, coldly mysterious scene that shifted about in front of them. Sometimes a small animal would flit like a ghost. A great white horse appeared shining at a crossroads. High walls of limestone flew by. They passed Jackie Bat, who raised his hand in the headlight, turning in at his own gate. Then the white, hooded figure of Mary appeared at the little flowery shrine by the turning to Rathmeelabo.

After a while they turned onto a narrow track running down into a broad shallow valley that sloped up to the foot of Rossa, where a stream came down and a scattering of empty cottages stood. Rathmeelabo had an oppressive air, with all the blind, lonely houses at the blind, lonely end of the track. Con drove down to the only inhabited one, Padraic's, large and austere with three little blue dormers sticking out of the roof.

'Here y'are,' he said, and Padraic got out. 'Luck!' he shouted, slamming the door and walking off towards his house, turning once as he crossed the headlights.

Bob knew the theory that the Irish were of Berber origin. Seeing Padraic in the headlights he thought it was true, for Padraic's face, he thought, was magnificent, transcending east and west. The man was not real, he was some kind of timeless essence of peasant, the mountainy man, Tomas O'Crohan's Islandman, Steven Dedalus' holy peasants at Clane, air and rain and turf and corduroy, reassurance that nothing had changed.

They turned back to the road. The headlights picked out a hollow tree filled with rubbish, bags, polythene, old tin cans. Bob closed his eyes and yawned and let the darkness echo and swoop in his head until he felt the car slowing down and heard the crunch of gravel. It was his own track.

'I'll walk from here,' he said. 'Thanks, Con.'

'Not at all.' Con was already swinging the wheel round. 'I wouldn't like to think of you in the ditch.'

They bumped down the track to the wagon and Bob stumbled

out. Con banged the horn loudly as Bob fumbled his way inside, reaching for the torch and swinging its beam crazily about the wagon. He heard the car roar away, lit the lamp, pumped it wildly for a few minutes then stood for a while leaning out of the half door, letting the silence settle and watching the pale night sky above the plantation. He remembered that the track through the plantation was said to be haunted by an ancestor of Con's, sixteen and simple, shot down there by the Black and Tans for running when challenged for being out after curfew. He remembered that a blow-in up near Kish claimed to have gone out one night to empty the shitbucket and seen a great black dog with red eyes watching him from the bank above. He remembered the shadow.

7

The shop in the village was owned by Davy Scanlon, a big bluff grey individual with hooked nostrils, who also owned his son's Tommy's bar, the garage, most of the land and the plantation near Quigs's. Apart from condoms, arms and restricted drugs, if you could think of it, the shop had it. It was crammed from floor to ceiling, the windows a madly surreal assemblage of tools and boots and seeds and cans of food and shirts in cellophane wrappers, and there were sheds and out-houses that stored the big stuff. Mrs Davy could lay her hand on anything within minutes. The shop stayed open till about ten every day of the year and gave apparently unlimited credit to anyone who asked for it, even strangers.

On Christmas Eve, Bob walked down to buy a bottle of wine to take up to Essie and George's party. Sometimes he dreaded the shop. You couldn't just go in and get your stuff and come out. It had to be a social occasion. If you were lucky you got just Mrs Davy and perhaps one other, but sometimes there'd be half a dozen standing there and you'd know you were in for a good half-hour of it. Irish time. He used to think it was a cliché.

He opened the door and the bell rang. Clyde was there, Sheila from Sheila's bar and a beaky old hag called Nora McBride who fixed him with her terrible eye and iced his blood. Davy himself, who never served, was mucking about importantly behind the freezer. Mrs Davy, a strong, square, motherly woman, cut a steaming berg of frozen fish with something that looked like a scimitar, and Siobhan sliced bacon on the machine. Everyone but Clyde and Nora McBride said hello to him. Sheila, a gargantuan, squinting, red-legged woman, wished him a Merry Christmas and asked after his mother's health. She'd already got her things and stood there holding the bag, towering over him. He thought his mother was probably on the way out but said she was fine, and that, yes, she was spending the Christmas with his sister in Salisbury and, yes, it was a nice place. Siobhan had been to Stonehenge. Davy and Clyde were holding a conversation about lobsters. Nora just sat there on a high-backed chair near the counter, all stiff in a brown coat, listening like an owl, eyes roaming. If you met her eyes she'd never smile, just stare. He'd been in her house once, she'd asked him to carry a gas bottle in. She lived in a rust-red grotto that closed its mouth upon him and made him want to run from the awful crucifix, the bloody drops pouring from the Sacred Heart, the Blessed Virgins with sepia faces, the desperation, the swooning eyes. He'd felt as if he'd stumbled into a Voodoo den.

'Can I get you anything, Bob?' Siobhan asked him.

'A bottle of wine, please, Siobhan. Red.'

'Come for your brack, have you?' Clyde addressed Bob aggressively, his stray eye wandering.

Siobhan handed over a bottle of Chianti for inspection.

'Give me one of them lighters, please, Dierdre,' said Clyde to Mrs Davy, 'and some of that chocolate. That big one, the nuts, and stick it on the slate, please, love.'

Mrs Davy opened a little book and wrote down what Clyde owed. 'He loves his chocolate,' she said to Bob and Sheila, smiling.

'Wouldn't it make you sick?' said Sheila. 'Thin as a rake. Oh well.' She bade everyone a Merry Christmas and went out with her vast high haunches swaying and her great, bunioned, flip-flopped feet slapping the tiles.

'Now there,' said Clyde with no trace of humour, 'is a beautiful woman.'

Bob paid for the wine and Siobhan rolled it deftly in a sheet of pink tissue paper.

'Would you ever do me a favour, Bob,' Mrs Davy asked, 'would you drop something in at Connie's for me?'

'Yes, of course.'

She went into the back. Clyde appraised an area to the side of Bob's left shoulder with faint contempt until Mrs Davy came back with three big round loaves wrapped in holly-sprigged grease-proof paper. One she gave to Clyde, two to Bob. 'That's yours, Bob, and the other you can deliver for me,' she said. 'You're a good boy.' Seven months he'd been here and he qualified for a Christmas brack.

He was touched. He picked up his things to leave and Clyde came along at his shoulder, familiar and threatening, his brack under his arm.

'Merry Christmas, Clyde. Merry Christmas, Bob,' Mrs Davy called.

In the dark street Clyde and Bob walked without a word as far as Tommy Davy's. 'I'd be careful if I were you,' Clyde muttered, slipped aside and went in.

Bob walked on towards the end of the village. It had been raining all day and had recently stopped and the air was fresh. It was the custom to put candles in the windows on Christmas Eve and they shone comfortingly here and there across the valley when he left the village behind, but the lights excluded him. He could hear streams running in the deepening night, millions of little water-falls that had appeared after the rain, gleaming blue in the moony dusk.

The lights of the Mullen farm lay ahead. He'd hardly seen Marie since the dance. She was never in now when he called for his milk, he just went in and helped himself, left the money, that's how things were; and sometimes he'd felt that she was upstairs being quiet, or lurking out the back waiting for him to go away, and he wondered if he'd done or said something really stupid at the dance. She'd be out now, of course, and if she wasn't he wouldn't stay. He rushed on and came upon her suddenly as she emerged from a gap in the wall just before the farm, frightening them both.

'Oh, Jesus!' she squawked. 'Oh, Jesus, my poor heart!'

'Sorry, sorry,' he said.

They laughed.

'I was putting the chickens to bed,' she said.

'Were you? I've got your brack from Mrs Davy.'

'Ah, and I have something for you,' she said, 'Come on.'

He followed her up the path and into the kitchen.

'I'll pay my bill, too, Marie,' he said, putting the bag down on the table, 'if that's all right.'

'It is, of course.' She gave him some mince pies in a bag, saying, 'There now,' and patting his hand as if he were a child. 'Have a cup of tea, it's just boiled. Will you go in and sit down?' She was all bright and excited.

He went into the room with the range and the TV and the shelf of family photographs and sat down in an armchair. Marie came and put a tray on a small table covered with a clean white cloth, poured him a cup and handed it to him. Then she sat down with her own tea.

'Did you not want to go home for Christmas?' she asked.

'No,' he said, 'not particularly.'

'Don't want to see your mum?'

He laughed.

'You're a funny lot,' she said, 'none of you getting along. I wish I had my mother back, I can tell you. You don't know 'till they're gone.'

'You may be right.'

'You should make the most of family,' she said. 'Me and mine are all scattered now, I never see them. People just get further and further away.' She was not from these parts, she'd told him once, but from some little town in Waterford. Her brother had kept a bar. 'And you're not going to your brother's?' she asked mischievously. 'Shame on you.'

'Ha ha,' he said. 'No. I shall spend a very relaxing day doing absolutely nothing out of the ordinary.'

'Have you seen the brochure?' she said brightly. 'Julia brought one home.'

'Brochure?'

She got up and poked about on the mantel shelf. 'There.' She handed him a little fold-up advertising brochure, the kind you see strewn about in tourist offices. Montsalvat, Dundreen, West Cork, it said, Affirmation Centre, and there were photographs, one of the circular meditation room, one of the rugged glory of the coastal view, and one of oh my God, James and Helen sitting in the slightly Gothic rusticity of their back door with their shaggy-maned sheepdog. They looked wonderfully happy. The dog looked wonderfully happy too. And they looked so nice, you couldn't help but see that they must have some of the answers. Bob burst out laughing.

She looked surprised.

'Spiritual tupperware!' he sneered and handed the leaflet back. 'James is completely mad. God, look at them. Posers. You know, when I first met Helen she had nothing on.'

Marie smiled.

'I knew her slightly at Oxford, you know. She had this boyfriend – this was long before James – and I went round one day to borrow a book from him or something and knocked on the door and heard all this scurrying about as if they were getting dressed, and then a regal call: Come in! And there they were, both draped prettily about the place with nothing on. Nakedness was all the rage that year, I seem to remember. Sixty-nine or thereabouts. It was a statement.' He laughed cruelly. 'Rich as fuck she was and drove about in an old banger trying desperately to look like a gypsy. A pose, just like this new thing is a pose. Fashion. That's all it is. James has had several poses, you know. Ernest young businessman. Pop entrepreneur. Did you know that? Managed a terrible band called The Cosmic Cucumbers or something ridiculous. He and Helen. Absolute crap. Of course that was in the days before they gave up booze and dope. Not sex, I don't suppose.'

The word *sex* hung between them in a little silence, and *nakedness* and *fuck*.

'Will you have some more tea?' she asked.

Bob said he wouldn't mind. While she poured he got into his stride. He railed against the smugness and stupidity of all that new age crap, said his brother was a patronising moron, that they all thrived on a sense of superiority and that went for all forms of religion – in England people who went to Church were just stupider and uglier than all the rest, a gross generalisation, he said, but fairly observable. 'Here it's different because you all go to Church, *all* of you, whether or not you believe. This country drives me mad sometimes, it's the same thing, the smugness, the sureness, you go in the bookshops here and look under religion and its just Catholicism. Everything else is lumped in with Philosophy or something. Outrageous country! Sin! People kill themselves when they get pregnant, babies get dumped, it's Victorian, unbelievable.' He leaned forward, taking out his cigarettes and offering her one.

Marie felt a little thrill. It's only me he talks to like this, she thought.

'You should have seen this house when I first came here,' she said, looking about. 'Con's mother and father were here then, and Therese. Oh, we had all the holy pictures up, you know.' She shrugged. 'What harm, though? We're not all the same, you know. I'm not a great believer, myself, but I can see the comfort in that kind of thing. You're just as bad as them, sure, you think you're right, just like them.'

'But I am,' he said, and laughed.

He was at ease. He looked like a boy. She could see him in a crowd of youths, on the edge, with limp hair and a nice face, the kind she wouldn't have fancied at all as a girl. Then after a while maybe she'd have thought he looked nice, but by that time he'd have been off with someone else, or he'd have done well at his lessons and gone away and that would be that. That's the kind he was.

'You see,' he said, 'I'd hate to think I was getting the illusion and not the real thing. It's the same with Ireland. It's easy to get hijacked by the image. Before I met any of you I'd look down here, the white farmhouse at the foot of the mountain, smoke curling up from the chimney, the sea behind and the sun going down and the washing on the line and the donkeys pulling carts and the nice friendly people and the horses still ploughing in the fields and the old blacksmith still plying his trade, and all that. Oh, we're suckers for it! English romantics in love with Ireland. And all the funny little stories we laugh about amongst ourselves about Ireland and the Irish. Oh, we're full of them, they're just killers at dinner parties.'

There was a long silence.

'Tell me about your book,' she said.

He said it was about a painter who'd been blown up at the age of thirty-two in a terrible explosion with all his life's work, apart from a handful of brilliant pictures which had survived. He spoke at length and rapturously about a painting of the Raising of Lazarus that he'd gone all the way to Warsaw to see. He'd got the train back to Vienna and —

'Vienna!' she said longingly.

'Yes,' he said, 'my girlfriend was working there at the time.'

'Oh, the dancer.'

'Yes,' he said,' she was a dancer.' He thought of some of the scabby dumps Nola had danced in and how always he couldn't wait to get home.

'Going up to Essie's party, are you?' she asked.

'Yeah. Come on up.'

'Ah no, I couldn't.'

'Why not?'

'Ah no, I'm too tired.'

'Essie said she always invites you but you never go.'

She smiled. 'All this about religion. Don't you ever get afraid?' she asked him. 'I do.'

'Oh yes,' he said. 'Isn't that called the human condition? But on a deeper level, no. I'm not afraid of death, you know, at all.'

He had a serious, steady, vulnerable gaze, and the corners of his mouth were stiff.

Simon came in.

8

Con came in angry. 'Stupid shites!' he said.

'Who?' Marie came out of the kitchen. Her hands were wet and she was smiling at something on the TV over Simon's head.

Con took off his coat and sat down in his chair by the fire. Julia looked questioningly at him but he scowled at her till she turned her eyes back to the screen. 'Bloody pine needles!' he grumbled, brushing the arm of his chair fussily. The Christmas tree, much denuded, overhung it slightly.

'Want some tea?' asked Marie, leaning over and pulling at Julia's hair.

Engrossed in MTV, Julia and Simon nodded.

Marie went into the kitchen.

Con followed her and pushed the door to. 'Do you know what they are saying?' he said quietly. 'Do you fucking know what they are fucking saying?'

She coloured visibly, turning at the tone of his voice, the kettle in her hand. Con never swore at home. 'What are you talking about?' she snapped. 'Why are you coming in here like that?' She walked about frowning, filling the kettle, plugging it in, running the tap to make a noise to add to the sound of MTV in the other room and drown out what they were saying.

'I was at Ma's,' he said, lumbering awkwardly after her with a clumsy, high-shouldered wheeling movement. 'Listen to me, Marie.' His anger was subsiding, replaced by embarrassment. 'She says you were walking down the street with Bob and there's been some talk, you know what they're like ...'

'What!'

'Now look, Marie, I am not saying ... I am not saying ... ah, you know what they're like, just don't you go giving them any excuse to talk, that's all. The bastards! Now, I am not saying ...'

'What!'

'She said you were walking up the village with him ...'

'I only met the man in the shop and was just walking back the way with him. He's a neighbour! He has to walk this way! What do you want me to do? Refuse to talk to him?'

'God, they love the fucking show. Sorry, Marie, I'm not mad at you. I just hate the way people talk around here. Now it doesn't matter that there's nothing in it, it's what some of them are saying, and it's got to stop!' He swiped the air bitterly with his forearm.

The kettle boiled. Marie flew at him, stopping an inch away and staring into his face furiously. 'Don't you dare!' she hissed. 'Don't you dare accuse me of anything! I've done nothing wrong and I will not have it!' She got into her stride. He wilted. 'I will not have your mother accuse me of anything. Talk? Talk? I know who's spreading talk! I'll go right there this minute and sort her out!'

And she turned for the door but Con caught her arm, desperate, and pulled her back. 'Christ, no!' he pleaded. 'Don't say anything to her. For God's sake, Marie! Don't say anything.'

'Oh no!' she said viciously, flinging about and making the tea. The steam made her face red. 'I never do, do I?'

'Christ, I wish I'd said nothing. Will we forget it? Marie?'

She wouldn't speak. Her mouth was hard.

'Come on, Marie. I'm not saying . . .'

'What are you saying, Con?' she shouted.' 'What *are* you saying?'

'Ssh! Do you want the whole world to know?'

She laughed. 'The whole world? In our house? If there's gossip I want to know, and I want to know who's spreading it, because it's all a load of rubbish and I'm not having it!'

Marie took the tea into the living room, shoved it on the table and left them to get their own, sitting down with set lips to light a cigarette. I was too angry, she thought, too angry. After a moment Con followed, looking sheepish and puzzled, and proceeded to pour the tea with exaggerated and slightly martyred care.

'What's the matter?' asked Julia.

'Nothing,' said Marie.

Simon accepted his tea, ignoring everything around him apart from the TV, his legginess all hunched up in one corner of the sofa, thumb in mouth.

'You two make me laugh,' Julia said.

'Oh, Julia, keep out of it!' Marie snapped.

'I'm only after . . .'

Con turned on Marie. 'You started this. Shouting out in the kitchen so they can hear and then telling them to keep out of it. Who brought them into it?'

'I started it?'

'And you,' said Con to Julia, 'you can keep your mouth closed. You've got some bloody silly ideas anyway, meditating, scrubbing your aura! Christ! What do you know?'

'Me? What have I done?'

'Start on her now,' said Marie blandly, leaning forward to flick ash into the fire.

'She wants to be up and off.' Con addressed Marie with grim
levity, jerking a thumb at Julia. 'Thinks she knows it all.'

'Oh, she doesn't know what she wants yet,' said Marie dismissively. Of course Julia would go to London, she thought. Out into
the world. And *she* would remain, an old woman in this house,
like Con's mother before her. 'She goes up there,' Marie said
lightly, 'meditating and the Lord knows what, and she's still a
swine about the house.'

Julia looked away disdainfully and watched the TV. Her long
thin wrists moved restlessly, twining a couple of stray threads of
her mother's wool.

'Let her alone,' Con said. 'She means no harm.'

Simon looked at his mother, took his thumb out of his mouth
and suddenly smiled. He had tombstone teeth and a big mouth,
wide, milky-blue eyes and a pale face lightly freckled all over.
'They're building a car park, Mum,' he said.

'A what, sweetheart?'

'A car park, at Dundreen.'

'What for?'

'And stop following George around,' Con said sternly to Julia.

'I don't follow him around.'

'Yes, Julia. It doesn't look right. I don't know what Essie
thinks.' Marie picked up her knitting.

Julia blushed deeply and her eyes filled.

'You don't want to be up there all the time,' Marie said.
'They're all a lot older than you. You want to be with your friends.'

'I only go up there when there's something on. What's wrong
with wanting to find out about things?'

'He does know a lot,' Marie said, 'I'll give him that.' Then she
laughed. 'It's him I'm worried about. You'll be going to his head.'

'Because they're expecting lots of people,' Simon said.

'What?'

'Up at Dundreen.'

'London!' Con said suddenly. 'What a terrible place for young
people to be these days!'

'Aunt Gretta's there,' said Julia. 'She's all right, isn't she?'

'She's a married woman with a family. She's a lot older than you.'

'So?'

'Now don't you be cheeky.'

'Does that mean I can't go? Tonight? Essie and George are picking me up.'

Con sighed.

'Oh, it's all right, I suppose,' Marie said.

'Ssh!' Julia silenced them peremptorily. A Prince video had come on. She was heavily into Prince.

'Daddy,' said Simon, 'can I drive the car tomorrow?'

'No.'

'Oh, let him,' Marie said, 'he's only crawling after the cows.'

'No.' Con sat down in his chair and put his feet on the hob. 'I dunno, I dunno,' he said wearily. Simon put his thumb back in his mouth and sulked, wrapping his arms about his knees.

The video was quite sexy and they were all embarrassed. Con didn't say anything but ignored the screen pointedly, coughing and rustling and slurping at his tea. Two or three videos later he began to grumble. 'Why do they always have the same ones on over and over again?' he asked. 'I've seen this one about fifty times. You don't want to watch everything fifty times, what are they playing at?' Julia and he began to argue. Marie said nothing at all, but laughed condescendingly every now and then at things that Con said.

After a while Con got his coat and went out grimly and did a few chores about the yard. The weather was warm and damp and a mist lay over everything. The foghorn sounded. Hedges dripped; moisture swirled about him with almost invisible grace.

He was still thinking about what his mother had said.

Con retraced his steps to the village. It was mid-afternoon and Sylvester's was locked up, but Clyde's dog, Molly, lay by the door. Sylvester came and opened when Con knocked and they went through to the kitchen, where Ger, Clyde and Tim Pat Malachi sat drinking whiskey at the big table full of dirty dishes and food slops.

'Now then,' murmured Sylvester, pouring him a drink and sitting down once more to peel potatoes.

'Well, you can't blame him,' Clyde was saying, 'fucking stupid bastards.' His gun was on his shoulder.

'What?' asked Con.

'Paddy Bawn,' said Ger, 'shot one of Ben Bowden's dogs.'

'The stupid, poncey-looking one,' added Clyde.

'Supposedly for killing a sheep. It wasn't his dog that did it, Ben's saying.'

'He would, wouldn't he?' Clyde snorted. 'Ah, come on. That thing was always out in the road sniffing about on its own.'

'Twas gentle though,' put in Sylvester, his smile constant. He put down one very blackened peeled potato and took up another. 'Sure, I saw Ulrica getting out of her car outside the shop and she was crying.'

'Oh, Paddy hates Ben,' said Ger cheerfully, crossing his legs and gesturing with an unlit cigarette. 'He'd say anything. Hates those dogs. He's a madman.'

'You've got to see his point, though,' said Clyde, chucking his lighter over to Ger who caught it deftly. 'Thirty years the house next door stands empty, then all of a sudden they move in with their stupid pet dogs ...'

Ben Bowden was desperate to belong, joined everything and worked hard at his pronunciation, but he hadn't quite cut the mustard with the locals.

Tim Pat laughed. He had a big, narrow-eyed face and neat brown hair. 'He has Ulrica to goggle at, though,' he said. 'She has better looks than Dan Hogan, anyway.'

Everyone laughed.

Con drank and had another and thought of coming in and seeing Marie and Bob Sawle together at the kitchen table. Companionable. They hadn't jumped apart or anything when he came in. I wonder, would she go for that refined type he thought, and his heart began to pound a little as the whiskey settled into him.

'What do you say, Con?'

'What?'

'Your new neighbour,' Clyde repeated. 'Is he after a kicking or what?'

Ger giggled, his handsome little face clownish.

Con went cold. They knew something. They were all talking.

The old woman was right. 'Why?' he asked as casually as he could. 'What's your bother with him?'

'No bother,' said Clyde coolly, 'only that he's put a fence across the back between Inchicora and Quigs's, and that's always been free access. Shit,' he showed his teeth and shifted the gun, 'it's getting like fucking England. Private. Fucking keep out. Fucking aristocracy.'

'Oh sure, Simon helped him with that,' said Con, relaxing. 'It's only that the cattle were getting down that way and churning it all up where he gets his water. He'll be putting a gate in. You can still walk that way.'

Clyde was unappeased.

'Rosanna says he's been sniffing round her,' Ger said enthusiastically.

'Oh, fuck,' laughed Clyde, 'he must be hard up.'

'Are you game for another?' Sylvester asked, rising with all the dirty potatoes in a wet cloth and walking to the sink to wash them.

'No thanks, I'm off.' Clyde got up and made for the door, hauling his game bag.

'After the bunnies?' Tim Pat smiled, standing and walking to the window to check the weather. He was huge and had to duck his head to look out. 'Bad day for it.'

Clyde did not reply. He hoisted the gun, pulled at the peak of his cap, slitted his eyes at the smoke from his cigarette and sauntered out, smiling knowingly. Con followed him. They walked as far as the old schoolhouse, derelict now, where Con and his sisters and all of the others had gone, then turned West, striking out towards the cliffs.

'Is it true,' Con asked. 'Has that one been coming it with Rosanna?'

'Course not! What do you think?'

Cattle materialised suddenly, close by, with a soft, hot clearing of the nostrils. Clyde's thin, hard-bodied dog loped along in front. 'He's in for a kicking, the bastard!' Clyde burst out viciously. 'Gets right up my fucking nose, he does. Thinks he's the big fucking writer up there. I wish to fuck I could shove this gun up his arse and pull the trigger.'

Con was shocked. 'What's the man ever done to you?'

'I don't know.'

They came to a place where a circle of stones leaned away from the sea, which boiled white amongst the rocks in great basins below the cliffs. Gulls and cormorants clustered on one grey gleaming peak.

'Well, I'm off to Vigo soon,' said Clyde, looking at the sea, 'off on the old *Mary Ellen*.'

The dog started nosing about dementedly, soft dugs dangling, tail wagging.

'Get much, do you?' asked Con, indicating the game bag hanging down over Clyde's back.

'Enough. She's a good dog.'

Molly ran wide to avoid the stones.

'Funny,' said Clyde, 'she'll never go near them.'

They walked along, hands in pockets, heads down.

'You'll get done for that one day,' Con said, nodding at the gun as their paths diverged.

Clyde grinned. 'They'll never take me alive,' he said.

Con grinned too and raised a hand, turning his face towards home. He felt better somehow. Least he wasn't crazy like Clyde. By the time he reached the farm he'd armed himself once more with his own good nature, his old sweet smile, his getting round her look. For a few moments he stood outside the door before going in, bracing himself for her righteous indignation. A cat padded over to him and rubbed against his leg with a throaty mew and he stooped to stroke its matted fur. From the shed came the sound of the heavy shifting of beasts. The sweet smell of dung was on the wet air and the mist gave to the rocks on the far hillside the appearance of a giant bare-armed woman hauling a man out of the earth.

The kids were out. She was making a stew and her face was hard. He went over to her and kissed her on the cheek. 'Sorry,' he said, shaking her a little.

Marie said nothing but ground her teeth. If she was a crying woman she would have cried, but she never did. As far as he knew she hadn't cried since she'd told him she was having Julia. She'd scowl, grind her teeth, work her jaws, bang pans, break things.

But she'd never cry.

'Come on, Marie! Oh, come on, please! Don't be like this.'

'Me,' she said drily, scraping a carrot viciously. 'I'm to blame. Always.'

'Ah, come on,' he said. 'Put your bloody knife down, woman.'

'Tell your mother, why don't you?' She flung the carrot into a bowl in the sink. 'Oh no! What? Tread on her toes? Oh no!' She grabbed another carrot and chopped its head off.

Con stood in the middle of the kitchen looking crestfallen, hanging his head and watching her from under his brows as she peeled and chopped and hurled things carelessly into a bubbling pot on the stove. From time to time he sighed ostentatiously but she ignored him. After a while she adjusted the gas and went into the next room without so much as looking at him.

Con went and stood at the door. 'Will I make us a cup of tea?' he asked.

'Suit yourself.' She was at the table working something out in a jotter with a pencil.

He walked over and stared at her until she was forced to look up, then said, 'I'm sorry. There. Now.' He bumped her briefly on the corner of the mouth, a good boy. 'Will I make us a cup of tea?'

He smiled in a way that would still have been charming if his mouth had not turned in so, she thought, then hated herself for having the thought and softened and put her hand on his arm. He looked embarrassed. I don't touch him any more, she thought. Did I used to? Yes, once, a long time ago. Another life. She took her hand away.

'Yes, please,' she said.

He went into the kitchen and she could hear him pottering. He began to sing with an exaggerated man-of-the-people delivery, deliberately waggish. She looked at the meaningless squiggles on the page, calculations for a waistcoat she was going to make for Julia. It was his own 'Ballad of the Poor Old Farmer', a thing he always used to sing to annoy his father.

Oh, me dear old father he broke his back,
And me aunt in America died.

> Me aged mother she took to her bed,
> And me brothers and sisters all cried.
> And we starved! And we starved! And we starved!
>
> Oh, me Uncle Patrick contracted tuberculosis,
> And me sister Peggy started to go blind,
> The landlord came and knocked down our house
> And we all had bare behinds,
> And we starved! And we starved! And we starved!

He came in with the tea, throwing added pathos into the last verse. He had a pudding-like quality, she thought. You could have him with custard.

> Me mother, it turned out, had some rare malignant disease,
> There was nowhere to go but the ditch,
> I was forced to leave me own dear little native home
> And it's all one hell of a bitch,
> And we starved! And we starved! And we starved!

It had been funny the first few times.

'You are a fool,' she said, smiling. His hand stayed on the back of her neck when he gave her the tea, resting there heavily for a moment with the trace of a caress before moving. Suddenly she knew she wasn't going to be able to get out of doing it tonight in bed, and she felt depressed. Her big heavy nightie put him off sometimes, but it didn't put him off enough.

9

A few weeks later when Bob was coming down the track with his library books, he saw Marie bringing the four cows down from their grazing above Quigs's. She was over on the other side of the gully, moving from tussock to tussock in a series of little runs and jumps, surefooted with her arms folded. A sheep-dog ran with her, and the cows moved slowly before, stopping to graze now and then. She had not seen him and he stood still for a while to watch her. She wore wellingtons and a grey skirt, her knees showing between, and a headscarf tied under the chin. Her hair bushed out from under it. When she saw him she waved, moving sideways to bring in a massive Friesian with a great white head.

They met down on the road. The dog ran to greet him and a cow's eye rolled pink. Marie was adjusting the scarf into a more becoming style. Her cheeks were flushed, shoulders square under a dark blue jumper. He walked with her to the farm gate, looking at the clear blue sky. Some early violets were coming out at the side of the road. Jackie Bat's dark bulk could be seen in the distance standing on the old pig run, two fingers in his mouth, whistling piercingly to his ancient dog, Rex, herding sheep far above. Before them the grimy tails swished and the cloven clopping feet lazily scumbled the dried dung along the lane.

She said now all the hard work started. The cows spread themselves over the home field as he followed her down the path. 'Come and see,' she said, and took him round the side of the house and showed him all the work she was doing in the garden. She'd planted larches round the edge and they were shooting up, she said. She'd got them from that place near Rossgarry. She'd just put down five lazybeds of earlies and walked along between two of them treading down the earth. 'What are your books?' she asked.

They were detective novels.

'I didn't think you'd read that kind of thing,' she said.

'Why not?'

'Oh.' Her knees went up and down as she stamped, 'I thought you'd have something more ... I don't know.'

'I read everything,' he said.

'So do I. Only I can never remember the writers' names. Do you know, I used to write myself once. Poetry and so forth, oh, terrible stuff.'

He watched her knees going up and down and a terrible yearning came upon him, filling him with horror. It lay between them for one awful obvious moment.

Then she came walking towards him, stepping over the potato ridges, smiled and said, 'Come on in and get your milk.'

They went round to the front, where a fine cockerel lording it before the door moved slowly away with a grudging drawn-out cackle at their approach. The house smelt of dinner cooking. She took off her boots inside the door and slipped on some shoes, standing and pulling off the scarf, pushing back her hair and smiling in a peculiar, reckless kind of way as if she had no control over it. She was fairly close and the sense of complicity was unmistakable. For a few seconds they actually swayed towards each other before recalling the watching walls, the eyes of the family photographs, Con's mother, Julia and Simon, Con and Marie on their wedding day, all pale and young.

She moved away. 'How long have you been here now?' she asked brightly, going into the kitchen to get the milk.

He thought. 'Ten months.'

'Ten months!' She returned, smiling. 'Is it really now? It seems longer.'

She put the container of milk on the table and sat down there, running her finger slowly across the icy beads of moisture on the rim of the lid. Bob put down his books and sat across the table from her and they smiled, saying nothing for so long that any pretence of normality foundered.

When she laid her hand upon the tablecloth, he covered it gently with his own and a thrill shot up her arm, tinged with a certain strange repulsion. She didn't even blush. I'm getting him, I'm getting him, she thought. Reeling him in.

They looked at each other. 'Marie,' he said quietly, 'what are we going to do about this?'

'Nothing,' she said, 'nothing, nothing, nothing.' The grip of his hand tightened.

Someone was walking up the path. Bob stood up with his container of milk. Con came in, dirty and tired, and greeted him civilly. Bob remembered with a shock that he liked Con.

'Well,' she said cheerfully, 'I hear you're going to England soon.'

'Oh, not till summer.'

She looked out of the window. 'The library's at the strand,' she said, 'it'll be in the village any minute.'

Bob took his milk and went on his way, declining Con's offer of tea. Con drank a cup anyway, lying back in his chair while Marie got his dinner out of the oven.

*

His car needed a service. He took it to Rossgarry and left it there and came back on the Strangarvan Sprinter, a ramshackle old bus that rumbled slowly along the sea-threatened switchback for thirty miles between the two towns. All the way he sat with his eyes closed and his hand over his brow to keep the glare off. Of course, Con might be in town too, but they wouldn't be together, they never were. She'd drive home before Con, leaving him to come on later with his cousins, that's the way it happened. And he would ... there was a changelings' graveyard somewhere between Strangarvan and Ballinaphuca, sheltering woods ... no, best to keep it as it was, courtly love, chaste, obsessed. He opened his eyes. Probably wouldn't see her anyway, or she'd be with Therese or ...

The fish factory came into view. Tall masts stood against the white sky. A tang of fish and the sea hung over the town. He climbed down from the bus in the square. People were thronging about market stalls. When the boats were in on a Fair Day Strangarvan was vivid, Spanish and Korean fishermen rubbing shoulders with mountainy men like Padraic South, blow-ins from everywhere buying in their bulk loads of wholemeal flour and organic brown rice from the back of a van outside Biddy O'Neill's on the quay. Livestock changed hands, sheep and cattle stood about in the painted, terraced streets, and there were barrows covered in baskets of live chickens outside O'Leary's.

He saw Marie buying apples from the fruit lady, turned and fled, ran into Ben Bowden at the cassette stall and ended up having a drink with him at Biddy O'Neill's. They stood outside with their pints, looking at all the activity along the quay. Ben said he was starting to sort his head out a bit now, get on with life. Two dogs sat looking up at him.

'I'm trying to affirm Paddy,' said Ben, 'what else can I do? I have to live with him.'

Shimmering silver fishes were falling from a chute. Armies of blue barrels stood on parade, great ropes slumbered. A bunch of Yorkshire sailors jumped in and out of a boat as if there were no difference between land and sea. Bob drank up and got away and went out past the rabies notices to where the harbour wall was nearly deserted, and sat down on a bench. It was chilly. He had to go back, had to face it, she'd be getting away. Two swans floated near the wall. A nun came along with a paper bag and started feeding them with strips of white bread. Jolly Irish accordion music drifted from the cassette stall in the square.

There was a changelings' graveyard somewhere through the woods. He'd had it in his mind that he must take a look at it some day. The nun brushed her hands and went away and he sat watching the swans delicately polish off the bread before paddling further out into the harbour. If she said yes, he thought, if she came with him through the woods, then she was his.

An elderly woman with bright red hair and too much make-up came out of a house on the other side of the road and threw a cardboard box full of rubbish into the water. The swans came back to investigate, but there was nothing for them, only plastic milk bottles, soggy packages, cans, bottle tops, a spreading flotilla of trash.

He went back and looked for her but she'd vanished. A man was beating a stubborn, stoically frightened cow into the back of a truck. A few drunken revellers caroused outside O'Leary's. He met Essie coming out of the supermarket and she offered him an apple ring. 'I've been trying to get the makings of a ratatouille,' she said. 'I do wish the locals'd cotton on that anything more than cabbage and potatoes is not necessarily decadent.'

Julia stood by the hot-dog stand queueing up with all the other schoolkids. Her eyes followed him all along the street and made him uncomfortable, as if she could have known his thoughts. He stopped outside the chemist, feeling flat, thinking: should've bummed a lift from Essie. Then he saw Marie walking past the church on the other side of the road. His heart gave a little jump. She crossed herself, automatic. Christ. She said she didn't believe but they were all the same, even hardened old sceptics like Feargal Breen did it: appeasing the local gods, he'd called it, smiling apologetically.

She saw him and smiled and he went over to her at once.

'Did you leave your car off OK?' she asked.

'Yes.'

She looked about. 'I thought you'd be here,' she said innocently. 'Are you looking for a lift?'

'If you can.'

'I can, of course. I've just got one or two more messages to do, then I'm off. The car's on the quay, see you there in, oh, a half-hour.' She started to walk away, but then turned. 'No, tell you what. I have to go to the Creamery, so God knows how long I'll be. Why don't you start walking and I'll pick you up along the way. If you don't get a lift before.'

Wiser indeed, fewer eyes. She knew, she knew, surely she'd been making plans of her own.

He nodded, walking away without a word.

He turned, shading his eyes as the car drew up alongside. He'd already turned down two lifts saying he felt like the walk. 'That was quick,' he said as he got in. He was cold and the car's warmth was welcome. A sack of fertiliser sat on the back seat like a passenger. They smiled noncommittally at one another and drove a little way in silence. Five or six miles out of town the woods began, the grounds of an old estate that had been allowed to run wild down to the sea for a mile or so. Once the whole of the land down to Caheradown Strand and Ballinaphuca Point and Anagar to the east of the bay had been woodland, but this little bit was all that had survived Oliver Cromwell and deforestation.

'There's a changelings' graveyard somewhere around here,' he said. 'Barney Mac was telling me about it. That man's a mine of information. He ought to do a Peig Sayers and make his fortune, you know, he's got it all. Do you know where it is?'

'I do,' she said, nodding towards the trees, 'it's just a little way ahead. It's a wild enough place all right. Very high up over the sea.'

'I'd like to see it.'

He looked at her as she drove. She had an eerie smile that never wavered and her eyes were sparkling. He thought she was going to say something, but she just kept on driving.

'Marie,' he said. 'Have we time? Could we go and see it?'

'OK,' she said.

A little later she slowed, then turned down a narrow, unfrequented track that bounced them along with the foliage scraping the car, to a widening and an opening, a gate with an orange rope tying it to a wall, dark and thick with new spring growth. She pulled in and they got out. She opened the gate, not looking at him, closed it, and led the way down a scarcely visible dirt track that led through a thickness of beech trees, holly and ivy, tall rhododendron, tiny purple flowers and strange fungal growths. The back of her fair head was plucked at by fingers of trees. After a while the growth thinned out and they heard the sea far below. They came out onto a long bare point of earth stretching out with the sea on both sides, flanked by other ridges, stony and bare. It was like being on the arm of a starfish. They walked side by side, three feet apart. Bob kicked a stone intently, walking along with his hands stuffed deep in his pockets. It was very cold out here and he felt exposed and longed to go back to the trees.

Suddenly the land fell away on their left and he gasped when he realised how high they were. Sea caves boomed: all around, a hollow roaring, an endless moan.

She turned and laughed at him. 'Stick to the path,' she said, 'and you'll be all right.'

He hated the height, the pounding space. Down into a dip they went, up again, out upon a knoll where fifteen or so tiny head-stones stood, some upright, some leaning, all grey and lichened and smooth. He walked silently among them. Not a name remained.

'They were the babies born with something wrong,' Marie said. 'They thought they were changelings. Poor little things!' She sat down away from the graves and lit a cigarette. 'They were put out here away from all the rest when they died. You can imagine what their poor mothers must have felt like. My little changeling out on the point.' She shuddered, looking towards America. Very far out on the cobalt sea, a single fishing boat hung as if sus-pended, a cloud of seagulls like midges about it. 'Poor little souls,' she said, looking up as if they hovered in the air above her head.

Bob went and sat beside her and took a cigarette from her and lit it from her own. He was trembling slightly.

'Well,' she said, 'here we are.'

What an impossible place, he was thinking. It would be obscene to make a move here, the poor little graves listing before them like tired children. The height made his teeth chatter. He thought he might run to the edge and jump off. The sky was an eye, the sea another. Open space boomed all around, a vast breathing spectator. God alone knew how he'd get back to the safety of the trees. They were more exposed here than in the centre of town.

'I'm sorry, Marie,' he said. 'I really am.'

She looked closely at him. 'Are you all right?'

'No.'

'It's OK, it's OK.' She put her hand on his arm.

'It's the height,' he said, 'I didn't realise it would be like this, it's some kind of . . .' his heart and his blood were pounding with the sea '. . . Oh, shit,' he said.

'Shall we go back?'

'I don't think I can.' A wave of nausea swept through him and he closed his eyes.

Marie put her arms round him, pulled down his head, put her mouth close to his ear. 'You're all right,' she said sensibly. 'I won't let you fall off.'

They sat there for several minutes, growing colder and colder. In the darkness behind his eyelids he kept seeing the tiny gravestones, nameless, and wondered if any one of them had a claim on anyone anywhere, no matter how distant, or were they all abandoned utterly to the terrible howling, forgotten completely?

'Now,' said Marie, 'you come with me.'

He opened his eyes. The stones were still there, blank, listing. The far blue line of the curved horizon crackled. 'Come on,' she said, and they stood up and walked side by side and arm in arm along the sloping ridge, down, up, back towards safety. His knees shook. When they reached the trees they hugged, then kissed, all tongue and clashing teeth, a real lover's kiss, hot and reckless, the kind she'd thought she'd never ever have. She hated tongue with Con. He'll remember me, he will, she thought, I'm not just anyone, there'll never be the chance again. Then they leaned back to look at each other and he smiled shyly, sliding his hands down her haunches and in under her buttocks, pulling her in to kiss again, licking her lips daintily.

'Oh, Marie, what a mess this is,' he said.

'I know. I know.'

It was pointless. It was cold, they shivered, the ground was damp. What could they do? They crouched down under a tree, huddling together, horrified at what was happening.

'Not here,' she said.

'No, of course not. Christ, it's cold!' He held her face, stroking her eyebrows with his thumbs. Then he kissed her between the eyes.

'It's wrong, isn't it?' she said. 'It's wrong.'

'Does it feel wrong?'

'Of course it does! It feels like hell. Doesn't it feel like that to you?' Before he could answer she said: 'Tell me about your girl-friend.'

'I don't have one.'

'Nola.'

'That's all boring.'

She pulled away and jumped up abruptly. 'I have to get back,' she said.

'No, you don't.'

'I do.'

'Right now?'

'Yes.'

He stood up. 'Marie,' he said helplessly, taking her arm and looking into her face. She grabbed him and kissed him, then pulled away again.

'I want to go home,' she said.

They walked about amongst the thickening trees, arms about each other, kissing, always in the direction of the car.

'I just want to see you sometimes. When?' he asked urgently.

'Ever? What do you want to do?' His tongue was thickening with fear.

'I don't know,' she said, 'what should we do?' She had this awful smile frozen onto her face.

The wood closed in like jungle. A path appeared through it. To continue it would be necessary to walk in single file. 'I have to get back or someone'll notice. We can't let anybody see anything or …' She walked on quickly ahead. He stood hesitating for a moment then stuffed his hands in his pockets and followed her down the narrow dirt track back to the gate and the car.

All strange and formal, she opened the car door. He just stood there.

'Can we be seen together?' he asked.

'We can, of course,' she said. 'It would look even stranger if we avoided each other. But not in a place like this. Go ahead, get in.' He did. 'Duck your head down for a second when we reach the road.'

They drove along the bumpy track, the engine whining. Just before the road he sank down, feeling as if he'd just found himself in a very bad thriller, and started to laugh. Marie joined in. 'Oh God, I feel so funny,' she cried. The road ahead was clear. 'OK,' she said, 'you can get up now.'

He sat up straight and they drove along smoothly towards Ballinaphuca. The woods ended and he looked at the sea. Marie drove quickly. After a while the engine warmed the car and their bones relaxed.

'You have to see that I don't do things like this,' she said, 'that I've never done this before . . .'

'Me neither.'

Mad dogs ran out on a corner and attacked the wheels, snarling.

'What do we do now?' he asked.

Marie shook her head, smiling at the road ahead. 'I wish me and you had met when I was young and you could have seen me then,' she said innocently as they came over the Gap.

'I don't want you then,' he said, 'I want you now.'

She didn't speak and her eyes were steady on the road. The village lay before them. The road snaked in and the road snaked out, the mountains gazed over its rooftops. Beyond was a knotty patchwork of small green fields, and one very big field that had been made by Davy Scanlon and changed the valley for ever. They sailed down the hill. At the foot of the village Barney Mac in his long leather apron was driving his cattle along and turned his head to watch them go by, raising his hand to their greeting.

'Oh, God,' said Bob.

'It's all right,' said Marie.

He wanted to say something more, anything, before they parted, but then there was her gate and Simon coming up the road with a dog and a big grin on his affable face, a woollen hat pulled down around his ears. So he said, 'Thanks for the lift, Marie, I'll see you soon,' and got out.

'Bye,' she said and waited for Simon to open the gate for the car.

There were worse lives.

She sat staring at Con's open mouth as he lay sleeping in his chair. Did she love him? Of course she did, she always would, he was indelible and that was that. And yet, looking at that open mouth there, the only mouth allowed to her for ever, she didn't want to kiss it any more, didn't want to touch him any more, didn't want anything at all from him in that way any more. She thought about Bob but couldn't really see his face. But she could feel the way she felt when he put his hands down under there, and she smiled and took in a very deep breath. Still, I wonder what he'd think if he saw me with no clothes, my stomach's gone now, she thought. Then: this is my only life, and she was filled with horror.

It began to rain lightly. She lit a cigarette and smoked it with deep, frightened draughts. I ought to stop this, she thought, I hate this bloody habit, I wish I'd never started it but, God, there's nothing, truly nothing, like the smoke going down your throat. Couldn't you just gargle on it? Con stirred and would wake soon.

There were worse lives.

She heard the yawn of a dog outside the back door, the pocks of rain on the window. The staircase hung down from the dark above. She was sleepy.

After all, what was it but a snog in the woods?

Con woke up when she rattled about in the range. He asked for a cup of tea, rubbed his eyes and yawned, then turned on the radio. Pascal Mooney was on, he was always bloody on. Con sang along to 'Four Country Roads'. Marie started to laugh to herself as she filled the kettle at the tap, slightly hysterical, remembering all over again what had happened in the woods.

10

She was avoiding him.

She was never there when he came for his milk. From a distance he saw her walking about in her yard, feeding the dogs or the chickens, but she always vanished as soon as he hit the lane. He lived in a state of permanent excitement, nervous like a dog, working all night, sleeping in the mornings, walking about the mountainside and sitting for hours amongst forgotten ruins, signs of a population gone, watching the mountain sheep crop the grass. He had to go away. It was the only sensible thing to do.

A week passed. He thought about cancelling his milk. Then he went into the shop one morning and there she was, hauling a sack of something with one of Con's cousins, a big fair boy with a walrus moustache whose name was Christy Pads. The shop was crowded, of course. Padraic South stood just behind them, old rocky face look forth, and Mrs Davy was asking him whether he wanted the mild or the matured.

Marie smiled brightly at him and asked how he was.

'The matured, Mrs Davy,' he said, and to Marie, 'I'm fine, I'm fine.'

'The Lannanshee's coming all right,' said Christy, smiling at him in a friendly way.

'You'd better tie down your wagon,' Marie said. Then she was gone.

That night he stood among the rocks in the blustery wind, looking down at her house. He saw her come out and stand for a while at the back door in the gathering gloom. Then Con appeared from the cow shed and she said something to him and they went into the house together. In ten years' time Con would be a fine fat farmer with a creased neck. Twilight was falling again, bloody sentimental twilight, making the light falling across the yard from their little kitchen window into a golden well of rural familic content. He put out his thumb and blotted it out, demonic, sowing decay.

He left it till late to call for his milk the next day, just to catch her in. Con was in the yard, Simon in the other room watching TV. They stood in the kitchen. She was in the grey skirt, the boots; her knees were bare.

'Well, you're not very friendly these days,' she said, rising from the fridge with a bland smile so that he wanted to shake her.

'How can I be friendly if you're never here?' he asked. She handed him the milk, saying nothing. 'What's the matter?'

'Nothing,' she said.

'Are you all right, Marie?'

'No,' she said softly, 'are you?'

They came very close with the milk container cold between them and kissed quickly.

'Not here,' she said, drawing back.

'There's nowhere,' he whispered despairingly.

'Con will be in soon.' She came closer and whispered: 'I'm lying awake at nights thinking about you.'

He passed Con and Simon on his way out and wished them goodnight, loathing himself. He was in the lane in the bloody twilight, she came running after him down the path. He'd forgotten his milk. She laughed at him. He leaned on the gate and the wind whipped the long grasses that stood on top of the wall. She looked slightly horror-struck, as if she might be going to cry. He'd made her look like that.

'Have you tied down your wagon?' she asked, 'it's going to be a wild night.'

'I'll hammer it down.'

A tear rolled down her cheek and he could do nothing, the night and the hedge and the gate and the road up from the village were all watching.

'Come up to the wagon,' he said. 'Some night. Please.'

She looked away, putting her hand across the gate for him to take. Briefly he held it. She wiped the side of her nose and sighed and pulled herself together and said: 'I don't know what to do, I just don't know what to do.'

'I want to touch your knees,' he said, and she laughed.

Someone appeared in the lane, a shadow near the water tank.

'Oh, it's terrible,' she said, controlling a sob in her throat.

It was old Dan Hogan the peeping Tom, a little black bat drifting down the lane, weaving crookedly towards the village. 'G'night!' he announced gruffly as he passed the gate.

'Goodnight,' said Bob.

'Goodnight, Dan,' said Marie cheerfully. 'I have to go,' she whispered, 'I'm in the middle of making the tea.'

Dan was fading down the lane. A light appeared up the path, Con going into an outhouse with a lantern.

'Goodnight,' she said, and turned to go. Con coughed; Simon laughed violently in the house where he was watching TV. She ran away up the path.

He walked quickly home. Everyone was saying the Lannanshee was coming.

He met Essie. 'Batten down the hatches,' she said with excitement, looking at the sky. 'Oh, I do love the Lannanshee!'

The wind was rising. He got home and hammered down the heavy ropes about his wagon in the growing dark, giving in to anger at himself and fate. He'd leave, he'd leave.

The wind blew all night long.

11

It had been building for some time.

It was something to do with the way they seemed to stop talking when he came into the shop, something to do with Tim Pat looming there with his big beaming face and his crinkly eyes studying the seed packets, Ger Sheehan swaying from foot to foot. Worry stirred in Con's stomach, like something bad he'd eaten a while ago that was only just starting to take effect.

The shop filled. Con left and walked down to Barney Mac's to hand in the form for his small farmer's allowance. The village was packed. Outside Barney Mac's, people were waiting to hand in their forms to the Guarda, local people and blow-ins, some in their cars, some huddled against the wind along the wall. Heads nodded as he passed.

'All right, Con.'

'All right there, Connie.'

'Con.'

He was in a foul mood anyway. Marie had gone off to town with the car and the fool of a dog had taken off again, probably after Clyde's bitch. He went and stood next to Jackie Bat against the big window full of shoe leather. Jackie nodded, drawing on a crumpled Afton. Old Rex, a grey-white-black-brown chaos of fur, grey-muzzled, lifted his leonine head and shook his grizzled mane. His eyes, one white, one green, were rheumy, two-tone nose dry as a bone. Heads in the cars parked over the road turned, blank faces, greetings, something else about them he couldn't put his finger on – something like guilt, he thought, the guilt you felt when you knew something bad about someone and they didn't know you knew. His cold cheeks burned.

The Guarda car was seen coming over the Gap and feet shifted. People were getting out of their cars. He saw Feargal Breen lean a little towards Ben Bowden and speak softly, and suddenly knew, just knew, that everyone was talking behind his back. He could say nothing, even when Christy came over and said as normal as you like, 'Howya, Con?'

He felt the kind of anger he'd not felt since he was a child, the kind where you wanted to cry or shout or kick your mother but couldn't do any of it. The car drew up and the young Guard got out and went into Barney Mac's back room. A ragged queue formed up the dim brown passage. Barney was in the room on the right, standing to one side in his long leather apron, filing away at the heel of a boot. The sparse whiskers on his pointed chin were very white, the slit of his mouth and the slits of his sharp eyes knowing when he smiled at Con. All of their eyes were knowing.

Con handed in his form and went down to the shop. That Ulrica was there, the one with the legs that he liked to watch dancing, and Ben and George and some others. He always got on well with the blow-ins and had to talk to them in a reasonably affable way for a while just to show willing, but he got out as quickly as he could and walked with his head down against the whistling wind towards the Post Office. They were talking, too, the blow-ins. Going home in their cars and talking.

The big mottled face of Mrs Shanahan in the Post Office was

insufferably knowing, but then it always was. The door kept opening, people gathering at his back. Con, who usually hung about leaning up against the display case where all the packets of bacon and the yoghurts were kept, chatting to everyone, shoving his hands through his thick hair, winking at the children, just turned and went out without getting what he'd come for and without a word to a soul, just walked on out of the village and down to the strand to see if there was any sign of the stupid dog, huddling down into his warm jacket and stepping out at a good pace. The wind blew straight in off the sea into his face, blew tears from his eyes. What was the matter after all? Nothing. Nothing at all had happened, it was all in his mind. After all, she was very friendly with lots of people.

It was freezing and he cursed her for taking the car.

Six or seven dogs were in the field above the beach, but not his own. He went down and stood near the beach house, his eyes scanning the strand. Dan Hogan wandered along the cold, flat sand like a blown rag, searching for spoils from the sea. His eyes, when he came near, were narrow and suspicious, mocking. Dan carried a polythene bag with a shovelful of wet cement in the bottom which he showed proudly to Con as if it were fine spoils.

'Fine, Dan, fine,' said Con distractedly.

Rosanna appeared in her doorway, hands stuck up the sleeves of a jumper that came down to her knees. The bitch pushed its nose out from behind her leg. She saw him and waved, smiling broadly, and he went over.

'When's Clyde back?' he asked. Clyde had been at sea.

'Anytime now,' she said. 'Ger saw him in Strangarvan.'

She had a bad cough and was hacking away helplessly, eyes swimming. Con told her if she saw his dog to chase it away home.

'Sure, Con,' she said and offered him a cup of tea, her watery eyes amused.

Con shook his head.

'Sure, I'll have a cup of tea there, missis,' said Dan gruffly, coming along behind with his limp bag of cement, and she laughed and ruffled his hair as if he were a child.

Con turned to walk east along the cold deserted beach. A sea-gull flew screaming by. A gathering of oyster-catchers sat in the sand, unperturbed by the weather. There was no sign of the dog, and after a while he turned inland and hurried away up the back road towards home thinking that he had to talk to Marie, had to do something about this horrible feeling that he had, like fear in his bowels, making him sick.

He met Jackie Bat, eyes watering, nose dripping, battling through the wind with a half grown lamb in his arms, Rex padding after. 'Hello there, Connie,' he panted, 'the poor creature's turned its leg.'

They walked along together for a space. Jackie's house was set back from the turn of the road, surrounded by fuchsia and foxgloves and great ranks of springing green swordlike plants. The house was crumbling, grey, the windows dingy. Con could remember a time in his childhood when there had been white curtains at the windows, and people had come and gone on visits from London and Liverpool and Manchester. No one came any more. And Jackie had always been there and Jackie had always looked the same.

'Tell me honestly now, Jackie,' Con said, 'have you heard any talk about anything I should know about?'

Jackie didn't say anything so Con knew something was wrong.

Their steps pounded on together side by side, and they looked at the ground. Then Jackie made a long catarrhal sound with his nasal passages and said breathlessly, 'Sure, isn't there always talk.'

God. 'What have you heard, Jackie?'

'Well, don't take it wrong now, Connie, I've heard nothing about Marie, only that the new fellow should be a little bit less familiar. Now that's not her fault, is it? Maybe if you just have a little word with him, he probably doesn't realise ...' Jackie spoke cheerfully, hitching up the lamb which hung there patiently, its small pointed black face upon his broad arm.

'What else, Jackie?'

'Nothing at all, nothing at all, Connie.'

He was not to be drawn, and a little further on said good luck and turned aside and crossed a field of sheep which were getting in behind the wall. Con walked on. The wind hit him in the throat and he almost gagged. It made him mad, pushing and blathering at him all the way home.

Marie had the radio on loud to hide the sound of the wind. The ironing board was up. 'Caroline in Navan, are you there?' shouted the DJ. Con stood for a moment sighing at the sudden warmth. He smelt turf and cooking and newly-ironed clothes.

When Marie looked up and saw his face her eyes were scared. 'What's the matter?' she asked at once.

But he couldn't speak, just went and sat staring into the fire. She looked at him and saw the flames burning in his eyeballs. His brow was tense under the strands of fair hair and his eyes looked like a scolded child's.

'What's the matter?' she asked again.

'He's not to get his milk here any more,' Con said abruptly. 'We haven't it to spare.'

There was a little silence. Her expression didn't alter. 'Fine,' she said softly, 'fine.' Then, after a while, added, 'It's all right, now, Connie, it's all right,' very firmly before going back to the ironing board.

Then they both tried to pretend that nothing had happened.

The Lannanshee came like a fist, hitting the house so that everything shook.

The sea took on itself the portrayal of grand passion, hurling itself up Caheradown Strand, over the sheep fields hundreds of feet above, covering the needle rocks at Ballinaphuca Point and Anagar, and the Puck Rock far out at sea. Over the mountain ridges, high up past Mishlin Lake, wind howled about the Mass Rock where the people had gone in the terror times to receive communion. Everywhere, everything rippled and strained.

Dan Hogan blew down the road like a leaf.

At Rathmeelabo, Padraic South stuffed an old coat over the gap under the front door, piled sods on the fire and blew it up with the bellows. With liver-spotted hands he put the kettle on, singing in a cracked voice: '*Hi-the-dithereeidledum, diddleyum-the-didledum, diddley-um-dum-diddley-aye-day.*'

Up at Inchicora, Essie and George stood together at the end of their garden. Around them the world waved and whirled. Essie sucked her tongue-stud happily; George had left his coat off deliberately and his shirt billowed out. His long and complex black beard, full of knots and ripples and only slightly grey, carried a pencil and some crumbs of old toast. Some old planks of wood lay discarded in the field. First one then another levitated miraculously and flew towards them through the air. They laughed and ran back inside, through their huge, gracious, cottagey living room with the Peruvian and Indian rugs and the chimes from Tibet, the sleeping cats, the variety of musical instruments that neither of them could play very well, upstairs to their crooked chaotic bedroom to watch the wind whipping up the bay like a demented cook from the safety of their long dormer window.

'There!' said Essie, 'isn't this a thousand times better than the TV?'

George just grinned.

Bob was sitting at his desk, vacantly stirring his coffee, staring at a mess of scribbled notes and thinking: I'll just take this lot and put them in the sea, recycle them, when something like a momentous stone rolled towards him across the sky, a monstrous meteor, a fire spreading, the apocalyptic horsemen charging. It hit. The wagon shook itself once with a yelp, then settled into a constant wary trembling. Bob looked up, saw the things on the shelf move, heard the shrill howling voice take up its scold, thought of the wildness of the mountain out there and hoped the ropes would hold. The Lannanshee took in a breath and rolled another bowling ball across the sky.

'Jesus Christ,' he whispered, feeling like a ninepin.

In the house on the strand Clyde held the gun to Rosanna's head. 'No one would hear,' he said, 'no one at all.'

She smiled at him, the sailor home from the sea. She was lying on the mattress, her eyes doting and full of tears. He made a sound in his throat like a gun exploding. He was bored already, his mind still full of the *Mary Ellen*, the decks shining and slippery with fish, the gulls, the cold, the waves in the Bay of Biscay. He put the gun to her fanny, finger stroking the trigger. Rosanna rubbed herself against the barrel. Then she started to cough explosively.

He jerked the gun away. 'It could have gone off, you fool,' he snapped. Tears streamed from her eyes. 'Christ,' he said, 'it's just one thing after another with you, you're never well.'

The dog Molly whinged by the door.

Only the most ardent of her suitors remained on the dunes above the beach. The Mullens dog was running home, head down, disdaining the lanes and heading straight across country. When he got to the farm everything was locked up, so he howled pitifully at the house door. Con flung it open and grabbed the dog by the scruff of the neck, dragged it across the yard with a mighty kick in the flank that made it yelp, tied it with a frayed rope to a post at the side of the house and beat it repeatedly. Then he marched back in and went upstairs without saying anything.

Marie was in the kitchen kneading dough, thinking this could not be true, this was a dream, that Con was not speaking to her and that she could not see Bob any more and nothing would ever be the same again. After a while she sneaked out and freed the trembling dog and put him in the shed with his mother. She did not stop to look up at Quigs's but ran back in, shivering, hoping Julia would get a lift back OK.

Julia was at Dundreen. Montsalvat, she always called it now. She was in the circular room with all the rest. Their eyes were closed. James Sawle, pale and frowning and gingery, had his finger on the switch of the cassette recorder from which a soporific voice guided their meditation. He'd already turned the volume up twice against the wind that shrieked and sobbed about them. Julia wore black leggings and a black T-shirt with a white swan's wing across the chest. Her wide greenish eyes were open, gazing out of the reinforced glass wheel in which they sat at the devilish waves reaching up to pull them in. A seal appeared and reappeared occasionally down there in all that boiling mess. No one will ever know my secrets, she was thinking. I'd die if anyone ever got to know my secrets.

The meditation ended and the switch was flicked and the due silences observed, then everyone went through to the kitchen for tea. The kitchen was huge, all pine and green, with a beautiful black-and-white tiled floor. Tartex and hummus sandwiches, egg and spinach roll, a cheeseboard, home-made bread, honey, were all laid out on a long table under a poster of Swan Mary, ancient, raceless, unsmiling, seamed like the rocks at Ballinaphuca Point.

They talked about the Moon's nodes.

Kester and Polly ran into the big round empty room and started to shout and leap about. Helen came and shushed them. 'Oh God!' she said, flouncing out her mossy black hair as she looked at the wild estuary. 'Sometimes I think we'll all just vanish overnight.'

Jackie Bat sat warming his steaming feet by the fire. The lamb was in a cardboard box. 'Aren't you the lucky one?' said Jackie, and chuckled. 'Aren't you the lucky one?' And thought of all the others out there on the field of the crown, which had once belonged to his father and grandfather and now belonged to Davy Scanlon, like nearly everything else around here.

12

The Lannanshee blew for a month.

There'd been a note on top of the fridge when he went into the empty house to get his milk: 'No more milk from next week, I'm afraid.' A week's notice, no less. She was good at disappearing.

And then in a little while you'd have thought nothing had ever happened: he'd see her in the shop or in Strangarvan or bringing the cows down and they'd say hello like neighbours and leave it at that.

So he just worked, just slogged and walked about the wagon in his dumb show, talking, reasoning, explaining. Sometimes he went up to Inchicora and discussed Rousseau or Nietzsche with George who, in spite of his appearance of grinning imbecility, was actually quite intelligent at times. But for the most part he became a recluse. He learned to love the wind and put himself in stupid places, tempting fate: the cliffs at the edge of the sheep fields, the strand, the ravined path that led out to Anagar, that wild green terrible place beyond the bay. Once he went walking along the beach in a storm and nearly got plucked out to sea by a freak wave that rushed him and gripped him past the knees. He stood in a raging sea, blinded by the spray, winded by the cold, listed like the stones in the changelings' graveyard to the land then seawards,

Americawards, as the wave washed back. He got away and went home and thought: I nearly died, and lay down on the bed all cold and wet as he was, and wondered how she'd feel if he was washed up on the shore. But then he laughed at himself, got up and stripped off his sodden clothes with frozen fingers. He had to go soon, soon as the wind stopped, if ever it did. Day after day, night after night it shrilled and bullied, and the constant movement of everything everywhere became a madness like a Van Gogh sky.

Then the wind was gone and there was Summer, full-blown, glorious. *A View In Delft* had defeated him. He was going to call it finished even if it wasn't because he couldn't stand it any more. He put the word about that he was leaving soon.

Marie heard when she was out in the bottom field doing the hay with Con. Simon told them, doing wheelies on his bike in the lane, smiling and showing off. He said it in with a lot of other things but nothing else registered. Con was on top of the stack and she was passing up armfuls of hay; she hated this work, hated it, stinking, sweating work in the blazing sun. Con scowled as he bound the hay into the pile, working seriously and breathing noisily, his round face dirty and intent.

After a while she stood up straight and arched her back, frowning in the sun over the yellow glare. She was worn out, shivering slightly as the sweat dried on her. She watched him cross the ropes on top of the stack this way and that. He was a perfectionist and had to get it just so, and it drove her mad.

'Pass me that stone,' he said, panting and coughing. 'Not that one, that one.'

They worked on, not speaking. When did they ever speak these days? Simon wheeled about in the road for a while then disappeared. The dogs lay nearby, their slitted eyes adorned by ticks in various stages of engorgement. The old one gasped weakly, the young grinned extravagantly. Marie took care not to look towards Quigs's. Soon the job was done, all neat and nicely finished.

'I could kill a cup of tea,' she said, smiling.

Con didn't speak.

They walked back to the house slowly. Bees buzzed around the door and the fly-paper hanging from the kitchen ceiling was thick with sticky black bodies. He came up when she was at the sink and grabbed her from behind, clumsy and desperate. Marie shrank. He flung himself away, going into the next room and flopping down in his chair with closed eyes and pained brow.

God, don't let him start that again, please God, don't let him start that again, please God, please God, she thought. What can I do, cut off my head? That's where all the thoughts came from. It was enough that she had to suffer them. She was here, wasn't she? What more did he want, blood? She'd done nothing, had she? Only wanted. He could keep off. She was here and that was enough. She almost hated Con at that moment.

'Here you are, Connie,' she said nicely as she gave him his tea. He said nothing.

She went upstairs and started running the water for a bath. He appeared in the doorway, his face all strange and strained; she was scared because of this and because of his size in the small space and his physical closeness. But he didn't try to embrace her, only reached out and pinched her very sharply and deliberately on the underside of her arm. She screamed and hit him across the face.

'You're a bitch, you're a bitch, Marie,' he said, and ran out with fingermarks and a horrified look on his face.

He wouldn't talk about it. They hardly spoke to one another all through tea and the early part of the evening. Julia and Simon, exchanging long-suffering looks, escaped as soon as they could, Julia to a body-awareness workshop at Dundreen, the butt of many a ribald comment in the bars, and Simon to his Aunt Therese's house. Con was pulling pints at Sylvester's.

As soon as she was alone Marie put down her knitting and turned off the TV. She went upstairs and looked at herself in the mirror, thinking: I'm only thirty-four, it's not fair. I'm all right, I still am, if I tried again I could be ... don't want to let myself go, and reached up to her hair and lifted it to the back of her head. Her arms were milky. She switched on the light and looked at the open pores on her nose. But that's nothing, she thought, and opened a drawer and took out a little bag of make-up that she hardly ever wore. Just a little touch, she thought and dabbed some on her nose. Then she put on a little mascara, just a touch, and bit and licked her lips and brushed her hair, and stood back thinking how nice she looked and how nice it would be to have to bother again, and she thought of all the boys and men she'd ever fancied or who'd ever fancied her, for real or in fantasy. This is how I really am, she thought, opening the wardrobe door so that she could see herself in the full-length mirror, taking off her horrible old clothes and standing naked, shivering though the room was not cold. It was very quiet. She looked at her full rounded stomach, large breasts with swollen purple-brown nipples, good childbearing hips. She looked OK, curvy and strong, really quite good if she held everything in. Marie turned this way and that, placed her hands gently in the small of her back and rubbed it where she ached from the haymaking. It was lovely it was, that flesh, like some beautiful statue or something in a painting. It would never be seen, never be touched with a lover's touch again. She ran her hands slowly over hips and breasts and buttocks, turning and turning. I would want to touch me, she thought, if I wasn't me, yes, I would. I swear I'm so nice I could fancy me myself, stroking the insides of her thighs. Then she wanted to touch herself down there. It was unbearable. She lay down on the bed and wriggled about.

It was not fair, not fair. The thought came that she could run up to the wagon and get it all now while she still could, everything there was to get, just this once, then she could think about it while she lived on in this touchless world, getting older, joining the ICA, knitting jumpers for the grandchildren when they came, ending up in that house in the village perhaps where Con's mother lived now.

She got up and pulled open another drawer and rooted about. Her underwear drawer was a mess, full of boring old knickers and mis-shapen bits and pieces of things. These red ones with the black dots weren't too bad, kind of thin at the sides. Best of a bad lot. She put them on, and her good peach bra with the open lacy bit at the top, then took from the wardrobe her yellow dress with the flower pattern, plain but showing off her figure. 'Do it! Do it!' she whispered, and laughed. We're all going to die soon enough, she thought. Anyway, it's a sin to think it so I've already sinned.

71

She looked at her watch. There was time. Get home before eleven just in case he's early, she said and ran downstairs, covered herself with her coat in spite of the warmth of the evening, and went out.

No one was about. There were foxgloves and purple loosestrife at the side of the roads, deep pink thrift covered the walls. She walked up between the gorse and fuchsia to the wagon, chamomile smelling like apples under her feet, the first traces of dusk creeping on. Padraic South's white horse grazed on the side of Rossa; far out over the Puck Rock a helicopter flew. She could hear voices from the other side of the valley and the soft distant bark of a dog.

He was in. The door was open. She nearly turned back, but instead brought him into her mind in a deliberate way, all her favourite images flicked through like a wad of photos, walking on and tapping softly on the door before she went in.

'Come in,' he said. He was standing by the cooker.

'I've come to say goodbye,' she said.

It was true, he was going, there were signs everywhere of disorder preceding a departure – shelves dusty and cleared, cardboard boxes, things set down in strange places. She went over to the desk where he'd been sorting through some pictures. 'That's nice,' she said, looking at a black-and-white print of a bird chained to a perch.

'The goldfinch,' he said. He came over and picked up the pile of prints, acting as if nothing had ever happened between them. 'Would you like to see some pictures?' he asked. 'Come on.'

They sat down on the hard narrow bed and looked: most of the pictures were portraits; he told her that that one there was probably Fabritius himself though it wasn't known for sure. He looked nice. Poor thing, she thought, poor nice-looking young thing blown to high heaven and younger than me, what's it all for? Bob's hand, turning up the pictures, was square and unremarkable. He was not meeting her eyes.

'Did you mind me coming up here?' she asked.

'Of course not,' he said, 'I was hoping you would.'

But he still didn't look at her, just showed her the picture of the Raising of Lazarus and told her that the poor young thing had been only twenty-one when he painted that, probably in Rembrandt's studio in Amsterdam, and that his wife and two babies had all died within the last year.

'Oh God!' she cried, 'what's it all for?' and looked anew at the picture of Fabritius and saw this time the suffering she knew must be there in the eyes, and saw how you could fall in love with someone who died four hundred years ago just for the sheer pity of his existence. What if you fell in love with a picture like this and then found out years later that it wasn't him at all? What would you have been in love with then?

'When is it you're going?' she asked.

'In three days.'

'Oh, to London?'

'Shropshire,' he said.

'Shropshire?'

'Back to my roots. I'll go there and finish the book. Loose ends, you know, that kind of stuff. And then, who knows?' He smiled.

'Are you looking forward to it?' she asked.

He shrugged. They just sat there for a while, doing nothing, saying nothing.

'I'm sorry if I caused any trouble for you, Marie,' he said and looked at her.

'No trouble,' she said and smiled. They put their arms round each other, lay down and stretched out, kissed. 'Wait!' she said, broke away, locked the door, closed all the curtains, took off her coat. She ran back. He held his arms open and pulled her down on top of him, grabbing the back of her head with his hand. He was trembling. Now I have him, she thought, and I can do anything I like with him, but she just kissed him gently. He seemed innocent and beautiful, at her mercy.

'Tell me what you like,' he said.

When his hand reached her naked knees he went all hard, and she put her hand on top of his and half led, half hindered a process up the inside of her thigh towards the red knickers with black spots.

'I love you,' he said. 'Tell me what you like. Tell me what you like, Marie, I'll do anything you like, anything at all.'

But she didn't know what she liked, she'd never once got it right, not really. She didn't even know what it was supposed to be like.

'I don't know,' she said.

Bob put his hand up under her red knickers, put a finger of his unremarkable hand upon the spot, the very spot, and did things there, very gently, kissing her lips and holding hard against her.

It was never like this with Con. Never.

13

Rosanna came into the darkened back room of Tommy Davy's where a bunch of them were watching *Dirty Harry* on video. 'Want to hear something juicy?' she whispered, leaning over Clyde's chair and putting her arms round his neck.

'Not specially.' Clyde was eating chocolate and drinking Guinness with whiskey chasers.

'I was coming down the track from Inchicora and I saw Marie going up to Quigs's,' she whispered delightedly. 'All done up, she was. Fun, fun, fun!'

Clyde said nothing. Rosanna started leaning on him and drinking out of his glass, draping her naked muscular arms all over him, giggling stupidly at inappropriate moments in the action of the film. He folded his chocolate wrapper neatly and stuffed it down the side of the chair, drained his glass and got up.

'Oh, lovely,' Rosanna said, falling into his chair and settling down with her legs over the arm, her limp old T-shirt riding up.

Clyde went into the bright bar where Tommy Davy wiped glasses. The room hummed with voices, the tables were full. Cars sped through San Francisco on the screen of a huge colour TV set high above the bar where Barney Mac and Christy Pads sat with their drinks. A picture of an old-fashioned girl with ringlets and a posy simpered on the wall and turfs burned on the fire in spite of the summer night spilling in through the open door.

'Same again, Clyde?' said Tommy.

'Just a Jameson's, Tommy.'

Tommy poured. Clyde watched, his elbows among the mats and ashtrays, thinking seriously. There might be a kicking in this somewhere, a good one. Got to think. He looked about the room. Jackie Bat was playing Snap noisily with some little tourist girls, his Lucozade on the mantel shelf behind him. Clyde looked for Ger or Tim Pat but didn't see them. Christy Pads was with his brother Mike. He caught his eye and nodded pleasantly.

'What do you think of this, Christy?' Clyde said quietly, shifting over towards him, 'Rosanna just saw Marie going into Bob Sawle's wagon.'

Christy looked at him for a moment, then shook his head. 'I'm saying nothing,' he said, tipping back his head to drink. His great moustache got all covered in foam. Tommy Davy and Barney Mac were listening.

'All done up,' said Clyde, 'like she's going to a dance or something.'

Christy lit a cigarette.

Clyde sat thinking, building up a plan, then knocked back the whisky with one sharp movement and left. The changes of high summer were well under way: a van selling chips and burgers in the layby opposite Sylvester's, bare-legged tourists drinking on the long wooden benches outside Tommy's. The light was fading and a haze lay over the sea. No islands were visible. He went next door to Sylvester's. Con was behind the bar.

'Con,' said Clyde, walking straight up to the bar and ignoring everybody else. There was something in his manner that made everybody take note. 'Can I have a word?' The two of them went and stood in the cool passage.

'Tell me to fuck off if you think I'm interfering. Marie's with Sawle in his wagon. Did you know? If you don't I thought you ought to.'

Con went white. He put down the towel he was holding and went back behind the bar.

'Sylvester,' he said, 'I have to go,' then walked straight out, looking at no one.

Clyde followed, summoning Ger who abandoned his drink, sensing danger. Outside, Clyde quickly put him in the picture. 'What?' said Ger, delighted, a half smile hovering about his face.

'The dirty bitch!'

Con was already at the end of the street. They followed. Nora McBride, sitting in a straight-backed chair in her doorway, hands clasped in her knob-kneed lap, followed them with her eyes to the foot of the village.

'Don't take him on your own,' said Clyde, coming up quietly behind Con near the Strangarvan signpost. The smell of silage was sickly on the air. It was darker here.

Con paused, his face absolutely blank, looking at them both. 'What are you two doing here?' he said coldly. 'This is nothing to do with anybody else,' and walked on, quickening his stride. But Clyde and Ger quickened too, falling into step alongside him, and Con allowed them to walk with him.

'Rosanna saw them,' Clyde said, 'and you know what she's like. The whole place knows it by now.' Clyde wished he had his gun. He was excited. He fancied a twanging guitar accompaniment. Ger was smiling.

When the wagon came in sight, its shuttered windows ominous, Con told them to stay back. 'This is my affair,' he said. 'I'll go in and if she's there I'll get her and take her home. That's all. I don't care what you do then.'

They waited near the mouth of the gully, watching. Con went straight to the door, stood gathering himself for a moment or two, then hurled his shoulder at it. It made a sound like a gunshot but didn't break. He went at it again and again. On about the fifth crack the lock broke and the door crashed open.

There was only one candle, which guttered but did not go out. Marie stood stiffly by the desk, Bob at the cooker. The three of them stared stupidly at each other.

'Con ...' said Bob.

'Shut up, I don't want to speak to you. Marie, get out, get out of here now.' Nobody moved. 'Get out!'

She moved sideways, awkwardly, and got her coat from the floor, then started fishing for her shoes with her feet.

'Con,' said Bob, 'just listen ...'

'Nothing's happened,' said Marie, having trouble with her shoes, her cheeks blushing furiously, 'nothing's happened.'

'Out, out, out,' Con said calmly, staring at Marie. 'Out before

I kill you.'

'Con ...' said Bob.

'Oh, fuck your shoes!' cried Con, and stepped forward and took Marie's arm and pulled her shoeless towards the door. 'Come on!'

Bob stepped forward but she pushed him aside firmly. 'It's all right, Bob, we're all right, we're going home, all right?' she said, and went out. Con went after her.

Bob ran to the door and watched their shadows disappearing through the gloom. She was walking ahead quite steadily, Con a few paces behind. He felt stupidly like running after them. For a moment he hated her and thought it was all just a game she had played with him. She would go back to her life now, quite unmoved, like his mother leaving him in dreams he'd had as a child, quite unmoved. The door hung on one hinge. He pushed it as nearly closed as he could get it and lay down on the bed, afraid, covering his face with his hands and wondering what he'd got himself into this time.

When the door scraped open he thought at first she was coming back, and then he was really afraid, standing up and blinking shortsightedly through the candlelight. At first he didn't recognise them, but after a moment Clyde spoke evenly.

'Now I'm going to give you a kicking, you bastard. Me and Ger.'

He didn't bother with resistance. What was the point? He was no fighter, this kind of thing scared him stiff. They moved very fast. He was on his knees on the floor with Ger behind him and Clyde in front, Clyde's knee jerked up under his chin and he sliced his tongue, tasted metal, then a fist crunched into his face and suddenly there was blood everywhere, spreading in long dark stripes down his chest and onto the rug. Ger got in a few kicks to the kidneys, Clyde hit his eyes. There was not enough room so they hauled him to the door and threw him sprawling and Clyde jumped hard from the top step, landing with both feet on his back. Something cracked audibly. Ger stood in the doorway watching as Clyde yanked Bob's head by the hair, rammed back the neck and smashed the face with a fist over and over again, heavy and relentless. Ger was reminded of someone hammering in a tent peg.

'Clyde,' he said uncertainly. 'Clyde!'

Clyde let go. Bob fell and lay face down, hands gathered in beneath him. He snivelled, retching once loudly like a dog.

Clyde stood, surprised at himself, panting, his prick hard. He'd had many a ruck in his time and you never could tell which ones would be the ones, the few out of the many that got you this way, gave you a kind of a buzz. This was one of the best, not the best, but near. When he was sixteen he'd hospitalised his stepbrother, Stephen, a hulking, big-nosed, fair-haired bastard he'd had to share a room with for too long. That had been a beginning, a revelation. He'd hated that fucker. Since then he'd roughed up a few, and sometimes he stuck one on Rosanna if she went too far, and now and then you got a good one, like this, that raked your hackles and made you wonder just how far you could go. He took a step back, then kicked this one right in the face, right up the nose. Yeah, made that connection. He'd noted a blackened fire pit with stones around it to the side of the wagon, and there was kindling underneath. He laughed softly.

'What?' said Ger. 'What? Come on, Clyde, don't kill him.'

Clyde went back inside and searched the desk, returning with a couple of box files. 'This is it, this is it,' he said excitedly, emptying their contents into the fire pit. Then he began building up a little pyre with kindling from under the wagon. Ger went over to Bob and looked at him. Bob's eyes were open, looking at him with no kind of an expression, but the lids were swelling fast, the wings of his nose were torn and his mouth had turned black and spread all over his face.

Clyde flicked his lighter.

'He's only bloody mad,' Ger muttered, 'only bloody mad, you know.'

Then the flames leapt up, suddenly roaring, and Clyde crowed and fanned it madly, adding more twigs, more paper, poking it all deeper and deeper into the centre. He got himself worked up good and proper then ran across and started kicking again, just anywhere, all over, dancing a little between kicks, and Ger was crying: 'That's too much, it's too much!' He tried to grab Clyde's arms but Clyde was mad and Ger was afraid of him. 'Clyde, stop

it now, stop it!' he cried, afraid there'd be murder and he'd be . . .
'CLYDE!'

Clyde stopped. 'He's passed out, the cunt,' he said.

'Mother of God, you've killed him!'

For a moment they were both silent, examining the mess carefully like doctors. The face, turned away from the firelight, was
dark and bloated, indistinct.

Clyde tipped over the water barrel as they left.

14

Marie just sat there. She'd cut her foot on something on the walk
back and it was bleeding steadily into a tissue she held to it.

Con sat in his chair, just as he always did, always had. 'I don't
want to know,' he'd said.

'Can we not talk at all?' she said finally.

Con covered his face and spoke through his hands: 'I can't
believe, I can't believe that you would ever, Marie . . .' and broke
off with a catch in his throat. He was an emotional man. He'd
weep at 'Spancilhill' sometimes and he'd probably cry at Julia's
wedding. Sometimes she hated his emotion and wanted to slap
him. Great breaths heaved in his chest. 'It'll be all right,' he
gasped. 'I know it'll be all right. In the end. It has to be all right
in the end. I'm not letting you do this, Marie. I am not letting
you do this. Too much is at stake.'

She suddenly saw Bob's face in her mind, a stranger's face, long
and rather plain, she supposed, but then she'd thought that he was
beautiful at certain times and now she had no idea. 'Oh, Con,' she
said, swallowing, hating herself. 'Oh, Connie.'

'Is that all you can say? Is that all you have to say to me? After
all these years? What have I done?'

She jerked towards him. Nothing happened, she was going to
say. It was true in a way. What was the point? There'd never been
a future in it so why upset the poor man any more? But then
Simon came in. Marie set her face further to the fire and Con
turned quickly away.

Simon's big smiley face was about to speak, but Con said in a harsh, jovial voice: 'Up to bed with you. Now!' Simon wavered then went upstairs.

At the top Julia appeared, seized his arm, and pulled him into her room. 'Ssh!' she said, though he hadn't made a sound. 'Now, tell me if you've heard anything!'

'Nothing happened,' said Marie. God in his heaven heard her lie so blatantly. She could still tremble before God. She put her head in her hands. 'How can I face anyone?' she whispered, and her face went dark with the effort not to cry.

'Fuck them!' said Con furiously. 'Let them talk!'

She jumped and stared at him. He's just the same, she thought, just the same, dear old Con. 'Nothing happened,' she said again.

They looked at each other with stricken eyes.

'This is our life, Marie,' he said, his voice shaking a little with the effort to stay calm. Maybe he believed her. 'You're not messing it up like this. This is where we live. This is what there is. OK? Come back down to earth, Marie. There isn't anything else. For Christ's sake, you'd better wash that.' He indicated her foot, then strode into the kitchen and returned with a wet cloth, which he pressed to the cut. He'd doused it with TCP and it stung. 'Pressure,' he said grimly, 'that's the secret, pressure. Where are the plasters? You need a plaster on that now.'

'In the table drawer,' she said.

Con went and got one, returned and pasted it over the cut. It would probably bleed through. 'It'll be all right, now, won't it?' he said, and started to cry wetly, open-mouthed like a child, and wanted to come into her arms. She could not possibly refuse him though she had to close her eyes and hold her breath to do so.

There was a furtive tap on the door. Con jumped up, rubbing at his eyes and wiping his nose. 'Who is it?' he called, collecting himself as he reached the door.

'Ger!'

'What does he want?' Marie asked, annoyed. Con opened the door.

She saw Ger's triangular white face hovering mysteriously in the dark out there.

'Better call a doctor,' the face said sepulchrally. 'Better call a doctor, Con. Best thing.'

She went cold.

'How bad?' asked Con.

Ger shrugged. 'Hospital bad.'

'Oh Christ!' The white face melted away and Con closed the door, then, turning, said to Marie: 'Do you see what you've done? Do you?' He went to the phone.

'What? What?'

But he didn't answer. When she heard him report a fight and that someone was hurt up at Quigs's she was suddenly sure that Bob was dead and that it was all her fault. She jumped up. He'd be on her conscience for ever. 'What happened?' she cried, 'What's Ger got to do with it?'

'He was there,' said Con, 'so was Clyde. They came up with me.'

They'd seen her walking along in shame without her shoes on. Marie broke up and shouted, 'You had no right to go killing a man for nothing, nothing at all, because nothing happened, it's gone too far, *nothing happened*, *nothing happened*, don't you understand?' She ran to the back door and started pulling on her wellies, wincing when her sore foot hit the ground.

'Where are you going?' he asked sharply.

'I'm going to see if the man needs help,' she said, just as sharply, 'and if you had any decency about you, you'd come, too.'

Con turned away. 'Go to hell,' he said.

She ran down the path. Someone was in the lane. If it was Clyde or Ger she'd kill them. She thought it was a man but it was only Essie coming back from a session on the beach.

'Something's happened,' Marie gasped, 'Bob's been beaten up, come with me,' and ran straight up the track to Quigs's without looking back. Essie followed. They saw the remains of a fire and a body with a blank black face lying in front of the wagon.

'Christ, what happened? Lie him on his side.' Essie drew back her lips. 'I can't stand this kind of thing,' she said.

They tried to move him but he moaned and sobbed and blood came pouring from his mouth. They got him on his side and he went on leaking into the damp ground. 'Rescue remedy,' said Essie briskly, rummaging in her stripy shoulder bag. 'It's all wet down here. He's soaking wet!' She sounded annoyed. 'Who the hell did this?'

'Clyde,' said Marie, 'Clyde and Ger.'

'Christ!'

'Con's phoned the hospital.'

'It's outrageous. There you are, darling.' She dropped liquid from a little bottle into the burst lips.

Marie just sat there on her heels looking and looking at him. She wanted to touch him but couldn't. It was all her fault. Everything. Her head felt strange and light. Nothing would ever be the same again.

Essie saw something incongruously tragic in her face. Well, well, she'd thought it was just gossip. She sucked her tongue stud and shivered. She'd been down on the beach all night, guitars, fire, baked potatoes, dope, full moon on the black water – and now this sordid little scene. She sighed. George was up at Montsalvat. He never came to sessions any more. She yawned. The sky was big and cold and she wanted to go home and get into bed and read a book.

'He'll be all right,' she said kindly, 'these things always look worse than they really are.'

And the two women kept the vigil, waiting for help.

15

Essie was in conversation with a nun in a nurse's uniform on the subject of body-piercing. 'Nine in that one,' she said, smiling proudly, twisting the ring in the upper tip of her ear, 'and eight in that. So that's seventeen. And then, of course, this one, and last but not least –' she stuck out her tongue.

'Ugh!' said the nun.

'Nineteen,' Essie said.

On the second day of the Fleadh, the yearly weekend when the streets of Strangarvan were full of music and drunken revelry, she'd visited Bob with a big sheaf of flowers from George's flower garden. Nobody else had gone near him as far as she could see.

He was a mess, face all yellow and swollen like an old rugby ball. They ought to lock Clyde up but he'd get away with it, he always got away with it. Someone ought to give *him* a good thump. He was only a little weed, when all was said and done; she could probably lay him out easily enough herself.

'Oh well,' said the cheerful young nun, 'I'd better get on, I suppose,' and stood up. 'OK?' she said to Bob.

'These nuns,' said Bob to Essie when she had gone, 'are fantastic. I take it all back.' It was hard for him to speak. He'd lost a good few teeth, she guessed.

'You really should press charges,' she said.

'Can't,' he said. 'You know.' Drag it all into the open, he meant.

'But the book?' she said. 'Couldn't you do him for criminal damage or something?' There hadn't been a copy. He'd been going to get one done in Cork on the way back to England.

He ignored that. He said his brother had been to see him and told him he was a fool and deserved all he got. Then he indicated a blank envelope on the locker at the side of the bed. 'Give it to Marie,' he said.

'I can't,' she said. 'I don't want to get involved.'

He nodded. 'Is she OK?' he asked.

'She's fine.'

It was time to go. 'Just take it, Essie,' he said when she stood up, 'then she can do what she likes with it.' She took it.

Essie walked up to the harbour and the square. The streets and bars and school halls of Strangarvan were alive, gay with coloured bunting. There was dancing in the square. Two men and a woman played accordions outside Biddy O'Neill's and an old man sang an old song in sweet cracked tones. It was a terrible thing that had happened. Poor Con, the innocent party, had impressed everyone: smiling as always, walking with Marie as if nothing had happened. Marie was toughing it out, looking everyone in the eye, subtly challenging. Clyde had gone away, no one knew where. But he'd be back, of course, he always was, and everything would blow over, roll on, as things always did one way or another.

Essie sat on a bench overlooking the harbour. She ran her big hands through her lawny hair, crossed and uncrossed her long legs. What the hell do I do with this? she thought, taking the envelope out of her pocket and looking at it. It's not fair, it's got nothing to do with me. They're neighbours, how can I ... Affirm. What? Accept whatever the universe throws up. All that used to seem so simple. To be fair, to be truthful, to do the right thing. Essie tore open the envelope and found it to contain only a Salop address. She threw it in the harbour.

Immediately she was filled with dismay. First she hated to see litter floating in the harbour, though this was organic and would soon break down; second, the futile realisation that the act of throwing it away was an intervention as surely as its delivery would have been.

Never hit seventeen when you play against the dealer
And you know the odds won't ride with you
Never leave your woman alone when your friends are out
to steal her
Years are gambled and gone like summer wages ...

Marie sang along to the radio.

The kids were back at school again and the turf was coming down from Rossa. Marie sometimes tried to write a letter on large sheets of lined paper torn out of Julia's exercise books. It would never be sent, so it shouldn't have mattered what she wrote, but even so she found it hard. Everything sounded silly on paper, the florid gush of a lovesick adolescent. She folded up the attempts and hid them at the back of her underwear drawer. Each time she opened it she saw the red spotted knickers and remembered what she'd done, sometimes standing there breathless with the pang of it. It was the loveliest thing that had ever happened to her.

She looked around. Nothing much had changed. Only the likes of Nora McBride and Padraic South still bothered to look askance at her, and Con's mother, of course. Well, that was no loss. She looked in the mirror. I must get into town and get my hair done, she thought, I could go in on the Sprinter. But there didn't seem much point now. For what? To get Con going? He left her alone now, thank God, and the pretence continued that nothing had really happened.

She stood for a while looking out of the window, thinking

about Con. He was always crabby in the mornings, now he was crabby more often, that was all. And none of it was his fault. But then a small seditious voice spoke up: None of it? None of it? Surely there is something. Let me think. Let me think. She saw him walking up the path, his big round shoulders and the thickening neck, the boyish fall of his longish hair.

Marie turned from the window and closed her underwear drawer sharply. She heard the sound of cattle being driven past the door by Simon, the swish of their tails and the soft heavy fall of their dung. She heard him talking to them in that familiar way he had. Downstairs the door opened and Con came in. He whistled, rattling the fire irons.

This was all there was and it was not so bad; she should have been content with it. All that other was a mirage.

She went down to make tea.

Part Two

Part Two

16

It was a week or so before Christmas. Rosanna had hung a curtain across the lived-in end of the house to keep the warm in, but
it didn't go right up to the apex so the cold came over the top.
Clyde lay watching her as she lit the old range, which she'd finally
got going after a fashion, and started to cook rice with lentils and
chopped cabbage. She was an excellent cook and could make
such things delicate and appetising. The room became cloudy.
Molly stretched like a rug before the range. Strings of dried field
mushrooms hung from the ceiling. It was getting dark outside and
Rosanna hummed as she drew the curtains. She sat down and
took up her sewing.

'You know,' she said meditatively, 'I would have been quite
happy in the middle ages really. Sitting about doing my sewing
with a unicorn at my feet.'

Clyde turned on the radio and fiddled with the dial. At this
time of night the airwaves were always laced with some Eastern
kind of music, playing along softly at the back of everything else.
He got RTE2, 'The Rock Show', and lay down and closed his
eyes, thinking of the new van he'd brought back with him from
Mick Madden's, a maroon Renault 4 laced with rust, the exhaust
tied on with string, but she went, she really went. One of these
days she'd be a car wreck of West Cork. Or perhaps Clare, or
Mayo, or some other place, who knows, maybe it was time to be
off again. He saw her take her place with all the others in his exhibition, magnificent, her blind windows framing the Skellig
Rocks. Rosanna was saying something to him. The van had
wiped him out, he needed to get some money. They'd passed Julia
in the road coming back from town. Tasty, reminded him of
Melanie Broadbent. He'd gone around with her for a week or
two in London years ago. Yeah, Melanie Broadbent, he thought
with a touch of sadness. London, sometimes he just wanted to

smell Paddington Station, see black faces, hear the echo of the Underground. Melanie Broadbent was a cow-bitch and he hoped she was rotting in hell. Julia though, Julia was something, still smooth like a child and she had those incredible muscles on her calves when she stood on tiptoe.

'I'm pregnant,' Rosanna was saying.

It finally registered.

'You are not,' he said after a while.

'Yes, I am, I'm pregnant. I should know, shouldn't I?'

It's got nothing to do with me, his face said. He thought rapidly. Could it be? Shit! He looked at her doubtfully. She was just as skinny as ever. 'Well, what are you going to do about it?' he asked, thinking: I could shoot her and chuck her in the sea, like in the song, ha ha ha!

She said nothing.

'Bet you're not,' he said.

'Oh, I am.' She was actually smiling, rather dementedly he thought. She was mad, she'd been getting worse and worse ever since he'd known her. 'I've been to see Dr Deasy,' she said. 'There's no doubt.'

'Deasy! You don't want him knowing about it. You wanna just go to England.'

She said nothing again for quite a long time, smiling over her sewing. She was just mad enough to try and keep it. He sat up and lit a cigarette, then moved towards her and smoked it leaning over her closely. She put down her sewing and kissed his pale bony face and he put his arms round her. 'I thought you'd been sleeping a lot lately,' he said. 'I thought it was just another of your ailments. How far gone are you?'

'About four months.'

'Jesus! That's quite a lot, isn't it?'

She laughed softly. 'I'm going to have it, Clyde,' she said.

He took his arms away and leaned back to look at her, revolted by the idea. This was horrible. It wasn't that he didn't want children – well, sometime, perhaps, one day – but it wouldn't be like this. For a start, it wouldn't be with the likes of her. He'd have his wagon or his bus, and the kids would be dark, gypsyish, handsome and surly, the chick calm and patient and sexy, able to drive the bus and cook and take care of them all. So she couldn't be pissed out of her skull all the time.

'You're not serious,' he said.

'Why not?'

'Rosanna!'

'What? Rosanna, what?'

Clyde thought again. 'Suit yourself,' he said then and lay back down, simmering slightly but not sure why. After all, it wouldn't affect him. Probably never happen, he couldn't see her with a kid. But then he thought of a screaming baby in this place, nappies, Rosanna when drunk. No, he'd just have to go, somewhere with boats, Killybegs, Galway. She got up and went to stir the pots and he watched her grinning as she sipped from the end of a wooden spoon. Anyway, he thought, she's much too old to have a baby, it's ridiculous, and suddenly felt sorry for her. But he couldn't go getting soppy now. Guilt, he was having none of it, he'd never chosen her, she'd picked him out then stuck on like a tick. Christ sake, he couldn't get her off! Do anything to her, she still clung on. Talk about a vampire. She walked about, tidying her books that lay here and there away into an old cardboard box that lay on its side. She had an old I-Ching and some things about religion and earth mother cults. She started up a thin, nasal giggling as she moved about. Irritating.

'I could even have it in here if it came to it,' she said, looking around. 'Our Lord in a stable, hee hee hee, the star over Caheradown Bay, the shepherds! Jackie Bat holding a lamb! The wise men! And you! You, Clyde, Joseph saying: "it isn't fucking mine"!'

Clyde smirked. 'It probably isn't,' he said. 'Could be anyone's, Dan Hogan's, Sylvester's . . .'

'Credit me with a bit of taste!' In fact, she thought, it probably was Clyde's, but it could also have been a Spanish sailor's, or Ger's, or Mike Pad's, or some bloke one night when she was gutting fish down at the fish factory in Strangarvan. She figured these were his fault anyway for not wanting it as often as he should. Everything was Clyde's fault really.

Clyde shrugged, pulled his cap down over his eyes and shifted the burnt-out match between his teeth. She felt like hitting him, hurting him. She went back to the range and danced about it to the music from the radio. Clyde tried to bring his mind back to car wrecks of West Cork, but couldn't. He kept seeing this stupid baby, this screaming pig-like animal, his, brain-damaged most likely or anyway totally fucked up. What else could it be?

'How to get a good start in life,' he said with a grim smile. 'Choose your parents well.'

'Shut up.'

'You know, I don't like this, Rosanna. I think I ought to have some sort of say in this.'

She stopped dancing and stirred the pots. 'It's all right, you prick,' she said, 'I don't expect you to stick around or anything.'

'Too right I won't,' he said casually, getting out his gun.

'Oh, don't start that.'

'You've not thought about this. How old are you?'

'I'm forty-three,' she said defiantly.

'There you are then! You can't have a baby at forty-three! There might be something wrong with it. Anyway, your health's crap, you've always got some weird thing or another.' He started playing along to The Smiths on the radio.

'Women my age have babies all the time these days,' she said. 'You're behind the times. It'll be all right. It'll have as much chance as anyone.' She gestured with the wooden spoon. 'Some of the truly great people had shitty beginnings. Strengthened their characters. I think I'd be a terrific mum to have. I'm a real person. Think how they'd always remember me. Aah! My old mum singing her old songs over my cradle. Aah! I'll go to the Council, anyway. They'll have to give me something if I'm pregnant. They always take care of a pregnant woman over here. They've got to, it's the religion.'

'Oh, yeah?'

'Yeah.'

'You're not right in the head,' he said.

The spoon was coated with steaming hot lentils. Rosanna flew at him and started beating him about the head with it, catching him a solid blow across one cheek. He jumped up and knocked it out of her hand and slapped the side of her head. Molly jumped up trembling, claws skittering on bare concrete. A deep, hollow baying filled the rafters.

'Shaddup!' yelled Clyde. 'Shaddup!'

Rosanna punched him in the throat. They slapped each other about for a bit with a certain ease of movement which came from long practice. Then they broke apart, scowling and pacing about in different parts of the room.

'Anything that came out of you,' he said, 'would be so mad it'd have to be carted off to some institution at birth. It'd be a drooling idiot.' Poor Molly caught Rosanna's glance, softened her eyes and dipped her head ingratiatingly. 'Deasy wants striking off for letting you have it!'

She came at him again and they fought, blow for blow, like boxers, breathing hard and deadly serious. She was a good, strong fighter and it was not easy for him to win, but at last he began to wear her down, getting in one or two good punches to the side of the head. She went down with her arms over her head. 'Hit me!' she screamed. 'Hit me! Hit me! Go on! Hit a pregnant woman! Hit me!'

He laughed.

She got back to her feet and stood in front of him, shouting into his face, her eyes swimming fishily with tears. 'Hit me! Hit me! Hit me!'

'Hit me with your rhythm stick,' he sang, laughing, then hit her hard in the mouth.

She reeled back and crouched, feeling to see if her teeth were still all there. They were. He stood a little way off, grinning stupidly. Rosanna went for his legs and knocked him off balance and the two of them went down, grappling and grunting at the iron feet of the range. She managed to squeeze his scrawny throat and smash the back of his head against the hob, to bite his hand and hang on with her teeth, drawing blood. He gave a great shout and threw her off, then they came together again and rolled around all over the floor while Molly growled in the corner. He slapped her head whenever he could. They began rubbing together and she groped his jeans, found his balls and squeezed them cruelly, twisting as much as she could with the meagre grip she could get. She laughed and sobbed. Clyde made a terrible strangled sound and kneed her in the stomach as hard as he could.

'No!' she gasped, 'not there!'

They rolled to the door. She kept trying to kick him in the balls but couldn't quite get to them. His eyes were closed and wet, he wheezed. It was getting out of hand. He was stronger. She was losing her grip and he was kicking her away, harder and harder. Let go, she thought. It wasn't fair, because he was always stronger in the end. He was on his feet, hobbling and doubled and furious, opening the door, kicking her out. It was very cold and dark out there. Clyde threw and kicked her as far as the road, then stood over her gasping for breath, both of them suddenly invisible in the total darkness. There was a moment's silence, then a muffled exclamation and a kick from nowhere to nowhere, surprising itself with its own ferocity as it connected with something both hard and soft, that yielded. Then Clyde felt sick and ran back into the house and boarded the door, trembling as he sank down upon the mattress.

The smell of all that good food was heavy on the air.

It wasn't his fault. She'd explained it to him herself once, one night when he'd been doing a heavy number: it was really his stepbrother Stephen's fault for being such a bastard. I mean, if you had to share a room with someone like that what else could you do but try and kill him? And it was his mother's fault, too, and Melanie Broadbent's. But it wasn't his. He just got mad. She knew that.

Rosanna lay on her side, winded and sick. The sea hissed in her ears, so close it was like a voice inside her head. Years and years ago there'd been a car crash, a serious one. She couldn't remember anything about it, but she remembered lying somewhere and hearing this very same hissing, though that time the sea had been nowhere near. Her face stung and there was an ache coming from somewhere. She was afraid to move but her mind felt absolutely clear, and she wondered if he'd really meant to kick her in the stomach.

After a while she sat up. Everything seemed to be OK. Her eyes were getting used to the dark. Bastard, she thought. Sod him, I'm not going back in there. And she got up slowly and walked a few paces experimentally. Still OK. She walked on slow and steady towards Ballinaphuca, keeping her knees together. She wouldn't go in Sylvester's tonight, *he* might come in. No, she'd go and sit by the fire in Tommy Davy's and have a good crack with someone. Her spirits rebelled. Bloody cold, it was, just this old jumper and no time to put on a coat. He'd pay for this. Oh yes, he'd pay for this. One day. Bloody freezing! She stuck her hands up her sleeves and started to sing softly:

> *I don't care if it snows or freezes*
> *Long as I've got my plastic Jesus*
> *Swinging on the dashboard of my car . . .*

She'd survive it. She'd go and get warm. She wasn't hurting that much. Funny thing, pain.

> *Comes in colours pink and pleasant,*
> *Glows in the dark 'cos it's iridescent . . .*

Funny thing. For as long as she could remember Rosanna had got off on the idea of pain. She liked to roll around in bed playing with herself and agonising luxuriously over fantasies of being tortured and fucked to the utmost limits of consciousness. She would pile on the agonies, the filth, the vile depredations, the abominable brutal desecration, picturing the gaping appreciation of a watching crowd, insultingly indifferent or rapt by her terror and suffering. But she didn't want real pain. She'd have a little drink and beg a paracetamol. She could handle it. She supposed the baby must be quite big now. Well, if it went, it went. Just don't hurt too much, she told it.

She went into Tommy Davy's. Padraic South and Paddy Bawn sat drinking morosely at the bar. No crack there. The TV was on low, nobody watching it. She got herself a Guinness and two paracetamols and went into the back room where a bunch of men were watching a blue video. Rosanna stood with her legs apart and shouted, 'Cor!' and, 'Wow!' and, 'Stick it in!' and suchlike till they yelled at her to shut up. Then she went back into the other room. 'You old miseries!' she cried at Padraic and Paddy. 'Come on, what's the matter with you? Come on, I'll buy you one! Tommy, stick it on the slate.'

'No way, Rosanna,' Tommy said, laughing.

Paddy Bawn turned his fat red face away from her resolutely;

Padraic sighed, blew his nose and slowly got up to leave. Rosanna drank. Christy Pads and his brother Mike came in as Padraic left and she begged a whiskey and sat down by the fire with them.

'All right, Rosanna?' Christy asked kindly. 'Are ye all right? You look a bit pale.'

'Look at this!' she said pulling up her jumper and showing them some bruising on her ribs with a kind of pride.

'Jeez, the pair of you!' said Mike.

'Don't take it,' Christy said. 'Why d'ye stick around?'

'Cos I love him,' she said prosaically, smiling.

'Ah, don't be stupid.'

Nice lads, these are, she thought, nice lads. She felt so much older than them, like the Old Woman of Beare or some ancient sybil. I could eat them, she thought. She started nibbling Christy's neck.

'Now, Rosanna,' he said, putting her aside.

There was no pain. Or was it there, waiting? Some of the men came out of the back room and she began to fool around and flirt with them. They laughed with her and gave her cigarettes. 'Sing us a song, Rosie,' someone said, and she started on 'The Little Skillet Pot', but on the line about potato cake a sharp pain shot through her womb, deep inside. Another, duller, began rolling like the sea inside her head, and an image of slowly running blood trickled through her mind. She did not finish the song but put her head down and gazed into the bottom of her glass. Her mouth had gone dry.

'Are ye all right?' Christy asked her again.

Something was happening inside her. She ought to get into town, get to Doc Deasy. She looked around at all their faces. Damn it all, she didn't want this lot knowing all her business! The pain clung close about the walls of her stomach and she hugged it, curiously protective, till it dimmed a little. Nice faces, she thought, good lads: how funny it would be if she should actually die here amongst these companions.

'All right? All right, Rosanna?'

She gulped down the last of her drink. 'Have to go.' She wiped her mouth with the back of her hand and got herself outside, holding her stomach. Abe, she thought, Abraham, the first child.

She didn't think about him much. The light from the Puck swept the mountains. She'd go and get Essie to run her into town. Once, many years ago, they'd been good friends in London. Essie tried to play it down now, but she had to help, old times sake and all that. Rosanna started walking. It wasn't far. The night was crisp and starry. A figure that could have been a ghost or the Devil or her Guardian Angel walked silently ahead in the dark of the lane. By the shrine to Our Lady at the turn-off to Rathmeelabo, that creepy dark place with its back to Rossa, she saw by the light from the single lamppost that it was only Padraic South going home. He was there for a moment in the light and then he vanished.

Rosanna stood before Mary, bowing her head. Abraham was simply the first boy's name she had come to in the name book in the library. She'd thought it was rather nice, Abraham Lincoln and all that. 'Oh Mary, help me,' she prayed aloud, 'I have strayed from the path but I have always loved you.' Then she looked up at Mary's gentle face in the lamplight, the smooth white hands open and forgiving.

She felt blood between her legs.

All the way up the track to Inchicora she talked to Mary. The pain returned and she wondered if the child inside felt it too. No, of course not, they don't feel the pain of childbirth, do they? Unfair to suffer pain even before you were born. Where did it all end? From deepest childhood Jesus came back to her, hanging on the cross and drawing it all in like a sponge. Another pain came, sharper, making her cry. She found herself falling over old potato ridges and realised she'd got off the road and was not far from Essie and George's back door. Then she found the yard and saw lights in the kitchen and the studio, looked through a window and saw Essie with her hands covered in clay, gazing at the floor with an abstracted look on her face. She knocked.

'I'm bleeding,' she said when Essie opened the door.

17

Essie had put on a long floral shirt in honour of Christmas. She was trying to ignore the fact that seven horrible children were trampling the garden and tormenting the cats. She couldn't stand children. Why people had to have so many she didn't know, it wasn't as if there was a shortage, was it? She had just followed a wonderful sequence of logic through her brain and worked out that it was all right to clobber George physically when she got hold of him, but she wouldn't, of course. It was Christmas Day and he'd invited hoardes of people to drop by, which they did throughout the long morning and early afternoon, bringing small gifts. There was garlic, bright yellow butter, carob cookies, a home-made crusty loaf that shone enticingly, a little corked stone jar filled with poteen, and finally a little box, elaborately and beautifully painted, which opened to reveal a single perfect white egg. Essie had made cheesecake and apple pie and soft yellow cornbread that melted in the mouth, and she handed out the comb honey they always gave. Jazz played. George himself had gone out for a box of matches early in the morning and hadn't returned.

'But, Ess!' he'd say happily when she complained, 'you could have gone out, too!' George and she had no tags on each other. Didn't she know him by now? He did this kind of thing to everyone and they let him get away with it because he was such a nice person, and clever too. He'd studied in Tibet and was an authority on world mythology. Everyone made allowances. The sun shone out of his arse and pearls of wisdom dropped from his soft red lips whenever he opened them. She had to live with the bugger.

Rosanna served drinks but had none herself. She wore a demure and old-fashioned blue dress with a white collar that had been given to her by the nuns, the sort someone's mother might have worn. She'd had another of her mysterious illnesses and wasn't supposed to drink. Only Essie knew that she'd lost a baby around midnight a week ago in the cottage hospital in

Strangarvan. Clyde hadn't stuck around to find out. He'd gone off with Molly in the old maroon van that same night and hadn't been seen since. Rosanna didn't want to go back to the beach house when she came out, so she was staying for a while in the old caravan down beyond George's bee hives. It was their meditation retreat so she was in the way, but Essie said that provided she didn't drink she could stay there till she found somewhere else. Everyone was waiting for her to crack and have a drink but she didn't. Instead she took her prayer book and went off to Mass.

'Christ, Rosanna!' they all said, laughing and shaking their heads. Her Catholicism was such an affectation.

People came and went. 'Where's George?' they all asked.

'Out somewhere.'

'Oh, when will he be back?'

'God knows.'

'Oh, what a shame.'

Bastard.

'Well, that's George, isn't it? That's just George.'

The smell of chestnut roast mingled with a heavily rose-scented pot-pourri. Ben Bowden played the guitar badly and sang in a high quavery voice. Feargal Breen had a row about James Joyce with Vincent, a bitter artist who sweated over vast blotty-looking canvases that nobody wanted to buy and scratched a few quid together now and again painting Celtic signs over pubs and shops and occasionally the prows of boats.

'Joyce is elitist,' Vincent said. 'You've got to have all this in-knowledge to read it. And all that intellectual guff he shoves in, all that deliberate obscurity, it's just like saying piss off, sucker, you're too thick to read this.'

'Well, perhaps you are,' said Feargal, stalking about with his big red nose and his beard stuck up in the air, a small cigar held aristocratically in a holder.

Essie had a conversation about Christmas with Felicity who ran the craft shop over by the Kish Pontoon. Essie said she hated the commercialism, that's why she liked to be out here. Felicity agreed. She'd not even bothered with a Christmas tree this year, she wasn't going to go and rob the plantation like everyone else, she'd just got a lovely piece of driftwood from the shore, a beautiful thing like a narwhal's horn, and stuck it all over with nice, natural things like pine cones. Essie thought it sounded stupid.

'You could sell it in the shop after Christmas,' she said.

'You never know.' Felicity laughed.

'Take *Finnegans Wake* now,' said Vincent. 'Completely unreadable as a novel.'

'It isn't actually.'

'Oh, come on!'

Feargal had read *Finnegans Wake*, of course, and understood it all.

Some people went and more came. There was a long talk about the Winter solstice and the pagan roots of Christmas. Essie ran out and rescued one of the cats from a fondly strangling toddler. The death of Christianity was discussed. Then there was a long and detailed dissection of all the building works that were in progress here and thereabouts, and the plans for Dundreen – Dundreen, Essie thought, I suppose that's where he'll have ended up as usual, but on Christmas Day? – and drainage and the everlasting problem of damp.

Rosanna came back and made filter coffee and the slightly burnt aroma filled the house pleasantly. Essie ran in and out of the kitchen, adjusting the gas here and there, lifting the lids of her copper-bottomed saucepans, checking on the brown stock. Everybody drank brandy and pulled crackers and told funny stories about droll things Jackie Bat had done or said. Children ran in and dispersed themselves loudly around the house. Essie got them out of the studio, terrified for her earthenware leprechauns, old women in shawls, ballad-singers, barefoot colleens, Irish cottages with removable roofs, Ballinaphuca mugs. She ran back to the kitchen to make the sauce and the little sods got back in again, messed about with the wheel and broke the panniers off a terracotta donkey. Essie yelled, Rosanna laid the table with the green and blue slipware and, at last, the diehards started to leave.

'Well, what a shame. It looks like we're going to have to miss George, doesn't it?'

'Yes, what a shame!'

'Hey, doesn't it drive you mad, Ess? I'd go bananas if Chuck went off like this on Christmas Day.'

Essie shrugged, arms folded. 'You know George,' she said. 'Good old George!'

The house looked like hell. Essie flopped down in front of the fire. The chimney breast was all pasted with pictures, photographs, Hokusai waves, Haiku, enigmatic calligraphy, the Desiderata. 'Thank God I never had kids!' she cried with feeling, then felt awkward, remembering Rosanna's condition; but Rosanna just smiled and started clearing up as if she were the au pair, and when some kind of order had been restored the two of them ate dinner, a chestnut roast with all the trimmings, Christmas pudding, the lot. Then they drank some more coffee, gave each other a foot massage and had a go at balancing each other's chakras. She's OK when she's off the booze, Essie thought. Poor Rosanna.

'Hell with it,' she said, 'let's smoke some dope.'

They played around with the tarot cards. Essie wanted to know if she'd get her exhibition. Some woman from a gallery in Dublin had written to her out of the blue, on a recommendation apparently, and she was going up to Dublin in a few weeks to take a few samples: not the tourist crap but the good stuff, elaborately sprigged ceramic sculptures like great dripping plants or peculiar mythical beasts. Essie loved them. Her heart raced when she even thought of them. It looked promising, Rosanna said. There was the Ace of Coins and the Star. Really very good indeed. But why was the King of Cups reversed? Who could that be?

'George,' said Essie, 'after I've strung him up by the heels.'

I am calm and in control, she repeated in her mind again and again to the anger simmering there. It would be nice to have a couple of days in Dublin, get away from him for a bit.

'The Ace of Coins!' Rosanna said. 'And up there, too, that's a pretty good position for it. Hey, lend me some, will you?'

Essie laughed. If she made any money she'd get a proper toilet. She'd been shitting in a bucket for eleven years and it was getting a bit much.

'You know, you're all right, Rosanna,' Essie said, mellowed by food and drink and dope. 'You're all right when you're not drinking and not with Clyde. He's the worst thing that ever happened to you, you know.'

'No, no,' Rosanna said, smiling, 'the best. All this,' she gestured vaguely towards her stomach and genitals, 'he didn't mean to do. He wasn't thinking, old Clyde, you know what he's like. He's a violent man.' She gave the hint of a shrug as if to say: there it is, what can anyone do?

Then she recounted for the fiftieth time the pathetic little story of how it had been love at first sight on the Liverpool-Dublin ferry, how there had been a terrible storm and the boat had heaved and pitched, the decks swimming with seawater, the toilets with vomit, drinks flying, people falling over, and how only she and Clyde (and the barman) had still been on their feet calmly downing the Guinness while the world went mad. How they had looked at each other, silent, one at each end of the bar, then without a word got up and gone and found an empty cabin and fucked till the boat berthed, and then – fate, of course – found they were both travelling to obscure Ballinaphuca, she to visit her old friend Essie who had no idea she was coming and would be horrified at the state of her after all these years, he returning from his mother's funeral. Only he hadn't really been coming back from his mother's funeral, it was just another of his lines, in fact he didn't give a sod about his mother, who was alive and well and living in Catford and not giving a sod back.

Clyde himself always maintained that he'd probably met her on the bus out from Cork City, or maybe somewhere up the west coast.

'You're mad,' Essie said sadly, patting Rosanna's knee. 'He's seriously dangerous, Rosanna. You didn't see what he did to Bob. That was horrible.'

'Oh, he asked for it. That wasn't really Clyde's fault, he was just sticking up for his friend.' She laughed to herself and lounged about on the floor: 'Well, I'm done for, I'm done for in the eyes of the Church, you know. It's not the drink they mind, it's the sex. Too much sex. Father Leahy loves it when I turn up for confession, you know. Settles down, he does, for a nice long listen. Oh, I'm a born confessor, me, I love it. Rosanna the Confessor. He likes me, you know, knows I'm straight with him. I thought about getting in as his housekeeper, you know. Cushy little number that'd be, eh? What do you think?'

She's tough as old boots, Essie thought, the way she recovered. I'd be dead if I lived like she did. 'When are you going to grow up?' she asked.

Rosanna just laughed.

'Oh, dammit, I'm going to ferret him out,' said Essie, rising. 'He can do the washing up and see to the animals. Damned if I'm doing anything else today. You going back to the caravan soon, Rosanna?'

'Can I just watch a little bit of TV while you're out? I don't often get the chance.'

'Yeah.'

Rosanna opened a cupboard door, revealing a little old black-and-white TV set. She turned it on and stretched out before the fire, yawning. A priest was talking to someone.

'I'd quite like to have a little time alone when I get back,' Essie said, getting her boots and slinging a long black coat on, 'so if you wouldn't mind . . .'

Rosanna climbed into an armchair and turned like a cat before settling in. She'll be here for ever, Essie suddenly thought, panicking slightly as she felt in her pocket for the car keys.

'Have you noticed how many priests there are on the TV?' Rosanna asked.

'I don't watch it,' Essie said.

'Yeah, primetime TV. All the chat shows have got one thrown in somewhere. Studio audiences are full of them.'

Essie breathed deeply a few times. Rosanna was the kind of person who drove others to assertiveness training. You could throw it all at Rosanna, every technique in the book, she was like a tank, unassailable, shooting them down as they came. 'Rosanna,' said Essie, planting her feet firmly apart and speaking calmly and evenly, 'I would like you to go back to the caravan in a little while please so that George and I can have some time to ourselves when we get back. I think we may need to talk. I'm sure you understand. If you like, you can come and have breakfast with us in the morning.'

Perfectly delivered.

'Gonna have a row, are you?' Rosanna said, not looking up from the jolly musical sequence that seemed to have burst in from nowhere. Then she looked up. 'Oh, sod off,' she said. 'I'm going in a minute.'

18

Essie stood before the house for a moment, gathering herself. She knew she was still a little drunk but decided to take a chance with the driving. The Guarda wouldn't be out today and there was hardly anyone around. The church bell tolled. The mist over the sea had cleared and the air shimmered.

Inchicora was beautiful. The track ran between crags of rock and heathery scrub, through the rising undulations of the mountain to an amphitheatre of ferns with a waterfall trickling down a rock-face and two old cottages standing together knocked into one. Both were painted white with yellow doors and windows, and a long studio extension had been built onto one end. A terraced flower garden, George's work, lay before them, in summer lush and riotous, humming with fat bees, now comely and sedate in its rough winter plumage. It had been a poor spot when they'd bought it sixteen years ago: big fat old Nora South had had it, then Davy Scanlon who'd let it go to ruin with the sheep grazing in and out and toadstools sprouting in the windows. They loved it so much they could never split up, she and George. It was more binding than children, who, from what she could see, didn't bind anything much any more. George was a child anyway, an idiot child she was stuck with.

She got in the car and drove down to Con and Marie's, the first place he would have called. Simon and Con were watching TV. Marie was in the kitchen dancing alone to a happy romantic pop song on the radio. She looked flushed and laughed when Essie came in. 'This is what I get up to,' she said. 'Will you take a drink, Essie?'

'No thanks, I'm driving. Has George been here?'

George had been in the morning, she said; he'd stayed for about half an hour and gone off in the direction of the village. Essie didn't hang about. She always felt guilty around Marie now.

It wasn't just the address she'd thrown into the harbour, it was a sealed letter addressed to Marie inside another addressed to herself that had arrived in October. She hadn't passed it on. Marie looked all right, why raise it all again for her? Better this way. And in a fit of curiosity, burning with guilt, she'd opened it and read:

Dear Marie, I'm sorry I caused you so much trouble. I'm sorry I got my head kicked in. I gave my address to Essie to give to you but either she didn't or you chose not to write. So probably this won't get to you or you'll throw this away, too. Maybe you'll never know that I'm sorry I caused you so much trouble. That's all I want to say. Dearest Marie, I'm still thinking of you. Bob.

The shame of reading the letter had made her angry and she'd thrown it in the range and tried to forget all about it. What was the point? Why bother her with it? It was like a question from Scruples, she couldn't work it out.

'If you see Julia,' Marie said as she was leaving, 'could you send her on home? She's out with the car and she's had long enough, her daddy'll be getting worried.'

They looked at each other. They're together, the thought struck both of them at the same time but nothing was said.

Half way to Strangarvan Essie turned from the road and wound her way across a mile and a half of James and Helen's land, towards the high cliffs of the coast. Sheep grazed among the tussocks and hillocks on either side. All this had once belonged to Jackie Bat's grandfather but it had ended up, like so much else, belonging to Davy Scanlon, who'd sold it to the Sawles. You got a legacy when you moved in here. You got Jackie Bat's grandfather or Nora South or Quigs and his sons in America. You got what was left of them in living memory, scraps that sat upon your hearths like familiar spirits. Land: a possession like anything else. Who really owns it? It didn't work out too badly. James and Helen, from obscure guilt, let the neighbours' sheep graze here now for nothing at all.

She sailed into the big earth car park they'd had made below the house. The Mullens' car was there and several others. She parked beside a battered orange Mini with conservation stickers and a flattish tyre and walked up. Dundreen overlooked a lovely wild stretch of the coast. The long grand house had come together elegantly around the bones of three abandoned cottages. Off to one side, attached to the house by a covered passage, was a huge ring of a room, a thick glass wheel with polished wooden spokes that clung to the very edge of high, cruel cliffs. There was a wide gravelled drive, a little pool where ducks swam, a great painted wooden wheel leaning up against the side of the house. MONTSALVAT, the brass plaque at the side of the main door announced respectably, AFFIRMATION CENTRE. An old sheep–dog with a spiralling mane lay over the threshold.

The door was open and Essie walked in, padding softly along the hall. There was a long wooden bench with a few leaflets strewn upon it. The carpet was soft and blue, the walls beige, the pictures abstract, many of them by local blow–in artists. An oil painting of Swan Mary hung at the top of a flight of stairs. She came to a large tidy sitting room with open double doors, and windows gazing across the great estuary towards far mountains and islands. The floor was covered with smooth white swirls of goats' hair and a few people sat here and there in the comfortable chairs and on the floor. It was a lovely room with well–loved and cherished old things, an escritoire, a book press, bowls filled with fruit, tall fluted vases of cloudy green glass holding dried wild grasses and flowers. Something by Suzanne Vega played faintly in the background. George sat cross–legged on the floor talking about the time he'd nearly fallen off a cliff, Julia was gazing at him, James weeping and grinning and wiping his nose. Everyone was laughing. A thin–faced man with very long straight fair hair sat cross–legged under the window. Oh dear, she thought, some big scene.

Everyone turned to look at her.

'Hi, Essie.'

'Hi.'

'Hi.'

'Oh, Essie, hello,' said Helen, jumping up. She had massive breasts and big wide lips that smiled voluptuously, the upper curling back on itself and revealing the gums. 'Would you like some tea?'

'I've had some, thanks ...'

'It's no trouble, there's plenty in the pot.'

She sauntered to the kitchen, grey leggings baggy, feet bare. Essie followed and leaned against the doorframe, watching her pour tea from a big Chinese teapot. 'This is jasmine,' she said. 'Is that all right or would you rather have ordinary?'

'That's fine. What's the matter with James?'

'His mother's just died. We got a phone call about fifteen minutes ago.'

'Oh shit!' Crap timing, Essie thought.

'Oh, don't worry.' Helen handed her the mug, still smiling broadly. She whispered, leading the way back to the sitting room: 'It's not that big a deal, really. He hadn't seen her for years – couldn't stand her actually – and it was expected. She was a wreck. Still, she was his mother. It's nice that there were people here when he got the news, takes the edge off it a bit. The guy over by the window by the way, that's Brendan, he's from Sligo. He's had a vision.'

Essie went over to James at once and took his hands. 'I'm ever so sorry,' she said, 'you must feel really strange.'

He laughed and pulled her towards him for a quick fraternal kiss. He was a thin pale man with a narrow, handsome, twisted little face with anxious blue eyes and a bulbous white forehead faintly veined with blue. 'I do, I do,' he said. 'Look at me, crying! I was just saying, I don't want any of you to leave or feel awkward on account of this. I'm glad you're all here.'

Everyone laughed awkwardly.

'On Christmas Day, too,' Essie said stupidly. 'Are you going over?'

'Yes, for the funeral. Bob's taking care of things at that end. Fortunately he was in London when it happened.'

Essie sat down on the floor and drank her tea. She said hello to Plum and Toni and Dave and Grania and Julia and Brendan who'd had the vision. George continued to talk in his amiable, chuckling sort of a way about other near-death experiences he'd had, here and in the Himalayas and once when he'd been shot at in California. She'd heard it all before and looked about, tapping her fingers on the side of her cup. Of course, he was upstaging the man who'd had the vision. Dear old George with his silky beard and big gooey eyes, they laughed at his charm, that particular combination of sad clown, child and God. He spoke familiarly of death, as if it were some good old pal from the sweet bye-and-bye, got enthusiastic, his eyes dancing.

Everyone laughed. Julia's mouth was huge, all teeth and lips. Too big, really, but that was part of her beauty. She wore long boxer boots, black tights and a lurid purple jumper, and she didn't look like anyone else but herself.

'Oh, George,' said Essie. 'Put a sock in it.'

'Leave him alone, Ess,' James said. 'He's keeping me sane.' He swivelled slightly in the big red leather chair, pushing a hand through his springy ginger hair, then got up and walked about near the window. He was small and faintly foppish, with long freckled white hands. A permanently ridged frown cut his forehead in two. One of his hands started wafting the air by his brow as if drawing forth ideas. 'I've always thought,' he said, looking down the estuary, 'the view down that way cries out for a room with a huge window. I have it exactly in mind. But what about this? What about this? My mother has just died and I keep thinking what I can do now with the money. Isn't that terrible? Isn't that terrible?' He wiped away another tear.

Sometimes all this blurting stuff out got her down. She looked at George who was grinning manically and wanted, really wanted, to hit him. She tried to reboard the train of logic from this afternoon but it had gone. Release what is within, they said. That's what Clyde did. That's what Marie had done. Where did it end? Children played outside, blow-in kids with mostly English accents, running and shouting on the rough lawn.

'I've got this idea now,' James said, 'and I can't get it out of my mind. You'll say I'm mad. I'm going to build the most beautiful house in the world for the glory of the light, and I'm going to invite Swan Mary to come and stay in it. I won't rest now till it's done.'

There was a short embarrassed silence. Essie thought how loaded his mother must have been. She'd seen her once, years ago, when she was over on a visit, looking like a man in skilful drag with a wide-brimmed white hat and pearls. The luck of some people, she thought. It's not as if they really needed it, is it?

Julia smiled at her.

'Oh, Julia,' she said, 'your mum says your dad's getting a bit worried, wondering where you are.'

'Oh, crikey,' said Julia languidly, pushing her fingers through her short flopping hair.

Everyone was ignoring the vision man, who had not moved or said a word, and during all the laughter had only smiled wryly. Essie felt sorry for him. 'I hear you've had a vision?' she said politely. 'What was it like?'

'It was like a pure white light,' the man said in a quiet Irish voice, turning towards her and smiling formally, 'absolutely blinding. It hung just above the table where I was sitting and I knew that in the centre of it was the source and final end of all things. But you couldn't look directly at it. It was too bright. No human being could live in light like that. It was terrifying.'

'My goodness,' said Essie, trying to pick up some feeling of holiness from him, something to mark him out from the rest. But there was nothing particular.

'Money doesn't matter,' said George. 'Everyone's scared to talk about it. What's money? Pshew!' He threw it away, smiling, his face a happy clown. His eyebrows were very dark and as expressive as his eyes. 'I'm not envious of your money,' he said sincerely to Helen, 'it's irrelevant to me. You're all naked. I don't see any difference between you and the beggar kids in Cork and Dublin. You take what life gives you! It gives you grief for a while, you take it!' He grew stern and emotional. 'You take it, man! It gives you love! Fuck-ups! Everything! The best and the worst, heaven and hell, you take it!'

Essie looked away.

'And if it gives you money, you take that too, and don't feel guilty, you use it, you use it, man, and you use it according to the light. It's as simple as that. If that means you give it all away, you give it all away, if it means you build a house, you build a house.'

The way Julia was looking at him. After all, thought Essie, trying to see him objectively, he is quite attractive in an ugly sort of way. He was free, of course, to go if he wanted to. They both were. A commitment had never been made. Everyone was laughing. Helen sat messing with her thick black hair. 'I love George,' said James. 'Yes, I do, I love George.' He wiped his eyes. Everyone beamed and George ducked his head, covering his eyes and grinning.

'That day in Okinochee,' said James, 'I knew, I knew when I saw Swan Mary that one day she'd come here. I saw it.' He closed his eyes fiercely. The knots and whorls upon his high white brow were painful to look at. There was another silence.

Essie found this kind of thing desperately embarrassing. George met her eyes, winked and smiled. Only she and Brendan who'd had the vision noticed. She did not smile back.

The children came running in from the garden, screaming.

'Sshhh! Sshhh! For heaven's sake!' cried Helen.

'Kester's frightening us!'

'Kester, don't!'

Kester was the big one.

'George,' said Essie, 'I think it's time we were going.'

George looked at his watch, a huge silver thing full of dials.

'I don't deal in time,' he said, getting obligingly to his feet.

George followed Essie down to the car park, rambling along with a bounce in his step and his knees turned out, his old Tao Te Ching under his arm. He stood sniffing the sea before getting into the passenger seat and sitting back comfortably, his head on one side. George did not drive though he could. The saggy old seat had moulded itself to the shape of his back.

'Do up your seatbelt, George,' Essie said.

She drove silently. 'About your father's business, were you?' she asked sourly after a while.

George laughed, a smothered explosion, then began to talk. 'Sometimes I get scared, Ess,' he said, 'really scared. I go in and in and in on myself like endless repetitions in a mirror, horrifically in the end. It's been going on like that all day.'

'We all get that, George,' she said. 'Feargal was over, and Ben and Ulrica, and Felicity, and Chuck and Sara, and Hamish and Paula. They brought some nice presents. There were hoardes of kids and one of my donkeys got broke. Rosanna's been OK. We left the washing up for you.'

'It's nice to have kids around at Christmas,' George said comfortably. 'What do you make of Brendan, huh?'

'Brendan?'

'Guy under the window.'

'Seems nice enough,' she said. George would have loved to have had a vision, she knew. The kamikaze dogs ran out and bit the wheels. 'You've got to put the animals away as well. What took you to Dundreen?'

'Oh, you know how it is. I just got to walking about, kept on meeting people, Dan Hogan, the Collins girls, you know, then Julia came along in the car and said she was going to Montsalvat so I got in.'

'Did you get the matches?'

'And yeah, you know, it's amazing. People just kept giving me things. Fantastic! Putting it all together here and there throughout the day, I must've eaten like a king. You know, there's a lot of good in people still.'

'I don't know why I put up with you.'

'Neither do I,' he said. 'It's a good job you love me, isn't it?'

There was a long silence. All the time she was aware of him grinning uncontrollably beside her. 'You know sometimes,' he said as they came over the Gap, sea and valley and sky unfurling, 'I think about giving up speech, like Meher Baba.' He giggled. 'They'd love it, wouldn't they? My fans?'

'Oh, don't give me all that, George,' said Essie. 'You know this guru stuff is driving me up the wall. I wish you'd stop it.'

They approached the village. She could feel him gazing fixedly at the side of her face and glanced at him. He smiled. 'Aw, come on, Ess,' he said, 'don't be mad at me.'

'Why am I never to be mad at you, George?' she asked.

'Essie,' he said, all serious again, 'This – admiration – is not something I chose. All I'm doing is saying what I think. I can't help it if people . . .'

'Oh, shut up, George! You encourage it!'

Nothing more was said till they were home. Rosanna had gone. The fire chuckled peacefully and the cats sprawled here and there among the rugs and cushions and cosy chairs. It was only about tea time, but Essie went and changed into her warm nightie and red woolly socks, her favourite things, sat down by the fire and told George to bring her a glass of sherry and a mince pie.

'Guess what they're going to do up there,' he said, bringing the goodies and setting them down by her side. 'They're getting a flotation tank.'

'You're joking.'

'It's true.'

'I've always wanted a go in one of those,' she said, eating and tucking her legs underneath her.

'And another extension for when they have speakers and what have you. Ha! Vincent's going to paint a mural all over the gable end. That'll be a disaster anyway.' He laughed.

'Julia fancies you,' she said.

'Yeah?' He looked pleased. 'You think she does?'

'Of course she does.'

He laughed delightedly, slapping his thigh. 'Oh man, oh man, I find that quite, ah, touching,' he said, 'the idea that she's chosen an old fart like me. I mean, look at her, look at her, man, beautiful, kind of thing you cream your pants over when you're fourteen. Anyway, there'll be a lot of work up there, building.'

'Oh, I'm sick of hearing about building! Only building job I'm interested in is getting our new toilet plumbed in.'

'And I'm gonna help out. I wanna get in on it. What do you think? It's good for the place, Essie. Anyone'll be able to go up there any time and use the library or meditate or just hang out or whatever. It'll be like a meeting place. Yeah, I think it's a good thing.'

'Hm,' she said, nodding her head.

'Joe and I went to this place in India once. Right on the edge of a great cliff on the side of a mountain. Bet that's the kind of thing they have in mind.'

Joe was his old hippie lover from years back. An honoured picture of him, unframed and evocatively tattered, was tacked to the chimney breast with all the other stuff: six by four head and shoulders, slightly sepia tone, saintly face, toothsome smile, softly parting fair hair. He was on a bus in Fresno. Other women had other women. Essie had Joe, the dream hippie. Where was he?

Lost. Lost and gone for ever. He had attained legendary status and looked down on them like Geronimo or Che Guevara or Bob Dylan. She didn't really know if he'd actually had sex with Joe, but he might as well have done.

'The money'll come in handy,' she said.

'What money?'

'For the Dundreen work.'

George sat down and eased off his boots. 'No money,' he said. 'Long as there's a patch of cement somewhere with my name on it. That's all I want.'

'What are you talking about? Work for nothing?'

He just smiled at her, then broke into a long, deep laugh. 'For nothing, for nothing, man. Pshew! Oh, Essie man, I knew you'd blow up!' Then he said, 'Hee hee hee!' falsetto and deliberate and slightly mocking.

'George,' she said, sighing, 'they are loaded. It's not some poor little co-op somewhere, they're filthy rich. You are not working for the Sawles for nothing.'

'Discipline,' he said, 'spiritual discipline. We did it all the time, me and Joe. Y'see, I said I would and then he got this call about his ma. Can't go back on my word now. See?'

'George,' she said, getting up and standing over him, 'you work for the Sawles, they pay you. I'll make sure of it. We can use the money.'

'What do we need money for?'

'A toilet, damn it.'

'I rather like the old shitbucket,' George said.

'God, I hate you sometimes!' she yelled.

George looked hurt. 'I've washed the feet of beggars in Calcutta,' he said. 'Do you know what that means? Do you know what that has done to me?'

'Sod off, George,' said Essie. She sat down again.

'It was serious,' he said seriously. 'It was real life. And some of us never came back. It's getting harder and harder for me to think in terms of the material, Essie. I try. I do try. I'm a different animal. I'm money-blind. It's like being colour-blind, I am congenitally incapable of being racist, sexist, speciesist, any ist you care to name, and that includes richist. They are people, Essie, just people.'

'Of course they're people, you stupid idiot,' she said withering-ly. 'Who said they weren't?' She went upstairs and turned on the fan heater in the bedroom. Books and clothes lay everywhere and the walls were covered with rugs and pictures. She started to clear up a bit. He followed.

'I'm going to meditate for a while,' she said, plumping up a cushion on the floor. 'Could you go downstairs, please?'

'I'll do it for money,' he said, smiling, 'for you, my little plant mired in the material soil. So you can shit in style.'

'I should think so too. Piss off.'

George went away and she sat down on the cushion and closed her eyes and sighed. After a moment she started to breathe deeply. She let her mantra come in. She let it go in and out with her breathing. She felt an itch at the back of her leg and scratched it. Her brows lifted. She sank a notch, consciousness bubbled over her head. She let the mantra twist and writhe like a leech, in and out of her long slow breaths. She sank again, and the anger dropped off her bit by bit, like rust off the wreck of a car. She let it go, saw it form rust-brown clusters in the sky over Rossa, sent it far away out over the Puck Rock and beyond to fall as rain at sea. She fell pleasantly. Her mantra went out into the sky and came back, she repossessed it, just went along for a while, she was happy, she was happy, she was happy . . .

Five or six minutes passed.

Then George put the telly on downstairs. There was no door on the bedroom, only a long red curtain, so the sound was very loud. A man's voice rose and fell, then a woman's joined in and a lot of people started to laugh.

Essie jumped up and ran to the top of the stairs. She felt all funny, as if she'd just been shaken out of a deep dream. 'Turn that bloody thing off!' she roared. He didn't so she ran downstairs. 'Turn it off!' she told the back of his head. 'Didn't you hear me? I said I was going to meditate.'

Essie hated TV; she'd read books laying out all the technical, medical, statistical and sociological proof about how it mentally lobotomised and corrupted and physically rotted the brain. George watched any old thing: the adverts, the *Late Late Show,*

Anything Goes, Hotel, the *Angelus,* that Canadian kids' show about loggers. That was pretty good, he thought, it was making points about Eskimo rights.

'You usually go down to the caravan to meditate,' he said casually.

'Rosanna's there, you know that.' It was only some silly comedy thing so she turned it off. 'I can't stand it,' she said. 'How can you watch rubbish? How can you waste your time? Here we are in this beautiful place and you sit there in front of that thing. Why don't you go outside and watch something real?'

'It's cold,' he said, and stood up, righteous. 'You know, Ess, this is a little bit patronising. Think about it. Millions of people enjoy this rubbish, as you call it, and what are you saying, that they're all stupid or something? Putting your judgement above theirs? Don't you think that's just a little arrogant? Don't you think that might be pride? Doesn't it make you feel just a teensy-weensy little bit ...'

'*George,*' she said warningly.

He spoke like someone on the TV, making the points with his fingers. 'Hell, Swan Mary herself watches television. She loves soap operas. Don't you see, there's a beautiful God-given meaning to everything. Jesus, this fucking reductionism, I'm interested in plastic and dirt and things other people don't even notice. Pshew! They scrape it off their shoes! But I see ...'

'Bullshit. That's not even original.'

'It doesn't have to be! TV's vital, it's the modern artform. What you're saying is pure elitism.'

'Oh, more of that.'

'Prejudice. Y'see, Essie, I'm not prejudiced. I'm not prejudiced against anything. I'm not even prejudiced against prejudice ...'

'George!'

His face creased into a big warm smile, soft-eyed and comical. She sat down opposite him. George said nothing but twiddled his thumbs in a manic kind of a way, beaming stupidly. Now and again he had to stifle laughter. He was like a cloud of humour that you could catch like a cold. To look into his eyes would have been fatal, so she looked at Joe of the beautiful serious eyes and small, becoming beard and hoped spitefully that he was old and boring and overweight somewhere in small-town America. Then George laughed explosively.

'Essie!' he cried. 'You can't believe it, man, it's incredible! You're sitting there looking absolutely — ' he laughed, 'like there are these, these great rays of anger shooting out of you. I can almost see them. You're like the aura round a mushroom cloud. White hot! Wow!' He slapped his leg and shook his head. High and merry, he laughed, clapping his hands as he ran to the back door. Essie ran after and thumped him in the back.

He put on his coat. 'I'm going for a walk,' he said, opening the door. It was soft twilight. George walked away, smiling.

'Fuck off, George!' she yelled after him.

He walked on, bending at the knees with that funny jaunty way of walking he had. There were some old planks lying down one side of the garden. Essie ran out, cold in her nightie, feeling the ridiculousness of her woolly red socks. She seized one of the planks and ran after him. At the gate she hurled it like a javelin. She saw that old fool Dan Hogan walking up the track to scrounge a little something. The plank clattered down well short of George's retreating, dignified back. Dan turned and started walking quickly back down to the road.

'Oh, fuck you!' she bellowed and ran back inside, slamming the door. She started to giggle uncontrollably, thinking of Dan Hogan's retreating back.

George walked a little way then turned back and pottered about for a bit, seeing to the animals before going into the garden and moving about expertly gathering winter flowers in the growing darkness.

Essie was sitting by the fire listening to Billie Holliday. He went into the kitchen and found a vase and put the flowers in water, then did all the washing up and cleaned around the place, smiling and humming to himself. Then he took the vase of flowers in and put them on the mantel shelf.

'Any of that Christmas brack left?' he asked.

'Plenty.'

'Want some? And coffee?'

'OK.'

19

George loved work. First he was on the Scheme, cleaning up the graveyard in Ballinaphuca in the wind and rain with Christy and Mike Pads, Vincent, Ben Bowden, Padraic South and Paddy Bawn. He loved that, couldn't wait to get up and go to work in the morning. It was a real trial of strength. The weather never let up, the rain dripped from your eyelashes; sometimes when the wind blew hail they'd get into a circle facing inwards, like yaks.

Paddy Bawn was ganger. Every day he had at least one furious jumping-up-and-down tantrum, the screaming bulgy-eyed throbbing-veined kind, quite stunning. All you could do was stand back in awe and wait for something to burst. It was not healthy in a man of his build and complexion, George thought, eating his raisins and shredded cabbage and red beans soaked in olive oil and herbs. He liked getting up early in the morning while it was still dark to make it and put it in his lunchbox. He loved working his way down the hill with his spade alongside Vincent, who moaned all the time. This was all a waste of time, Vincent said. He wanted to be doing some serious painting, gazing intently into a six by eight foot canvas that just looked like a lot of grey blobs. He spoke witheringly of those pretty little landscapes – cattle grazing, Rossa, ruins in mist, that kind of thing – that he did occasionally manage to sell. Some blow-ins had bought the old schoolhouse in Ballinaphuca. They were turning it into a craft centre and he was going to try and flog a few through them in the summer, he said. They were quite nice little paintings, George thought. Essie had bought one and hung it up in the kitchen. It looked OK. Vincent nearly cried if you said you liked it. *Et tu, Brute*, his eyes said.

They worked in twos: George and Vincent, Christy and Mike, Paddy and Ben. Paddy and Ben hated one another. Some sheep had been savaged high up near Weeping Rock, a vast grey slab by the old road over Rossa from which the emigrant leaving for America would turn for a last long look at the valley. Paddy had poisoned the carcases. Ben swore his dogs had been locked up the whole time but Paddy didn't believe him. Now if Paddy wanted to tell Ben to do something he had to shout across and go through Christy Pads.

You had to see the funny side of it, George thought. You had to get the most out of things. It had been just like getting drafted, not that he'd ever been around to get drafted but how you'd imagine it, thrown together with these people and having to get on with it. What a learning experience! And wow, wasn't it all worth it just to see Padraic South in his black oilskins standing apart from it all against a leaden sky with his scythe, like Old Father Time. Times George had seen him coming down from the Mass Rock above Inchicora, looming out of the mist on a big white horse like King Arthur. He must have some sheep up there. Essie wanted to do a bust of him but daren't ask him to sit. He'd only refuse, of course. A camera, that's what was needed, with a good zoom lens so that you could home in on them from a distance, catch them when they were unaware. Like big game photography.

At the top near the road were the newer graves but they got older and older as you went down the hill, becoming unreadable; and then brackens and gorse and brambles began and they got older still, more fundamental, dwarfed and ravaged, leaning and lichened, fungoid, ivied.

Two septuagenarians died that winter. They were carried the traditional route about the churchyard before being interred into the bleak black loam. The work parted around them, then went on.

But all that was coming to an end now. George was going to work at Dundreen.

Spring came. Essie drove to Dublin to see about an exhibition. She felt pretty certain the show was wrapped up, photographs had already changed hands and she'd spoken a few times on the phone with Sandra d'Arcy, the woman who ran the gallery. Sandra said she was just dying to get her hands on a few samples, and it was a good excuse for a trip. Essie could visit friends in Bray while she was about it, check out the shops, see a film.

The gallery was central, small, classy and super-casual. Sandra d'Arcy was a small dark woman of about forty in a long silver and black dress, with a huge swathe of wiry glossy black hair. She greeted Essie like a dear and trusted friend and took her into a little cluttered office papered with black and white pictures of movie stars and famous writers. They put the samples on the floor and on the desk and Essie gazed at them proudly. She even smirked a little, she couldn't help it, they were gorgeous: slightly sinister, indecipherable, snake or cactus, footed like hounds, extravagantly sprigged, dripping with cobalt and apple green. Sandra was efficient and wildly confident.

'Oh, aren't they marvellous!' she said in a throaty Anglo-Irish voice. Essie smiled. Sandra got out some fizzy white wine and they sat down and talked about the art scene and Aosdana and the Europe effect on the Irish economy. She was OK, Sandra. The door was open and people kept wandering in and out of the office, a gorgeous pouting sexy boy in a limp T-shirt, a haggard woman in hotpants, city people. It was exciting. Essie felt like a country hick but nicely.

'You know, what's so wonderful,' Sandra d'Arcy said, pouring more wine and sitting back all casually elegant, 'is that you can look at these things for ever and still ask: what is this, is it human, animal, mineral, mollusc, butterfly, vegetable, ether . . . oh! I don't know, that's what's so wonderful.'

Essie drank and basked. Sandra offered her a two-man show in October. Two-*person*, Essie thought automatically. Some guy who did the most amazing paintings based on themes from Irish mythology, Sandra said. She jumped up enthusiastically and took Essie into the store room and showed her three of his canvases: vast swirling maelstroms in bright primaries with minuscule figures wallowing lost here and there. They had no effect on Essie whatsoever, but she said with feeling: 'Oh yes! Oh yes!'

Then Bob Sawle wandered into the room and started poking about among the racked pictures as if he lived there. 'Hi, Essie,' he said.

No, this isn't right, she thought, he shouldn't be here.

She blushed with guilt, then rallied. It was nothing to do with her, the letter, all that. All she'd done was do nothing. 'Hello,' she said. 'What are you doing here? Are you back in Dublin now?'

'Not completely. I'm teaching,' he said. 'London. It's half term now, I'm just over for a few days.'

Should I tell Marie? she was already thinking. He wasn't surprised to see her. 'What a coincidence,' she said.

'Not really. I knew you'd be here. Did you give her a show, San?' he asked. He seemed jumpy, more elegant than before. A thin scarf was wrapped around his neck.

'Of course I did,' said Sandra.

'These are horrendous, don't you think?' he said, waving his hand at the huge canvases.

Essie laughed. 'It's not the word I'd choose,' she said.

'Ignore him,' Sandra d'Arcy said, smiling. They moved back to the office. A show, thought Essie, a show! I've got a show! They finished off the wine. He just stood looking at her samples while Sandra and she compared dates in their diaries.

'What do you do with them?' he asked.

'You put them on your mantelpiece,' said Essie dryly, 'and look at them.'

'I think they're fabulous,' Sandra said.

'You eaten?' he asked Essie.

'No.' She looked at her watch.

'Fancy a Chinese?'

'OK.'

'Not you, San.' He handed her his empty wine glass. 'I just want to talk to Essie about old times.'

'Sure.' Sandra sat on the desk and lit up a small cigar. 'I'll just sit here and eat my humble cheese sandwich.' A look of amusement passed between them. They knew each other very well, that was clear. She was attractive, Sandra d'Arcy, with big painted lips and sacs under her eyes. Her head hair looked pubic. It crackled.

It was nice to be a little drunk in Dublin in the middle of the day. She grinned as she walked through the streets with Bob. 'I've got a show, Bob,' she crowed, 'I have got a fucking show.'

He smiled, lips closed. 'How's things in Ballinaphuca?' he asked.

'Oh, fine.'

He rushed along with his hands in his pockets. Shouldn't have read that letter, she thought, that was a rotten thing to do.

Everything else was OK, but not that.

They went to a restaurant near the gallery. 'Let me buy this,' he said when they were sitting down with the menus.

'Don't be stupid.'

He shrugged. He was awkward, looking all over the place but at her. They ordered wine and Dim Sum and talked about Ballinaphuca. He said he'd bought a flat in London. He was writing the book again. God, she thought, some people are suckers for punishment. Poor thing. Then he said he'd got someone interested and named a publisher she'd heard of. She was impressed. He said it was much quicker this time, and much better than before. He felt good about it. He drank very fast as if deliberately trying to get drunk. 'I'm fuelled by anger,' he said. 'Do you know why I'm angry?'

'PMT?'

'Don't be facetious. I'm angry because of what happened. I had my jaw wired for a month. I certainly don't see as well as I used to. I still get a lot of pain. I have nightmares. I'm not some macho man, you know, I'm just anybody. I was terrified. Christ, I know what it must be like for you women when you get raped . . .'

'No,' she said seriously, shaking her head, 'you don't know that.'

'I was stuck in that hospital afterwards feeling like death and I could hear the Fleadh going on and all the drunks shouting and I was terrified. Let's have some brandy.' He looked around for a waiter and knocked over his wine glass. 'The nuns were very nice to me, you know. They knew all about me but they were very nice. Shame they were nuns. The world could use more women like that.'

'Yes, it was terrible,' Essie said. 'It was appalling. Clyde's just a nutter, you get nutters all over the place. You don't want to judge the place too harshly. You weren't totally innocent, were you?'

He frowned. The brandy came and he lit a cigarette. They clinked glasses, both of them pretty drunk by now. 'Listen,' he said, taking out a sealed letter and placing it on the table near her elbow. 'I want you to give her a letter. I know you didn't pass the others on, but I'm going to tell you why you've got to do this.'

'No,' she said.

'How is she?'

'She's fine, Bob. She's OK.' She pushed the letter back towards him but he did not pick it up.

'Really?'

'Well, of course she is. What did you think?'

'How do I know?'

'Please, Bob, don't try and involve me in all this. It's like asking me to take sides, these are my neighbours, I have to live there. Honestly, she's perfectly happy, I can assure you. Please, just don't involve me.'

'Listen,' he said, leaning forward and looking directly at her for the first time. His eyes were cold. 'This is excruciating. Do you really think I want to be sitting here talking to someone I hardly know about my private life? And that's just the point. Whatever happened or did not happen between Marie and me it was private. It has nothing to do with you or anybody else. But you are taking it upon yourself to deny her the chance to respond or not, as *she* decides, *she*, not you. You have absolutely no right, knowing as little as you do about the whole situation to make her decisions for her.'

Essie was stunned. 'You've twisted it!' she cried, slamming down her glass.

'I'm angry,' he said, still cold. 'You lot always make me angry. You're all into being open and all that crap but when it comes right down to it . . .'

'Open? Open?' Essie laughed. 'Sneaking letters behind my neighbour's back?'

He gestured floppily. 'I manufactured this, you know that, don't you? I gave your name to Sandra and I made sure she got you here at half term. Now, all you have to do is deliver a letter.'

'Oh, I get it,' she said, sitting back and folding her arms. 'I get a show, you get a pimp, is that it? Well, thanks a lot! And offering to pay for the meal! Ha! What the hell do you think I am?'

He turned away, knocked back his brandy with one disgusted jerky movement and stood up, reaching into his inside pocket. 'Here,' he said, discarding a couple of notes onto the table, 'my half of the bill. I would have got you the show anyway, and if you don't believe that, fuck you.' He walked out.

She picked up the letter and put it in her bag. Centre, she thought. Centre, keep still, don't let them rattle you.

20

West: darkness, the small towns, the shrines, the little yellow lights of houses appearing and disappearing. It was three hours drive back to Ballinaphuca. The last thirty-five miles, twisting and tortuous, were always the worst and seemed to take twice as long as all the rest of the journey put together.

She got back to Inchicora around ten and sat for a moment in the car outside the house, feeling that slight relief she always felt at the end of a journey – ah yes, survived again – then went inside. She wanted to get into her nightie and red socks and have a cup of chocolate in bed with the radio on. She'd go mad if the TV was blaring. But it wasn't, it was in the corner with a big jagged cartoon hole in its screen. Julia and George were sitting by the fire, one on either side, Julia eating pasta out of one of Essie's more functional bowls. The place smelt cosily of coffee and incense.

'What the hell . . .' she began, ignoring them and going over to the TV.

'Essie, love,' said George, jumping up. 'Coffee? That was Rosanna. How'd it go?'

'Rosanna?'

'I'm borrowing again,' Julia smiled. 'Books, this time.'

'Hey, come on, come on. Get a show?'

'Of course I did.'

George clapped his hands together and did a little dance, feet and knees turned out.

'What the hell happened to this?'

'Banjaxed,' said Julia.

'Rosanna.' George chuckled. 'I was just sitting here watching the *Late Late Show* and she comes in and sticks her foot through the screen. Last night. Good job she was wearing boots or she might've hurt her foot.' His laughter splurted out of the sides of his mouth.

'She's mad,' Julia said, smiling. 'She's just like an old witch.'

Rosanna was drinking again, mostly in the bars of Strangarvan, coming and going eratically. sleeping about probably, turning nasty at times. She'd got thrown out of Biddy O'Neill's for pulling a knife on a sailor.

Essie flopped down in George's vacated chair.

'She said it was for you,' George called through from the kitchen. 'Are you hungry? Want some pasta? We're pigging out. Said you'd taken out a contract on it.'

Essie groaned.

'That's grand about the show,' said Julia, 'I'm sure you deserve it.'

'Oh, I do, I do.' Essie started to laugh. 'Oh God, Rosanna's got to go. Oh God, look at it. Do you know, Julia, Rosanna was a nice girl once. Do you know, we used to work in a bank together. Oh God, before you were born! She wore a pink suit, she was very good fun. Everyone liked her.'

George returned with a mug of coffee for her and one for Julia. 'Where can she go?' asked George.

Essie sighed.

'You're right, Essie,' Julia said, finishing the pasta, 'she can't stay here for ever. She takes advantage of you. No one else'd want her. You've been so good to her, the pair of you, and she throws it back at you.' She licked her fingers casually, hanging onto one and gnawing at the nail. George darted a very stern, obvious look at her.

'What?' she said defensively.

Essie sipped her coffee, wrapping her fingers right round the mug. Here we go, she thought.

He built up a nice little pregnant silence then said: 'The Zen fool, Ryokwan, one of my superheroes, made a poem about the thief who broke into his hut one stormy night and left empty-handed because there was nothing to steal. Ryokwan, you see, had nothing. And he lay awake in the night worrying about the poor thief all alone on a road somewhere in that terrible night with nowhere to lay his head. He at least had his hut, the roof of straw above his head. What a man, hey? What a man! And when the little green shoot of a tree came up through his earth floor, what'd he do? Does he dig it up like you and me woulda done without a thought? Does he fuck! He lets it grow. Beautiful! And it grows up and up and up and he lives with it and watches it 'till in the end it goes right up through the roof and breaks the hut in half!' George laughed. 'No home. No home in this world.' They all laughed. Then there was a little silence.

'Tell you what, George,' Essie said, 'she can have the house and we'll move into the caravan. How about that? Happy now?'

George got up and danced about in front of the fire, clapping his hands and chuckling. 'Right! Right!'

Essie jumped up and threw him down into a chair. 'You shut up,' she told him. 'You're cracked.'

Julia stood up too. 'Well,' she said, stretching, 'I'll be off. OK if I take these books, Essie?'

'Sure.'

George tapped his head dementedly. 'Think, Julia!' he urged, 'think!'

It happens. Youth and Age. He's flattered, inevitably, Essie thought.

Next morning she meditated for half an hour psyching herself up for two confrontations, first Rosanna, then Marie. And I came here for a quiet life, she thought, going down with resolute stride through the brown bracken and the beehives to the caravan. It was warm and moist, what the Irish called a soft day.

Rosanna was up, she looked as if she'd never been to bed. Her hair was long and witchy and she was sitting on the bed peering up through the dry tangles balefully, just sitting there doing nothing as if she hadn't moved for hours. Essie felt a touch of fear, very faint.

'Rosanna,' she said, 'you were out of order breaking the TV. Now enough's enough, love, you really must start looking for somewhere to move onto. Me and George'll be getting cabin fever soon, honestly, we used to use this old caravan a lot. Two weeks, Rosanna, yeah? All right? Rosanna?'

Rosanna said nothing at all, just yawned as if she were terribly, terribly bored, and lay slowly down, turning her face away. There was a sour smell in the caravan and cobwebs growing thick on the windows. All the pretty little things of George and Essie's that lay about, the Kali, the globe, the old Peruvian rug, all sad, downtrodden, neglected. Essie felt depressed when she came out into the grey air. She needed a little walk and went down to the strand. She walked along past the deserted beach house and thought: she could always go back there, I suppose, oh bloody life, why can't people look after themselves? Along the beach, breathing to the rhythm of the sea, gazing along the sublime raggedy arms of the bay towards the distant high headland of Anagar where sea birds nested.

After a while she felt composed enough to go up to Marie's. Half way up from the beach she met Jackie Bat and Rex tearing along towards the village, a look of sheer horror on the poor man's face as if his entire family had just this moment perished. 'Sure, they've all gone!' he burst out as if he could not contain it. 'The lot of them. Dogs. Not a one left alive.'

It took a moment to realise he meant his sheep.

'Oh, Jackie!' she said helplessly, then again, 'oh, Jackie!' because she didn't know what to say.

There were weak tears round the margins of his eyes. Jackie rubbed his great red nose with a dirty hand, all cracked and calloused.

'Did you see them?' she asked. 'Oh, that's terrible! Oh, Jackie! Oh, I am sorry!'

He shook his head. 'They was on the field of the crown,' he said, ''tis a fine field.' Then burst out again: 'The little things! All lying there with their necks all torn. Oh, 'tis a terrible thing to see!'

Essie went cold. Jackie rushed on to the village and she continued on her way, shaken. She suspected this was ruinous, catastrophe. What would he do now? Oh Jackie, poor Jackie. You couldn't do a bust of Jackie. Big features but too indistinct. She looked back. The road shimmered all silver and grey and misty and Jackie strode on, a broad dark figure putting up its hand to its face from time to time. What could she do?

'Come in,' Marie said gaily.

Oh God, Rosanna was there. She was everywhere.

Marie was combing out Rosanna's hair in the living room and

126

drying it with a hair-drier. The two of them were laughing about something and Rosanna's clean red hair flew about her head, all bright and new, the ends kicking wildly in the air like the legs of insects. 'Hi, Essie,' she said as if nothing had happened.

'Congratulations!' Marie called over the noise of the drier. 'An exhibition!'

Of course, everyone already knew about it. The jungle grapevine, not much slower than light.

'There,' cried Marie, 'isn't that better, Essie? Shampoo and blow dry, I ought to set up in business. What'll we do with her, Essie?' She tapped Rosanna's head. 'She says she hasn't used shampoo for nine years. Can you beat that?'

'Soap's soap,' said Rosanna as if she was talking to idiots. She did not smile. 'It doesn't matter what you use, soap, washing up liquid, it's all the same thing with different labels on. Shampoos are the same, only more expensive.'

'Rubbish,' said Marie. She turned off the drier. 'Would you hand me that comb? There now, you're lovely.'

Rosanna stood up and looked at herself in the mirror and burst out laughing. 'It's gone all fluffy,' she said.

'There's nothing like getting nice and clean to pick you up when you're not feeling great,' Marie said, going into the kitchen and putting the kettle on.

'You funny thing.' Rosanna laughed dismissively and started walking about in a vaguely menacing way, hands in pockets, poking her nose into corners and kicking her feet against the range and the legs of chairs.

'I just saw Jackie Bat,' Essie said, loud enough for Marie to hear in the kitchen, 'dogs have killed all his sheep.'

'All?' Marie came and stood in the door, taking a pack of cigarettes from a pocket in her sweater. 'Mother of God,' she said seriously, tossing one to Rosanna, 'he'll be destroyed, the poor man.' She left the pack on the sideboard and put her head on one side to light up, then stood there with her arms folded, smoking with great hungry sucks like an alcoholic falling on the neck of a bottle.

'Whose dogs?' asked Rosanna.

'He didn't see.'

'Well, it can't be Ben and Ulrica's this time. Those poor mutts are in a canine Colditz.' Rosanna laughed. 'Well, everyone'll be rushing for their licences now.'

'Poor Jackie,' Essie said, 'isn't it bloody typical? The nicest people get the rawest deals.'

'Yeah,' said Rosanna to Marie, 'look at me. She's throwing me out.'

'I don't blame her,' Marie said quickly, smiling.

'Oh, that's nice. That's friends for you.' Rosanna was smiling but her eyes were cold and steady.

'Well, you couldn't stay here,' Marie said, friendly but firm, 'you'd have me mad in no time. I couldn't stand all the noise.'

'Good God!' Rosanna hit the sideboard and the things on it jumped. 'How old are you? You're younger than me and look at you! You're middle-aged! And you. What's the matter with you all? You're so old! You're getting boring!'

'Stop it, Rosanna,' Marie said sharply. The kettle was boiling so she went in to make tea.

'*This* is getting boring, Rosanna,' Essie said, 'you being like this is getting boring. Please, love, think what you're doing to yourself.'

Rosanna laughed. 'Don't be so bloody dramatic,' she said. 'Marie! Why don't you stick some music on? Why is it always so dead around here? God, what's the matter with you all? Give us a couple of fags for later, Marie? OK if I take a couple? Sod you lot, I'm going to find some action. Someone must be alive around here.' She took a couple of cigarettes from the packet on the sideboard and walked out with her head down, bristling with challenge.

Marie came in with the tea. 'How do you stand it?' she asked. 'Turns in a second, doesn't she?' She sighed. 'Poor old Jackie!'

'It was that little field at the back. Does he own that?'

'No, that belongs to Davy.'

'Does it?'

'So. How was Dublin?'

'Dublin was fine,' said Essie. 'I met Bob in the gallery.'

Marie stopped pouring the tea for a second. 'You're joking me,' she said and began to smile in a peculiar half-embarrassed, half-brazen way.

'No, really.' Essie regretted it already.

'He's in Dublin? How is he?' She went on pouring the tea.

'He's fine. He's working on his book again. That's nice, isn't it? We had lunch together. He's fine, really. He seems to feel quite bitter about what happened to him, but he's OK. He said he was going back to Shropshire. Did he? Yes, I think he did ...'

Marie was listening very carefully. 'That's funny that, isn't it? You meeting him in the gallery?' she said.

Essie pulled a face. 'I don't think it was accidental, Marie. He wants to get in touch with you. He gave me a letter to give you and I just didn't know what to do. I thought I'd leave it up to you. I've got it with me if you want it. If not, we'll just say no more about it. I really had no idea what to do.'

'Oh Jesus,' said Marie weakly and just stood there at the table looking down at the steam rising up from the tea. She gave a little laugh. 'Well, this has taken me by surprise.' She sat down.

Essie got her tea and sat down, too.

'Tell you what,' she said, 'if you want to think about it for a little bit I can come back later.'

'No, no,' Marie said quickly, 'of course I want it, it's for me, isn't it? Of course I want to see what he has to say for himself. What did he say to you?'

'Oh, you know, just what he was doing and so on. He's teaching, he said, he was just over from London for a few days. He asked after you, of course.'

'What did he look like? Did he look the same?'

'Oh yeah, well, no, a bit different, I thought actually. Kind of more ... city ... I suppose. But then he would, wouldn't he? Here,' she said, producing the letter. Marie took it and sat there looking down at it as if it were a surprise cheque in the post. She turned it over and over in her fingers.

'I'll go now, shall I?' Essie said, putting down her nearly untouched tea.

'And he's writing his book again?' Marie smiled. 'Oh, isn't that ... think of all that work...'

Essie stood up.

'I'm sorry, Essie,' said Marie, jumping up, 'you don't have to go.

Finish your tea, for God's sake, I want to talk to you. Are you angry?'

'No,' said Essie.

'You are, I can tell.'

'I don't want to be a go-between, Marie. I really don't want that.'

'No, of course not. I'm sorry, Essie, I didn't realise.' She blushed deeply and put one hand over her face in sudden shame.

Essie felt terrible. 'It's all right, Marie,' she said quickly, 'I don't mind just this once.'

'Have you told anyone? Have you told George?'

'No,' said Essie truthfully.

'Please don't say anything to anyone, Essie, please, not even George.'

'Of course I won't,' she began indignantly, then saw with horror that Marie was on the edge of tears. Her nostrils and eyes had gone all red. 'Marie,' she said, putting a hand on her arm, but Marie moved imperceptibly away, not wanting to be touched.

'It's just that he was nice to me, Essie,' she said. 'That's all. He was just nice to me. Nothing happened, y'know. Not really.'

This was terrible, thought Essie, getting pulled deeper and deeper in.

'Please, Essie,' Marie said sincerely, 'I know this is all very awkward.' Then she gave a small shrug and the peculiar smile crept back again.

As soon as Essie had gone she ran upstairs, holding the letter with both hands at arm's length, grinning madly. In the bedroom she dropped down onto the bed, panting a little and just looking at it, savouring it for a second more, then she fell at it and ripped it open with her nails and yanked out the letter, a single page, the writing small and peculiar like printing, and read:

When you get this letter I'll probably be in England. You would not believe the struggle it's been to get this thing to you. If you want to, you can always reach me at the address at the top of the page. If I'm not there, they'll send stuff on. It was finished so brutally and there were things I still had to say to you. Are you OK? Against all odds I can't believe that what we did was wrong. Write to me. I get horny just thinking of you.

Just that.

It all came back, everything. Marie lay down on the bed and read the letter again and again. Then she placed it on her chest and closed her eyes and just lay there for a long time doing nothing while the day trickled along, and all the things she had to do before dinner-time piled up against one another. Of course she'd write back. She wasn't a great one for writing letters but she'd do it. But then if Essie wouldn't take it, how could he reply? Oh, Essie would. She'd have to take her into her confidence. She'd cry if she had to, say, Essie, please, what can I do, you're the only way ... she wouldn't trust the Post Office, certainly not in Strangarvan, maybe Rossgarry but that would be ridiculous. For how can we stop now? she thought. *She* wouldn't, not now she'd set her foot on that path. She smiled and rubbed her nipples with her palms, then with the letter itself. A second chance. Thank God. She was rock hard, dilated, ready. It had happened so easily, just like turning on a tap. Her spirits soared. When she sat up and went downstairs and looked out the back door everything was beautiful. She sang as she went about the rest of the day.

21

When Rosanna left Marie's, she went down to the village and into Sylvester's. It was full. Con was there, and Ger Sheehan and the Pads and one or two blow-ins, and Padraic South sitting in his eternal corner with the *Southern Star* and a pint. Ger and Con were talking about Jackie Bat's misfortune.

'Hi, Rosie,' Con said, reaching under the counter for a glass.

She felt funny, kind of light, a little dizzy, as if she might float up to the ceiling or throw up or something. She swallowed, breathed carefully. Something was coming, viral maybe. She smiled broadly, playing with all her lovely clean hair which shivered electrically about her head, glowing on the outskirts of vision. Marie had made her have two lathers and God knows how many rinses. Hanging over the sink with Marie pouring water over her head from a jug, the lather gathering in her ears, she'd had a flashback to being about five: her mother telling her not to open her eyes, the heat from a pipe, with a funny bulgy bit she could see as clear as day, that ran along the wall next to the sink, and the smell of that place, the stamp of it, the tang of the time, as if it had never gone. She was filled with panic.

'He's been crying like a babby over the sheep,' said Ger.

Rosanna went into the back while the first instalment of her drink subsided. Sylvester was in the kitchen scraping chip fat off the porridgy-textured floor. Ash tumbled from the long end of a cigarette hanging down from his meaty lip, peppering the grease.

'I've got to find somewhere to live,' she said casually. 'Can I kip down in the back of here, Sylvester, if I have to?'

'Bit of an accident with the chipper,' he said apologetically, smiling. 'What happened to the caravan? I thought you were well and cosy up there.'

'They want it back. Call themselves fucking holy.'

'Do they?' he asked, rising heavily to his feet and sighing. 'Watch your feet now, darling, it's like a skating rink down there.'

'It wouldn't be for long. Just while I get sorted.'

He stood swaying slightly. He was very drunk and his blood-shot eyes were heavy. 'Sure, if you're stuck,' he said, stubbing out his dead cigarette in a saucer on the table, 'but only for a night or two, mind. I have to watch the reputation.' He pulled himself up grandly, pushing out his chest, and laughed.

'You're a pal.' Rosanna crossed the passage and looked into the living room. Boxes of crisps were stacked along one wall and Sylvester's dirty shirts were piled up in one corner behind the TV. Against the dim floral wallpaper bloomed the Sacred Heart of Jesus and a very beautiful picture of Our Lord in the garden of Gethsemane. Her chest tightened and something thumped like a rabbit's foot. Oh Jesus, palpitations again. Steady as she goes. Life was full of possibilities. She went back into the bar and sat down. The palpitations receded. She started to drink. Sylvester came out and got himself a little tot of whiskey.

'Oh well,' she said, fussing with her hair, 'I suppose it'll be back to the beach in the end. I'm being kicked out, you know,' she told everyone. 'Anyone got a place for a wee orphan?'

There were no offers.

'What were you up to in the back there, Rosanna?' Ger Sheehan asked with a sluggy smile. 'Leave poor Sylvester alone.'

'Sod off.'

'Oh, you've got a dirty mind indeed,' Sylvester said mildly.

'The punk's barn's empty,' said an American called Chuck, standing next to her to buy his cigarettes.

'Really? Out on Anagar?' Rosanna thought of Anagar with a chill of delight, the sheer drops, boiling waves in grey chasms, rocks like witches' fingers, screaming, devil-faced birds. Then she remembered there was a drop of cherry brandy, nicked from a bottle in Essie and George's cupboard, left in the little Martell Cognac bottle in her pocket, but didn't want anyone else to know she had it; so she moved to a spare table and turned to the wall and drank quickly. Oh yes, that was good. Leave a bit for later. She capped it and tucked it away warm against her hip and went back to the Guinness, licking the foam from her lips, pushing her glass about. The punk's barn, she thought, and a funny feeling grew inside her that that was where she wanted to go.

The punk had come and gone, hanging about for a while in black leather and bondage gear, showing his bare bum on the Kish Pontoon; he lived in half a barn with some friends, roughly did it up and practised black magic in it for a time. Now he'd gone and would never come back. Couldn't take the pace and the fact that everyone was polite to him and tried to involve him in conversations about worm drench and weather and Wimbledon. The barn had stood empty for two years. It was desolate, facing the utmost edge of Europe, gazing over the empty sea towards America, the New World, Tir na nog, the Land of Youth, Hy-Brasail. Ah yes! The fairy music came again, drifting over the fields, the back door open, her mother saying: 'Listen.' It really did happen. She started to croon to herself, and the talk went on without her. To be there, alone, facing it all, madness or salvation, a wolf taking a leap into the very moon. There it would all come true. What? What? She believed in magic. The back door, the moonlight on the empty fields. 'Listen. Fairy music.' Faintly drifting in from the fields when she was a child hundreds of years ago. She could do magic out there, oh yes, she could, she could do a spell and get Clyde back. She'd have a black cat and a toad. Hares with thorns in their pads would come to her back door. She'd grow herbs and have a well, and she would be wise and stern and beautiful and everyone would fear her knowledge. She'd fucking show them, oh yes, she would.

She kept picking all her hair up and shoving it on top of her head, then letting it fall lazily and ticklishly about her shoulders. She finished off the cherry brandy and smoked her last cigarette and wondered who she could get some more off, forgot what she had been thinking about and some time later found herself studying the rings the porter made as it sank down the sides of her glass. She thought she must have passed out for a time.

When she looked up no one was taking any notice of her. Perhaps she wasn't there. It was a queer, frightening sensation, as if she was just fading in from some other channel but hadn't quite got here yet. She might fade back, go out, just like that, and these bright shiny drinking faces would survive her. How dare they ignore her! She jumped to her feet with her empty glass in her fist and shouted: 'Look at me!'

Everybody did.

'Bugger you,' said Ger. 'What do we wanna look at you for?'

Rosanna went to the bar and asked for another drink.

'Go easy, Rosanna,' Con said.

'Enough,' said Sylvester.

'What you fucking talking about?' she said nastily. 'Give me another. I've got the money.' She hadn't.

Sylvester hesitated for a moment, then shook his finger at her. 'You've had enough,' he said as if his mouth were filled with treacle.

She burst out laughing. 'Look who's talking!' she cried, then with a peculiar balletic leap hoisted herself half over the bar, grabbed him by the top of his baggy beige jumper and nutted him between the eyes. She just felt like it. She'd never nutted anyone before and had often wondered what it must feel like. Should have been Clyde really.

Sylvester bled. He ran round the bar, spraying blood, grabbed her arm and started shoving her to the door, his face furious. She struggled and he slapped her face and she screamed and fell back into a corner, covering her head with her arms.

It all went quiet. She felt that her eyes rolled back in her head, and up to replace them from inside the machine came a new pair, stone-steady, deadly. Gorgon's eyes. She raised her head slowly and stared, but no one turned to stone.

'Are you all right now, Rosanna?' Con asked her.

'Fucking bitch,' Sylvester said. 'Anyone can go too far.'

'Miserable bastards,' she said venomously, then like a witch cursed the valley and the sea and the mountains and all of them, bitterly and vilely, for being dead on earth, she said, all of them dead on earth.

'Ah, hold off, Rosanna,' said Con.

'That's right.' Ger grinned and leaned on the bar. 'No one wants to hear you now, Rosanna.'

'I'm Cassandra!' she cried, 'I'm Cleopatra, but you're all too stupid to see!'

'Out, Rosanna,' said Sylvester, and took her by the arm and tried to walk her to the door, but she shook him off again. 'Get me a drink!' she yelled.

'Fuck your drink!' Sylvester roared.

She kicked his shins. Con stepped forward. Ger Sheehan grinned. Sylvester slapped her once hard about the head and pushed her to the door.

'It's the only way she can get a man to lay a hand on her these days,' Ger Sheehan said.

A slightly malicious, slightly pitying snigger ran round the room.

'I heard that!' she bawled from the door, struggling fiercely.

Sylvester slapped her again.

'That's enough!' cried Padraic South severely, making everyone jump.

'Oh, fuck off, you stupid old bugger!' she sneered at him, not realising it was an intervention on her behalf.

Ger ran to help Sylvester, a broad grin on his face. The two of them, struggling, gave her a good fling out into the road, then leaned against the door and locked it, laughing.

She heard them laugh inside as she sprawled on her face. She'd thought it was heavy night in there and was surprised to find when she sat up, daylight, people walking about, Barney Mac driving two red calves, Paddy Bawn by the signpost looking back, Sheila from Sheila's bar walking up from round the bend, a washing up bowl pressed under the wildly spreading flesh of her arm. They all acted as if she were invisible.

'Don't fucking help me, you bastards!' she screeched. 'Don't help a woman that's just been assaulted. Hit me round the head, he did! I'll have the guards on you! I'll have the guards on you, Sylvester, you cunt! Hear me?' She got to her feet unsteadily. Her palms and chin were skinned, knees trembling, one twisting a little.

She reeled stupidly about the village street. 'Hear me! Yah! You bunch of fucking wankers! Fucking wankers! Wankers! Wankers!'

Voices came from here and there:

'Ah, shut up!'

'Go home, can't you?'

'Rosanna!' It was Mrs Davy. 'Go home, now! Don't you dare behave like that! There are little ones about!'

Sheila came along behind her like a bulldozer. 'Now, now,' she said in a deep voice, soothing as rain, 'time to go off home, Rosanna.'

'Oh, fuck off!'

Rosanna ran out of the village. She wanted another drink. No chance of getting one here now. She finished the cherry brandy, barely a taste, plodding on through the mist, her knee giving out every now and then. Palpitations returned. She met Ben Bowden with his two remaining dogs leashed, a little black mongrel and a big sandy thing.

'Why should they have to suffer?' he asked her, aggrieved. 'They've done nothing. If I hide them away it's like an admission of guilt.'

'Give us a fiver,' she said, 'I always put in a word for you.' A great anger was boiling in her. If she'd felt just a little stronger she might have nutted him too, but he got away light. Sucker. She got one pound fifty out of him. Better than nothing. She set off in the direction of Strangarvan. Violets and celandines bloomed at the sides of the road. Ahead of her she saw through the soft drifting white mist a certain formation of rocks that looked like a bare-armed woman drawing a dead man out of the ground. She used to think of it as some pair of tragic legendary lovers from deep in the Celtic twilight, but now she saw that it was a *pietà*: Our Lady holding Our Lord. Passing Marie's she turned in at the drive to see if there was anything going.

Simon was watching TV. Marie sat by the window, her feet upon a stool, smoking a cigarette and drinking coffee. She was miles away.

'Nothing to do, Marie? Dossing, are we? What's on? Ooh, cartoons!'

'Hello, Rosanna.' Marie smiled faintly, suppressing a yawn. 'Hair looks nice.'

'You would not believe it. They fell at my feet in the pub. Lend us a little drop of Powers in this, will you, love?' She held out her little empty Martell Cognac bottle. 'I'll call by after dole day and let you have it back. OK?'

Marie looked at her for a second, still smiling absently, then shrugged and said, 'Suit yourself. You know where it is.'

Rosanna did, of course. She went straight to the sideboard and filled up her stash, had a quick nip and stowed it away in her pocket. Turning, she saw the back of Simon's head, the brown slim stem of his neck bowed as if for the blade, the sweet springing hay of his hair. I wonder does she ever fancy her son? she thought. I wonder if I met Abraham now and if neither of us knew ... She used to take him to parties in a plastic bag. She'd put him in the corner. He'd sleep through anything, sex and drugs and rock'n'roll. She fell down and kissed Simon's neck quickly.

'Agh!' he cried, nearly jumping out of his skin. 'Get off!'

'Rosanna, leave him alone,' Marie said wearily.

'How are you these days, Simon?' she asked. 'How's school?'

'It's all right,' he said, smiling.

'I bet you can't wait to get out of it, can you?' she said. 'Can't wait to get over to London and start sniffing something and beating up old ladies like any self-respecting young hooligan.'

'Now come on, Rosanna,' Marie said, 'there's no need for that kind of talk.'

'Can't wait to get away from all these Catholic girls who keep their legs crossed.'

'Rosanna, he's only fourteen.'

He was crimson.

'Fourteen? Why, you ought to be ashamed of yourself, young man. Why aren't you out there on the front line saving the world? Why is your soul not full of rebellion?'

'Rosanna!'

'He's gorgeous, Marie,' Rosanna said, leaning forward and trying to cuddle his head. He squirmed. 'How can you resist him? Don't you ever get the urge to lick him like ice cream?' She put out her tongue.

'That's it.' Marie got up. 'I'll not have that. Out, Rosanna, if you can't behave yourself.' Marie went and opened the door. 'Out.'

Rosanna stood up and put back her shoulders, then strolled over to Marie in an easy, menacing way and stared into her face. Marie was frightened, she could see that, but she was trying not to show it. Of course, she thought, I've still got my Gorgon's eyes. She clenched her punching fist down by her side and smiled. Smug bitch, Marie. 'Don't worry,' she said softly, 'I wouldn't hit *you*, Marie.'

'Oh, Rosanna,' Marie said with a great show of exasperation, 'what is it with you? No one wants to be horrible to you, but you make everything else impossible.'

Rosanna pulled a blade, a little silver penknife.

Simon ran up behind her. 'You leave my mother alone!' he cried in his breaking voice. 'Don't you touch her!'

She turned and looked at him once admiringly, put away the knife, and walked out leaving the door open. She heard it close behind her. 'Shoo!' she cried, chasing the chickens all over the yard. The dogs began to bark excitedly. 'Oh, shut up!' she yelled at them, 'who do you think you are? You're only bloody dogs! Cringing, craven mutts! Crawl back to your holes. Holy Mother of God,' she said, standing at the gate. Where to go? Where to go? She might go on the road with Iko's lot if they came around again, but they hadn't been since last summer. There she was again, that woman pulling her son out of the ground. She could walk up there, walk about on the woman's arms, on their ancient heads, go somewhere wild, up to the Weeping Rock, to the Point, to Anagar. But it was getting late. The rabbit kicked in her chest. Her stomach felt funny. Either it was too long since she'd eaten or she was going to get one of her dodgy stomachs again.

It was Saturday night. There'd be something on at Dundreen. Food. She could liven things up a bit for them. So she set off in that direction and rain began, beautifully singing as it hit the hot earth, which hissed and exhaled. Over there the sea's little white tongues licked the shore. She began to think that she would never leave this place now, that she would die here and be buried on a lonely headland, looking out towards that twanging indigo band upon the horizon. Funny that she'd been born so far away and gone through so much just to come here for that. Destiny. She sang to shorten the road, all four or five miles of it, shiny and grey and flinging on ahead through the deep dark greens and the glistening rocks. Sheep and cattle stood patient through the downpour, long ferns, montbretia, fuchsia drip-dripped. She sang in the old Sean Nos style she'd learned from her father, 'Slieve Gallion Brae', so sweet and yearning, for her Irish father. She always thought of him as that, even though she'd worked it out once that he must have actually been only about one-eighth or so Irish. But he'd kept the faith as it were and sang the old songs beautifully. She'd always been a sucker for them. Just like him.

She drank from her bottle as she walked, and wept. 'My daddy,' she whimpered, 'my little daddy.' Abba, Abba, the poor man on the cross had cried, poor child crying for his daddy. My daddy, my daddy, my little lost daddy. And from that she got to missing Clyde again, and a great terror covered the world, a great wing: the delicate white bones of his face appeared before her, his head in a glass jar and she weeping, weeping over it night and day. Too late he had realised. One look, one final understanding, then goodbye for ever.

She was weak at the thought of him.

22

She came to Dundreen. A mural was in progress on a gable end, scaffolding was up. It appeared to be a single flower, thirty foot high. Off to one side at some distance a building site had materialised. They were building, among other things, a house for this old crone with a face like a prune and a platitude for every occasion, who had not yet agreed to come, the idea being that positive thought and action would draw her to the place by some kind of cosmic law.

Montsalvat, Affirmation Centre. The door was open. A notice pinned to a board said: WELCOME, WILKOMMEN, BIENVENU, CEAD MILE FAILTE! She slipped in and followed a sound that led her to an open door and a room where children watched a Postman Pat video. Somewhere else a distant voice droned on. She walked through a huge kitchen where something simmered on a big Aga and a table was spread with small sandwiches and bowls of crisps and dry-roasted peanuts. She walked on and out, into a long corridor high above the sea, all window on the sea side, all books from floor to ceiling on the other, a comprehensive range of fiction, religion, philosophy, art and politics. Some little booklets were fanned out along a ledge, most of them bearing a flying swan logo, and a few glossy paperbacks: *God The Child, The Seed of Being, Drops of Rain on a Wire: the teachings of Swan Mary, The Doctrine of Eternal Resonance, Swan Mary: The Early Years* with a cover photo of the crone in youth looking sternly beautiful.

She emerged at the back of the great round room with the awesome views. People sat about on little white mats all over the shining floor. Essie and George were there, and Julia, and loads of other people. There was old James Sawle sitting off to one side like a headmaster, frowning in a scholarly kind of a way, his lips all pursed up. They were watching a video of life on a ranch somewhere. Pretty children were bottle-feeding baby goats. The voice-over was female, calm and deep and American. Rosanna sat down, knackered after her long walk. No one had noticed her.

'Children are very important at Okinochee,' the voice said. Then a man with long neat grey hair and very black eyes sat at a computer and spoke straight to camera, saying that the kinds of questions people asked – her age, racial origins etc – were the first casualties of true enquiry. Then he was walking on a lovely lawn by a river with pine trees over the water and a big house in the background. She'd been old, he said, when she first became a presence thirty years ago, here in this very place. That is Okinochee Creek. The legend took hold first in the neighbouring villages, that there was a woman up here who kept swans as if they were geese – shot of swans on creek – that she sometimes slept amongst them on the lawn – this very lawn – that they rallied round her when anyone approached, shielding her with their great wings. Rosanna fell asleep. When she woke up the video was over and they were all talking. Some of them had seen her at her last big gig in Miami. Her presence, they said, was awesome. They spoke of techniques for freeing the eagle, liberating the spirit, plumbing the depths, scaling the heights, lying happily ever after in the everlasting arms, the Mother's Arms. It sounded like a pub. Rocking the baby. Someone was coming to show them how to do it.

'What are you all on about?' Rosanna asked, sitting up.

They tried to explain, everybody chipping in. It was a technique for contacting the first you, the first I, the great baby we all are, the tyrant soul, essence and source and origin of all things, for so placating it with love and understanding that it was bathed in glory, and a permanent state of inner happiness and well-being was produced. It sounded great and was very simple. There were other techniques, too, but some of them sounded like heavy going, and it got expensive.

Rosanna started to sing 'Rock-a-bye Baby' and some of them joined in. She got into it and sang it again. How profound the words seemed. 'Of course the fall from the treetop is the loss of innocence,' she said. 'Growing up.' Everyone agreed. Rosanna sang it again. They went on talking around her and she lay down in the middle of the room and curled up foetally with her thumb in her mouth. 'Look, this is how you do it,' she said, 'it's dead easy. Then you dribble a bit and shit yourself.'

George laughed.

Rosanna sat up. 'Look, I need a place to stay,' she said. 'Anyone got any ideas?'

There were a few mumblings.

'Come on,' she said, 'a fellow traveller.'

'Rosanna,' said James in a remote and fatherly way that got right up her nose, 'why don't you go to the Council? I'm sure they'd treat you sympathetically.'

'Time,' she said, getting to her feet awkwardly. The room whizzed about her head like something on an elastic string. Sickness surged up her chest, didn't quite make it to the throat. Not yet, ha ha, she'd hold it there, her secret weapon. Splat! 'It's them,' she said, pointing to George and Essie, 'they're chucking me out.'

'Sit down, Rosanna,' said James, standing up. He was small but he did have a kind of authority. His eyes were slightly humorous.

'Out,' she said, 'into the cold, cold –'

'Come on now, Rosanna, take it easy, sit down ...'

'To wander the roads and beg my bread, ochone. Oh, to have a little house! Och! but I'm weary of mist and dark and roads where there's never a house nor bush ...'

'Rosanna ...'

'Well, fucking hell!' she suddenly shouted, 'What are you going to do about me? Eh? What are you going to do about me? Here I am! I've got nowhere to go! *I'm* the poor and homeless! *I'm* the fucking needy.'

'Rosanna,' said James evenly, 'everyone wants to help you but you have to learn to take responsibility for yourself. You're not a baby.'

She laughed. 'I thought we were all babies.'

'That's facetious, Rosanna. You are deliberately misunderstanding. We do want to help. Come on and we'll show you. Here, calm down.'

He got her to sit down in the middle of the room, then people closed about her in a protective circle that made her shiver. Essie and a few others didn't join in, but the rest Ommed and celebrated her till she felt her head ringing like a bell. They went on for about five minutes. Their smiling faces frightened her. Ye

Gods. The ones around the outside were starting to look faintly embarrassed. One or two here and there were starting to laugh, now more. How long, oh Lord, how long? Ten minutes, surely? She began to think that this was all some terrible joke at her expense.

'Stop now,' she said, but they went on, so she jerked forward and made as if to nut Felicity Rawlings but was sick instead.

Felicity got out of the way just in time, yelling 'Oh, my *God*!'

It was mostly booze and bile, rather boring, really, but it splashed quite dramatically and made them all scatter, anxiously checking their clothes. Essie and Helen started trying to rush her out to the kitchen but she shook them off, whirling her arms about and shouting, 'Leave me alone!'

'Oh, for Christ's sake, Rosanna!' Essie scolded.

'You can fuck off for a start,' Rosanna spat. 'You're throwing me out. Think you're fucking holy. Holy, arseholes, what about the homeless? Eh? What about the poor in spirit? Eh? What about the fucking meek? I was walking the roads before you lot was born. What are you going to do about me, what are you going to *do* about me, huh? Throw me out, you bastards, go on, throw me out, I can't believe it. What are you doing?' She was roaring. 'What are you doing? You all go off to your little beds and dream, but *I'm* under them, oh yes, I am ... Remember this night! Remember this night! Remember this night!'

She screamed and ran at the windows as if she was going to leap through, out into the lovely deepening blue of the estuary. She did in fact hit the glass, but it was reinforced to withstand the weather up here, and her fist just bounced off.

'Enough!' cried George. 'Rosanna, Rosanna, go back to the caravan, please. It's still there for you. You don't have to go any-where, honey, you know that. You know you're a pain in the ass when you drink, you know it, you make it so no one can be with you. We love you, honey, just go home and sleep it off and when you wake up everyone will help you. Come on, Essie'll drive you.'

Rosanna scowled around for a moment then walked out abruptly. She stood for a second in panic in the corridor of books, seeing her reflection now in the long black window, forgetting for

143

a moment where she was. Suddenly she realised how cold she was, how wet and how very, very hungry.

Essie and George and James and Helen followed her out.

'Come on,' Essie said sulkily, getting out her car keys.

'I don't want your lift.'

'Don't be stupid. You're going home.'

She laughed. 'I don't want your lift. I don't want your shitty little caravan, it's cold and it leaks. I'm going somewhere else. I've got places I can go, you know. I've got people who could sort you out. Look, I'm not drunk. What do I want your fucking lift for? Sod off. If I wanted a lift I'd ask for it ...'

'Oh, don't be so bloody silly, Rosanna,' Essie said coldly and went back into the meditation room. George made a peculiar helpless gesture with his whole body and followed her. Rosanna started crying.

Helen approached her briskly and gave her a tissue. 'You'd better go,' she said calmly. 'Sit in the kitchen and calm down a little and someone'll take you home.'

Rosanna looked at her. 'It's all right for you,' she said, 'with your big tits and your black hair.'

'Yes,' said Helen, 'it is all right for me. Now, go and sit down.'

Rosanna went into the kitchen and picked at the crisps and dry-roasted peanuts while Helen got out the cleaning gear and ran hot water into a bowl. James came and lounged in the door. 'Oh, Rosanna!' he said sadly, shaking his head.

'Help yourself to whatever you want,' said Helen, waving a hand over the food. 'Take a doggy bag for later. We'll try and sort a lift out for you. And don't you ever come here in that state again. I mean it, Rosanna. You are welcome here any time you want when you're sober, but you don't turn up in my house like this again. Do you understand?'

Suddenly Rosanna was sober and reasonable. She ate a sandwich, some peanuts and raisins and three oat cookies, then filled her pockets. Distantly she heard the sound of talking. 'I don't want a lift,' she said. 'I want to walk.'

They watched her take a final handful of nuts and James followed her as she wandered slowly through the house in the direction of the front door, looking into rooms as she went. At the children's room she stopped. 'What you playing?' she asked.

Kester and Polly and a few other blow-in kids were there doing something on a computer. They'd heard all the shouting and were afraid of her.

'Can I have a go?'

They stood back to let her, but James said, 'That's enough, Rosanna. Time you were on your way. Take it easy now.'

She could hear Helen clanking along with the cleaning gear. Should have done it on these soft blue carpets, she thought, finding the door. Left a stain they'd never get off. Rosanna woz 'ere. She went out and stood on the path in front of the house. The air was tangy. It had gone dark. She hung about till her eyes were used to it, unsure of the path. It started raining again. She realised that her lovely clean hair was plastered flat to her head, tried the door again and found they'd locked it. So she went round the side and stood in the scrub, looking up at the high shining glass of the big round room sitting like some alien craft about to take off over the lonely arm of the sea.

'Hypocrites!' she bellowed. In the quiet night she knew they'd hear every word. 'I know your guru, Essie! The Marijuana Mushroom! You'll never sell that crap! You'll never sell it! George! What are you up to? Fucking little girls? Eh? Is he good, Julia? Is he good? It's a sin, you know! Why don't you slosh her one, Essie? Why don't you smack her right in the teeth? That's what you want to do! Hypocrites! Hypocrites!'

Rosanna ran cackling away into the dark.

Part Three

Part Three

23

Marie had never rebelled as a girl. There hadn't been time. Julia did, sort of. She dyed a tiny ringlet of hair purple and wore it down one side of her face. She'd discussed nose-piercing with Essie. Marie liked the ringlet but thought a ring in the nose was just stupid, though she didn't mind it on Essie. Her own rebellion, late as it was, was simple: she just started wearing make-up any old time, whenever she felt like it. There was comment.

'Off somewhere, are you, Marie?'

'Hello, Marie. You look nice.'

Marie stared them out, smiling in her bland friendly way. Only Essie seemed really shocked. 'Oh God, love, you don't need that stuff,' she said as if it were a drug. But Marie liked to see the lipstick on her cigarette. She bought magazines and looked at beautiful clothes on weirdly beautiful women, all long and slim, and read about clitoral orgasm. I'd've had one of those, she thought, that night if we could've carried on. Con had never done that for her, not properly anyway. Just a quick once over then in.

She smiled, peacefully ironing as she listened to pop music on the radio. She did, in fact, feel drugged. A slave army of nerves was on the move, marching up and down all over her, kicking its heels in her soft bits. She was getting letters. There they were, stashed at the back of her underwear drawer, well covered in rolled up tights – *if you can get to Dublin, or Cork, if we could meet* – Dublin, Cork, life, oh life. Funny, he'd been so stiff and shy when he was here but his letters, his letters ... She was thinking up another reply. She wasn't good at letters. His were all passion, hers all the farm and local talk. She just told him things in a big jumble. Con wasn't talking to her. Julia was making a Madeira cake with lemon peel on top. He said he was sick of London. He'd got a commission to do some kind of art textbook but he had to finish this one first. He was going out a lot. He seemed to know a lot of people. Sometimes she felt sick when she thought about them all. He might as well have been on the moon. And he wrote that he remembered the line of her body, one beautiful sweep up through hips and arms as she hung the washing on the line in the yard when he was going by in the road. He'd love to see her again.

Marie went out to hang the next batch of washing on the line. I'm not a fool, she thought, I know what's what, all that being in love doesn't last and real life goes on, but I don't care. I'll go up to Essie's exhibition. She pegged out the washing, flapping it out before she hung it.

She went back into the house and up to the bedroom and wrote that she would be going up to Dublin in October for the opening night of Essie's show, and that she'd have to stay the night at Con's sister's in Terenure. Perhaps if he was in town they could have a drink? She put the letter in her bag all ready to post when she went into Strangarvan and ran downstairs all breathless and made herself a cup of coffee and sat down with it. My God, she thought, what if it really happens? What am I doing? She picked up a magazine and looked at a picture of a stunningly clean and peachy bloom of a girl in a little skyblue dress with a neck so wide it just about fell from her shoulders. That's what she'd be wearing when she met him, and she'd get some earrings ... her fingers touched the simple gold sleepers she wore in her ears. Then she looked down at her wedding ring and the engagement ring with the three little diamonds sitting in a row.

Next day she went into Strangarvan and posted the letter.

A whole week passed. Well, that was all right, give it three days to get there, three days back, and some more time and then ... Friday week, and another week gone, and she was all sharpened up, snapping at the kids and feeling sick when the green post van went sailing by the turn-off for Inchicora. Nothing again. And every time she saw Essie she got excited then deflated, and then came a horrible suspicion that maybe Essie was holding something back. What if she'd got sick of passing them on, anyone could see she hated it, the way she slid them across all furtive in the kitchen as if she was passing drugs.

'You wouldn't keep a letter from me, would you?' she asked

Essie one day.

Essie coloured. 'Of course I wouldn't,' she said.

Well, she thought, looking out of the door at the line of Rossa against the sky, what was the point anyway, it could never have come to anything. I never knew that I was going mad till he came. I suppose I'll have to stay here now for the rest of my days. Suddenly she hated the place, hated the view out of the door.

Next day another letter came. As soon as Essie left she was off upstairs again, tearing it open: He was drunk. He said his book was finished. He said he thought of her naked all the time. He walked down the street thinking of her naked. All the time. *Right now* he said, *while you're reading this I'm probably thinking of you naked.*

She read it standing over her underwear drawer so that she could shove it away quickly if need be. Someone opened the door downstairs. She put the letter away and went down. It was Simon, coming in from working up at Dundreen, like a man with his long legs and big hands, all covered in dirt and white dust, cement in his hair. He asked her to get it out for him, so she stuck him in the sink and poured and scrubbed away at his poor little head. Bob was walking down a street in London thinking of her naked. London. Full of women. Oh no, I'd never leave you, darling, she thought, wanting to kiss Simon's neck. But I could go just the once and do everything and then never again. Don't I deserve that much?

24

Clyde came back towards the summer's end. Con met him in the shop.

'Block of Whole Nut, please, Dierdre.'

'Clyde! When did you get back?' cried Con, smiling, turning at the voice.

'Coupla days ago,' said Clyde, shifting the peak of his cap.

'Where've you been, man? Out on the road?'

'Up around Clare,' said Clyde. 'Thanks, Dierdre.'

'You're welcome, Clyde.'

The two of them went outside. It was a fine, fragrant day. Clyde peeled the gold foil from his chocolate, broke a bit off and offered it to Con. His dog sat gazing up at the chocolate with soft, hungry eyes. Clyde had his rod and tackle on his back. He said he was staying at Ger Sheehan's but had to look around pretty quick because the old lady didn't like him.

'How about the place at the strand again?' asked Con.

'Nah! Another winter there? Joking. Anyway there's some Americans in there. There's this guy in Strangarvan with a place down the back road that should do. Needs a bit of work on it, but it's sound enough.'

They sat on the wall between clumps of thrift. Across the higgledy-piggledy little fields the sea was dark blue and absolutely clear. The Puck looked as if it had a mouth, the lighthouse was distinct. A brown horse ambled over and put its head between them. Clyde fondled its nose.

'Rosanna's out at Anagar,' Con said. 'What a place to live!'

'I heard.' A tick had installed itself in the soft skin inside Clyde's elbow and was not yet big enough to be easily removed. He stuck his hand up his sleeve, fingering the lump with fascinated revulsion. He hated ticks. Rosanna always used to get them out for him.

'What is it with her?' asked Con. 'She's acting crazy.'

'She's mad,' said Clyde. 'She wants to kill herself, let her. You working with all the others up at Dundreen?'

The horse tossed up its head, snorting softly. 'No. Simon's up there on Saturdays. Will you look at that little madame?' Con sounded annoyed but proud.

Looking up, Clyde saw the Mullens' car coming up from the Post Office with Julia driving. Con swore and flagged it down angrily. 'Get over there at once,' he scolded, yanking open the door and making her move across into the passenger seat. 'Don't you know the Guard was at Caheradown this morning? I'll drive back.'

Julia looked over his head at Clyde, smiling very freely with her big wide mouth. Her hair was simple apart from this little purple bit down the front of one ear. She'd come on in nine months. Clyde thrust out a hip lazily and tipped his hat, spitting out his match.

'She'll get me arrested,' Con said. 'See you, Clyde,' and they drove away.

Clyde stood alone in the empty village street. He'd known Julia since she was about eight. She'd always been a looker. Into his thin nostrils came a gentle breath of autumn. He was glad to be back. Seeing her about the place now she was getting older would be one of the pleasures of living here. She wouldn't stick around. She was out of the mould. She had a refinement, she did, not like her mother. He'd sussed that one for a randy cow first time he'd seen her. Liked the smarmy type, obviously, any bitch who'd go for Sawle ... But not Julia, she was refined. That's what he liked. He liked those songs Rosanna used to sing where the girl was always sixteen come Sunday, or had little white feet or a nice little boudoir where she'd soothe you with her fan. All he ever landed were these mad bitches like Rosanna.

He stroked the ears of his hound. He'd bought her for an eighth of dope from some travellers, old Molly. His gun was in his tackle bag. He felt pretty good.

'Clyde!' Ger was calling him.

Clyde gave him a lift back in the old van, still valiant against all odds. Ann was giving him the cold shoulder at Ger's so he didn't stick around, just got his stuff and drove into town and hassled about for a couple of days until he was installed in a shed down the back road, watertight, fairly clean; hassled about some more and got together a mattress and a heater and all the bits and pieces he possessed that were stowed here and there with friends about the area.

It was pretty good. Nice to lie back and just look up at the beams and do nothing while the tilley lamp slowly dimmed. Nice to be alone and quiet. Sometimes all he did was lie there like that all night, thinking and thinking, and in the morning never knowing what it was he'd been thinking about. He never looked backwards. It was good when it went on like that. But at some point after a few days he would slip into a phase of abject staring terror, then he would start to want a woman, and then he'd go back to Rosanna and the whole thing would start up again. He didn't want to do that this time. The thought of her made him miserable. That was no good, was it? She was like this tick here in his arm still, its head burrowed well in, its fat wrinkled body a sack of blood, disgusting, the colour of old women's corsets in glossy catalogues of the fifties, the kind his mum had got her clothes out of.

It was not his fault that he encountered Julia a few days later near Weeping Rock up on the high path over from Kish to Ballinaphuca. It was just one of those things. He had his gun on his back and he was carrying a big horse mushroom the size of a dinner plate. Julia was all wrapped up in anorak and wellies, coming back from her Aunt Therese's. He ran a hand over the high white dome of his forehead and through his thin brown hair as he approached her, getting a funny feeling in his gut, nerves, a sudden raciness of the senses; threw back his head and hardened his jaw and prepared to nod his head as he passed her. But she came on with her big smile, and they dithered faintly for a moment before stopping. She leaned down and patted Molly.

'Hello there,' she said, 'Hello, girl.'

'Here,' said Clyde, 'do you want a mushroom?'

She laughed.

Clyde smiled a thin smile, raising his brows and looking down, shifting his shoulders. Nothing like the old bad-boy-shows-his-soft-centre to get them going. They love it. Beauty and the Beast and all that. It works. So she's young. So what? He was – what? – thirty-eight, thirty-seven, something like that, not ancient. Some of them like it. Not as old as that stupid hippie halfwit.

She asked him where he'd been this time on his travels and he told her Clare.

'Oh, it's lovely up there,' she said. 'Did you go to the cliffs of Moher?'

'No,' he said, 'I'm scared of heights.'

'Me, too,' she said, 'you wouldn't get me near them.'

Then she just stood there with her arms folded, smiling at him. He could think of nothing in common for them to talk about. 'I'm living in Strangarvan now,' he said.

'Handy for the bars,' she said smartly, turning and looking back at Ballinaphuca.

He watched her fiddling with her hair, the ends of her fingers all bitten down like his own.

'You bite your nails,' he said.

'Oh, that's a terrible habit.' She looked at her fingers critically then held them out to him, saying, 'Look at 'em, look. Atrocious.'

'Look at mine.'

They compared nails. 'So you don't grow out of it?' Julia said, 'I thought I might, but you haven't.'

'No,' he said, smiling, 'I haven't.'

She knew it, he thought. She knew what she was doing to him. Pity she was into that new age crap. He could cure her of that. Yeah, Clyde and Julia, Bonnie and Clyde. She was like something in a magazine, something you'd take home and lie down with and have a nice long wank over. Jesus Christ, he was getting a hard-on, here it came, banging and flashing away down there like a neon light on this bleak hilltop.

'Well, I'd better be on my way,' she said. He tipped his hat and they parted. Weeping Rock gleamed. She raised a hand as she went down the track and for a second he got a flash of all the partings of the ways there had been at this place.

He whistled low and soft to Molly and went on, and a little further along turned off the path and sat down among the rocks with the dog leaning against him. He would have loved a drink of cool water. Nothing else. Straight types never went for him. In the songs, the elegant, the dovelike ladies, the pretty little missies, they always ran away with the railroad man or the gypsy or whatever; but not in real life. In real life only cranks went for him. Melanie Broadbent hadn't been a crank, though, and she'd liked him, but that was a long time ago.

He'd met her in a room above a pub. There was a band on a stage. Those were the acne days. He touched his face. He'd just been walking through the crowd and her long straight brown hair had got caught up in a button on his jacket. It had taken a while to untangle and some of the hairs had stayed there for weeks. She'd really gone for him. They'd stood out in the hall talking and drinking. She drank Cherry-Bs, and wore this little brown mini skirt that just covered her bum. She was fifteen. He walked her home. 'Sorry,' he said when he kissed her goodnight, 'I've got these spots.' She was so smooth and babyish. She'd laughed. She said that didn't matter, it was the person inside that mattered. He fell hideously in love with her, a terrible sickness deep in his bowels. They walked along by the reservoir, stood in doorways, sat in dumps of cafés, kissed. She couldn't kiss for toffee, he'd had to show her. She gave him love-bites on his neck. It lasted six weeks. Then she said she didn't want to see him any more, said it all nice and friendly. Bitch. Should have blackened both her eyes.

Clyde remembered the lower bunk in the box room, staring into a magnifying mirror at his scabby, pustulant face, a flaming plague. He burned with shame. Stephen turned over in the top bunk. The room stank of bad feet, aftershave, farts. He had to get out or he'd vomit. He'd kill Stephen, that's what he'd do, he'd kill him if he didn't get out soon.

Clyde touched his face. He still had the marks. Julia, he thought. Yeah, Julia didn't know what she was missing, stuck out here. He'd take her to London. They'd ... no, what would they do there? He didn't know anyone there any more. No, they'd go to America, they'd buy a trailer. He'd lie down with her at nights in a sleeping bag, under a prairie moon.

25

'Saw Clyde,' said Julia, sitting at the kitchen table colouring in a mandala in her exercise book. Marie was skinning a chicken and dreaming. 'He's got a thing about me,' she went on, 'I could tell.'

'Who has?'

'Clyde.'

'Clyde!' Marie was disgusted. 'He's not!'

'Yeah.'

'Why, what's he said to you?'

'Oh, he's not said anything. I can always tell.'

'Oh, you can, can you?' Marie stopped what she was doing and looked at Julia sitting there with her head on one side, eyebrows lifted all superior, all sure of herself. Look at her, just look at her, she thought. What if she got pregnant? 'You think you're older than you are,' she said.

'Clyde's horrible,' Julia said, 'he's all slimy.'

'The man's a psychopath. You keep well away from him.'

'Daddy likes him.'

Marie said nothing. Oh God, she thought, October, October. 'What is it with you and these old men? You're always with people twice your age. Why, Julia? I can't work it out.'

'Young people are stupid,' Julia said and got up to leave.

'Don't you go running away when I'm talking to you,' Marie said in her stern voice.

'I know what you're going to say, you don't like it 'cos George thinks I'm intelligent enough to talk to. You think I'm still six years old.' A swollen, pouchy look came about her, familiar since childhood.

'Peel the potatoes, Julia.'

'It's not fair.' Julia pushed her hair about. 'Nobody takes me seriously. I'm not allowed to have my own ideas. Everybody laughs at me.'

Oh well, thought Marie, she'll be back at school soon. Con and Simon came in, Simon all dirty from Dundreen.

'What's this?' asked Con.

'It's a mandala,' said Julia, peeling potatoes.

'A what?'

'A mandala.'

Con snorted. Julia burst into tears. Marie raised her eyes to heaven.

'What have I done?' cried Con.

'There's not one of you here has any respect for me!' sobbed Julia.

Simon turned on the radio and walked about grinning and whistling slightly through his teeth.

'Turn that shite off!' barked Con.

Simon turned off the radio and went upstairs and ran himself a bath. Marie walked about the kitchen with haughty eyebrows and a hard mouth.

'What's the matter with you?' Con asked.

'Nothing.'

It was something in her tone.

'Julia, get upstairs,' said Con. She laid down her knife and left at once.

Con came over to Marie and took her by the arm and held it very hard, sticking his face right into hers. 'You are a disgrace,' he whispered, 'a disgrace, carrying on like this in front of the children. Pull yourself together!'

'Like what?' She looked back at him defiantly.

'Now, I don't care how you're feeling,' he said, 'I've had it to here with your selfishness and your moods, and I'm sick of playing nice when you don't even try. What is it you want from life, Marie? Is it not all perfect then? Is it not all roses? Well, it's what it is, Marie, and you'd better just get used to it. There's no going back now. No going back.' His grip tightened and his blue eyes filled with angry tears and his hand shook and she felt that he wanted to hit her. 'You say nothing happened,' he said fiercely. 'Then why has it all gone wrong for us since he was here? Even if you didn't do anything, you wanted to. Deny it! That's adultery anyway, Marie, that's a sin of the mind.'

He was far too close and for one horrible moment she thought he might be going to kiss her. She couldn't help it, she turned her face away with a tiny shudder of disgust.

Con just went into the other room, turned on the TV and sat down in front of it.

That night she had to let him on her because he got so upset about it. She just had to grit her teeth and go through with it, and she didn't think he got much out of it, either. Afterwards she lay awake for ages watching the Puck light come and go on the wall. If doing it in the mind was a sin anyway, what did it matter if she did it for real? And after, she'd knuckle down to real life. Con, hot and heavy, snored softly. This one shred of freedom, she thought. He owes me, and he'll never know.

26

October. She felt odd and furtive when Essie and George dropped her off at noon near Trinity College to catch the bus. She was staying at Con's sister Maura's tonight. But she didn't get the bus. She looked at her watch and walked very quickly to the bus station and went into the ladies toilet and changed out of the jeans and jumper she'd had on for the trip into the yellow dress she'd not worn since that terrible night. She wrapped her coat back around her and stood by the mirror feeling like a spy. This coat wasn't good enough but it would have to do. She checked her face, messed with her hair, lit a cigarette and smoked it nervously. She looked tired. She'd been up since before dawn, standing at the back door smoking a cigarette and listening to the cocks crowing to each other across the dark valley. She'd left everything ready for breakfast for the others but she'd been too excited to eat anything herself. Now she was hungry. Her heart pounded.

She went out and saw him leaning against a kiosk. She'd forgotten what his face looked like. He hadn't seen her for the moment so she got a good look. Why, he's nothing special at all, she thought, surprised. Probably not as good looking as Con. He was wearing putty-coloured trousers and a grey jacket; his hair was flat, his eyes serious and unfocused. She walked over to him and he saw her and smiled.

'Marie,' he said civilly, as if they'd just met in the shop and Mrs Davy and a brace of villagers were standing by.

'Hello,' she said.

All the things they'd written lay between them. There were some little scars on his lips and eyebrows. He was very gentle about the eyes, that's what she remembered now, that's what she liked about him.

'How long have you got?' he asked.

'I have to be at Essie's gallery at eight,' she said, 'then back to Con's sister's and home in the morning. How about you?'

'Oh, me,' he said, 'I've got nothing but time. Have you eaten?'

'Sort of.'

'I haven't. Come on, let's go and get something.'

'No,' she said, 'we shouldn't be seen together.'

He laughed. 'This is Dublin, Marie,' he said. 'It's OK.'

'There's one or two up for the opening,' she said, 'you never know.'

He laughed. 'Then how are we to get to the car?' he asked. 'Do you want to walk ten paces behind me? Come on.'

It was a fair walk. They didn't touch. She looked about. She could live in a town all right, odd times at her brothers' or here she'd always liked the sodium lights at night, the buses with strange names on, even the fumes and the noise in a funny sort of way. There was a kind of romance about it all. They reached the car and she waited in the passenger seat while he went to get a take-away pizza from somewhere. It was all familiar, the old red leather, the big wooden dashboard. I'm glad, I'm glad, I'm glad, she thought, now that I've seen him I'm glad I came. She looked out at the young people walking by. He came back soon with a Hawaiian pizza in a box, all neatly divided into farls.

'Listen,' he said, offering the box, 'what do you want to do? I've got the use of a friend's flat for the rest of the day. We could just go back there, or we could go somewhere, do something, I don't know. The day's yours, Marie.'

'Let's just go back there,' she said. Got the use of a friend's flat. It sounded so seedy.

He nodded. 'Good,' he said, 'that's what I hoped you'd say.'

They ate the pizza, threw the box into the back of the car and pulled out into the heavy traffic. 'It's not far.' He put his hand on her knee for a second and squeezed and it gave her an electric shock to the roots of her hair. Of course they both always knew they were going back to this place for sex, all this talk of doing something else was just a sham. They chatted as he drove. He said he was waiting for proofs. He'd got peanuts for the book in the end, still ... at least he was through with it now. It was scheduled for April. 'You know, it's bloody good, Marie,' he said. 'I do know that.'

'You must be very nervous,' she said.

'No,' he said, 'I'm not nervous, why should I be nervous?'

She laid her hand on his leg for a little while.

Soon they stopped at a Georgian house in a flash, slightly run-down square, with steps running up to a red door with a big brass knocker. He took her hand as they crossed the road. There were four bells. If this were real, she thought, would I live in a place like this? But it wasn't real, so she could do anything she wanted just like in a dream. The front door was unlocked but he had a key to a door on the first floor landing, where the floor was polished wood and a great mirror hung upon the wall, so clean and bright that their reflections seemed more substantial than themselves.

The flat itself was tiny, one big room with a small kitchen half hidden behind a partition, and a bathroom; but she'd made it beautiful, whoever she was, for it obviously belonged to a woman. It was all blue and purple, dark, vibrant colours. There was a large red bed at one end, a desk and a swivel chair at the other, and between them two lovely old easy chairs and a bright Oriental rug. The room was full of beautiful things, sculptures and paintings and little antique knick-knacks, everything clean and shining. 'Oh, what a lovely room!' she said, walking in and looking about.

It was cold. He lit the gas fire. There were lots of big expensive shiny books. I'm as good as anyone, she thought defiantly, I'm worthy of anything. 'Who lives here?' she asked, taking her coat off.

'A friend of mine called Sandra.' He came over and stood a little awkwardly before her. 'I can't believe that we're finally doing this.'

'Neither can I. Who is she? Are you staying here?' He had the look of someone at home in a place.

'Oh, you'll probably see her at the gallery tonight,' he said.

Then she remembered and said, 'I was so sorry to hear about your mother.'

'Well,' he said with a rueful smile, 'these things happen, you know.'

She touched his scars.

Much later she said she ought to go back to Maura's for tea before the opening. Her legs were about his waist, he held her buttocks. 'You don't,' he said, 'we've got food here. You don't have to go anywhere.'

'No,' she said, 'I don't.'

She rang Maura and said she'd see her about ten, she'd met an old friend from her schooldays walking up Grafton Street, would you believe it? Anyway, they could have a good old gossip in the morning.

161

'Suit yourself,' said Maura, sounding offended.

Marie panicked. She'd be found out. Her heart pounded. Bob was in the kitchen making coffee, naked. He was lovely naked, moved more freely. He was not a fighter, anyone could see that. They should have left him alone. I just did all that with him, she thought, I did it. Had him hot, hopeless, helpless. Glory hallelujah. Warmth, wet, seeped between her legs, lovely. Marie, Marie, she thought, is this you? She looked down at herself, her big white naked body with the telephone flex coiled about the hip, licked her mouth and tasted sex. 'See you later, Maura,' she said.

She went into the bathroom, a narrow black box full of peacock feathers. They stuck out of thin mother-of-pearl holders set into the walls, shivered fastidiously in the jaundiced glow of the mirrors, made of the toilet an oriental throne. Hundreds of them, must have cost a fortune. It was twilight in here. Marie sat and peed daintily. Her thighs were all sticky so she washed them down standing in the seagreen bath. The soaps were all different colours, like shells and fruit and flowers. She tried to imagine this peacock feather woman, tried to see herself meeting her, sitting down and drinking a cup of tea with her. She couldn't. This world was not hers. She sniffed enviously, stepping out of the bath and checking herself in the mirror. In the gloom she looked wan and mysterious. You'd have a hard time getting your make-up on in here, she thought.

He'd got back into bed. She saw him watching her walk across the room. Smiling, she kneeled upon the bed. She didn't care about a thing. She wanted her coffee, grabbed it gratefully and drank.

'You seem to know this woman pretty well,' she said. 'Are you staying here?'

'No, I'm staying out in Bray. Much too far for us to have gone and hundreds of people around.'

'So who is she?'

'She's an old friend,' he said, and grinned. 'You're not jealous, are you? Don't worry about her. She goes away a lot and sometimes I flat-sit. I could be here next year. She's off to America for about six months.'

God, these people, she thought, what lives they lead.

'You could come and see me,' he said.

But she imagined him talking to this Sandra woman, this old friend with her fancy soap and peacock feathers, discussing her.

'Marie,' he said, 'you're unrivalled.' He turned back the duvet for her to get in with him. The mess of the sheet! What's this woman going to say? And suddenly she was dizzy, reeling with the magnitude of what she'd done, and it all burst in on her, the strange city, the unfamiliar traffic sounds from the street, Essie's show and Maura's back bedroom and tomorrow and home and real life and the impossibility of it all, and she turned away and started to cry. He came from behind and put his arms and legs about her and pulled her into a long, leaning, backwards embrace, caressing her all over and twisting his neck to kiss her face, telling her everything would be all right. She dreamed, closing her eyes and letting the tears dry on her face. They'd have this brilliant affair. He'd write about her, she'd be a major influence. She'd go to London.

'You can't go back now,' he said. 'It's impossible.'

In London she could see her brothers. She could make new friends. She could get a job. What people were they? She couldn't imagine. She couldn't see any of his friends, or London, or anything. She couldn't even see her brothers any more. What would they say about her leaving Con and the kids? It was shocking, like murder or suicide, not to be contemplated. What had Con really ever done to deserve that?

'It's half past six,' she said.

'So?'

'I'll have to go soon. Time I started getting ready.'

'No. You don't have to go to that stupid exhibition. You've seen it all.'

'Ah yes, I do. I have to go.'

'You don't have to go.'

'Of course I do. What could I say to Con?'

'Oh, of course,' he said, with a rather stupid laugh, 'I forgot about Con.'

They looked at each other for a moment.

'Do you still have sex with him?' he asked.

'No,' she lied immediately, 'never.' You couldn't really count those horrible fiascos every three months or so. 'We haven't had it for years.' It was true in its own way.

'What if you got pregnant?'

'I won't,' she said, 'I can't any more, not since Simon.'

'Oh,' he said, then, 'I just wish he'd die.'

'Don't say that!'

'I'm sorry. I don't really mean that. I just wish he wasn't there, that's all.'

'Well, he is. And so are the kids.'

'They're not the problem,' he said slowly. 'I realise that now. Con is.'

She sat up in the bed and got her bag from the bedside table and took out a mirror and some bits and pieces and started examining her face. 'My God!' she said, and got out of bed and stood straightening her hair.

'When are we going to do this again?' he asked.

'We have to be realistic.'

'Yes.'

'This is it. It's as far as we can go.'

'You can't just vanish on me again. Not now. Can you really just go home after all this and forget about me?'

'No.' Marie started dressing in front of the mirror, holding her own eyes.

'Then what are we to do?'

'I don't know.'

He got up too and dressed sloppily and came over and put his arms round her.

'I told myself before I came,' she said, 'this once and once only.'

'That's not fair on me,' he said. 'You can't do this to me and then just walk off.'

She was afraid. Every move took her deeper in. She went away and sat down in one of the chairs and put her head in her hands. 'I don't know what to do,' she said, 'I just don't know what to do. Maybe if the kids were just a bit older ...'

He came and kneeled and held her hands and kissed her. 'It's all right,' he said, 'I won't lean on you, but I won't go away either.'

'I have to go,' she said.

He sighed. 'I'll take you. It's only ten minutes in the car. Don't worry, I'll be discreet. You need to eat before this thing, there'll be lots of wine. You've got time. I'll make you something.'

He went into the kitchen and she put her feet up underneath her and curled in the chair listening to the hissing of the gas fire. He's so nice, she thought. So nice. It occurred to her that all along she had carried the notion of having it all, of living in harmonious chastity on the farm with Con, while Bob remained just offstage, ever ready with love and devotion and sex. It had always been impossible.

He came back with a tray of bread and cheese and pâté and wine and they ate together before the humming fire, then wrapped up and walked down to the car. In the car they kissed modestly and drove without speaking through the dark, gaily lit streets to a place not too far and not too near to the gallery.

'Here's lookin' at you, kid,' he said.

27

Clyde hung about town on Fair Day. The schoolkids were on their lunch hour and he sloped around stopping now and then to speak to people he knew, keeping an eye open all the time for Julia. Lately he'd been having these lovely slow wanks about her while listening to the radio very late at night in his shed down the back road. He kept remembering what she'd looked like when she was eleven or so. Even then she'd had that supple sexiness, even then she'd looked at him like that, she'd always looked at him like that, or so it now seemed, though he'd not really noticed it at the time. Of course, he didn't stand a chance there, he knew that, he didn't care. He was a realist. He'd have to use rape to get anything there.

Clyde had never raped anyone, but he'd thought about it. He didn't think it was so bad really, so long as you didn't go over the top. After all they didn't die or anything, did they? And if they just

165

lay back they might even enjoy it, if they'd let themselves. Sometimes he raped Rosanna, but that didn't count because she wanted him to. They were always at it in the songs: she said no, he freaked. And there were bloody corpses, all beautiful.

He leaned against the celtic cross in the square, surrounded by the noise of the market, one leg bent at the knee, hands in pockets, squaring his shoulders and looking soulful; and saw her standing alone looking in a window, leaning with an air of truculent schoolgirl laziness and chewing big-lipped on some kind of sticky red licorice. Of course he wouldn't really do it. Not to her. It would kind of spoil something to do that to her, and anyway he wanted to stay around here a while longer. A blue jumper came down below her hips, longer than her jacket, and a bag hung from one shoulder. Without thinking, he ran across and stood in front of her and said, 'Hi.'

'Hi, Clyde.' She looked surprised.

He didn't know what to say. Julia turned away, then looked back and smiled right at him, just gave it to him like a knife in the gut. Dazzled, appalled, he gazed into the funny old window full of goods all faded by the sun: tea-towels bearing thick Irish jokes, place mats sporting Irish beauty spots, flowery birthday cards, confirmation cards, playing cards, holders full of jaded spills, plastic doilies, little girls' manicure sets; and centre-stage the plaques and statues and rosaries, the holy pictures in little sheaves all held together with elastic bands, prayers to the various saints for this, that and the other.

A crate of chickens on a cart by the side of the road chuckled and complained.

'Gonna buy one?' he croaked loudly.

'What?'

'One'a them.' He indicated the holy gear.

'Now, why would I want to do that?' She was dismissive and slightly amused.

'Well,' he said, shrugging arrogantly. 'You Catholics.'

She leaned towards him. 'Let you in on a secret,' she said, 'I'm not a Catholic,' and smiled again. A moment of complicity. He could not believe that she did not like him.

Then her mother came out of the butcher's next door and

looked right through him and made everything awkward. 'Is Con around?' he asked bluntly.

'No,' said Marie, looking into her bag and frowning.

'Oh.' He went away. Marie was a cow. Looked at him like shit since he'd landed Sawle in hospital. It was turning cold. He felt horny and wrathful when he went into O'Leary's. For a moment he could not see in the dark, smoky bar.

'Hey, Clyde.' It was Ger. 'Just warning you, Rosanna's in the back.'

Clyde's vision cleared. He leaned back slowly and peered around the glass partition. There she sat in her old camel coat with her back to him, at a table with Iko and Dolly and Boz and Chris and Mig and Sally and Terry and Fabian. They were all laughing. The air crawled with smoke. The kids, brown and filthy, had a table of their own, full of fizzy drinks and apple rings and something like Bombay Mix. The baby stood on a chair. Nice to see Iko and that lot. As for her, he'd been giving her the cold shoulder since he'd been back. Well, he was damned if he was leaving. He ordered his pint then went over to the table and sat down and exchanged greetings with all of them except her, then rolled and lit a cigarette with deliberate slowness.

Boz was doing a Jackie Bat take-off: 'Holy Mother of God, says he! That's desperate bad! 'Twould be like lying down in your coffin!'

Everyone laughed.

'Flotation tank,' said Iko by way of explanation, licking the edge of a cigarette paper. 'Up at Dundreen.' He had dull blond dreadlocks, tattoos and a white hatchet face. His guitar lay over his knees.

'Huh,' said Clyde.

'Too right,' said Dolly, 'you wouldn't get me in one. I get claustrophobia going to the toilet.'

Rosanna had one of those permanent drunk smiles plastered all over her face. She fixed it on him. He crossed his legs and shifted his shoulders about, inserting a match between his teeth. She needn't look at him like that. Like what? You couldn't tell what was going on with her any more. Ger came and sat looking over her shoulder at Clyde, grinning malevolently.

'Well, I want a go,' she said. 'I think it would do me good. After all I've been through.' She giggled insanely.

In a funny sort of way that kick had done some good, he thought, blowing smoke. The thought gave him some surprise and a vague sense of regret. Couldn't wish her on anything for a mother; anyway, whatever she gave birth to probably wouldn't be fit to live. Some poor idiot. Call me daddy, ha! Clyde winced visibly.

Iko strummed his guitar softly, a smoking roll-up shoved in amongst the tuning pegs. Rosanna sang 'Kitty of Coleraine'. They were good together, those two. Dolly got out her knitting. A very small, very dirty girl with a shock of white hair came and sat under the table. Clyde's anger went onto the back burner. Rosanna sang that old thing she'd always been driving him mad with in the beach house, he'd never even got the name of it, the one about the beautiful girl lying dead: the hairs on the nape of his neck rose up. He felt slightly light-headed and a sweat broke on his high, furrowed brow. The Guinness and the jovial fug had made all things possible. The tailor ran away with the red man's wife. The wee weaver pined away and died. The lady bedded the railroad man ...

Rosanna was as familiar as an old bed. She looked across at him and smiled as she sang, all forgiveness and invitation. She wasn't so bad sometimes, old Rosanna.

He gave her this lingering look, kind of hurt, disdainful, the kind of look she couldn't resist, then finished his drink and got up and went outside and leaned against the cross. He smoked a roll-up, slit-eyed, menacing the square; stood there for about ten minutes, running a hand through his thinning hair from time to time, but she didn't follow him. A stiff breeze was tugging at the canopies of the stalls. The hurt look got settled into his eyes. He looked sourly about, seething and aimless. No Julia, all the kids had gone back to school. A ram tied to a post across the road had got the knots in the rope stuck over its eyes and was blinking painfully. Clyde stuck his hands in his pockets and raised his collar. Fuck her. Marie walked past and got into her car, alone. Fuck her. For a second her eyes met his but there wasn't even a blip of recognition. It was just as if he didn't exist. Up yours, you snotty big-arsed bitch.

Rosanna came out of O'Leary's and walked over to him.

'Clyde, love,' she said soberly, 'what's going on? Are we talking or what?'

He looked over her head, silent for a second, then spoke softly. 'We seem to be.'

'I've got a bottle of Paddy's at my place,' she said. 'Want to get out of your head?'

After a while he turned his face and looked at her, his stray eye wandering badly. 'No,' he said sadly, 'but if you like, I'll come and watch you doing it. What's it like out there?'

'Lonely,' she said.

The cattle getting bought and sold were lowing.

Clyde put out his hand and touched her cheek for a fraction of a second. Her eyes went soft.

'I'll run you back there,' he said.

Anagar was a wild green roaring place, a high spit of land a mile long with a knobbled backbone like that of a goat. Its shaggy, ravined splendour could be seen across Caheradown Bay, towering cliffs, arches with legs like Ozymandias set firmly in the sea, great caves with soaked grey howling mouths and wrinkled vulvae. A narrow track, just big enough for a car, dawdled along it about half way up, skirting sheer drops into the sea; and at the end was a fist of land preceded by a smooth green womb where sheep nibbled. The punk's barn stood here, stark, surrounded by low ruins and ancient potato ridges from before the famine.

The track ran out just before the barn. Here Clyde parked the car.

A huge white puck goat perched on a rock high up near the distant ridge, motionless. When they got out of the car Molly ran a little way towards it, dancing and whinnying and shaking her tail, till Clyde called her in. In she slunk. The wind was getting up. The huge Western sky was murky, the swollen sea heaving and baying, the air full of the endless shrilling of a huge colony of seabirds that lived on a massive rock a little way from shore. They wheeled heavily above, cackling and giving the evil eye.

'Isn't it just too much?' Rosanna shouted over the din of wind and sea and birds.

Clyde said nothing. He was thinking with a kind of awe of her living here alone. He didn't think he could do it. Good place to go mad in, he was thinking, with a quick vision of Rosanna running straight out the door and over the cliff one dark night. Toss her over, he thought. Who'd know? He could. Just like her to come back and haunt him.

They went into the barn. It was small but had been made into two storeys joined by a ladder. The ground floor was so low it was like a goblin house. The walls were painted black and bore a series of rather lurid felt-tip abstracts that on closer inspection turned out to be graphic depictions of genital organs, male and female. A cupboard without a door displayed a ram's skull, also painted black and with glittering glass eyes. 'Christ, Rosanna!' he said, annoyed. 'What the hell is that thing?' It gave him the creeps.

Rosanna was lighting both rings of a two ring cooker that stood beneath the ladder.

'That's Satan himself, of course,' she said lightly, 'I've found my perfect partner at last. He was in here when I came. So were the pictures. "Rosanna, love," he said, "Come in! Pull up a chair! Oh, sorry, there are none. Here I am, my dear. I've been sitting all alone here for ever so long, just waiting for my princess to come and kiss me. So come and kiss me." So I did. And now I'm done for.' She shrugged and ran up the ladder.

Clyde's shoulders itched. He wanted to get out of here. He left Molly sighing forlornly below and went up the ladder. There was no window, you were in the roof. At first he couldn't see a thing but she lit candles here and there till the room glimmered eerily. It too was painted black, with a ledge running round it at knee height and nothing else but a bed at one end, the curtain drawn back, its two or three bright blankets rumpled. A few books were strewn by the bed, and a huge plastic crucifix, brightly coloured, hung above. That gave him the creeps just as much as the skull.

'Fucking cold in here,' he grumbled.

'I know,' she said, taking a very dirty old Paddy's bottle out from under the pillow and getting into bed with it, not even bothering to take off her coat or wellies. There were a good three inches left in the bottom of the bottle. 'No heat in here. Awful, isn't it? I should ask for a reduction in the rent, don't you think?' She giggled. 'If you sit over the ladder you get a bit of warmth from the gas rings.'

This was getting seriously depressing. Clyde didn't think he could stand it. He strode about uneasily, scratching himself and messing about with the peak of his cap. He grabbed a cup from the peculiar ledge, speckled with mouse shit, that ran round the room, and went and sat down on the bed, poised as if to run. 'Gimme a drink,' he said.

Rosanna leaned forward and poured with a smile, then she threw her arms around him and tried to pull him in close, kissing him relentlessly and longingly about the side of his head, the bottle hanging from her fingers a weight against his back. 'I love you, Clyde,' she said, 'I do. I do, I do.' But Clyde just sat there stiffly, letting her do it but not responding, drinking his whiskey. She gave up.

'When you gonna sort yourself out?' he said gruffly. 'You can't live here.'

'Where *can* I live, Clyde? With you?' She lit a cigarette, snuggling back against the pillow. She got a hair stuck on her tongue and drew it out slowly, squinting at it. 'This place is really something, I can tell you. This place is like heaven and hell, God, it's dreadful here at night on your own, can you imagine? Can you really imagine, Clyde? The devil's out there after dark. Don't you believe it?' She tittered. 'He is, you know. Sometimes at night, dead in the middle of the night, I can hear him breathing at the door trying to get in and he could, you know, he could if I let down my guard, and do you know what my guard is? Do you? Do you, Clyde? My guard is ...'

'Don't start!' he ordered, looking despairingly about. 'I should have known you'd never change. You love misery, don't you? You really fucking love misery.'

'Christ,' she said, sitting up and shouting it strangely, frightening him, 'Christ, Christ, Christ, Christ, Christ, Christ ...'

'Stop it!' He'd forgotten how creepy she could be. Sometimes in the beach house she had prayed, kneeling, eyes closed, hands together like something in a picture. He didn't know people still did that kind of stuff. Not normal people, anyway. It was horrible.

He looked instinctively for a window to see the state of the light, but there was no way of telling. Had to get out of here before nightfall. You never know, mess around with those kind of things, the Devil and all that. What if it was true? Out here in the middle of the night, what if ... terror rose at the back of his neck. I believe in it, he thought, horrified. What if she's like a vampire, what if things happen here in the middle of the night? Something stirred below and he started, then remembered poor Molly down there with that bloody awful ram's skull.

'For God's sake!' he exploded. 'You must be mad living here. This is awful!'

'I know,' she said steadily, looking at him. 'What am I to do?'

'Why are you asking me?' He glared angrily into her pale face. 'Why are you always asking me? You're not my responsibility, Rosanna. It's nothing to do with me. I never ... I never ... Christ, how did I ever get into this?' He looked at his watch. What time did it get dark these days anyway? Early.

'Clyde,' she said, leaning forward, 'I don't want to stay here. Can I come back with you, please? I can't stand it out here. Something terrible's going to happen, I know it, I know it, I just feel it ...'

'Ssh!'

'Stay with me, Clyde, stay with me, stay with me, please, Clyde, stay with me, please, I'll go mad if you leave me, please Clyde, stay with me, stay ...'

Clyde took hold of her and lay down with her to keep her calm. He was trembling, whether from the cold or from terror he didn't know. It was so freezing he had to get under the blankets with her, coat and boots and all, just as she had, and lie very close to stay warm. She was getting old, you could see, the looseness about her chin, the bags under her eyes.

'Sometimes,' she said, 'the birds start up in the middle of the night, all of them, all together, with a scream of terror as if something's coming.'

'Nothing's coming,' he said, starting to kiss her with the same fussy little kisses he always used to start with. It was much too cold to take their clothes off so they just undid their pants and fiddled about with each other for a long time with neither of them com-

172

ing. At length they gave up and lay panting and swallowing into each other's ears, wordless and blinking. Molly yawned downstairs. Clyde rolled onto his back and looked up at the bloody cross, eerily kitsch with its thin plastic hands and the long thin splashes of blood from the wounds carefully painted. The hanging figure wavered in the candlelight. Clyde looked at his watch. Ten to five. Could've been the middle of the night for all you could tell in here. He couldn't stick it, not this, the ceiling was not even an arm's length away, it was hideous, like being trapped in a two-foot seam under the ground. He lay staring into the blackness of the A-frame for a long time till he realised she had fallen asleep.

Clyde found himself flooded with a vast directionless emotion. He remembered a long time ago, midnight in a marquee in a field somewhere up the west coast, an electric band playing reggae, nice women dishing out food, dogs lying everywhere, kids running about, loads of drink and dope and everybody loose. Iko, Dolly, Willy the Wheels, Cherrio, Lips, Jethro, Pedro, Josh, Rosanna. That's where he became Clyde. This cool-looking dude had walked up to him and asked him his name. 'Clive,' he'd said. But the dude misheard, perhaps deliberately: 'Clyde, man, have you got any skins?'

'Yeah.'

And he was Clyde, cool Clyde.

It was like peeling back a layer: campfire, faces, Rosanna's voice from someone's tent singing the one about the girl, sixteen and dead and beautiful. The guards, of course, coming to look them all over and standing to listen, one of them saying: 'Lovely, lovely.' What would she be dying at sixteen for? First he knew of her, the voice, the one thing she had. It wasn't on the bloody boat like she said, wasn't on the bus. Maybe then, in the tent. Maybe in Ben Bowden's kitchen threading beads. Hundreds of years ago. 'Sold!' said Ben Bowden, beaming, 'to the lady with the long brown hair!' Rosanna saying it wasn't brown, it was red. She'd always been stroppy but she'd been all right then. A long, long time ago.

He thought about Julia's creamy face, big mouth and eyes. He imagined walking down the street with her, her hanging on his arm like that chick on the cover of *Freewheelin'*. Then he thought about Melanie Broadbent's nice little tits. She didn't know what to do with them. He only ever got to touch the little fatty bits round the sides where they started to swell upwards, just kind of rubbed against them with his arms. Every time he kissed her he felt like apologising for the puss oozing from his volcanoes. That fat slob in the upper bunk, that stinking creep, he was the one that got to feel those tits in the end. So what that it was a long time after? So what that they did their best to hide it from him? So what anything? It wasn't his fault. Rosanna had explained it to him. It wasn't his fault, he just got these feelings. A cracked arm, a pounded face, it'd just been like playing in the dirt, shoving your hands in shit. What else could he do? Had to do something, didn't he?

'Rosanna!' he said, shaking her by the shoulder, but she didn't wake.

The wind was louder. He rose on one elbow and looked down at her. It would be dark soon. His heart raced. He got up and stood edgily rolling a cigarette with freezing hands, wondering what to do. He could wake her and take her back into Strangarvan with him to his shed in the back road. In about two days' time, if not before, she would drive him mad. He lit his roll-up and went down the ladder to look out of the window. To his horror it was completely black downstairs apart from the ghostly blue flames of the two gas rings burning low. Molly made a strange strangled sound. He pictured the black skull with its glittering glass eyes staring at him through the darkness, panicked and blundered to the door.

Outside, it was not quite dark. The puck had come down from the ridge and now stood on a rock just at the back of the barn, a huge beast, looking down on him with its strange eyes and long white beard blowing. Molly went on standby. He heard the screaming of gulls, the roaring of sea, saw treacherous paths, goat-tracks leading up the slippery near-vertical sides of Anagar, a sleeping giant that need only twitch in sleep to pitch you off, down into the foaming caldron, the mouth of hell.

He saw his little van waiting for him on the track, facing town. He could do nothing for her. She was going down long before she met him. The puck could be Satan himself, for all he knew.

What could he do? He ran to his car, Molly loping along all cheer now that they were leaving, and got in and drove away as quickly as the narrow track would allow.

Half way up Miley's Gap he realised he'd left his cap behind, but was damned if he was going back for it now.

28

One night standing at the back door, looking out over the fields towards the Malverns, her mother had called her. 'Listen,' she'd said, and Rosanna had heard distant music, very high and slow and swirly. She was about twelve. Her mother told her it was fairy music. It was one of those things she always remembered.

When she woke, only one candle was still alight. The bed was cold. She still had this thing about her mother in her mind. She got up with a blanket wrapped round her and went and sat at the top of the ladder to get the heat coming faintly up from the two gas rings below. He was gone, of course. Doesn't matter, she thought, I'll get him in the end. You can't duck fate.

The wind moaned. Mice scurried whispering below. Later they would come up, her tiny companions, sharing her meagre store, looking at her incuriously while she stayed still in the bed. She got her rosary and went down the ladder to find more candles, taking her one light with her. There were just a few bits and pieces stuck about the place, the wicks all sunken in. She gathered them up, then stood looking at the ram's skull with its powerful trilobite horns, its jagged black nose and missing grin, the candlelight catching the glass in the eye sockets. She really did believe it carried some malignant power. 'Hssss!' she spat at it. She'd considered moving it but didn't dare.

The one small window showed blackness. She hadn't got a watch and had no idea whether it were merely late evening or deepest night. She climbed back up the ladder awkwardly with her candles and placed them about the room at intervals along the ledge, lighting them as she went. Then she got some books and climbed back into bed with her whiskey and pulled the blankets round her. Clyde's cap was unearthed and she pressed it against her breast, rocking slowly and wallowing in memory.

The boat tossed wildly. They were throwing up all over the decks. The Ladies was awash with it and someone retched behind every cubicle door. The rubbish bins were being sicked into also. She strolled about like an arrogant child, rolling with the rolling of the sea, adoring it. She had no idea what she was doing on this boat. Yes she did, she was going to see the place of the songs, the songs her father used to sing; she was looking for the old boreen and the apple tree over the well, for the Coolin, for the little black rose, for young Thady footing it with Eily Moore at the cross-roads. Somebody must have given her the money for the boat. She couldn't remember. And there stood Clyde frowning in lonely contemplation against the bar, one foot hooked about the other, drinking a pint of Guinness with artistic relish.

Night was more profound out here.

She tried to read a book but couldn't. One or two of the candles had already died. Shit. Get some more first thing. Too many draughts in here, that was the thing, and with the wind gusting like that – malicious it sounded, whining, carping, malicious –.

Rosanna got up and walked about, lay down again, read, blew on her hands, let the whiskey warm her throat, mumbled aloud to herself complainingly, whimpered, told her rosary beads. Her eczema was bad these days. It was in the joints and round the back of her neck. Something was here on Anagar, something so vastly greater than herself that she trembled. It was in the banshee shrieking round the barn – I believe, oh I believe – and in the skull – oh, save me – and in the slick brown beads moving under her fingers. It was horrible, she was going to burst with it all. It was not possible that she was here all alone, that she'd come to this. When the Devil creeps with his long red nails, pray, pray, what else is there to do, fall at God's feet and grovel, beg.

Rosanna could pray, oh Lordy, how she could pray, prostrate upon the bed weeping in abject terror, reduced to an atom, pleading for deliverance from evil, for the rescuing arms, for love and salvation and freedom from the fear of death. She went on and on, remembering: distant chimes, other beds, other nights, other prayers, an hour a day nonstop, sometimes two, falling on God as onto a sword. Sister Francis tapping at the door and telling her that was enough now, come on down. Thinking about that poor bloody man through these nights on Anagar, her ears singing constantly as if voices swirled in the eye of a distant storm. Sometimes it was OK, the voices were just friends, the goodies: God, Our Lord, Our Lady, mummy and daddy and her Guardian Angel. She talked to them a lot out here. Other times, it seemed that the sound was the far voice of hell, speaking through the wild shells on the brow of the monstrosity downstairs. It was the sound she had first heard after the crash, impassive, indifferent. She remembered Tommy Kenny's music shop on Shoe Hill. Tommy Kenny was her father. He died with her mother in the crash. She remembered their two heads in the front of the car, side by side, eternal. He always drove very fast, she loved it.

'Daddy, daddy,' Rosanna said, and closed her eyes. She sat in the back, just as she always did, urging him to go faster. She was fourteen. He laughed, putting his foot down, he was like that. But Mummy hated it.

'Tommy,' she said, 'don't you go taking no notice of her.'

And that was the end of them.

She woke up alone, with a sound inside her head.

A little grey mouse pottered about the floor, unawed by the night and this thing out here on Anagar. It was darker. The candles at the far end had all gone out. An orphan! All alone in the world! Oh, there was mileage in that, no doubt about it, charmed a few in its time, didn't it? I should get a cat, she thought, a black-and-white mouser, I could call it Dinah ... Rosanna dozed for a while, woke as if startled on watch, tried to read some more but couldn't. They were out in force now, the mice, hurrying here and there, chittering at one another. She didn't mind the little ones, it was that big fellow over there she had her eye on. She crossed herself, praying constantly under her breath as the night progressed. Fear sweated on her and gave her a tang she could smell. She drew the bed curtain across to keep the cold out but of course it made no difference whatsoever and made her scared of what she couldn't see. So she drew back the curtain. She felt like a bell about to ring. Whatever was coming up from below she would face it, not wait for it to stretch out its hand and pull on the cord. The wind blew right through the barn and the flames flickered. How long would this night last? The whiskey was going, going. Clyde was a bastard to leave her here like this on her own. She'd do for him one day, she'd do for him, let him think he could ever get away with anything, *she'd* get him. She believed in magic. There was power in a place like this. She'd get him, she'd get him, oh yes, she would.

Another candle went out. A strange sound came from below and her heart jerked. Then she realised it was only the flickering sound of the flames slowly guttering on the gas burners. The cylinder was running out. More light would go with it. Fear of the night grew maddening. She looked up at the crucifix on the wall and prayed and tried to work through the stations of the cross in her mind. You had to put yourself up there, that's what you had to do. And what happened then? Because it had to be a man, didn't it? Couldn't be a woman. You did all that to a woman. it would be pornographic. Rosanna squirmed like a worm. It must be pornographic because it got her going, it really did, thinking about having those things done to her. Ended up just another horror show. Having a long, slow one. Ach, stop this! She didn't know when she'd last eaten. Hunger, too, was terrifying. There were no arms for her, anywhere in all the wide world, anywhere in the universe.

The last candle flickered wildly for a moment then went out.

Endless empty darkness, for ever and ever amen. She crouched upright in the bed, sobbing. Hours passed, every inch unbearable. The horrors of eternity unfolded. The cold bit through the light blankets and she shivered like a dog seeing a rabbit. Sleep was impossible. Mice, and something bigger, scuttled across bare boards, skittered on bare concrete, and her tongue whispered on, growing stiff and dry in her head, the prayers of her childhood.

She must have slept because it came to her suddenly that she had been dreaming for a long time. Someone was coming up the ladder, she knew it though she neither saw nor heard a thing.

The fear was gone like the sudden ending of a terrible pain, wiped away like a stain. She was caught in something, helpless.

She knew in the pit of her soul that Jesus was coming to her through the darkness, naked and beaten and torn. She was his mother, he a pup running for the dugs. They had done these terrible things to him. There was no pity. He came and put his arms around her so that she didn't feel the cold, and then she went inside his body, or he went in hers, she couldn't tell, and they occupied the same space, limb for limb. Though she did not see him, she saw him. Though she did not hear him, she heard him. This must be what nuns get off on, she still thought distantly, this must be what makes the old itch bearable. Oh! 'Tis love, 'tis love ...

There was a light somehow. Mice fed peacefully about the place on some old crumbs.

She thought she understood love, sharpened like the point of a nail, killing as it saved. She understood because she was inside him and he took everything into himself as into a fire, burning constantly, the fire of love, the fire of hell, burning side by side constantly ...

Rosanna woke up crying and saw with wild gratitude the first light seeping up from below, in through the chinks and cracks in the roof and walls.

She slept again but they woke her up, slapping her face, sticking her on this cross, driving these great fierce nails through her palms and through her feet ...

She woke up cramped, her stomach aching with hunger, Clyde's cap still clutched in her arms. The gas had long since run out and the cold was intense, penetrating the blankets. The wind sobbed, the sea howled, the mice had mostly gone. She sat up, wide awake. What a sleep! Her hands were blue. He *was* here, she thought, he was here, he was! Surely he'd stay with her now. She'd go to Mass, she'd be good again. Oh, there was nothing like it, church, the smell of the flowers, the streaming of the light through the stained glass, the swinging of the censer, the sweet heady incense. She'd go back, she'd go back to all that. Sniffing, wiping her tears away, she got out of bed and went downstairs and out, stuffing Clyde's cap into her pocket.

The sky and waves were tossing white. The sea sucked and blew and hissed and keened and birds blew about like rags, savage faces appearing and disappearing, beaked like vultures. They sailed low alongside, seeing her off the premises as she walked along the track towards the mainland, huddling into herself, stuffing her hands right up her sleeves.

'Oh my good Angel,' she said, 'whom God has appointed to be my guardian, enlighten and protect me, direct and govern me during this day.' What was it? A dream? What? She kept drawing in great breaths as if in pain, then laughing to herself and running a few feet. The grass on the hillside was alive, rippling like skin. It was four miles to the village. By the time she reached the first house and the milking sheds her joy had dissipated into the firm presence of another day. But something happened, she kept saying, something happened, something happened.

She hung about waiting for the shop to open. Old Dan Hogan came along the street with his willy hanging out. Davy appeared, all gruff and square, and opened up the sheds. When the shop opened, Rosanna went in and rubbed her frozen hands together in the sudden warmth that set them burning. The smell of baking was rich already from the kitchen at the back. 'Cold today, Mrs D,' she said.

Mrs Davy and Siobhan bustled about behind the counter, frowning and distracted. Mrs Davy looked up and smiled. 'Hello, Rosanna,' she said, 'isn't it awful? I get depressed with this weather sometimes. Don't we get enough of this wind? Are you frozen out there?'

'Is the Arctic cold?' asked Rosanna.

Mrs Davy shook her head. 'Siobhan,' she said, 'would you go and see if Tom's got the van ready and give him these.' She handed Siobhan a carton of something. 'Now, Rosanna.'

'Is there any bread yet?' she asked.

'Another hour or so, Rosanna. There's none fresh but I've a bit of soda bread left from yesterday, or a sliced ...'

'Oh, the soda bread, Mrs D.'

Mrs Davy went into the back. The smell of bread rising, the warmth, the higgledy-piggledy shop, it was all wonderful, wonderful ... she had survived the howling mouths of hell and lived to fight another day. How wonderful it would be now to sit in Mrs Davy's kindly kitchen and drink a cup of tea and let this good woman, this good mother, fuss about her and offer things. Her throat constricted. It was good just to be alive. Let his goblin glass eyes glitter on an empty barn, she'd never go back there now. Not even to get her books. She'd live a new life. She'd be good and holy and they'd see what she was and take care of her. She'd ...

Dan Hogan came in with his willy still hanging out. He nodded stiffly at Rosanna.

'Your willy's hanging out again, Dan,' she said fondly.

He ignored her and went and shuffled about, all small and jerky and frowning, at the back of the shop behind the seed packets. Mrs Davy reappeared with a big fat loaf of soda bread. 'Now, Rosanna,' she said, 'is that all right for you?'

'Lovely,' Rosanna said. 'On the slate, Mrs D?'

'Away with you,' said Mrs Davy, smiling and waving her hands. 'It's stale. I couldn't charge you for that. Will there be anything else, Rosanna?'

Rosanna thought. 'I couldn't have half a packet of butter, could I?'

Mrs Davy cut a packet of butter in half. That went on the slate. But she slipped a couple of rashers of bacon into the bag and said nothing about it. Old Dan Hogan was peeing behind the seed packets as Rosanna left. Mrs Davy clapped her hands, shooing sternly at him as if he were a hen.

Outside she stood for a moment, assessing the temperature and the state of her health. She was probably coming down with something, that would account for the weird shivers. Or the bloody change – oh, don't say that. She had to get a drink so she went first to Sylvester's, woke him from a deep sleep, got into the bar and nicked a fill-up of whiskey for the little brandy bottle in her big pocket, then went up to Inchicora to fry her rashers. Sylvester's stank, she felt too pure for it. She chewed on a hunk of soda bread as she walked and had a little drink on the way. The back door was unlocked so she just walked in and started frying her rashers in the kitchen.

A few minutes later Essie appeared in the doorway in her dressing gown and red socks, wary and furious.

'What are you doing?' she demanded.

'Having some breakfast,' Rosanna replied, taking out her

penknife and cutting into the soda bread. It wasn't too stale.

Essie sighed and put her face in her hands for a second, then stood very upright, arms folded. 'Rosanna, what are you doing, what are you doing?' Her nostrils dilated. 'Oh, not bacon. All that horrible grease. I can't stand this. What did I say? What did I say, Rosanna? You just don't listen, do you?'

Essie's face was all pinched about the nose, all long and sullen and ... scared. Rosanna was glad about that. It made her angry and the anger was strangely soothing, like brandy, a familiar heat in the belly. It unfurled its fingers slowly. Rosanna smiled. She felt her eyes go white and dead again, infernal. Essie saw it too because she quailed, something just visible but quickly controlled. Rosanna still held the knife in her white, stiffly clenched hand, a chipping of pale rock-like butter cleaving to the thin blade.

'How long have we known each other, Ess?' she asked reasonably.

'You don't listen!' Essie's voice shook a little and she started rubbing her nose-stud nervously. 'I said you are not coming in here in that condition.'

This had a familiar ring. 'What condition?' Rosanna asked, hardening.

Essie walked in a little circle of exasperation. 'Pissed out of your stupid head!' she said. 'It's just awful what you're doing, Rosanna, it's just awful!'

'What is? I'm only having my breakfast.' She laughed then spoke angrily. 'Oh, go and sit down, woman. Make a cup of tea, go on, make a cup of tea and let me have my breakfast and then I'll be on my way. Don't worry, I'll go, I'll go.'

Essie just looked at her for a moment. 'OK,' she said expressionlessly. 'I'll make a cup of tea and you can eat that crap. Then you're going.' She went over to the sink and started to fill the kettle.

Rosanna looked at the bacon spluttering reassuringly in the pan, the smell of its frying rising up from weekend mornings when she was a child, and thought of Mrs Davy slipping it into her bag, saying nothing. That crap, she says. She looked at Essie's smug square back and thought about sticking the knife in it. It's all right for you, she thought bitterly, and her eyes filled suddenly with tears of self-pity; you've got this nice twee little house with cosy cats and a big turf fire and a bloody washing machine for Christ's sake, and your picture in the *Cork Examiner* for those crappy ceramics. And I've got nothing and you begrudge me a bit of breakfast. Call yourself a friend?

'Shouldn't leave your door unlocked when you're in bed,' she said lightly, flipping the bacon onto a plate. 'Where's George?'

'Work,' said Essie. 'Dundreen.'

Rosanna strolled into the living room with her plate, settled down by the peacefully crackling fire and ate with her fingers, washing the food down with sips of whiskey. Essie came in with the tea and sat down opposite, still sulky. A cat leapt onto her knee and she stroked it stiffly.

Rosanna checked her bottle. Roll on dole day. All that strange elation had gone and she was scared, terrified. 'Last night,' she said, 'Jesus visited me in my barn.'

'Did he?' said Essie, affecting boredom.

A tear rolled down Rosanna's cheek and her eyes turned very blue. 'Clyde came round last night,' she said. 'It had been so long. He was mad for me.'

Essie leaned forward. 'Look,' she said earnestly, 'you've got to stop this, Rosanna. Please.'

'What? Stop what?'

'Stop drinking, Rosanna, please. It's got out of hand. It isn't fun any more, it's a nightmare. Rosanna, please.'

Rosanna gulped down her tea. She thought yes, yes it is a nightmare, but she was in it and it wouldn't stop so she just had to go on.

'You've got to stay on the straight and narrow in the end,' Essie said, 'if you want to survive.'

'Jesus didn't.'

'Jesus didn't survive.'

Rosanna jumped up and walked aggressively about the place, swaggering. She went and stood in front of the picture of pretty hippy Joe and started to sing to it, pushing her hair up on top of her head and swaying her hips. Essie covered her face.

He's a tramp, Rosanna sang crudely, *but they love him,
Breaks a new heart every day,*

183

Essie had been looking forward to a morning in bed. She stood up, arms by her side, legs apart. 'OK, Rosanna,' she said, 'you've had your breakfast and a little bit more. I've got an awful lot to do this morning so I think it's time you ...'

'Jesus!' Rosanna whirled about, nearly falling over. 'What is this? Why are you so horrible? What's happening to everybody? Come on, lighten up, you boring buggers, lighten up. Look at the weather! I can't go out in that!'

'Well, you should have thought of that, shouldn't you, when you decided to come up here. I told you. I told you not to come ...'

'I'm not drunk! I am not drunk! Listen!' She flung her arm out dramatically. The wind sobbed. A few spots of rain spattered the window.

'Just go,' said Essie, 'please.'

'Who's going to make me?'

'Don't do this, Rosanna. Please, just go.'

'Fuck off!'

'Please, Rosanna.'

Rosanna reached out her arm, ripped the picture of Joe from the chimney breast, leaving the corners behind, and tore it in two. 'Stupid bastard!' she yelled, throwing the two pieces down.

'For Christ's sake, Rosanna!' Essie dashed forward: Joe the golden, the saintly youth, the everlasting smile, the sweet dead days beyond recall. It was as if Rosanna had killed a child before her eyes. George would die.

'Call yourself a friend,' Rosanna said, and left, weeping.

29

Bloody awful weather.

She passed the Grotto and fell down before Mary. 'Help me!' she cried. 'Help me!' She drank the whiskey and it warmed her up. A car came along, it was Tommy Davy going into town. He gave her a lift. She said she felt scared that the end of the world was coming.

'Well, now, if you look at it one way,' he said, 'we're all a second away from the end of the world at any old time. I mean, someone might crash into us on this next bend.' He smiled.

Rosanna shivered. The bend zoomed up to meet them and they sailed round.

'Faster,' she whispered. But that was fast enough now, he said, and turned on the radio and the car was full of mid-morning DJs. Then some sloppy old song came on and she sang along till the bungalows outside Strangarvan began.

'Look after yourself now, Rosanna,' he said as he dropped her in the square.

She spent all that day and well into the night trying to borrow money, scrounging round the bars, getting a drink here and there, running out of money again, panicking, making up to some Korean fishermen, pulling a knife on a woman in O'Leary's because she said something, got thrown out of there and went somewhere else and got thrown out again and found herself in the late hours walking along the harbour's edge, dodging ropes and contemplating stowing away in one of the boats, of sailing with the fishermen to Russia or Scandinavia or Spain, fed, fucked, drinking, merry. The smell of fish and the sea was seductive and she dug up a shanty or two. The weather had eased. Life was not so bad after all. She started looking for a bed. Find a man to sleep with was the quickest way. She couldn't go back to the barn, couldn't. She'd die alone out there with nothing to drink.

The Guards picked her up walking down the middle of the street shouting obscenities. She fell asleep on the back seat of the car, so when they got to Anagar they carried her out and into the barn between the two of them. There was no light, so they shone their torches around.

'Awful place. Awful,' said the young one.

'Where shall we put her?'

She was a dead, snoring weight.

'Anywhere. Here for a minute.'

They put her down like a parcel on the bare black floor and stood looking about, breathing loudly. The torch light touched the eyes of the skull.

'Nasty thing,' the older man said.

They crossed themselves. 'Will we move it, d'ye think?'

'Ah, no. Leave it.'

'Are ye all right now, Rosanna? Are ye all right?'

'Push her over like this.'

She mumbled angrily. She was too awkward and heavy to get up the ladder, so the young one went up and brought down the blankets to throw over her. 'Is she all right, d'ye think?' he asked.

The older man sighed.

They left. After the droning of the engine had died away, there was no sound but the moaning of the sea and the cave's mouths.

The first thing she saw when she woke at first light frozen on the floor, was the ram's skull, and she screamed and screamed for her mummy and daddy, but nobody came.

30

There were two pictures now on George and Essie's chimney breast. One was of Swan Mary, who, against all odds, was really coming in the summer. It clashed with the Fleadh but she couldn't make it any other time. George had put the picture up and Essie didn't mind. She thought Swan Mary had a nice face.

The other picture on the chimney breast was the old Joe picture, lovingly repaired and restored, wearing its scars bravely. George grew mournful still when he looked at it. His eyes would mist over. 'Oh man,' he would say softly, 'Oh, Essie, man,' and he would reminisce for an hour or so about old times. Sometimes he'd cry, smiling.

Then he'd talk about Rosanna. 'We've got to help her, you know. We've got to help Rosanna.'

'She'll drag us down.' Essie rubbed her tired eyes. She was standing near the mirror, noting how wrinkled her eyes were getting.

'Doesn't matter, we've got to help her. What's the point of survival if you leave your friends to sink?'

'Oh George!'

'It brings me down, you know,' he said. 'That toilet, it brings me down. You're putting blue stuff in it.' The new toilet was wonderful. It was aquamarine and wobbled a bit when you sat on it.

Essie came and shook him. 'Stop it, George.'

'I mean, what's it all for, Ess? All that work, all that beautiful human creativity, all that running up and down to Dublin, all those months and months . . . for money! For money! For what? For a thing to shit in! Ha! Talk about the material world!' He was off, hooting with bitter laughter.

Essie didn't pursue it. His family were fairly free with the cheques from America. 'I'm worried about you, George,' she said sincerely. She was. Lately his daftness seemed tinged with desperation.

'Did you know,' he said, 'they're talking about getting Julia to present her with a bouquet when she arrives.'

'Who?'

'Swan Mary.'

'I thought we were talking about Rosanna. Settle down, George, stop walking about. I can't talk to you.'

'They're going wrong, Ess. They're going wrong.'

'Who?'

'That bunch. The Dundreen bunch.'

'I thought you were one of them, George.'

'Ah, come on, you know me better than that. Essie, listen. I have got more genuine understanding than any of them, listen to this. They just keep expecting human beings to be gods all the time, that's what it is, but they haven't got any idea . . . now, this poor woman, Swan Mary . . . you know, I only have to open my mouth these days and they all shut up and listen, and they come up to me afterwards and say I've really got 'em thinking and I've changed the way they see the world and all that kind of thing, and all I'm doing is blathering, Ess, just blathering. Now, I could do a Swan Mary if I wanted to, I could. Cinch. You gotta look nice. Gotta make 'em feel good when they look at you. Gotta . . .'

'Well, I want to see her,' said Essie, 'I'll go. Won't you?'

George laughed.

There was a knock on the door. 'That'll be your girlfriend,' Essie said.

George went to the door, beaming. But it was Con; he'd been fishing off the Point with Christy and had brought them some fish. He was like that, a nice man, a decent neighbour. He came in and drank a cup of coffee with them in front of the fire. Essie watched Con closely. For the first time in years she fancied a cigarette.

'That's her,' he said, nodding at the picture of Swan Mary. 'Julia's got that picture. She's got it up there with all the pop stars, would you believe it? I don't know, she says it's not a religion. What do you make of it all then, Essie?'

'It's not a religion,' said Essie. 'It's more like a ... philosophy.' Then she explained that as far as she understood it, it claimed to actually transcend and include all religions, including atheism, which was also considered to be a religion. But it was complex. 'At least she's a woman,' she said. 'Why they all have to be men, I don't know, about time a woman got a look-in.'

'Aha,' said Con.

'Actually,' said George, 'there's been a whole lot of women,' and he started to reel off a list. Of course he would know.

Then he and Con discussed the state of things at Dundreen. The house was taking shape and it was incredible, they said.

'It's aligned to the magnetic poles,' said Con.

She wished he'd go home. She was beginning to feel subtly angry against Con, and that was not fair at all. She didn't want to know all the things about him that she knew, all the things Marie confided in her. Because, of course, she had to confide in someone, didn't she? And she couldn't tell Therese, because she was Con's sister.

There was a verandah, a series of huge arches looked out across the estuary, they said. 'Aw, man,' said George, 'it's beautiful.'

'Turn it easht, turn it easht,' Con said gormlessly, doing a take-off of poor old Jackie Bat mixing cement. He was hopeless, they both said. Con was laughing heartily. I am colluding in your betrayal, she thought, looking at him. I know you pee the bed sometimes when you've been drinking at Sylvester's. She thinks you're getting fat and she's gone right off you. She wants someone younger and thinner, she wants a clean chin. She asks me what she should do and I think stop now, stop everything, but I muster all my counselling skills and say something absolutely non-judgemental and leave her to work it out for herself. I carry his letters. He's putting the word around about me, I think, there's even been a mention in the Irish Press. It's all very casual, I just hand the letter over and she says thanks and sticks it away somewhere. I'm just doing my job, guv.

31

Spring came. A whole bunch of them were working up at Dundreen on those pink and white clifftops full of thrift and bladderwrack: Jackie Bat, the Pads, Simon Mullen on Saturdays, and a few blow-ins. A lot of the time it was a shambles, full of sulking and backbiting and long delays. They grumbled about the wages and made fun of James, whose serious, worried little face hovered about the place continuously getting on people's nerves. James just couldn't get into drains and all that like the rest of them, but he did like to show an interest.

Jackie Bat, lost to time, sweated in an old jacket that was much too small for him, leaning on his spade smoking and looking out over the sea. He seemed all pulled out of shape, beefed up like a bull by time. Occasionally he'd mop his brow, panting. Old Rex lay sleeping nearby, breathing in a dry, laboured manner, his cracked tongue protruding puppyishly through a gap in his dreadful craggy teeth. The Sawles' big sheep-dog roamed the lawn, geese gaggled, grasshoppers sawed. Jackie had chronic catarrh that clicked audibly like rifle shots in his nose.

'For Jaysus sake,' Christy said for the thousandth time, 'do something about that.'

Jackie just smiled. He was doing the drains with George. George loved drains. It was just like being a kid again, and he worked with a smile on his face. But after a while he got a migraine and had to get out of the sun and go and lie down for a bit on the big sofa in the drawing room, and that's where Helen found him when she got back from picking flowers along the cliff path.

'What's this? What's this?' she cried. She had a big purple band round her head, very striking against her black hair, and purple lipstick that matched exactly.

George said he felt like shit.

Helen became serious and sat down next to him on the floor and tried to draw the headache out of his head with her fingers. George, eyes closed, could see the shadows of her fingers dancing against the light as she palpated an invisible dome about his brow. 'There,' she said every few minutes. 'There. Can you feel that? Do you feel a slight ... ?'

'Well, yes, Helen, I think it might be just a little bit better. Just a little bit.' He had his eyes closed, chewing gum.

Helen shook her hands as if shaking off water. 'Jackie's quiet,' she said. 'Have you noticed?' She went on massaging the air around his head assiduously. He felt too polite to say it wasn't working.

'Hey, do you remember,' said George, 'how Jackie used to talk?' Then he drew in a sharp breath against a sudden pain that stabbed the back of his left eye.

'Try not to frown. Lift those brows. Come on now, go with it. That's it. Go with it.'

'Used to be he never shut up.'

'Yeah.'

They were silent for ten minutes or so. Helen worked on, tireless.

'He-ey,' he said slowly, smiling, 'it's starting to work. I really do believe it's starting to work.'

'Is it?' she asked, excited. 'Is it really?'

'He-ey.'

Ten minutes later he felt able to sit up and drink a little jasmine tea.

It was dinner time by now and they all came trooping into the kitchen and queued up to wash their hands. The plates were stacked on top of the Aga. George was already sitting at the table.

'Look!' beamed Helen, pulling on oven gloves with fish faces. 'I've cured his headache. He's fine now. Aren't you, George?'

'I sure am.'

'Skiver,' said Christy.

Helen drew from the great oven two steaming casseroles and three long loaves of dripping garlic bread and stood back to let them help themselves. Some had brought their own sandwiches, but Jackie was tucking into the stew with the best of them and she watched him as he ate. He could hardly close his mouth because of the congestion, but he ate with a curious delicacy. A fair portion of their land had once belonged to his grandfather. Of course, nothing like that really mattered, she knew that, and they'd known nothing about it when they bought Dundreen; but still. Jackie owed a fortune at the shop. We ought to be paying him more, she thought, but they couldn't really do that without giving all the others more, too, and that would be ridiculous: the others were all carrying Jackie as it was.

Some things were just too difficult. She wished she was more like James. 'I don't have a problem with that,' he'd say. And he really didn't.

'Oh, Jackie,' she said to his lumbering back when the lads were going back to work, 'have you got a minute?' She was collecting the plates.

He waited. ''Tis very bright,' he said, indicating her bandanna. His nose made a sound like water running down a sink.

'Mm.' She smiled. 'Jackie,' turning from the sink, 'are you all right? You seem a bit – '

'Oh, I'm grand, I'm grand, Helen.' He always addressed her boobs as if they were the source of intelligence. She'd meet him in the lane. 'Hello, Helen,' he'd say, homing in on them.

'Only I think, I mean, we're neighbours and everything, so . . . well . . . I just thought if there was anything. You've been so quiet lately, Jackie, and it's not like you.'

'Ah well,' said Jackie, blushing furiously.

'I was thinking,' she said, 'I've got some really good stuff that might help your sinuses, it's a homoeopathic kind of thing.'

'A what?'

Helen started poking about in a cupboard. 'Oh, where is it? Here.' She gave him a little bottle. 'Take . . . oh, the instructions are on the side.'

Jackie looked gratified. They went to the door and Helen sighed, looking out at the flower bed and feeling rather foolish. 'What do you think of my poppies?' she asked.

'Oh, they're grand, they're grand.'

She followed him out and stood looking down at the crushed petals. 'George did all that for us. He's a marvel, isn't he? Aren't they lovely? Oh, look at poor old Rex!' She squatted and took the dog's face lovingly between her hands and kissed it between the eyes. 'He always seems so sad.' The dog's tail shivered and his eyes, encased in a snotty gum, rolled bashfully. His breath stank of decay.

'He's an old dog, all right,' Jackie said, taking out a packet of Major and offering her one. She shook her head. He lit one himself. 'Sixteen. His mother was a good dog. I'd be lucky to get another like that, I suppose. Connie's got a dog for me.' He exhaled. His nose cracked. 'Come on, Rex.' Rex pulled himself up with an audible groan.

'Amazing,' said Helen. 'Still going strong. I've seen him up Rossa bringing those sheep in line like nobody's business.'

Jackie smiled.

'Wait! Wait just a second,' she cried and ran back inside. Jackie slipped in after her. She ran upstairs and returned a few minutes later with a little bottle and an eye dropper. 'Give him some of this,' she said enthusiastically. 'This'll brighten him up. Three or four drops, you just drop them onto his tongue now and then. Does wonders, honest.'

Jackie held the tiny bottle in his huge hand. 'Drugs, is it?' he asked with a grin.

Helen laughed. 'No. Nothing like that, Jackie, all good healthy stuff, honestly.'

'For the dog, is it?'

'Yeah. Poor soul, he's depressed.'

Jackie looked down. 'Aye, he is that,' he said, then lunged awkwardly forward and tried to put his arms round her. Helen danced away from him, smiling wryly and turning away her face. He tried to get a kiss, chasing her purple mouth with his lipless slit. 'Just one,' he said in a strange calling tone, 'just one.'

'No, no, no,' she said sternly, pushing him away. He stood back, grinning. 'None of that now, Jackie, that's enough.'

'Thanks, missis,' Jackie said, putting the little bottle into his pocket.

He went back to work.

32

The primroses were out on the high bank at the back of the house. Sheets were spread out to dry along the hedges. Marie often stood at the back door thinking of the seasons changing and nothing resolved.

'I could do with getting into Cork sometime soon,' she said to Con, he and Simon stamping about in their turf-spattered boots in the kitchen behind her. 'I don't have a thing to wear for the summer.'

'Sure, Davy's a bastard,' said Con, and laughed, washing his hands.

'What now?' she asked, coming in.

Con didn't speak to her. He went to the cupboard and rummaged about for biscuits. 'Put the kettle on,' he said to Simon.

'Poor old Jackie.' Simon ran water and washed his filthy hands.

Julia came in, saying nothing to anybody.

'Where've you been?'

'Nowhere.'

'Sitting at the guru's feet,' Con said scathingly.

'What?'

'George.'

'No!' she said scornfully, 'George is confused.'

'Fickle child,' Con muttered, smiling.

Marie stirred something on the stove. They were all getting in each other's way. Con went and sat down by the fire, waiting for his tea. 'You hungry?' Marie asked Simon. She got the toaster out.

'She's given the dog some drops,' he said with a cracked laugh. 'Jackie's old dog. She only says it's depressed.' He was always bringing these funny little titbits from Dundreen.

'So?' said Julia.

'So,' said Simon.

'So you think you're clever. You've just got closed minds, all of you.'

'So?'

'So.'

'Stop it, the pair of you.'

Simon, big for his age, sprawled with manly grace at the kitchen table, the wide boots on his long legs pointing this way and that like hands on a clock. The dust became him. Marie served him tea and toast, then took some in for Con.

'Dinner won't be too long,' she said.

Con spat into the fire.

'Oh God, Con!' she said, screwing up her face. 'That just makes my guts heave up ...'

He just looked at her, swallowing, sour. She couldn't remember the last time he'd smiled at her. Julia came in and looked from one to the other. Again? her look said. Idiots.

'Will I go out again?' she asked pointedly.

'Aw, Jule, is it that bad?' said Con softly.

'You're worse than children.' Julia turned away, bored.

'That's enough,' Marie snapped.

'Leave her alone,' said Con to Marie.

'Oh, shut up.'

'Who are you telling to shut up?' he shouted.

'I don't believe this,' said, Julia rolling her eyes.

Con sighed and turned on the TV and slumped in front of it with his chin on his chest. His mouth sneered and his eyes glowered. After a while he turned towards Marie with a look of dislike and profound disappointment. His chin was fat, his face broad. I can't live like this any more, she thought. She went up to the bedroom and pretended to be sorting through the laundry basket, listened carefully, then stole inevitably across the room and opened her underwear drawer and put her hand to the back. The wad of letters was thick now. He said he loved her. He said all sorts of things. In the dead of night she lay awake thinking of the things he said. Invisible fingers stole across her skin. He said one day they'd be together. It is written, he said. She drew out the

194

latest letter and read: 'Now that I'm back in Dublin I keep thinking I'll just get in the car and drive down and get you and we'll
go away. Would you come? If I turned up at your door now,
would you come?'

Yes.

He was living in Sandra d'Arcy's flat. She was in California.
Marie smoked deeply, thinking of him up there on his own with
all those other women, him with money and a book coming out.
Those women at the gallery, they all knew what to wear.
Anorexic legs and hair all dyed, all vivid. They were out there.
Dancers and things. They had posh deep brittle voices. He knows
these people, she thought.

33

And then Essie delivered an advance copy of *A View In Delft*, and
it was much too big to go in her underwear drawer so she had to
stick it at the bottom of the big bedding chest on her side of the
bed. At the first opportunity she got it out and examined it. She
felt immensely proud, almost as if she'd done it herself. The
cover, all shiny and new, was Fabritius's goldfinch, chained to its
perch. Robert Sawle, it said, and there was a picture of him on
the back flap. She gazed at it, realising it was the first photograph
of him she had and wondering why she'd never asked for one
before. He was looking away from the camera, slightly amused.
She hugged the book against her breast. Then she sat down on
the bed and started turning the pages. He'd signed the title page
for her. She smiled. But then she turned another page and read
with a desperate sinking sensation, the dedication: To Nola.

She did not write to him. She didn't weep but she felt as if a
little hot coal burned inside her chest. She read the book whenever she could when she was alone in the house. He was a wonderful writer, she could see that it was good, not that it was the
kind of thing she'd read if she didn't know the author though. It
was too sad, much too sad, but it had really happened. And then
as she read on, slowly and carefully, pleased with her perseverance

because it wasn't an easy book, something dawned upon her. He'd put her into it. She was his second wife, Agatha, the one with the crazy sister. Then the terrible suspicion, no, certainty, that the first one, the dead mother of his dead babies, was Nola. It was horrible. She hated him. But wait, it couldn't be her, he'd been writing it before he'd ever come here. And she read on and on and the woman *was* her, right down to the things she'd said.

Then the horror increased because another advance copy of *A View In Delft* was doing the rounds. It must have originated at Dundreen. And then she thought, oh God, they'll all see, they'll all know it's me, and the sex and everything, it's me, it's me, oh God, how can he do this to me? She was ashamed to go out.

But no one noticed. No one said, my God, isn't that Marie to the life? Feargal Breen and George really liked it but most people had a hard time getting into the book at all. Heavy, someone said. Boring. It jumps about all over the place.

Why haven't you written? he wrote.

Marie didn't write back. A terrible time began. All the news got around and back to her in the end. He was in London. London, Dublin, your head spins with him, why can't he just stay in one place like everybody else? He was getting good reviews, so good that they were pinned to the notice board in the kitchen at Dundreen with all the good bits picked out in luminous yellow. *What's the matter, Marie?* he wrote.

Was he really that stupid?

I want to save my marriage while I still can, she wrote back. *Please respect my wishes and do not write to me again*. Her hand hovered. She wanted to add something more, something a little sweeter than that. But no. *To Nola*, a dancer with a flat stomach. He could suffer for that.

The foxgloves bloomed around the Mullens' yard along the hedge where the hens laid. He didn't write. Sometimes she lifted her skirt and looked at her thigh, pink and slightly dimpled round the side. Nola, she thought. Dark-haired, not like me at all. Even the name was fancy. Con didn't speak to her any more unless he had to and he gave her these looks all the time, looks that chilled her to the bone, as if he wanted to kill her. Somehow it had all got worse when she wasn't looking, and now her house was like hell.

Simon said, 'Ma? Are you OK?'

'I'm OK, sweetheart,' she said, kissing him.

Julia sauntered in one day and poked about the kitchen as if she was the boss.

Marie was hanging some washing up over the range. 'Where have you been, Julia?' she asked.

'Nowhere.'

'Huh,' said Marie, 'there again, eh?'

Julia went into the next room and stood staring truculently at herself in the mirror, pushing her hair up. Marie stood in the doorway, lighting a cigarette.

'Remember Bob?' Julia said, looking at her in the mirror.

Marie said nothing. It was always there between them: Did you do it with him? She thinks not, Marie thought. She thinks I'm over the hill.

'There was some talk about him up at Montsalvat,' Julia said. 'Some friends of theirs over from London said they'd seen him and he's quite the thing these days. Getting his picture in the paper, going on the radio. He's taken up with his old girlfriend again, that's what they said, the one that threw him over. Wouldn't you think he'd have more sense?' She turned and looked at Marie, peculiar and awkward, arms folded stiffly. Marie just stood there smoking and looking back, not thinking anything but starting to feel sick deep down where she'd felt all those other things. Put her in her place all right, didn't it?

'They said he was stupid. They said now he'd got a bit of cash and a book out she's back.'

She knows, Marie thought, she's doing it on purpose. Twisting the knife. But it doesn't hurt, it doesn't hurt at all, just makes me feel sick. 'Well,' she said with a hint of a shrug, 'some are just born fools.' Then she saw with a shock that Julia was crying, gathering her breath, pulling her mouth all out of shape. 'What's the matter,' Marie cried, moving towards her and standing at a loss. 'What's the matter?'

'Nothing, nothing,' said Julia forlornly.

Con was coming up the path.

'Come on in here.' Marie put her arm round Julia and led her into the kitchen and wiped her eyes with the dish cloth. They heard Con taking off his boots. 'There,' Marie said softly. 'There. You just tell me all about it.'

Julia shook her head and pulled away. 'It's nothing,' she said, 'it's nothing, I'm OK now.'

George, Marie thought. Girl of her age crying like this, got to be affairs of the heart. What's new? 'Look, Julia,' she whispered, 'it's only a crush, it'll pass. Believe me, it'll pass. Sure, I've had hundreds.'

Julia blew her nose.

'He's too old. Look at all the nice lads your own age ...'

'Oh, don't be silly.'

'Julia, he's married.'

'Oh, don't be *silly*. George is stupid! He only thinks he knows things. He hasn't got the answers.' Julia walked out, bumping into Con and disappearing upstairs.

Con saw that Marie was alone in the kitchen, scowled and went out again.

34

Marie got by. She thought about him all the time: walking up the mountain for the cows, doing the turf with all the others on Rossa, Con and Simon cutting, she and Julia spreading, hour after hour in the fierce sun, just thinking about him. In a way she hated him: she'd been all right before he came along. Now she never knew what anyone thought of her. She'd offered Nora McBride a lift one day. 'I'll walk,' the old woman said without a smile. Thinks I'm a slut, she thought. Of course, no one really bought the official line, they just pretended to for the sake of a peaceful life and to protect Con's feelings. Everyone knew something was wrong. Everyone blamed her, even the ones like Therese who were being nice to her. It was all there in their eyes.

Then the turf was done and it was lovely drying weather, perfect, hot with a sweet breeze, and meadowsweet frothed out of the ditches. Acres of tall pink and yellow flowers sprang full-blown overnight. Herons flapped their slow flights along the river. Tents came and went in the fields around the strand, and ice cream was sold from a kiosk in the beach house.

Marie sometimes cried alone at night in the house.

The phone rang. She wiped her eyes, always good at pulling herself together, and went into the kitchen and picked up the receiver.

'Is he out?' said a voice.

He's mad, she thought. 'Yes.'

'Are they all?'

'Yes.'

'Can you talk?'

'I don't know.'

There was a silence full of telephone hum while they listened for the faint wheezing breath of Mrs Shanahan, the presence on the line.

'It's all right,' he said.

'Ssh!'

'If you're there, get off the line, you old bat.'

'Ssh!'

This was serious.

'I think it's all right,' she said after a while.

He sighed. 'I'm drunk,' he said, 'that's why I'm calling you. I'm feeling reckless. Are you all right, Marie?'

'I'm fine.'

'Really?'

'Yeah.'

'Good. Good.'

There was a silence.

'Oh well,' he said, 'that's about it really. Just thought I'd ...'

'Are you going to do this regularly?' she asked sternly. 'What did I tell you? Do you really want to make trouble for me?'

'No, Marie,' he said softly, 'I'm sorry. I just wanted to know that you were OK, that's all.'

'Well, I am. OK?'

Another silence.

'How about you?' she asked.

'Huh?'

'You. How are you?'

'Oh, I'm OK. I'm in Dublin at Sandra's.'

'Is she there?'

'No, she's still in the States. I'm kind of messing about with this new book.'

'Oh.'

'You know,' he said, after another long pause, 'you never even told me what you thought of the book.'

'It was very good,' she said.

He laughed uneasily.

'Is Nola with you?'

There was a shocked silence. 'What are you talking about?' he asked angrily.

She said nothing.

'Whatever gave you that idea?'

'We're not completely cut off down here, you know,' she said sourly. 'Did you think I wouldn't hear?'

'That's crap!' he said. 'Absolute crap. For God's sake, Marie, I saw Nola in London. She was around for about two weeks, then she went back to the States. I saw her once for about two hours. She bought me lunch to thank me for the dedication. That's it. That is it. And anyway, even if that wasn't it, what am I supposed to do? Do you want me to sign in at a monastery for the rest of my life?'

'So what happened?' Marie said. 'Did she throw you over again?'

He hung up.

Marie stood looking at the receiver stupidly for a moment before putting it down. Then she went next door and sat down looking into the fire, dazed as if someone had hit her. A sense of weariness came over her. Oh God, I wish all this were over, she thought. The phone rang again. She wouldn't answer. But it went on and on ringing till she went back into the kitchen and picked it up.

'This is the most ridiculous way to conduct an affair,' he said. 'It's impossible. We have to meet again. Tell me where, I'll go anywhere. I'll come down there if you want.'

'No!'

'Why not? It's a free country, isn't it? I could come down for a holiday.' He laughed.

'Now, you listen. This stops right now. You're ruining my life.'

That stopped him. She thought about putting the phone down but didn't want to lose him again so quickly.

'Are you still there?' he asked.

'Yeah.'

'I'm sorry,' he said.

'Yeah. Put the phone down now.'

'You want me to?'

'Please.'

He put the phone down. She replaced the receiver and flopped, then dreamily started making herself a cup of coffee, allowing her habits to carry her along. She'd not let him go. Oh no she wouldn't, not this time. She was all shaky, had to just sit down and smoke a cigarette and pull herself together. She believed him. Nola was dead ground. She could have all that again if she wanted. Or she could grow old and the children would go and she'd sit all day with the fire eating her legs, like Con's mother.

Half an hour passed. He rang again. He was drunker than before. 'Listen,' he said, 'we'll be dead soon. You're miserable, I'm miserable, he's miserable, we're all bloody miserable. What's the point? You can come with me. It's all right, I'm not the demon lover, you know. This Nola thing is crap. It's crap. Believe me, Marie. Believe me.'

'Why did you dedicate the book to her?'

He sighed. 'It was a promise I made a long time ago,' he said, 'and I always honour a promise.'

'Very noble.'

'Marie, I do mind being alone,' he said. 'Can we meet?'

'No.'

'Go to Cork. I could meet you there.'

'No!'

The back door opened. Terrified, she slammed the phone down. She heard Con coughing. Heart thumping, she cocked the receiver a little in its cradle so it couldn't ring again, then put her head close and listened for the gnat-like hum. She ran to the sink and stood there, swallowing fear. Gazing down into the greasy washing-up bowl, she started to cry.

'What's up with you?' Con was standing behind her.

'Nothing,' she sniffed.

He came close, smelling of beer. Marie wiped her eyes.

'Well?' he said.

'Nothing.'

'Come on.' Con took her arm and led her through into the other room. 'Sit down,' he said seriously, and sat himself down opposite her, leaning forward with his fingers linked. 'Well?' he said again.

'What?'

'Oh, now, Marie, come on! You know what this is all about.'

She looked at him, his heavy shoulders, his face all red and shiny from the sun, his eyes that lovely pale blue like a slightly washed-out sky. When he was a boy there'd been a charm about him, a teddy bear quality. It was lovely to put your arms up under his coat and feel him, slowly squeeze; he was solid all right, he was always solid. But now he's soft, she thought. I don't like a soft man. A man's body should be hard, a woman's soft. That's what's wrong, we're both softening up together now and there's no difference. Her eyes filled with tears again.

His face started to break up. 'Oh, Marie!' he said, frightened. 'What's happening? I don't understand!'

'I don't either,' she gasped. She could never leave Con. They had to make something of this.

'What have I done? What have I done?' Tears streamed down his face and his nose ran. Marie watched, horrified. She'd have given anything for a man with a stiff upper lip at a time like this. 'Jesus Christ,' he said, 'I know I'm not perfect, but what is it you want out of life, Marie? Sure, nobody's perfect. I've been good to you. It just isn't fair!' Tears dripped off the end of his chin.

'Don't, Connie, don't, please don't!' she whispered.

His eyes were terrible. 'You did it with him, you did it with him,' he said.

She didn't know what to do so just stared back at him and the tears wouldn't come out of her eyes.

'I love you, Marie, Marie,' he cried, 'I never thought it would come to this.'

But he didn't love her. It was very clear suddenly. What he loved no longer existed. And if that was true, she was free. She wished she'd never gone to Galway, never met him. But then, she thought, she'd probably have met someone else.

'You know,' he said, 'I hate all this. I just hate these scenes, I don't want them. You never cry. Please let's just stop it, Marie. I can't take it.'

'Neither can I.'

He got up out of his chair and she did too, defensively.

'I never get near you,' he said, gripping her by the arms. 'You never want it now. Never.'

'I'm sorry,' she said, turning her face away ever so slightly.

'What do you think I am?' he demanded. 'I'm only flesh and blood. What are you doing to me? I hate you. I can't stand it!'

Marie was frightened. She jumped back. 'What can I do?' she shouted. 'I just don't want it. What do you want me to do, lie? All I'm doing is not lying. Do you want me to lie, Con? I don't want it and it's the truth and what can I do about it?' I'm staying with you, aren't I? she wanted to shout. What more do you want?

'I hate you, I hate you, I hate you, I hate you, I hate you, I hate you, I hate you,' he said and went and stood in the corner.

They did not speak for a long time.

It was just past ten. Soon the kids would be back. 'I'm sorry, Con,' Marie said. 'Will we not just try and be friends for a while? It'll be all right. Please, Con, let's just try and keep the peace, please.'

Then she went upstairs and washed her face and cleaned her teeth and went to bed, drawing the curtains across to keep out the light that was fading fast across the yard and over Rossa. She thought he might go down to Sylvester's now or turn the TV on, but instead he came thumping up the stairs and jumped on the bed and grabbed her arm. 'What are you doing?' he hissed. 'You have no right to walk off in the middle of it all like that. I hadn't finished.'

She sat up. 'Oh please, Con, I'm so tired.'

His face was set and furious. 'It's your fault,' he said, 'you sort it out.'

'What?'

'Whatever it is that's wrong! I don't fucking know! You're the one that started all this!'

She closed her eyes.

He shook her. 'Marie!' he said, 'we've got to sort this out.'

'Will you leave me alone for a little while, please?' she asked.

'No. No, I will not.'

'Oh, leave me alone!' She screamed it and pulled the covers over her head.

Con sat on the side of the bed and wept quietly with his head in his hands. She was shaking. She knew that if she touched him, even a little, he'd try and turn it to sex. She looked at his back, his bowed shoulders in a blue pullover that she'd knitted for him seven years ago. It was hopeless. She lay there steeling herself, wishing it were over, and after a while he lay down beside her and started to caress her all over nervously through her thin white cotton nightie. It was getting dark in the room. His lips were all over her face, greedy and gobbling. She was rigid, she couldn't help it. He pulled at her nightie, clutching and hauling. All she had to do was get through it, get through it. Here came the tongue, the cold wet tongue. He sighed. She stuck her face over his shoulder and gritted her teeth, clenched her eyes, dug in with her nails in desperation but this only spurred him on. He sat up with a grunt of anticipation, undid his trousers, yanked them off and returned. Marie closed her eyes.

'You don't know what that means to me,' he said later as they lay in the darkness. Then he got up and dressed again and went downstairs. The TV went on. Julia came back, then Simon. Marie looked and looked into the darkness. Much later when the house was quiet and he was sleeping beside her, she was still looking.

'Hey, this phone's off the hook,' Simon said, 'must've been off all night.'

Con was over there by the plantation making a wall, the dogs lying by him. She could hear but not see Jackie Bat: a sharp shrill whistle. On Rossa his old dog herded four or five sheep. She watched them run this way and that for a while, then went upstairs and took all the letters from her underwear drawer and brought them downstairs and burned them in the range. She didn't linger over it. Then she found paper and pen and ran back upstairs and wrote quickly on a piece of paper before she could change her mind: *Dear Bob, I'll be in the Savoy, Cork, at three on the seventeenth. I'll come away with you if you are there. Love, Marie,* and sealed it at once in an envelope.

35

Rosanna sat in the corner of Sylvester's bar, wearing Clyde's old cap, the worse for wear. No one had bought her a drink. Sylvester was there, Ger Sheehan, Con, a few others. Now and again someone spoke or a laugh rose up. Rosanna ignored them all. She just sat there, whispering to herself.

'She was in church anyway,' Christy said. 'I saw her.'

Con was mopping out the passage. He came out and lifted the flap, went over to her table and sat there for a moment. She ignored him. 'Go home, my love,' he said. 'Sure, I'll give you a lift, if you like.'

Her eyes flickered briefly. Home. Anagar. The mouths of hell. A fine sweat covered Rosanna's forehead. Her lips began to move again unbidden, reflexive: 'Holy Mary' she was saying soundlessly, 'Mother of God, pray for us sinners now and at the hour of our death ...'

'She's gone again,' Ger said.

'Rosanna, Rosanna my love, are you all right?'

'We ought to do something about her,' said Christy, 'it's time she was off to Rossgarry again.'

'... blessed is the fruit of thy womb, Jesus ...'

'I think a drop of brandy might help,' Sylvester said, 'What do you think?'

'Couldn't do any harm.'

A large brandy appeared before her and she gulped it down. She looked at them as if she'd never seen them before. 'Help me,' she said, 'help me, for Christ's sake. What do I have to do? Die in front of you?'

Night would come again. She'd sleep in someone's shed with the cows, or in an open barn, she didn't care. Now the weather was fine things were easier. She couldn't remember the last night she'd spent at Anagar. She couldn't remember much else. She thought she'd slept in a bed a few times but she couldn't remember who with. It wasn't Clyde. That's why she was here, she was waiting for Clyde, she'd heard he was around with Molly after rabbits.

'Look, Rosanna.' Con and Christy were sitting with her. 'Time for the wagon again.' Their silly big faces peered at her.

'Something's happening,' she said, suddenly afraid.

'What is?'

'Something.' She grabbed her mouth with both hands as if to keep something in.

'Do you want to go to Rossgarry, Rosanna?' Con asked. 'We'll help you. You know, you are a case.'

Both of them laughed and Christy put out one hand and patted the side of her head fondly. Shit, she wasn't going back to Rossgarry. Boring. Something was happening here. There was an awful rumbling of excitement in her belly, worse than hunger. She got up and walked about the little room looking at everyone, making people uneasy.

'Sit down, Rosanna,' Sylvester said.

'Fuck off.'

'Come on now, Rosanna,' said Con, 'there's no need for that kind of ...'

She gave a little jump as if waking up on her feet, slammed her fist down on the nearest table, picked up a glass and hurled it over the bar, where it shattered against the inverted spirit bottles. Sylvester ducked the spraying glass.

'That's enough!' he roared. 'You'll get a hiding!'

Con and Christy tried to hold her elbows. 'Easy now. Easy,' said Christy. She shook them off violently and ran to the door.

'Don't follow me!' she cried dramatically.

Ger laughed. She turned and glared at him. 'Clyde loves me,' she said.

'Nobody loves you,' said Ger.

'Jesus loves you, Rosanna,' Con said kindly.

She stuck two fingers up at them and slammed the door as she went out. It was a beautiful summer afternoon. These days she never knew what time of day or night to expect when she stepped out of a door. There were tourists about. Someone was coming out of the old schoolhouse craft centre. Jackie Bat was talking to Barney Mac near the Strangarvan signpost. It was all so ridiculous, life going on.

Rosanna went up to the end of the village. People melted away as she walked. She went on towards the great rocks, the heaped green shoulders, the little waterfalls here and there. There was a cloud lying round Rossa like a stole and in it she saw again, set there when the glaciers rolled, Christ and the woman, Christ's shoulder just pulling free of the earth which sucked at him like quicksand. His head lolled back, dead or dying. She'd thought it was a *pietà* but now saw that the woman was Mary Magdalene and began to feel all weepy again because he'd never returned, he was leaving her to die after all. Jesus, please come back. Don't leave me this way. Jesus loves you, Rosanna. But he's dead now. Seeing herself up there was funny, cradling that poor dead creature, the only one who'd ever cared for her. Dead, and the world cold. The rock face mourned.

Rosanna walked up into the mountains quite without thinking, up to Mishlin Lake and beyond. Sheep raised their heads to watch her go by. At first the earth was full of small flowers, pink and yellow and white, and tiny orchids of all colours. But she walked on to where the ground was starker, up the great jagged crack that divided the highest slope of the range. Here the rocks were treacherous, with sudden pits where water ran away, drops, teeth, small reed-filled bogs worn like crowns upon causeways. I want Jesus back, she thought. She reached a place very near the top, a throne-like formation with a seat of shining rock and sides the nibbling sheep had cropped to slippery lawns. Quite obviously Queen Maeve had sat here looking out across the Western ocean in the Celtic twilight. Rosanna walked upon the seat. She was tired. She saw the sky turn silver near the Puck Rock, shiny, blackened at the edges, saw rain suddenly falling on one spot far away, like something in a child's picture. Here it was warm and dry, but soon the rain would pass over.

Rosanna sat down and did nothing and at some point fell into a peculiar state unlike anything she'd known before. She thought she was probably asleep and dreaming, but in the dream she was wider awake than she could ever remember being, so wide awake that she wondered if she were dying. She lay down in a corner of the throne, curling up on the warm hard rock like a caterpillar on a stone. The earth ticked. The deep blue sky boomed in her ears like blood. All of a sudden the birds began to sing unseen, and it was as if somewhere out over the sea a great hand was poised to turn back a page. He was coming again. She didn't see him, but suddenly he was there inside her again.

'What was it like?' she asked him.

'What?'

'The crucifixion.'

She was extinguished yet something remained to see a man's body torn and ruined like something cats had been sharpening their claws on. It gave her a sense of *déjà vu*. Then she was it, suffering, pierced, streaming blood. Pain moved upon the face of the waters. The sky was darkened. Jesus cried for his daddy and Rosanna cried for hers. Then she was just Rosanna again, and it was raining, beating down upon her as she lay on the rock, beating her into the rock. She passed out.

When she woke up everything was clear again and she was drenched. Church bells rang distantly. She thought she'd go there, wanted the smell of the candles and the thick, sweet incense, the little arrowy flames, the coughing of the congregation, the lovely murmurous Latin, *benedictus qui venit, benedictus qui venit, benedictus qui venit*, the whole heady, terrible beauty of it.

She sat up on the gleaming rock and watched the sun begin its slow descent into Caheradown Bay. Soon it would be dark. Self-preservation drove her down the mountain.

By the time she reached the road forty minutes later the lights were coming on across the valley and a deep gloaming lay over everything. Looking back she saw that a round yellow moon had risen over Rossa, sharply defined against the sky, which deepened as she watched from indigo to navy. She stood still in the moon-lit lane, wondering what to do, feeling that something terribly important had happened to her but not sure what. Everything seemed different now. She was afraid. She thought perhaps this funny feeling meant death, and she wanted company, wanted to tell a friend. But really there was no one, only Clyde. If she was going to die he had to be there.

She walked towards the village and met Feargal, then Ben, then Julia Mullen. Nobody had seen him. Perhaps he'd gone back to Strangarvan. She stuck her head in at Sylvester's as if nothing had happened. It was fuller now, with tourists, and Sylvester didn't want any trouble. But she was changed again somehow, they all saw that, the woman was a Jekyll and Hyde; she just asked after Clyde and someone said he'd gone off with Ger Sheehan and away she went.

Ger's wife, Ann, opened the door, saw her and said, unsmiling, 'Yes?'

'Is Clyde here?'

'Yes.' She just stood there.

'Clyde!' Rosanna shouted and started in but Ann, a big woman, squared up to her. 'I think you'd better talk to him out here,' she said quickly, 'I'm getting the child off,' and closed the door.

Rosanna waited in the yard for five or six minutes. An ancient fury swirled in her chest, so palpable she felt she could spew it. She wanted to cry. She knocked again, waited a minute, then beat her fist against the wood.

Ger stuck his head out of a window. 'Go 'way, Rosanna,' he said. 'I can't make him come out. He doesn't want to talk to you just now.'

'It's something important,' she shouted.

'No, Rosanna!' He closed the window sharply.

Rosanna ran to the wall and climbed up onto its broad flat top and stood there amongst the thrift and toadflax, facing the house. She sang the 'Benedictus Qui Venit' as loudly as she could. When it finished she started again. Then again. Clyde came out and stood in the yard watching her finish the third time around. The moon was very bright and they could see each other clearly.

'Go away,' he said coldly, 'no one can take you when you're like this.'

She laughed. 'Like what?' she said. 'You don't know what I'm like.'

Clyde sniggered. 'Don't know? Look at you,' he said in a tone of disgust. 'Pissed as a fart. Piss off, Rosanna.'

She jumped down from the wall and ran towards him but he ran back to the door with what seemed like genuine fear, picked up a fair sized stone and held it ready. 'You don't get in here,' he said.

A dreadful deep voice came out of her mouth, frightening them both. 'Don't you care?' it wailed. 'Don't you care at all? I have no one.'

Clyde threw the stone at her and it hit her on the forehead just between the eyes. For a moment she was stunned and felt for her eyes. Blood ran down her face. She stood surprised in the yard.

'For your own good, Rosanna, go away. If you're going to die, die. I can't help you.' Clyde went back inside.

Rosanna screamed. She ran out of the yard and through a field of dock and ragwort, fell on her knees and ripped at the earth with her nails. She tried to dig up a dock with her hands but it was impossible, so she took her penknife and sawed away at the thick root curling vigorously in the earth like a white worm, till she'd cut off a good length and hauled it up by its broad leaves and shaken off the soil, then held it aloft to the full moon and said, 'This root is Clyde.' With the other hand she ripped a thick strand of her own hair out by the roots near the nape of her neck, never flinching as the pain shot through her. The blood that slowly seeped from the empty pores felt cold. She wrapped the hair round the dock. 'This is me,' she said, 'and I swear by my own blood that as long as these lie buried together he'll suffer for me what I do for him.'

Then she replaced the root with the hair clinging round it, stamped the earth down all around and stood there panting, exhausted.

She tried Sheila's, Michael Ruagh's, Tommy Davy's, Mrs

Costello's, the Rock. None of them would have her. She did the rounds, walking, getting lifts when she could. She tried Plum and Toni's, Dave and Grania's, Feargal Breen's. She shouted a lot and beat on doors, but none of them opened. Vincent's door was on the latch and she just walked in, stole a bottle half full of vodka and went on her way drinking it. Ben and Ulrica let her in but ordered her out when she started tearing up books. At the Haven, Felicity's place, she defaced Vincent's Celtic script sign – Wholefoods, Snacks, Local Crafts, Original Ceramics – and stood outside laughing and shouting: 'The Haven? Some fucking haven!' Then she headed back to the village, stopping off at Mike and Therese's, Tim Pat and Dymphna's, Con and Marie's. None of them would let her in. Even George and Essie drove her away.

How had she turned into poison?

She walked aimlessly about the empty lanes, going nowhere with her bottle of vodka, rambling, falling about, singing hymns and old songs, 'Star of the Sea', 'Come back to Erin', 'I Know Where I'm Going', till somehow she got off the road and found herself down in the deep dark swampy basin that lay between the village and Rossa's western flank.

Suddenly she remembered Jesus. He'd buggered off like all the rest of them. Teasing her, he was. She shook her bottle at the moon. Thick blue clouds had come from the east and moved at a steady pace across the sky. 'Go on then!' she shouted, 'love me like this, you bastard, it's what I am, do your stuff and love a sinner!'

The ground gave way and she fell four feet or so into mud, the bottle flew from her hand, the moon was eclipsed. Rosanna howled like a dog. Here and there she went on her hands and knees looking for the bottle, but of course when she found it it was empty. She got up. There were reeds, hard and stinging, cutting her as she pushed through them. For a long time she wandered about in a boggy sucking mess, till she found a road again, some road without a trace of a light, with a howling empty sky above. She walked, full of fear, faint and sick and shivering, till suddenly she fell heavily forward, scraping her knees and palms. It was a bad fall, headlong, the kind she remembered from childhood when her mother would come and pick her up and kiss it better. It wasn't fair. Her eyes filled with tears. She got up and ran, terrified of this unknown place, but the cloud thickened and the road grew darker and she couldn't see a thing and fell down heavily again, this time into a deep ditch at the side of the road, where water ran gurgling merrily.

The clouds had passed over the moon. She saw it above, and the outline of the grasses dangling over the ditch. She heard her mother's voice quite clearly: 'Where's my little girl?' it said across time. Here! Here I am, Mummy! Mummy, please, come and get me! And in a lucid moment she remembered how her mother had always come to the gate and waited to see her coming safely home from school, how she had set a place so nicely for her at the table and always cooked the food so nicely too, just so, just as she knew she liked it. What would her mother think, seeing her like this? Rosanna sobbed and prayed, helpless in the ditch, thinking she might never get up again.

She fell asleep. Jesus came again. This time he was a bee, and he stung her palms. Someone was saying the Act of Contrition into her ear.

Part Four

Part Four

36

Padraic South, walking home from Sylvester's late at night, heard a peculiar coughing sound in the darkness at the side of the road and stopped short. There was nothing more, but he had a sense that he should look in the ditch. The moon showed him that it was the dirty woman who sang, dead drunk presumably and lying there in a disgusting state. Why was she here? He was annoyed. The road went nowhere but to Rathmeelabo, and no one went to Rathmeelabo but him.

She was mumbling and frowning in her sleep and there was blood on her face. It was not a place to lie all night, not for anyone, so he dragged her out. She was heavy and smelly, soaked with the slime of the ditch, and she moaned aggressively but didn't wake. Padraic stood there and swore, the way he swore at his dogs sometimes. What was he supposed to do with her? It was chilly for all that the days were so warm, and he couldn't leave her there; so he overcame the creeping of his flesh, hoisted her up onto his back as if she were a sheep and walked the small distance to the track that led down to his house.

He put her on the flagstones in the kitchen. She was out, pale face dirty, hair all matted with blood at the back. Couldn't leave her there, so he took her and put her on the made-up bed in one of the empty rooms upstairs. She'd ruin the linen. Then he thought he should have put her on the cart and taken her back into the village, or not heard her in the first place. He listened to her breathing: it seemed sound enough. Sleep it off a bit and she'd be fine. Then get her out quick, didn't want them all knowing she'd been in here. Scowling, he fetched water and a cloth and cleaned the worst of the dirt from the cut on her forehead and the raw patch on her head, which bled afresh, tut-tutting and shaking his head. She frowned and winced but didn't wake up.

Then he looked about and swore again. He always kept a bed made up in here out of habit, in case one of the family should turn up. But as the prospect had grown dimmer and dimmer he'd changed the sheets less often, twice a year, then once, then perhaps three years ago. He hadn't been in here for a long time and now the bed was cold and damp and the whole room smelt stale. His own room over the range was warm, that's where he ought to put her, she was a neighbour after all and she was ill, in a way. He thought of his own unwashed sheets and the state of his feet sometimes when he got into bed and felt ashamed. Quickly and clumsily, he moved her again.

In his own room her face seemed to have turned a horrible yellow. He thought he might be bringing on the poor woman's death shifting her about all over the place like this, so made her as comfortable as he could and whispered a quick Act of Contrition into her ear just to cover himself in case she died in the night. Then he went downstairs and sat down on an ancient easy chair by the side of the range. He was tired and wanted to go to bed but didn't feel right about undressing and getting into his nightshirt with her in the house. Anyway, his nightshirt was in there with her and he wasn't going back again. She was dirty and foul-mouthed and he was frightened of her. So he sat downstairs for a long time listening to the radio playing softly before doing his rounds and then finally creeping up and going into the cold damp back bedroom. There were dirty big stains on the bedspread and traces of blood where it rose over the pillow. Padraic rolled the bedspread up and threw it into a corner, then took off his shoes and climbed gingerly between the cold sheets with all his clothes on, wishing there was a lock on the door.

He couldn't sleep. It had been so long since anyone else had slept in the house.

37

When Rosanna woke up her head pounded. She lay for a long time looking at a cracked ceiling the colour of old putty. The bed was much too soft and her back ached. Jesus Christ, she'd found a bed. Glory be. She couldn't remember a thing but knew that what she couldn't remember was foul. She'd crawled up to the light of this room like a worm out of a dog turd. She felt sick. When she sat up – slowly – very slowly – the room began to spin with an awful kind of minimal jerk at the end of each revolution.

She looked about. Grey blankets and a threadbare pink candlewick bedspread covered her. There was blood on the pillow and the sheets were grubby. The room was low and dim, with faded yellow flowered wallpaper and a small dormer window. Above a tiny unused fireplace a little statue of Our Lady prayed between gaudy tapestries of the Pope and Padre Pio.

Rosanna got up slowly and went to look out of the window, moving stiffly in her filthy clothes, which seemed to have been wet and then dried upon her. She saw ruins: along the stream, up the wild slopes of Rossa, down along the ferny valley sprawled tumbledown walls, cottages with gaping mouths and eyes, shrubs growing out of the windows and roofs, overgrown foundations slumbering in the earth. A townland had once thrived here. She was in Padraic South's house at Rathmeelabo.

She walked carefully to the door, feeling her head and swallowing impatiently. Had to get some liquid. When she opened the door she was on a bare brown landing with four doors. Stairs went down. Rosanna listened. The house was quiet. She tiptoed downstairs into a flagstoned hall with lots of dusty shelves. Padraic South was shaving in the sunlight by the open front door, looking at himself in a small mirror that hung from a nail on the wall. He had not seen her. Through an open door she saw a dark room, chairs, a table, a range, a sideboard with framed photographs and a large statue of the Virgin in a blue robe.

'Padraic,' she said.

Padraic turned briefly and gave her a sour look, said nothing and continued with his shave.

She was faint. She sat down on the stairs and bowed her back, letting her head droop over her knees. After a long time, hearing nothing but the scrape scrape of the old man shaving, she raised her head. She'd never felt so weak in her life. This time it must be something serious.

'You can ride in the cart to the village,' he said, taking down the mirror and lying it flat on the shelf and walking out. She felt terror. She couldn't go out there again. The abyss was out there. She got up with shaking knees and a sick stomach and tottered into the room where the range was, made it to the largest of two armchairs and sank down into it, drooping all over the arm like the dying swan. Back to the village, to Anagar. Like this. All she needed was a place to hole up for a day or so, get back her strength. It had never deserted her like this before, never. She opened her eyes and saw what looked like a man's hand, dirty and trembling. It was her own, lying on the threadbare brown arm of the chair.

Padraic appeared, pulling a lumpy old jacket over his shirt and waistcoat. He did not look at her as he tinkered with the range. Then he started complaining: 'A shocking state! Shocking altogether! To be in such a state as that, and a woman! Take yourself away from here now and I don't want the bother of you again!' His voice had risen, gone high and nasal. He stamped to the door and out again.

She didn't think she could move.

'Give thanks that you're alive!' he called back from the hall.

She closed her eyes and drifted. When she opened them again, Padraic was peering into her face angrily. She saw deep cracks in his skin, open pores on his livid nose, frayed veins in the whites of his eyes. He muttered something furious and went away again. Clouds of grey kept billowing up in front of her eyes and she had to keep blinking to clear them. Distantly she heard sounds, clinkings and clangings, homely kitchen sounds. Padraic was making her a cup of tea, she thought, and wanted to laugh at the idea. Then there he was, placing a cup and saucer down on the range beside her with a scowl and standing back to light his pipe. The cup was thin old china, dainty and rose-patterned, but the saucer was plain cracked white with a blue rim. Rosanna lifted herself slowly and picked up the cup with her big trembling manly hand: sweet red tea slid down her throat.

'If it's illness you must go into town,' he said, 'and see the doctor.'

She sipped the tea.

He stood for a moment then went out. She began to feel a little better. 'Oh, thank you,' she said when he returned with of all things a plate and a little jam slice from the shop. She couldn't eat it but she nibbled the edge just to show willing. 'Padraic,' she said, knowing she had to be careful, 'I'd be ever so grateful if you'd just let me sit here for an hour or so. I'm sure I'll be fine then and I'll go on my way. There's no need for the doctor.' Deasy'd have her back in Rossgarry soon as look at her.

He shook his head.

'Just an hour, Padraic, please,' she said, terrified. Till her strength returned. It would, it always did.

He hesitated then said gruffly, 'I'm off to my work. Finish your tea and go,' and left abruptly. She heard the front door close and saw him go by the window and down the track with his dogs following.

She sat for a long time. Gradually becoming aware of a soft tick-tock, she looked up and saw upon the shelf above the range a heavy wooden clock, fifties style. It was ten past nine. Simultaneously, she was aware of a dull ache at the dead centre of each palm, where the bee had stung. The sun slanted in across the table under the window, a dense beam swirling with dust. The room was dim, formal and sparse, yet with the odd touch of show: photographs clustering round a statue, old, slightly nicotined antimacassars on the backs of the chairs. The walls were bare except for one or two very small holy pictures.

Rosanna stood up and found she was stronger now and could walk, if she pretended she was on the steep slippery slopes above Anagar and didn't look down. She went into the hall and stood listening, as if there might be someone else in the house. The shelves were full of things like pliers and old boxes of nails and balls of twine and mouse traps. A door led into a fairly large kitchen with scrubbed stone and white walls and shelves all but bare. It was so clean that she began to itch as if things crawled inside her clothes. She started scratching, looking down and wondering how on earth she could have eaten the jam slice with those hands, feeling as if she'd eaten dirt, shuddering and brushing at herself with quick, disgusted movements. The filth was leprosy eating her. In panic she pulled at her clothes, which were not bearable. Neither was her skin. She ran here and there in the hall, putting her hands to her face and recoiling from them in horror. She was going mad. The aching in her palms had increased and she thought it was the pains of crucifixion, but this was not imagination, a self-induced tingling such as she had often felt while making the stations of the cross: this really hurt. But she was stronger now. She went upstairs to the room she'd slept in, took off her clothes and stood completely naked, scratching and scratching wherever she could reach on her body, till her skin was red and whealed here and there.

Then she started on her scalp. It started bleeding afresh where some hair was missing at the back. But she still itched. Nothing worked. She must have water. She looked around: an old man's bedroom, it smelt a little of socks and sweat and something less definable. There were dust balls on the floor, cobwebs up in the corners, faintly moving in the soft air from the window. She saw her clothes in a heap on the floor and knew she couldn't put them back on – it was unreasonable, no one could expect a human being to have to put such filth back on – she had to wash them. That was it, get clean, get strong, then face it, whatever it was out there, but not yet. She pulled the pink candlewick bedspread from the bed and wrapped it round herself, grabbed her old clothes and ran downstairs into the kitchen. Had to be quick. There was a big enamel sink with a single thin brass tap. The water was icy. She filled the sink. There was a bar of yellow soap and she tried to make a lather, rubbing and splashing at herself quickly, hands, arms, neck, then discarding the bedspread swiftly, washed all over as quickly as she could, making a puddle on the floor.

'Heart of Jesus, burning furnace of charity, have mercy on me . . .' she said.

Her flesh burned with all the scratching and the icy water. She could only see one small hand-towel and didn't like to use it, so she just wrapped the bedspread back around herself, wet as she was. Her teeth chattered. 'Heart of Jesus,' she said, 'desire of the everlasting hills, have mercy on me . . .'

She ran fresh water and washed her hair with the bar of yellow soap, sticking her head under the tap for the rinse. Blood ran down the sink with the water. Her head ached with the cold and she could hardly breathe. She wrung out her hair and let it hang dripping down her back then took down a packet of Daz from a shelf, filled the sink once more and tried to wash her clothes, but they were so dirty and the water ran so black it was ridiculous. She was weak again. He'd be back any minute, she thought, and panicked. What would he say? It was funny, kind of thing you sat in the bar and told people about. She laughed out loud. She hoped he was onto a good water supply, she was using gallons. She washed and washed, laid the things out one by one upon the grooved wooden board and soaped and scrubbed them. 'Heart of Jesus,' she said as she beat them, growing weaker but continuing, 'loaded down with opprobrium, have mercy on me. Heart of Jesus, bruised for my offences, have mercy on me. Heart of Jesus, pierced with a lance . . .'

The water ran black and black and black, then grey. It would never be clear.

She cleaned the floor about the sink, crossed the hall and hung her clothes to dry on the rack above the range, then stood back, tired. She had to do something, couldn't just wander about like this, bare-shouldered, give him a heart attack. So she looked about and saw a very large grey shawl draped over the back of the big armchair in which she'd drunk her tea. She took it and draped it round herself, crossing it tightly over the front so that it covered everything and made her warm. Then she sat down and rested. The chair was soft and spreading and the shawl smelled ancient. Through the window she saw Padraic's white horse grazing. She was clean, an impossible luxury. The turfs shifted in the range from time to time and the old clock ticked. The aching in her hands had faded a little. She sat for a long time, forgetting how she'd come there, closing her eyes and drifting, jerking now and then. She could have used a drink.

Padraic liked a drop. She got up and started looking in likely places, the kitchen, the cupboards, the sideboard, which was full of old jugs and bottles and bits of leather, dog-eared packs of cards, ancient ledgers full of accounts. But nothing anywhere to drink. Just a nip, that was all she wanted, just a little nip to get her on the road again. She closed the big wooden doors and stood up too quickly and the grey clouds returned. When they cleared she found herself looking at the little set-up on top of the sideboard: the Virgin surrounded as if by priestesses by framed photographs of Padraic's father and mother and brothers and sisters — at least, so she presumed — all faded grey and sepia.

He was coming back. She sat down again quickly. 'I'm sorry,' she said before he could speak, 'I'm still here, I had to wash my things. I'm very sorry, Padraic, I'll go as soon as they're dry, I promise.'

He said nothing but his eyes darted about quickly as if to see if she'd moved anything, took in the clothes drying over the range, the shawl she was wearing. He looked stern but not as angry as before. 'I'm sorry, Padraic,' she said. 'I will go.' Then she put her hands up to her face and covered her eyes. 'I feel so terrible,' she said, letting her voice crack a little. 'I feel so stupid and so terrible.' He turned and went into the kitchen and put the kettle on. A wave of fear rose up. He'd turn her in and she'd have to leave. She took down her hands and stared in terror, rubbing the centre of each palm in turn with her thumbs.

After a while she smelt bacon frying. It made her feel sick and hungry at the same time. Padraic reappeared, standing in the doorway, drying his hands with a dishcloth. 'Is it a doctor you're wanting?' he asked querulously. She shook her head. 'If you're not well, you must see the doctor.'

She couldn't find words. He came and stoked the range.

'It's as if I'm hiding,' she said desperately. 'I'm not ill, I'm getting better all the time. I just need time. Just another night, please, Padraic. I'll clean the house for you if you like. Please, Padraic, I've got nowhere to go and I just need somewhere to sit still for a while. I'll stay in one of the rooms upstairs if you like . . .'

'No,' he said.

'You won't even know I'm there. Just another night. I won't tell anyone. Please, Padraic, please. I don't know what I'll do.'

'You must see the doctor.' He shook his head and went out.

Five minutes later he gave her a plate of bacon and onions, which she couldn't eat, and left her alone with it. He's probably eating in the kitchen, she thought, scared to come in. This was no good. She looked up at her clothes. They'd be dry by this evening and she'd have to go. Didn't look any better than before she washed them.

Padraic didn't come back in but went straight out of the front door. Rosanna sat on in the chair, clutching its arms for dear life and trembling slightly. She was still there when he returned an hour later.

'Tis a fine day,' he said grimly from the hall, leaning a stick against the wall. 'Twould do you good to get out.'

Rosanna smiled. He'd mellowed.

He stamped in and out from the hall to the yard and back again. Rosanna stood up and wandered through the room, crossing the shawl tightly across her chest. 'Just one night. You won't even see me,' she said.

He came in and poked about in the sideboard for something, ignoring her.

'Who are they all?' she asked, nodding at the pictures.

He glanced up. 'Family,' he said after a while, then went out again.

She went after him to the front door and stood looking out across the yard. 'Do you remember when people lived in all these houses?' she asked, looking at the ruins.

'I do.'

He walked off and stood at the end of the track and called his horse down from Rossa.

38

At tea time he lit a fire and put a light bulb in the back bedroom and hung the covers over the range to air. He told her she could stay in there tonight and go first thing in the morning. Rosanna crept upstairs and there she stayed, quiet as a mouse. What she did he could not imagine.

The next day he got up very early and kept out of the house till dinner time. He thought she'd gone, for there was neither sight nor sound of her when he got home, but later, after he'd ridden over to Strangarvan and back, she was there again, he knew just by the feeling in the house when he stepped over the threshold. The grey shawl had been returned to the chair. She'd eaten and used the teapot, and things had been dusted, the floor swept, the turfs neatly stacked in order of size. He stood listening. Surely he was wrong, the house was empty. She was gone. He crept upstairs and listened at the door of the back bedroom. There were small sounds within. He was afraid.

He rapped angrily on the door. The sounds stopped then the door opened. She was dressed in her old clothes again and she was white. 'I'm so sorry,' she said very nicely, 'I was rather sick this afternoon and I just didn't feel able to ... I'm sure I'll be much better tomorrow, just one of those tummy bugs, you know, I'm fine now, really, only it's just left me a little weak, and I thought ... oh Padraic, I am sorry! I'll make this up to you somehow. When I get my next dole cheque ...'

He stormed out, went down to Sylvester's, and got some chips and sat drinking alone by the door, worrying. He prayed she'd be gone when he got back but knew she wouldn't. What if she were really ill? Should he tell someone she was there? Why was she there? He didn't dare go home till about ten, thinking he'd take her into town himself in the cart tomorrow, or at least to the main road where she could get a lift, if she were better that is. She'd looked ill. She could have died up there for all he knew. But as he opened the front door he heard singing upstairs and stood for a while listening in the dark, chilled. The house was haunted. His tipsy brain rested. She was singing 'The Little Skillet Pot', a song his sisters had sung many years ago. She could sing a song all right. He'd always thought that.

Company after drinking was a thing dimly remembered from the past. He turned on the light. 'Missis!' he called at the foot of the stairs. 'Missis!' Rosanna appeared at the top of the stairs. 'Will ye come down for a cup of tea, Missis?' he said.

She came down the stairs very slowly, leaning heavily on the bannister. Her face was white and serious, the lines in it like cracks in china. She was frightening, like a ghost, and for a moment it occurred to him that she might really have died up there. He indicated that she should go through and sit down and wait while he made the tea, and when he brought it in she was sitting once more in his big chair by the range. He sat in an unaccustomed place, very stiff and straight-backed, and they drank their tea in silence for a while.

'Oh, the drinking of tea,' she said, smiling faintly, 'what a wonderful ceremony that is.'

He said nothing.

'I'll be gone tomorrow. I'm much better now. You've been ever so kind and I do appreciate it. I'm awfully sorry if I've been a nuisance.'

Padraic nodded. He took out his pipe and lit it. There was a long silence. The clock ticked.

'It's very quiet,' she said.

There was another long pause, then he cleared his throat. 'I have a radio,' he said.

'Oh, Padraic,' Rosanna smiled, 'where is it? Why don't you fetch it and we could see what's on.'

Padraic got up and went upstairs and came back with a small black transistor, which he placed on the sideboard. When he switched it on, some late night easy listening show was playing 'Moon River'. It made Rosanna smile, thinking of her and Clyde listening to 'The Rock Show' in the beach house.

She and Padraic listened intently, sipping their tea.

'Is anyone asking about me?' she asked. 'Down in the village?'

'No.'

She shrugged. 'How many were there?' she asked, 'living in this house?'

His blue eyes were milky, he scratched the white whiskers on his chin. 'Eleven. Eleven maybe.'

They listened to 'Laughter In The Rain' and 'Little Old Wine Drinker Me', then Rosanna said she had to go to bed. 'I'll be on my way tomorrow,' she said. She went upstairs quickly, stumbling a little.

Next day the same thing happened. He was helping Tommy Davy

with the hay and got his dinner over there, then in the afternoon went into Strangarvan with Con Mullen for one or two things. He had a long wait for Con coming back and drank quite a lot in Biddy O'Neill's. When he got back she called down the stairs: 'I'm on my way! I'm on my way, Padraic!'

It was four o'clock in the afternoon. He wanted his house back. He didn't know what to do. 'See that you are!' he called grimly and went out again. He did some work in the low field then wanted his tea and cursed her. He'd threaten her with the law. He swore repeatedly as he rode into Ballinaphuca, left his horse to graze on the pig run and went for a drink in Sylvester's. Clyde and Ger came in and he thought about getting Clyde to come and move her but couldn't bring himself to tell anyone she was there.

It was dark and he was well drunk by the time he got home. She was still there, hiding upstairs again. Panic overcame him. She had to go, now, at once. But first he went in and raked the turfs about in the range.

She came down anyway. 'I tried to go,' she said immediately in a frightened voice. 'I got just down the track a bit and my knees went funny. I had to sit down. I think I'll be all right tomorrow. I'm sure I will.'

She looked horrible, her hands shoved under her oxters as if she was very cold. 'Has anyone mentioned me?' she asked.

'You can't stay here! I've told you to go. You're well enough to get into town, you can get into town!'

'Yes,' she said. 'I'll pay you for what I've eaten. If you can just wait till . . .'

'You will get out now!' he scolded shrilly.

She looked so badly frightened he faltered. There was something not right about the woman. 'Has anyone asked about me?' she asked again.

'I've seen no one.'

'Haven't you been in the bar? Which bar were you in?' She seemed very nervous and suddenly he was sorry for her and for the way he'd shouted. He didn't answer but walked out. She was stuck here now for the night anyway and he fancied a drop himself, so he went and got out a bottle of brandy that he'd wisely put away from her on the first night in a locked cupboard upstairs. Good for the nerves. A small drop now might sort her out.

'One only,' he said when he came down, getting out the glasses and pouring.

This time she sat at the table. 'That's your chair, isn't it?' she said as he sat down in his old chair by the range, 'and I've been hogging it. I am sorry.'

The brandy was good. Padraic kept it by him and relaxed in his old chair. She sipped her drink. Sometimes he didn't think she was so bad. Tomorrow he'd send her on her way.

'This house has been a haven to me,' she said. 'I think I would have died, I really do.' She looked around, got up and went over to the sideboard with her drink. 'Where are they all now?' she asked, looking at the pictures.

He thought carefully. Sometimes he forgot who was dead and who alive. Two were in London, he said, one in Dublin, one in Vancouver.

'And what about these three?' She picked up a photograph of three smiling dark-haired girls.

'Dead,' he said.

'Are they your sisters? And who's this?' She turned to a broad-faced elderly lady. 'Is she the same as the one in the middle?'

'My sister, Dolores.'

'Ah, Dolores!' Rosanna said as if she'd known her. 'She has a nice face.'

Then she sang:

Did you ever eat colcannon made of lovely pickled cream,
Where the greens and scallions mingled like a picture in a dream,
And did you ever make a hole on top to hold the melting flake
Of the lovely creamy butter that your mother used to make?
Oh you did, so you did, so did he and so did I
And the more I think about it, sure, the nearer I'm to crying,
Oh, wasn't they the happy times, when sorrows we knew not,
And our mothers made colcannon in the little skillet pot.

His blood ran cold. She got the most out of the dawdling old tune, making it graceful and plaintive, so that the words took on a hue of every loss that had ever been lost. His sisters had sung this

227

song when he was a small child, the spoiled baby of a big family. He could not help it, his eyes filled up. Rosanna finished and there was a little silence.

He turned on the radio. They sat through 'Big Spender' and 'I Left My Heart In San Fransisco'. Then he poured her one more little drop. She smiled but her mouth was pale, almost blue. She started to fidget about and clench her teeth strangely, sang along fitfully with 'Send In The Clowns', then broke off and grinned horribly. 'I don't need a doctor,' she said tightly, 'this has nothing to do with the doctor. Oh, Padraic, I'm so sorry to have involved you in this but God sent you, you see, and there's nothing we can do about it. You're a good man, a Christian in the best sense of the word. I always liked you.' He was mortified. 'It's my hands,' she said, and her voice shook. 'I'm frightened, Padraic. I can feel the nails. I'm scared of pain. I can't stop it. What can I do? I don't think I can stand it.'

Padraic turned his face away, horrified. He shook. He could not be expected to bear this. She was mad. He'd get Deasy first thing.

'Do you know what it is?' she said. 'His nails echo through time like ghosts, and if you're susceptible they get you. They choose you, you can't do a thing about them. Like Cupid's dart.'

A feeling of nightmare came over him. He crossed himself. 'That's enough,' he said, rising, 'I'll take you myself in the cart tomorrow,' and staggered upstairs to hide the brandy away once more.

She was crying when he called her down next morning and said he'd take her to the village in the cart. She nodded and sat down to wait, a hopeless look about her.

'What's wrong?' he asked

She just shook her head.

This was ridiculous. He couldn't be seen with this crying woman in the back of the cart. He made her sit by the window to get the fresh air and brought her some breakfast. 'One more day,' she said. 'Please, Padraic, just one more day.'

'You have no sense,' he grumbled as he placed a cup before her, carefully correct with the spoon just so in the saucer. 'You're no better than a child. If you'd had more sense you wouldn't be as you are!' But he didn't say no.

39

Two days before the Fleadh, James and Helen awaited the arrival of Swan Mary. It was very hot. Helen decided to make some iced mint tea to calm herself down. The kids were driving her mad. They'd gone to a party at lunch time and Kes had thrown up all over the kitchen floor. Polly bitched at him:

'Ugh! Serves him right, doesn't it? He ate meat! Ugh!'

'Oh, shut up, Polly!'

'I'll sick it on you,' he mugged.

'What have you had?'

'Jelly and cake and a lollipop and sausage rolls and a cream egg and a green thing and . . .'

'Oh God,' whispered Helen.

'*I* didn't have any meat,' said Polly. '*I've* not been sick.'

'Oh, shut up, Polly.'

'That's enough, Poll,' said James, 'you're not perfect, you know.'

Helen got them changed and told them to get lost, then carried her iced tea outside and sat under the big sunshade on the lawn. Dundreen was ready. The new house on the cliff was large and white and low, with a broad verandah running round three sides, a pantiled roof and a conservatory. Before it lay an area of rockery and running water and alpine flowers; inside everything was cool apple green and creamy fawn, the furniture old and elegant and beautiful. Fresh flowers were everywhere. Helen breathed consciously: one–two–three in, one–two–three–four hold, one–two–three out. That felt better. She could smell the sea. She felt slightly proprietorial about the estuary and kept thinking with a kind of fear of all the people who would descend with tents on their land the day after tomorrow.

James came out and sat down with her. She wished he'd stop wandering about pretending to be so calm.

'I really don't know how I'm supposed to act when I meet her,' she said. 'I suppose it's a bit like meeting royalty or a famous film star.' James smiled seriously. He looked very pale and his coppery hair was ragged. She knew he was nervous because a coldsore was coming up on his lower lip. Good, she thought meanly.

'It'll be OK,' he said, 'I just don't understand your discomfort. She's really very nice. Very humorous. Quite ordinary, really. What are you expecting?'

'I don't know.' But she wriggled. There was this slight sense of dread. They sat and watched a gannet skim the air below them, wheeling and sailing. Two fishing boats stood far out upon the sea. 'Hope the food's all right,' she said.

'Of course it is.'

They watched the gannet's crooked dive as if it were a firework display then caught each other's eyes and started to laugh.

'Oh, look,' said James, excited. 'Would you say that was a dolphin? A dolphin! There, look.'

'Oh, look, there's another one!'

'Daddy.'

'Well, there's a good omen if ever I saw one!'

Helen laughed.

'Daddy.'

'What?'

'Oh, look at your shoes!' cried Helen. 'What have you been doing? I told you to stay clean.'

'Kester says it's all wet at the side of the house.'

'What's all wet? Look, Poll, dolphins!'

Polly ran yelling with delight down the lawn.

Kester approached circumspectly. 'Oh, Kester!' Helen groaned. 'Just look at your trousers! What did I tell you?'

'It's all muddy round the side of the house,' he said in an aggrieved tone, 'I told her to tell you.'

'What do you mean, all muddy? It hasn't rained for ages.'

'Well, there's a lot of water there now.'

'Where? Under the playroom?'

'Not our house, the new one. Where the men were working.'

'Shit!' James jumped up and ran in the direction of Swan Mary's house. In a moment he came running back, his face stricken. 'It's the drain,' he said, breathing hard, 'all silted up somehow. Turning into a bog. Someone's been running water in the bath and it's all filthy and they've been in the conservatory. What did I tell you two?'

Helen put her face in her hands.

'Kester! What did I tell you?'

'I don't know.'

'He was washing his skateboard,' said Polly.

'Oh, brilliant!' Helen jumped up and flung her cup down onto the lawn. 'We've only got one of the greatest spiritual leaders of the world arriving any minute and suddenly it's imperative that his skateboard gets a bath. You stupid child!'

Kester stuck out his lip.

'Tell him off, Mum,' said Polly.

James started to laugh.

'Well, go on then,' Helen said, 'get a shovel.' She liked things to go smoothly. 'You little swine, Kester.'

'Not to worry,' said James, looking worried, 'I'll go and ring round. The bathroom needs a bit of a once over, Helen.' He ran into the house. The kids mooched away. Why couldn't he just grab a spade and do it himself, she thought, irritated. He was useless at anything like that, probably make things worse. She sighed, looking down at her clean simple dress, modest though rather elegant and stylish, carefully chosen for the occasion, and thought about cleaning the bathroom.

After the third or fourth call, James was getting panicky. Of course they were all on Rossa with the turf, perfect day for it. He looked at his watch, ran outside and got in the car and drove quickly down the track to the lane and headed for Ballinaphuca. Someone must be about. He passed a couple of tourists who waved at him, then the latest batch of men at work on the Scheme, digging out the foundations for a small picnic area overlooking the sea just below Miley's Gap. Paddy Bawn raised a hand grudgingly, his face a startling puce. Just over the top the luck changed: there was the wide stooped back of Jackie Bat, there was old Rex pacing along by the hedge.

He rolled down the window, smiling up into Jackie's broad red face. 'Got an hour, Jackie?'

Jackie leaned in. 'All right, James, all right? Glorious weather, it is, glorious all right.'

Oh God, he thought, Irish time. 'It is, Jackie. Got an hour, have you?'

'Ah?'

James explained what had happened.

'Tis strange the drain is blocked,' said Jackie reflectively, and the thought occurred to James that in all probability it was something Jackie had or hadn't done that had caused it. After all, most of the other cock-ups along the way had been down to him. 'Look, there isn't much time,' he said.

'Aha.' Jackie nodded, shifting his weight and taking out his cigarettes. A trickle of sweat ran down one furrowed temple. 'I don't suppose the cattle have got in there, have they?'

'Of course not.'

Jackie tapped his cigarette upon the box. 'Tis strange,' he said again.

Eventually Jackie was in the car, his old dog stretched lordly along the back seat, dreadlocked tail all tangled with dried dung. James offered a fair sum as they sped back to Dundreen. 'Ah no,' said Jackie, who hated talking about money, but James insisted. He'd be glad of the money now the big job was finished. Then Jackie said something which James couldn't catch, in spite of having lived here for ten years.

It was probably a joke, so he laughed.

Jackie worked hard, digging steadily in the hot sun, redirecting water mysteriously, stopping occasionally to wipe sweat from his eyes. The blood came more and more to his face till it was slick and shiny like the red face of a child's devil in a book. He refused the iced tea but drank gallons of home-made lemonade that Helen brought to him at regular intervals.

She sat on the verandah of Swan Mary's house chatting to him as he worked, sipping her tea. She'd cleaned the bathroom and got changed into some of her nice old Indian clothes – to hell with fashion, they still felt good – with indigo scarves in her hair. Swan Mary wouldn't care what she wore anyway, what did it matter? She'd calmed down a lot. Rex leaned against her, panting ador-

ingly as she carefully and patiently untangled his mane and skilfully picked fat pink ticks off his eyelids. In a way she missed the
men and boys out here building, the noise and general fun of it,
the radio playing and the tools pounding or doing whatever tools
did. Nice to watch craftsmen at work. But not Jackie, he wasn't a
craftsman. Dear old Jackie. He smelt. Thick white woollen socks
could be seen folded over the tops of his enormous wellington
boots. It made her sweat to look at them.

'You mustn't stay away, Jackie,' she said suddenly, 'just because
the work's finished for now. You must pop in and see us, you
know, whenever you're passing.'

'Oh, I will, I will, that's nice,' he said. 'You'll have your hands
full over the weekend, I'd say? Ah?'

Up flew the shovel again and again. He was going at it heartily.

Rex scratched fiercely at a certain spot. 'Oh, poor boy!' said
Helen, kissing the dog's grey whiskered nose and the scarred,
scraggy, mobile bits above his closed, delirious eyes. She scratched
him vigorously and he shivered with joy. 'Yes. God knows how
many'll turn up. I feel a bit scared about it, Jackie, if you want to
know the truth. It's a bit like being hostess at some very important party.'

'It is that.'

She'd been going to say: you know how it is at parties, you're
always secretly glad when it's over. At least you are if you're the
hostess. But then she realised that Jackie had probably never been
to a party in his life, at least not the sort she meant. 'Thank God,'
she said, seeing that the job was nearly done. 'You've saved our
lives, Jackie, you really have.'

Jackie laughed. 'It'll be all right now,' he said cheerfully.

'Come to the kitchen when you're finished.' Helen stood up.
'Have a good sit down and a bite to eat before you go.' She
strolled off looking at her watch.

The mural was finished on the gable end of the main house
across the lawn. A subdued *Book of Kells* style border framed a single nebulous image, mother-of-pearl, that might have been a lily
or a cirrus cloud or a great silver wing, an angel's perhaps, or that
of a swan or a mythical flying horse. Thank God they weren't
early. She hated it when people were early. She went and turfed

the kids out of the television room. They'd watch hours of end-less crap if you let them. She wasn't having her kids illiterate and bug-eyed with an attention span of half a second. No, sirree.

Then she went into the kitchen.

The big sheep-dog began to bark and old Rex joined in hoarsely. Helen looked out of the window and saw a long slow black car like a hearse coming up the snaky track. 'Jesus Christ,' she said, 'they're early.'

James jumped up.

'This is it,' said Helen.

'Well, I'll be on my way.' Jackie drained his tea.

So it was that when they went out and stood in the gravelled space before the house to greet her, Jackie was with them, dirty and sweaty, wiping tea from his mouth. Helen smiled hysterically. It was better this way, just the two of them – three – not the whole bunch.

There were seven in the car. Another was following. Four of them would stay in the new house, the rest in the extension. A burly young man in jeans and bright T-shirt jumped out of the driving seat, nodded at them and began opening the car doors. People spilled out: a round bespectacled man who could have been a lawyer, two brisk elderly women in sensible clothes and a very tall, striking young woman in a gorgeous long black summer coat, who crooked her arm to the back seat and helped out Swan Mary.

It was unnerving. A dozen familiar photographs come to life, Swan Mary's face: serious, intelligent, possibly Asiatic, with high-bridged nose and eyes like an old Spaniel, mobile and liquid and full of tragedy. She was small as a child, very thin and fragile and rather hunched, with a grey shirt that reached her knees, grey trousers, white pumps on bony brown feet.

'Welcome to Montsalvat,' James said, holding out his hand.

She shook firmly, smiling sadly, hands smooth and small like a child's. 'Good afternoon,' she said quietly. Her voice was gender-less American, full of throat.

Introductions were made.

Swan Mary smiled at Jackie Bat.

'And this,' James said, 'is Jackie, who practically built the house you'll be staying in ...'

'Ah,' said Swan Mary, putting out her hand, 'the house that Jack built.'

Everyone laughed. Jackie dipped forward heavily, shooting out his grimy hand and shaking hers firmly. 'I'm very pleased to meet you, very pleased to meet you,' he said. 'Did you have a nice journey?' He was short of breath.

'Oh indeed I did,' she said, leaning towards him and holding onto his hand for a moment. 'This is my first time in Ireland, you know. It's very beautiful.'

'Oh, it is, it is. Did you come the north road or by Strangarvan?'

Swan Mary said she had no idea.

Her travelling companions wandered about the cars, looked at the view. James and Helen caught each other's eye and smiled. This was it, suddenly everything was OK because it had to be: Kester had washed his skateboard so that the blockage in the drain would be revealed, so that Jackie Bat would come and fix it, so that he would be here at precisely this moment to meet Swan Mary, who was early. Perfect. One for the archives. If only they could have got a picture of it.

'Well,' said Jackie, 'I'm off for my tea now.'

'Don't run off, Jackie,' Helen said softly.

But Jackie said he had a nice bit of boiled bacon waiting for him. 'Nice with cabbage,' he said.

Swan Mary was uncompromising on the subject of meat. It was wrong and that was that. But Swan Mary, of course, just smiled and said, 'I do hope you enjoy it,' with no trace of sarcasm. Helen looked at the two of them standing there and thought that this was very profound, the old order and the new. One had to make allowances. And then she realised that in her heart of hearts she had always felt that she was superior to Jackie, no, not superior, simply more highly evolved. No blame. He was not a barbarian because he ate his boiled bacon with his big rough hands. He was just a dying breed.

Jackie strode away with a wave, cheerfully declining a lift from James. A third car was approaching. Jackie lifted his hand in salute as it drove slowly past him, coming into the yard. Too late, James remembered he hadn't paid him. The car stopped and disgorged three men with beards, a villainous-looking boy and a motherly woman who smiled a lot.

Helen started to panic. There were so many of them.

40

Jackie soon wished he'd taken the lift. The road seemed longer than usual, the sun hotter. The shadow of Rex, drooling from the tongue, stumbled beside him. He kept mopping his brow, rubbing his lips, sucking at a constant catarrh that shifted about in the centre of his face. At the top of Miley's Gap he rested, sitting down on the wall at the side of the road, his heart hammering. When it had stopped he lit a cigarette and smoked it, watching the faraway boats in the bay; a nice little English tourist girl came by, out for a ride on a hired bike, and sat down and talked with him for a while. She said her grandfather was Irish, leaning over and petting the dog. This place was Paradise, she said, looking out over the sea.

'It is when the weather's fine,' said Jackie. 'Smoke?'

'Oh, yes please.'

It had been an interesting day. One thing you could say about the blow-ins, they brought a bit of life back to the old place.

'I live in Birmingham,' she said. 'My grandad came from Kildare. I love Ireland. I'd love to live here. I'd feel as if I'd died and gone to Heaven.'

She was all young and clean. Young tourist girls were always telling him these things. Summer brought them. The summer, breeding Paradise, lay all about them as they sat there peacefully on the wall smoking their cigarettes. It was nice the way the girls always told him these things. Jackie smiled, rubbing his neck. Then she picked up her bike and said she was going back to Strangarvan. 'I'll be down that hill in no time,' she called, waving as she sailed away.

The sea was silent, things hopped in the grass at the side of the road. Jackie sat on for a while then got up heavily. It was down-hill from here to his house, but as he walked he laboured, sweat-ing. Hu–hu–hu–hu–hu endlessly went the breath of old Rex, and his head drooped to the ground as if he were in shame. Jackie looked up to the high ridge that ran out to Anagar and remem-bered his sheep running up there. It could still bring tears to his eyes – the bloody dogs, the bloody dogs!

He'd worked hard and was very tired. The road ran on and on, up and down, till it took him home. He was so tired he went in and just sat down at the table where he could look out of the open back door at the dog lying across the stones, at the field of the crown where Davy Scanlon's cattle now grazed, and at the wide open sparkling sea of Caheradown Bay. A gunshot sounded somewhere in the hills. He was so tired he forgot that he hadn't eaten, forgot everything he was supposed to do and fell asleep for God knows how long, till someone crept up behind him and touched him on the nape of the neck.

Jackie jerked awake, startled. His heart exploded, shaking him, so that he touched his chest anxiously, but no, he was still all right, though he felt a little peculiar. He looked round slowly, over his shoulder, fearing a presence. But there was nothing there. 'Oh my God,' he whispered, panting, 'I am heartily sorry ...' he'd been out on the field of the crown, he was sure of it, but then he saw through the open door that the sky had turned purple while he wasn't looking.

Rex still lay with his head on his paws, his old closed eyes twitching, and a cloud of midges danced ... it was a beautiful summer evening, the sea glimmered, the evening star appeared over Caheradown Bay. Young people were passing in the lane. Rex opened his eyes, turning them up without lifting his head. Around the yard were tall, lusty foxgloves, growing out of the walls. Jackie remembered them, foxgloves from the past, remem-bered his family, wept a thin tear for his mother, the only woman he'd ever kissed, thought he saw day and night revolve over Caheradown Bay, the field of the crown full of sheep with their lambs. He thought he saw thousands of yards flicker upon this yard, every day of his life, passing and changing like the running man in those little books you flicked with your thumb.

He felt like company. He'd go to Tommy's tonight for a Lucozade. But he was very tired. Much too tired really to walk down there. A filament of fur entwined with another in some dark arterial night, and there was pain, killing, till everything stopped.

Rex looked up when he heard Jackie move, stirring himself with a long yawn. But Jackie just turned to the left, folded up tight like a great fist closing and released one deep, lingering breath. After that, he didn't move again.

41

'It's Father Leahy you must see if it's troubling you that much,' Padraic said again.

She'd been crying for two days and he was frightened. He didn't know what to do, couldn't possibly tell anyone now that the woman had been in his house for six days. He wished he'd never found her in the ditch, wished she'd go. That she was mad he had no doubt. In the night she called out 'Clyde!' and 'Jesus!' and 'Abraham!'

Rosanna lay back against the creamy old lace of the antimacassar. This nice old man was bringing her another cup of strong tea and she didn't want to leave him. Her face was all red and white and swollen. She wore a kind of long shapeless dress knocked up in an evening from a swathe of old curtain material she'd found all moth-eaten at the bottom of an old bedding chest.

'If you ate your dinner,' he said roughly, 'you'd feel better.'

'Tell me,' she said, 'have you ever thought of becoming a priest?'

'Will you shut your mouth now.' His finger wagged. 'You are not right in the head.'

She looked scared. 'I'm not, am I?' she said. 'What's wrong with me? Am I really that bad?'

'Of course you are. You're not like other people. Think what it would be like if they were all like you.'

That made her laugh, but she stopped and a spasm of pain

showed in her face. She fingered her sleeve. 'To think this used to hang in the windows.'

'It didn't.'

'It didn't?'

'No. At Inchicora. My sister lived there. It came back after she died.'

'Essie's place?'

'Inchicora.'

'Was it Dolores?'

'Nora.'

'Nora,' said Rosanna. 'This place is full of ghosts, isn't it?' She was pale and short of breath and started crying again. 'I have to go, don't I?' she said.

He nodded sharply and went out to bring the cattle down for the night.

She went up, one hand steadying herself against the wall, to what she thought of as Dolores' room, though this was only her fancy. She'd made it nice, a bunch of meadowsweet and purple loose -strife in an old milk jug on the windowsill, the window open to the fragrant mountain air. Upon the wall Jesus pointed to his Sacred Heart, his big dark eyes bruised, brown hair gently parting.

She lay face down on Dolores' bed and closed her eyes, praying for help against the pain in her hands, but it didn't go away, it swelled like a freak wave, unpredictable, impossible. 'Oh God,' she gasped, then couldn't speak because she couldn't breathe. She squirmed and drew everything in like a snail retracting under its shell, but the pain stretched her out again, a stake ran in her heart and she was pinioned. Rosanna stretched her body like a starfish then recoiled, clenching everything. Her eyes popped open. She was nowhere, she was dying. Roses bloomed before her eyes. The pain wiped her out and she died and went into a pale seamless place where Jesus came again. This time he was naked, torn like an old rag, all dark and sweaty and bloody, five great wounds weeping. He bowed down his head. The crown of thorns was on his brow, pushed down hard against the bone so that the long spines had scraped furrows and raised excrescences in the skin before finally lodging. He snapped her heart like a pencil. She heard the sound of a gunshot, distant.

When she came to, she was trying to rise from Dolores' bed, calling out incoherently as if rising from an anaesthetic. Up she swam. She saw the room, felt her body return to her, struggled to sit, looked down and saw that blood was streaming from her hands and staining the old quilt. She gawped stupidly. Her mouth opened wide, and a great, deep gasp, almost a yawn, burst from her. From one to the other she looked, disbelieving, faint, an imbecile child letting the mess get all over Dolores' faded red quilt. What would Padraic say?

Of course she was still asleep. She felt Jesus whispering in her heart, his lips tickling in the physical organ, telling her he loved her in spite of it all. She had to stem the blood. It ran frighteningly, pure, lovely red, with the calmness and constancy of a settled rain, soaking the old curtain she was wearing. Rosanna brought her poor, familiar, blood-blown hands towards her face and stared into them, afraid to touch the centres and find out what was there. She turned them and looked at the backs. In the middle of each was a small shock of broken veins that itched and throbbed angrily. Then she looked at the palms again, daring to touch, but the wounds were tender and wouldn't be probed.

She was stronger now. She got up and stood swaying. The pain persisted, less piercing than before but still dreadful. She went downstairs, walking slowly and very carefully, slumping along the walls with her shoulder because she didn't want to mess up the wallpaper. When she stood against the sink in the kitchen, blood ran over the cracked white enamel and down the plug-hole. She should be fainting from weakness. Of course, she was still asleep, this was not real. But the stones of the kitchen floor were real, the weave of the dishcloth, the bleating of a sheep on Rossa. She swallowed. The clicking of her throat, the shifting of her tongue was real.

He must keep something somewhere she could use as a bandage. Blood ran down her wrists as she reached up to open cupboard doors. At last she found some old cleanish dusters and made long pads of them and wrapped them around her hands. Then she went and sat down by the window, rocking slightly and breathing shallowly. She felt the blood run under the dusters, closed her eyes and set her lips. Jesus whispered.

It was dark outside when Padraic returned half an hour later. He stood looking in at the doorway, taking off his boots. All his fear of her returned. She was death's-head white and her eyes had darkened, staring at him too directly like a child's. He put on his slippers and approached her, frowning. There was a thin sweat on her forehead and her lips were very pale and dry, fading away at the edges. She spoke as if breathing was hard and gave an impression of fine quivering, as if she were the tip of a cat's whisker.

'I'm all right,' she said, steady-eyed and smiling faintly, 'don't worry, it'll be over soon, I'm sure. I'm not exactly the stuff of saints, am I?'

'What?' he croaked.

She unwrapped the dusters carefully, soaked through already, heavy with it, and showed him the wounds in her hands. Padraic knew at once what they were. She gave a quick disbelieving laugh, he crossed himself.

'I can't bear the pain,' she said.

He moved as though in a dream. 'Up,' he said, 'up.' He led her by the elbow to his own chair next to the range and made her sit there. Then he fetched clean lint and bandages and knelt on the floor to wrap up her hands.

'I got blood on your sister's bed,' she said breathlessly.

His hands trembled. Now he knew that this had gone on long enough: he would have to tell someone.

'I can't bear the pain,' she said again, but Jesus whispered in her heart, telling her he'd never go away again, and it was worth it for that.

42

Something was going on at Rathmeelabo. Father Leahy and Doctor Deasy were both up there till late into the night and again the next morning.

'Padraic OK, Father?' Barney Mac asked, catching the priest at the end of the village.

'He's grand, Barney,' Father Leahy replied. He didn't stop to talk.

Later in the morning Padraic came riding down to the village and left his horse on the pig run just as he always did. He stood in the shop with a dour expression and declined all conversation, which was nothing unusual. He bought two loaves of bread and a packet of tea and went home.

'You don't suppose he's got an incurable disease, do you?' Christy asked. They were all in Tommy Davy's. A Bob Marley tape was playing loudly on Tommy's expensive music centre.

The door opened and Davy Scanlon came in, his face stony. 'Turn that off, Tommy,' he said softly. 'Jackie's dead.'

'Jackie Bat?'

'Jackie?'

'Aye,' he said. Then his eyes flooded with tears and he brushed them away.

They crossed themselves.

Not until about four o'clock did word get out about Rosanna, as word always does. She might have been seen standing at the back door of Padraic's house by someone after sheep up Rossa, or it might have been the young guard who a day or two ago accepted without a word her dole form from Padraic's hands. But anyway, word got out that she was there. And now when everyone thought about it, it seemed ages since she'd last been seen. Had she been there all this time? Rosanna and Padraic? *Padraic?*

It was a relief in a way. It gave them something to take their minds off poor Jackie lying up there in the house all night with his old dog beside him and the door wide open. Padraic? they said. The dirty old dog! And they laughed about it and shook their heads in Tommy Davy's.

That night Dan Hogan wandered away from the village where he'd been drinking and started on his rounds. He did the back road first, standing in the Mullens' back yard for a while and

242

watching Marie doing something at the sink, then passing on along the lane towards the light of the grotto. Something was going on at Rathmeelabo. He turned his face towards the darkness of Rossa and followed the lane along its twisting way till ruins appeared, then the lights of Padraic's house. He went down the gravel track and came up to the house and tried to look in the windows but the curtains were drawn tightly across, so he went round the back. There was a good chink, a fine generous chink, and he looked in: the mad woman was sitting on a chair with Padraic kneeling before her unbinding a thick bandage, all rusty red, from one of her hands. She was white like a corpse and smiling. The hand, revealed, was covered in blood. She gazed down into it, smiling still. Then Padraic unbound the other hand, till at last both lay palm-upwards on her lap. Rosanna and Padraic just stared and stared at the blood which, even from here, could be seen to be flowing, streaming, rising steadily as if from a spring. New dressings lay in a paper on the floor. It was starting to get dark. The blood, running and running, frightened him and he ran away.

Much later he came lurching into Tommy Davy's and sat down by the fire, shuddering and mumbling, crossing and recrossing himself.

'What's the matter, Dan?' asked Christy, going to sit opposite him. 'Jesus, man, you look as if you've seen a ghost.'

Dan looked sulky and affronted, staring at the fire. Tommy came out from behind the bar and sat down too, looking at him closely. There were a few tourists in, watching with interest but trying to look as if they weren't.

Dan held out his hands and shook them. 'Blood,' he said.

Christy and Tommy looked at one another. From the back room came the soft intermittent sound of snooker balls hitting off each other. 'Dan,' said Tommy quietly, motioning with his head, 'come on in the back.'

Dan got up with a sudden movement and blundered, head down, into the back room. Tommy and Christy followed.

43

Marie had done her eyes and tied back her hair and was waiting for the sound of Tommy Davy's horn at the gate. He was taking her into town for the noon Sprinter into Rossgarry to catch the Cork bus. She hadn't slept. She kept forgetting what she was going for, that this was the end.

Con had come in from the field in a foul mood, saying he was coming down with a cold. That was good. Easier to leave. He was angry because she was off to Cork for the day for the sale. She was amazed at her hardness. This was nothing, she could leave them all ten times a day and not feel a thing, all you did was just that, not feel. It was easy, you put it in a bag and put it out there, away from you, as she'd done with her fear on her one flight to London. After all, what's the point? Can't stop it now.

They were out there, all of them, arguing as usual. Julia was going to something at Dundreen this afternoon, and Simon was full of all this rubbish about Rosanna. Marie went and stood in the kitchen doorway, folding her arms and listening seriously.

'Oh, for Christ's sake, Marie,' said Con, 'don't look like that. It's not the Second Coming, you know.' He blew his nose furiously and scowled at the tissue.

'Of course it's not,' she said. 'She's done it herself. Sure, I always knew she was going mad.'

'Poor woman,' said Con. He fell back into his chair. 'Are you making the tea, Marie?'

Marie didn't move. The phone rang and she answered it. It was Felicity to say she'd pick Julia up about two. Julia received the message with a nod, standing at the mirror and gently back-combing her hair.

'Are George and Essie not going up?' Marie asked.

'No. George has been going round slagging off Swan Mary.'

'Swan Bloody Mary,' said Con.

Julia sighed. 'Intolerance, I hate it,' she said proudly. 'You wouldn't like it if I laughed at your beliefs, would you?'

'You do,' said Con, laughing.

'Yes, *you're* intolerant, Julia,' Marie joined in.

'No, I'm not.'

'Yes, you are.'

'I'm not.'

'For Christ's sake, make the tea,' said Con.

Marie went in and made the tea. For the last time, she thought, the greasy old kettle, the brown teapot, the view out of the window. Simon followed and got himself a cracker and stood eating it. His arms were slim and tanned, the sun had turned the hairs on them golden.

'They were all going on,' Julia was saying, 'about superstition and hysteria and ...'

'What do they know?' snorted Con. 'Bunch of bloody heathens. Sure, don't they worship any old thing going? What about Ballinspittle? Mass hallucination, they said. They'd say that if the Holy Mother Herself came down on top of Rossa. Ger Sheehan was at Ballinspittle and he saw the statue move with his own eyes. Everyone did, Protestants and all. For Christ's sake, I'm dying for a cup of tea!'

Marie stood waiting for the kettle to boil. They were not so bad, Con and Julia and Simon. Simon smiled at her as he chewed. He was the one, the only one she could not leave. He raised his eyes and gave a little tut. How often this look had passed between them. Look away, she thought, don't look at me today. She couldn't remember Bob Sawle's face. Not at all. Wasn't that funny? But she still had to go, there was a reason, though she couldn't remember what it was. She took in the tea and poured it out.

'Well,' said Julia, turning from the mirror, 'I suppose everyone's entitled to an opinion.'

Con cleared his throat crudely. 'They are not,' he said, holding a hand out for his tea.

Julia made faces. Con laughed.

'I'm thinking for myself,' she said. 'You can't stand that, can you? I'm enquiring. It may sound stupid to you but what you believe in sounds stupid to me.'

Marie lit a cigarette. Did they have to argue these things during her last hour? If they knew ... She inhaled. Back and forth, back and forth the argument went. There was a hollow ring to it all, though each of them was very sure. What did it matter? Julia still went to Mass, things went on.

'Can we not just agree to differ?' asked Julia.

Con slammed his cup down, got up and went out into the yard, coughing ostentatiously. His eyes were watery and his nose was turning red.

Julia gave her mother a long, hard look. 'You are one of those voices,' she said, 'that's always saying negative things in my inner brain. It's always you.'

Marie laughed. 'I thought we were supposed to be on the same side.'

'What are you getting in Cork?'

'A pair of boots. You won't forget the pudding, will you?'

'Not at all. We can manage without you, you know.'

'And if you can bring the laundry down . . .'

'I will.'

Marie smiled and got up and hugged Julia awkwardly, surprising her. 'I know you can,' she said. A horn sounded at the gate. Marie took her big shopping bag from by the door and stepped out. Julia went after, lounging on the step in her best jeans and black sweatshirt. Her hair was getting longer, nearly down to her shoulders now, and it hung all over her eyes so that she kept having to fling it back with a dainty movement. She was so beautiful, Marie thought, not just because she was her daughter, but there was something about her as if she knew exactly how to move, how to shift her eyes about, everything, a great sense of her own presence. She'd be all right.

The rim of Rossa was a bright blue line against the sky. She waved to Tommy and started down the path. Con stood spitting phlegm out of the shed door. He looked at her but didn't smile. Why should he? It was as if he knew. No sign of Simon – a sudden stab in the heart – for the best, for the best. I've done it, thought Marie, I've broken the family. I'm a wrecker. The decay of society and all that, that's me.

44

Strangarvan was crowded. They were putting up bunting and fairylights for the Fleadh. Clyde stood in the bright sun outside O'Leary's with his drink, watching the people go by. The peak of his new cap shaded his small pale face. He was sweating a lot these days and wondered vaguely if he'd picked something up that last time in Vigo. Christ! he thought, and shuddered. You never knew these days. He saw Marie coming down the street on the other side and sharpened up, wondering if Julia was about. Seemed as if he went around forever looking out for her from the corner of one eye. He kept having these fantasies where she sucked him off in a field of corn at gunpoint. He stored it up in his mind as something that might happen for real one day if he ever decided to leave this place for good. After all, it wouldn't be as if he'd hurt her.

Marie walked into the square and got on the old red bus that was parked by the cross.

And after all, he thought, what was there to stay around here for, really? Handy for the boats. He had money to jingle in his pockets right now. But then he could go up to Killybegs or somewhere, or back to England or ... A new name again. Back on the road. Yeah. But it was OK here. People knew him, the guards weren't too bad. If only Rosanna wasn't around it wouldn't be so bad, mad bitch, he thought, what's this latest crap of hers? Could get rid of her really easily, take her out to Anagar and push her off the cliff. Simple. Accident. It's the wounds of Christ, says Barney Mac, that's why Father Leahy was up there. Wounds of Christ? Wounds of Christ? says Ger. On her? Jesus. Christ must be hard up! And everyone laughed. What was she up to? Wounds of Christ. Superstitious dread washed over him, cold in the hot sun, but he shook it off. She looked mad that night, standing on the wall singing hymns. And then in a way, he thought, it might have been me that brought it on, giving her that kick like I did, set her off on something, sent her over the top, so now if she's got some sort of religious thing it's down to me. That struck him as funny.

But he wouldn't kill Rosanna. Poor old cow. He knew her too well to kill her. He could kill a stranger, no problem. Just do it and don't think, like a Mafia hitman. Businesslike, no problem. Or someone he hated. Could easily have killed Stephen. Could've killed Bob Sawle, come to think of it.

The clock struck noon. The people on the bus, mostly old women and tourists, sat looking out of the windows. Marie had taken a little mirror out of her bag and was looking at her face in it. The driver of the bus climbed aboard and took off his jacket, wiped his big red sweating face, started the engine and let it idle while he wrote something in his little book.

And Clyde drifted back to Julia as he always did, into another little scene where she came to him quite willingly, in fact couldn't help herself. He wandered away to the harbour dreaming it, staring into the dazzling blue sky, and she just couldn't help herself, she was all over him with those big dark lips. Swans nuzzled the oily water in the bows of a fishing boat. Clyde heard in his mind the chords from *Paris Texas*; they rippled across the sky, which should have been sunset but wasn't.

45

'Away with you,' Padraic said, standing in the doorway, impassable.

It was Mike Pads and Tim Pat Malachi, fresh from the bar. 'Is she all right, Padraic?' Tim Pat asked jovially. 'Look here. We brought her a few flowers. Put them in her bedroom and she can look at them.'

'I'll give her the flowers,' Padraic said brusquely, holding out his hand.

'Aw, go on, Padraic.' Tim Pat stepped forward. 'Can't we just say hello? Kind of pay our respects, like?'

'She's not well,' Padraic replied. 'She's not to be seen. Away now.'

'Is it true, Padraic?'

'Is what true?'

'That she's, you know, bleeding?'

Padraic's mouth clamped shut.

'From the palms,' Mike added.

'Away with you!' Padraic was red with anger. 'She's ill. You've been told and that's the end of it.'

'Ah, come on, Padraic!'

Padraic shut the door and stood in the hall looking down at the flowers in his hand.

After a while she called down the stairs: 'Padraic? Padraic?' He sighed. She appeared at the top of the stairs. 'You won't let anyone in, will you? I'm scared to sit downstairs.'

Padraic locked the door and went in and drew all the curtains across at the front of the house. She came down. 'Sit,' he said, and went out and came back with a great wad of lint and a bottle of TCP and some of the bandages Doctor Deasy had left.

'I don't understand what's happening.' She sat bundled up by the range as if she were cold, her bandaged hands together, protective of one another. Her teeth were chattering a little and she seemed to be in great pain. 'They know, don't they? How do they know? I just wanted peace and quiet and now they won't leave me alone, will they? What am I supposed to do? I don't understand what's happening.'

Padraic sat down opposite and laid out the bandages on top of the range. He believes in it, she thought. He absolutely does.

'Come on, come on,' he said as if she were one of his animals, and she held out her hands, palm upwards, and let him unbind one of them carefully. The blood emerged.

'It's eased off a bit,' she said. The wound looked ragged and angry, active.

Padraic gave a deep sigh and started swabbing it very gently with TCP. She gritted her teeth. He did it briskly and efficiently, applied wads of lint and bound it back up with clean bandages. Then the other one.

'When I'm better,' she said, 'I'll cook you a meal the like of which you have never had in all your life.' She winced.

'Sorry,' he said.

They were done. 'Thank you, Padraic,' she said and sat back in the chair weak with the pain, which was unbearable, absolutely unbearable, but she was bearing it anyway. The look in her eyes was fixed, unblinking, and gave her an appearance of innocence or stupidity.

There was no doubting the pain. Padraic patted her hand once briefly.

46

Heat beat through the window of the bus. Marie sweated. Half an hour had passed and they were still sitting there in the square while the driver and another man messed about with the engine. A woman called Joan Sullivan was sitting in front, sticking her elbow on the back of Marie's seat and turning round to make conversation with her.

'Typical,' Joan said. 'Are you for Cork, Marie?'

'Yes.'

'Oh, you'll make it. The other bus'll wait. I'm only for Rossgarry myself, so it doesn't really matter for me.'

Marie smiled. She'd have been all right if it hadn't been for the delay but now her heart had begun to beat sickeningly. She wished she was alone. She needed peace to work on Bob like a picture she was drawing in her mind, trying to make him real again. It was so long since she'd seen him. His image had vanished. She smiled broadly at Joan, fighting an awful desire to laugh. All this time he'd been stuck in her mind like a growth and now that it really mattered, he'd gone. What was she running away to? A ghost? Behind the shield of her big shopping bag, skilfully packed with essential clothing and toiletries and one or two things she could not bear to leave – some photographs, her father's pipe, the children's first shoes – she moved her hand and touched herself down there. It was something to do with that. Touching it brought him back. Yes, she thought, and remembered what she was going for. Love and happiness.

'No, it's true, we all saw them. Moving lights on the side of Rossa ...'

They were not talking to her.

'I myself saw them,' someone else added.

Omens. Her heart pounded. God was here in the valley looking at her.

'Going in for something special, Marie?'

'Shopping,' Marie said, and smiled.

The driver got on and said jovially, 'We're off!' Everyone cheered. Joan took her arm off the back of the seat, faced forward and got comfortable as if she was settling down for a film. Marie sighed, leaning her head against the window. So she'd get there after all. Would he wait if she were late? Then another thought: what if he didn't turn up? After all, there'd only been one brief note in two weeks, just to say he'd be there. What if she waited and he didn't come, and then they'd find ... too late she remembered she hadn't left the letters. One for each of them, telling the kids they could come and stay with her, saying sorry to Con. They were still stuck at the back of her underwear drawer. God, how stupid. The bus shuddered and started, rolled out of the square. Enough. It's decided. She stared amazed at the street going by, the faces she knew, the boats in Strangarvan harbour, the green mountains. She could still get off. It was too hot, she could say she felt sick. Go home. Make Con's dinner. Poor soul, he was a baby when he had a cold. He'd give Julia hell.

'Anyway, Father Leahy's keeping out of it all right. He's saying nothing. Mike Pads went right up to him and asked him straight out. "Father, what's going on?" says he. "There's a lot of talk, you realise." "Michael," says he, "the world's full of talk. The woman is ill, she's under the doctor. That's all there is to it."'

47

A knocking at the door: 'Rosanna! Rosanna!' Ger Sheehan's voice.

Rosanna looked up from her chair by the range, where she had been sitting in silence for an hour, lifting the dressings carefully from time to time to check on the wounds. The bleeding had all but stopped but they remained like squashed berries in the middle of her palms. Padraic had ridden over Rossa to get the horse shod and she was alone in the house, the curtains drawn, the doors locked.

'A message from Clyde!' called Ger.

Rosanna closed her eyes and rested her head against the back of the chair. Sly one, she thought.

'Are you in there, Rosanna?'

She smiled.

'Rosanna!' Tap, tap, tap. 'Can I just have a word? Hey, we're all worrying about you.'

Rosanna sat forward, reaching for a pair of large fingerless gloves that lay upon the range. It was agony manoeuvring them on over the bandages.

'They're all asking after you, Rosanna,' Ger called. 'Clyde's asking after you.'

She got up slowly and went to the door, unlocked and opened it and let Ger in. He looked first at her gloved hands, then her face, curiously and with slight embarrassment.

'Hello, Ger,' she said, going back to her chair. 'What is it you want?'

Ger did not sit down but stood about the place awkwardly with his hands in his pockets. 'Is it true?' he asked. 'Is it true? Go on, Rosanna, you can tell me, sure you can.'

'Oh, it's true,' she said.

Ger stooped and came close, staring into her face. He thought she looked not altogether there.

Slowly, smiling, she peeled off the gloves, unwound the bandage from her right hand, unwound the bandage from her left, propelled her palms into his face till they almost touched his cheeks. His sharp eyes darted from one to the other.

'Tell Clyde,' she said. 'Just tell him what you saw.'

As he watched, a new bead of blood welled slowly from the centre of the wound in the right hand.

'Jesus!' he whispered.

48

'Are you all right, Marie? You look as if you've seen a ghost.'

'I'm OK,' she said. 'Too hot, isn't it?'

Up and down, up and down they bumped, the old bus rattling and gargling. The back of the driver's neck was purple. Marie closed her eyes. She tried to see the future but it was impossible, like trying to imagine dying. The bus was limbo. She yawned.

After what seemed like ages the bus slowed down and she opened her eyes. They'd just passed a townland, an affair of three or four houses, no more. Some demented old woman with wispy grey hair was flagging the bus down. The driver stopped and let her on and she sat mumbling and moaning to herself in the front. It grew hotter still and they crawled on and up, on and up, the bus straining like an old horse pulling a wagon. The old woman turned and slid her disapproving eyes over the people on the bus, lingering on Marie. Marie stared insolently back. The road evened out, they gathered speed and the woman turned away, muttering peevishly. They sailed down the hill.

A few miles further on the old woman demanded that the bus be stopped. Grumbling and groaning, she clambered out and wandered distractedly up and down at the side of the road. The people on the bus watched her. She fell down and got up again. There was no village near, no farm, only shoulders of mountain, grassland sloping to the sea, hedges of old fuchsia. The driver cut off the engine, got out of the cab and went after her. They saw him take her elbow and speak gently to her, leading her back to the bus.

Marie looked at her watch. Con had bought it for her years ago in Dublin.

'What time's the Cork bus?' someone asked.

'Will we make it, d'ye think?'

'Oh, sure.'

The driver helped the confused old woman back to her seat, where she sat staring out of the window and talking to herself. Then he got back in the cab and tried to start the engine, but it just coughed hoarsely.

They shifted about in the heat while the leather on the seats burned and the engine tried and failed miserably, again and again and again.

'Give it some choke,' someone advised.

The driver shook his head sadly, got out and looked in the engine. A couple of men got out and joined him. The tone of their voices was not encouraging. God didn't want her to go, everything was telling her that. She hated this bus, hated it. If she'd had a knife she'd have slashed it to pieces.

'Sorry, folks,' the driver said with a slight shrug of the shoulders, appearing on the steps, 'I think that's it.' He took out a big white handkerchief and mopped his brow. 'I'd get out and stretch your legs a bit, if I were you,' he went on kindly, 'I'll walk on into Ballybrack and get them to send another bus. Anyone for Cork here?'

'Marie. Marie's for Cork,' Joan Sullivan said loudly.

A few others said they were, too.

'Well,' he said, his face implying it was hopeless, 'I'll ring through and see if I can get them to wait a bit.'

Then he left, plodding wearily down the shimmering lane.

They all sat waiting for another bus to come. Some got out and walked about. The old woman was silent now. No need for her to say any more, her task was done. Marie stared at the back of her head, ill-wishing her. After half an hour, she knew she'd never make Cork today. She felt nothing, peculiarly drained as if she'd just had a good cry.

An old maroon bus with green curtains at the windows pulled up, heading back towards Strangarvan and Ballinaphuca. It was that hippy lot, the one with the wild blond hair was driving. He stuck his head out and said if anyone wanted to turn back and go with him, they were welcome. Three or four took up the offer and Marie found herself with them. The seats had all been taken out in the bus and it was like the inside of a caravan, full of dogs and children, little wild things who'd been gutting rabbits since the age of two. She sat on a kind of a bench with Joan Sullivan.

'Oh well,' Joan said, 'so much for that. Doesn't it just make you want to spit, Marie?'

'It does,' Marie agreed.

When she got home, Con was there alone. He said not a word about her wasted trip, her weariness, her obvious disappointment, just sniffed and snorted and moaned about his cold.

She went into the kitchen and made a cup of tea. She saw Bob walking into the Savoy, looking around, sitting down with a drink and waiting. What would he do when she didn't turn up? What would he think? She'd have to write to him and explain, tell him it was over. Funny that, soon as she knew it was all over he was back in her mind again, clear as ever.

After a while Julia came in. 'I did the laundry,' she said in a defiant tone, standing there in the doorway and looking strangely at Marie. She knows, she knows, Marie thought, then: impossible, how can she know?

'OK,' she said as Julia just went on staring at her in that way. 'What are you looking at?'

Julia flounced out and went up to her room. Then Simon came in and turned on the TV and lay down on the sofa with his feet up on the range.

Marie looked out at the familiar line of Rossa as she peeled potatoes for their tea.

49

'That's what I hate about the Roman Catholic religion,' Ulrica said. 'This awful dwelling on pain and horror. It's so negative.'

A group of them sprawled on the back steps at Montsalvat. Swan Mary had gone for a walk along the cliff path with James. Brendan, who'd had a vision, perched atop an upturned painted barrel, playing a flute, the same three or four notes over and over again. His long yellow hair hung over his fingers.

'Of course, that's why Rosanna's into it,' said Ben, 'all that misery. Right up her street, this kind of thing, self-mutilation and all that.'

George, who had not been invited but who'd turned up anyway, sat cross-legged on the lawn a short distance away, alone, picking his nose in a damn-you-all kind of way, grinning and squinting towards the glare on the sea. He wore dusty baggy old clothes and his hair was dirty and tangled.

'The idea of Rosanna as a holy woman ...' Julia said.

There was laughter.

'Actually, though,' said Feargal, 'when you come to think of it, I can sort of picture her in a wimple, you know. I can see her being very harsh and a bit frightening the way some nuns are. You know the type.'

'God, yes, we had this horrible one,' Felicity said, 'Sister Mary Francis. For Maths. I hated her, she had eyes like a goat ...'

'It's like cutting your wrists,' said Chuck, 'a cry for attention.'

'You're all wrong,' said George, standing up. 'Julia, what's the matter with you these days?'

Julia blushed.

'Poor old bloody Padraic,' Feargal laughed.

'I bet she's got him under some kind of spell,' said Ulrica. 'There always was something witchy about Rosanna.'

'Twaddle,' said Felicity, 'there's nothing at all supernatural about it. It's all desperately sordid if you ask me.'

'Precisely.' Feargal nodded with a knowing frown.

George hopped from foot to foot like a little boy dying to go to the toilet. 'Precisely what?' he cried. 'What's the matter with you lot? Look at you all. Have you looked recently? You're looking down your noses at me, I can see what you're thinking. Why hasn't he had a wash? Why hasn't he changed? Look at you all in your casual cleanest best. I am the only real person among you. Listen to me. You don't need a guru, you saps. Look, any fool can converse with Jesus and Buddha and all that, I do it all the time. It's easy. When are you going to claw the cobwebs away?'

'Oh, come on, George. All that unwashed stuff went out with the ark,' said Felicity.

'Fashion!' cried George. 'Oh, you slaves of fashion!'

'What do you think, Vincent?' Julia asked Vincent the artist, who'd just appeared on the steps.

'About what?'

'This Rosanna business.'

'All I know,' he said ruefully, 'is that she nicked my last little drop of booze from me.'

Everyone laughed apart from George. Vincent was jealous because Essie was doing well and he never came up to Inchicora these days.

'Have you ever seen those horrible pictures?' Felicity said. 'Old nuns with blood pouring down their faces.' She shuddered. 'Disgusting.'

'Primitive,' said Ulrica.

The sound of the flute's three or four notes ceased suddenly and everybody noticed it for the first time.

'Julia, man,' George blurted into the silence with tears starting from his eyes, 'I was a little bit in love with you, you know.'

Julia cringed.

'*You've* got to tell Essie. You wouldn't believe it, my old Essie getting wound up by all those stupid stupid things like jealousy. She won't speak to me now 'cos I told her that. So what happened to honesty? Ha?'

There was a short embarrassed silence.

'George,' said Julia. 'This is nothing to do with me.'

George laughed and slapped his forehead. 'Pshew! She says that!'

'George,' said Feargal, 'this is embarrassing Julia.'

Helen came out on the steps and sat down with her face between her hands. Old Rex padded after and leaned against her, a look of imbecilic devotion on his face. She looked as if she'd been crying. 'George,' she said warningly, 'you're not going to spoil things for us, are you?'

George laughed again. 'How can the truth spoil anything?' he asked, then just stared at her.

She read his mind. After all the work he'd done on the house, he was thinking, all the money he'd spent on the flotation tank, the flowers he'd provided. Not even an invitation.

A small procession was coming up from the cliff path, Swan Mary and James walking slowly and thoughtfully and giving an impression of some deep conversation just completed. Behind them, two by two, came half a dozen of the entourage. There was a subtle coming to attention among the people upon the steps.

Swan Mary wore a long white cotton dress and a big-brimmed straw hat that shadowed her face. James looked a little drawn. Helen came down the steps. 'Lunch is ready,' she announced, smiling brightly.

'Hey, Swan Mary,' said George, butting in familiarly, 'we've just been talking about this appearance of the stigmata in our midst. What do you make of a thing like that?'

She seemed very tiny and frail today, like a thin grey spider, and her hunch was more pronounced. 'Ah yes,' she said, smiling faintly, 'James was telling me about it. Fascinating.' All her movements drew their eyes, even the most minute. 'Well, I don't know,' she said, and chuckled softly. 'Not all stigmata are divine, but most of them are real.'

'What do you mean by real?' asked Julia bravely. Swan Mary had noticed her, she knew. She always got to sit near her.

Swan Mary laughed and smiled pleasantly at her. She had a wonderful laugh, very free and natural but quite refined. 'Real,' she said, 'is rather a large word.' Everyone waited for her to go on but she seemed to lose track of what she'd been saying, taking off her hat and fanning herself with the big straw brim. No words came.

And then George did a terrible thing. 'Speak! Speak, oh, mighty one!' he implored, and giggled, turning to the people around him for approval, like a child. It was horribly embarrassing and no one knew what to say.

Swan Mary handled it like a pro, turning a calm steady look upon him. 'If you would like to know whether your friend is to join the ranks of St Francis of Assisi and the priest of the Gargano, you must go and see for yourself,' she said.

'Know your stuff, don't you?' he replied, jogging from foot to foot.

'Of course I do,' she laughed, and everybody joined in the laugh, relieved.

George ploughed on. 'I just wanted to know,' he said, 'what you think about it all. This Rosanna, you see, we all know her and she is not – ha ha – she is not what you'd call the type.'

'You know her, do you?' Swan Mary said sharply. 'That is an error. Know yourself before you presume to know another human being.'

George giggled. 'See, it's how you *say* it that's all-important,' he told the little crowd cheerfully. He threw out one arm and declaimed like Mark Antony stirring up the Romans: 'Know thyself!' Then, assuming an idiotic stance, switched to a fast Donald Duck adenoid: 'Hey man, you've got to know yourself!' He roared with laughter. 'Same thing, see? Same thing exactly, man, only different delivery, see?'

The awful thing was, it was funny. Swan Mary laughed. Everyone else laughed, too. Then Swan Mary was serious again. 'I knew a man who received the Crown of Thorns,' she said, addressing George alone, 'and the wound in the side from the spear that pierced Jesus Christ. It really is irrelevant to me whether you call it hysteria or religious experience. We must not underestimate. It is an extremely painful process and I am certain the woman has suffered greatly.'

George just nodded and smiled.

Then James offered his arm to Swan Mary and led her into the cool of the house. The others followed in their ranks. Helen was shaking slightly; the catering was getting to her. George did not go in, nor did Brendan, who put the flute to his lips and blew softly again, same old thing.

'Hey, have you noticed,' said George, glancing in at the back door, 'it's always the same ones that get to sit next to her? Julia and Feargal and James and Helen. And all the others are really pissed about it.' He sat down again on the steps, fingering an imaginary flute along with Brendan. After a while he drew a little leather purse out from somewhere and took out a small photograph. 'Me and my old friend, Joe,' he said affably, edging over and showing it to Brendan, like a soldier in the trenches showing a picture of his wife and kids to a comrade. Brendan went on playing the flute.

'See that?' George said. 'That there behind us is the window of our room in Pandharpur. And that, hey, that's Joe's old Tarot deck. No kidding, man, that old Tarot deck was alive. A card would just jump out at you without you doing anything. Weird. Course, he'd had it for years. Those old cards were so well used they were twice their original thickness.' He sighed. 'God knows what he's doing now.'

Brendan smiled as he played.

George put the picture away and gazed at the sea for a while. Then he got up and crossed the lawn and went walking alone along the cliff path in the other direction, towards the camp-site that had sprung up over a ridge in the land. Tonight when it got dark there would be camp-fires, guitars, camaraderie. He'd stay there with the people. Essie should be here, she would have loved it once.

50

Essie came to visit in the early evening. First she had to face Padraic, who looked her up and down with a faint sneer and left her standing on the step while he went in to consult with Rosanna. After a minute or so he returned and nodded her in, then stamped away and busied himself in one of the sheds at the back of the house.

She breezed in like a hospital visitor, bearing an armload of flowers from George's garden. Rosanna was sitting by the range. 'Rosanna,' she said, 'oh, Rosanna, Rosanna, what have you been up to? You look, you look, lovely! Really lovely! What a lovely dress! Is it a dress? What is it? You look, different. Are you all right?'

'I'm fine.'

'I'll just put these in water.' She went into the kitchen and looked about for something to put them in. God, she thought, what is this? Of course, she'd taken in at once the bulky gloved hands, the pale stubby fingers protruding, the pallor.

She'd never been inside Padraic's house before. Who had? She looked all around curiously. Poor old soul, she thought, poor old soul. He's bitten off more than he can chew.

'So how are you?' she asked, returning. 'Can I use this? Will Padraic mind?' She placed the flowers on the table and flounced them about with her fingers, then drew up a chair and stared into Rosanna's eyes. Different, yes, different. Rosanna's pale blue eyes looked back at her, guileless. 'What is it, Rosanna?' she asked seriously.

Rosanna gave a little laugh. 'These,' she said, turning up her hands with a slight shrug. Essie didn't know what to say. 'I thought you'd have been up at Dundreen,' Rosanna said.

Essie laughed. 'Not invited,' she said. 'Neither was George but he went anyway. Poor old George. I don't know, I'm getting fed up with all that stuff, I just want to get on with my work now. I've got another show coming up and there are these people from RTE coming.' She paused and sighed. 'Oh, I'll go along tomorrow, I suppose, see what she's like. Reel in George. I've been giving him a hard time but he deserves it. Oh well.' She smiled. 'So how do you feel?'

Rosanna just smiled.

Playing on the mystery, Essie thought. 'I went to the funeral yesterday,' she said. 'Padraic looked wonderful, carrying the coffin. He was at the front with Barney Mac. Round the graveyard the way they do, you know, and all the old boys there following on. I wonder how they feel? I wonder ... can't help feeling we're in at the end of something. Jackie's house will be all closed up now, I suppose. Sold. Probably to foreigners. Davy doesn't own the house, does he?'

'No. There are brothers and sisters somewhere. I suppose they'll have some say in it.'

'Yes. It's a lovely house. Have you been inside? And that view! Is there anything you want, Rosanna? Is there anything I can get you? You're so pale!'

'No. No. Nothing.' But Rosanna had closed her eyes and seemed to be in pain. Her eyelids fluttered and her throat convulsed. 'I wanted Clyde to know,' she said with difficulty, 'that this is real. That's all. The birds were singing all night. A wild puck came down from Rossa and looked in at the window. All these things are signs.'

'Signs of what?'

'Signs that Jesus is actually here now, in the valley. That God is in the valley.' Rosanna drew in her breath sharply, moaning a little.

Essie felt afraid. 'Is it terribly painful?' she asked.

Beads of sweat appeared on Rosanna's forehead. 'I feel it in my hands and feet and heart,' she said, 'but the physical wounds are only in my hands. It's not bad at the moment. It gets worse before they bleed, sort of builds up. Then when the blood comes it eases off. Dr Deasy came again, and another doctor. They don't know what to do. They want me to go into Rossgarry but I won't. Father Leahy told me to pray and be patient and not say anything to anyone – '

She broke off with a sharp gasp. Essie tensed, holding out her arms as if to catch her.

'Essie, I don't know if I can bear it,' she said. 'I'm scared. I'd say hold my hand, but it hurts too much for that. How long will it last? Wait. Wait. Wait a minute.'

Essie sat paralysed, watching as Rosanna bowed her head, struggling inwardly to regain some kind of normality. At last it seemed to have passed. Rosanna breathed steadily and deeply. 'There,' she whispered, 'there. I'm all right now.' She opened her eyes.

A few moments passed. Essie could not take her eyes off the thick-fingered, gloved hands. 'What are they like?' she asked softly, scared but fascinated. 'Can I have a look?'

'Oh, well,' said Rosanna, 'of course, if I was you I'd want to have a look.' She turned her right hand palm upward. 'Help yourself,' she said.

Carefully Essie removed the glove and undid the bandage. As she came closer to the skin, brown stains appeared. Then the bandage was off, and there it was. The wound was dry. Something like the head of a nail, dark-blooded, lodged in the centre of a swollen mass of shattered veins. 'Jesus,' said Essie, 'what's that?'

Rosanna steeled herself and touched it with a finger of her other hand, wincing and drawing in breath between clenched teeth. 'See, it moves,' she said, depressing the thick lump of solid blood, which re-emerged slowly by itself when she withdrew her finger.

Essie felt sick.

'Padre Pio's lasted fifty years, they said. Fifty years! But then some others just go away, just like that. I keep praying that they'll go away. Well, there you are. Now, do it up again.'

Essie's hands trembled a little as she obeyed. The room was hot and stuffy and she wanted to get out. 'When do you think you'll be coming out again?' she asked. 'What are you going to do, Rosanna? You can't stay here for ever. Even with these.'

Rosanna's eyes closed again. 'I don't know. One day perhaps. I don't honestly care.'

'What will you do now?'

'Stay here.'

'How? I mean, *can* you? What about Padraic?'

Rosanna smiled, then she laughed. 'You know, Padraic needs a housekeeper. He isn't getting any younger. Oh, don't look like that! He agrees. I need shelter. It's a perfect arrangement. I'll be better soon.'

'People will talk,' said Essie.

'Of course. People do.' Rosanna laughed again, quite merrily. 'It's the first pure thing I've done in my life,' she said, 'and people will talk.'

51

Later that night Marie went out to fasten the gate. Since she'd come back she'd measured everything in time. If I'd gone, by now I'd be ... Where? Someone was coming down the lane but she couldn't make out in the darkness who it was. 'Good night,' she said to the approaching figure.

'Listen,' said a gravelly voice. It was Nora McBride, probably coming back from her daughter's. The stick-like old woman stopped at the gate. 'Hear it?'

Marie listened. A chorus of birds was singing in the night.

'I've heard this before,' said Nora. 'At Medjugorje, at Fatima.'

'How strange,' said Marie, feeling faint. The birds sounded distant, muffled. How strange that she had not noticed them before.

'They'll sing all night now,' said Nora. 'They know.' She walked on.

Marie crossed herself and ran back up the path.

52

Bob checked out of the hotel at nine-thirty in the morning and knocked about town for a while aimlessly. There was a little group of kids sniffing brown glue out of polythene bags down by the bus station. One of them looked only about six. Good God, he thought, hungover and depressed, and sat down on a bench and just watched them for a while as they careened slowly and aggressively up and down the street in the wake of a fat girl of about twelve who appeared to be in charge of them. For a moment he felt quite lost. No one was taking any notice of them. On their fifth or so stagger-past he met the peculiar pale squinting eyes of the girl. She tried to say something which was probably fuck off, and one of the boys lurched against him. 'Here,' he said, giving them a few bob, 'go and kill yourselves,' and his eyes filled with tears. This was awful. Off they went. He'd been angry since yesterday and that had just made it worse.

He got up and walked about. Traffic poured over the bridges. On Patrick Street the pavement artists did the Pope and Mother Teresa. He went into a café and chewed aspirin with his tea, ate something and felt better.

The wall was mirrored – terrible idea that was – and his face in the glass was ugly with big pale half moons under the eyes. I suppose I'm getting old at last, he thought. Of course she hadn't turned up, he'd known after the first ten minutes or so that she wouldn't. He'd waited till half past four. Now was the time to just give up on the whole thing. But he was sick of being alone, sick to death of it. Someone somewhere had to be sacrificed, why was it always him? He never got what he wanted. What was she doing? When he felt angry he felt better. After all he'd suffered for her, he deserved something back.

He went out and found a phone and rang her number recklessly, not knowing what he'd say if she answered, but it was engaged. He tried again but it was still engaged. He went and found his car and got in and sat there for a moment before setting off for Dublin and that poky little flat. She probably just chickened out, he thought.

Then somehow he ended up heading west.

He turned on the radio and sang along with the daytime pop music, slapping the wheel, driving too fast for the roads, pushed on by a sense of urgency. 'Oh, young Lochinvar is come out of the West ...' he murmured as he drove, a wry look about the mouth. An hour passed and the mountains grew wild, great glens opened. He pulled into a layby and got out and breathed that first full breath of western mountain air that was always like an enema of the brain. He must be mad to come back here. Just got to keep out of that nutter's way and he'd be all right. Get there about two. For what? Con was often out then, she might be on her own. He didn't know what he was going to do, just see what happened, play it all by chance, sniff the glue, fall over the edge. This was her last chance. It's not as if she was happy there.

The car, he suddenly realised, was instantly recognisable. Turn back, he thought, but didn't. Maybe he'd just keep driving, get there and never stop, straight on up the north road and back across the top. Kind of a fishing trip, see if anything stuck on his hook on the way. Another hour passed. Little bleeding hearts drooped in the fuchsia hedges endlessly lining the roads, dogs ran at the wheels, neat white houses were carelessly scattered over the hills. An old man in tattered clothes, black dog at heel, raised a hand as he flew by. It was all coming back, everything, and with it came a defiant kind of fear. Then the sea came up blinding on the left.

He just kept on.

It became apparent the nearer he got to Strangarvan that something was going on. Then he remembered: the Fleadh. Oh God, the Fleadh, hundreds of people, of course she'd be there, with Con probably, and everybody else would be there, too, of course, and the whole situation was impossible. He thought fast and turned down a lane that struck inland. But there was no way to Ballinaphuca without touching the tail end of the town. All lanes inevitably led back there, so he just drove regardless, looking as much as possible at no one and trusting to luck. He didn't see anyone he knew till he saw Paddy Bawn's fat red face angrily conducting a sack race in the playground. Little girls in green dresses and clumpy shoes step-danced poker-stiff with flailing legs in the open space before the old dairy, and a burst of swirling pipe and drum came into the car.

Suddenly he was very scared. What was he doing? To Dundreen, he thought, panicking. At least they wouldn't kick in his head there.

Some creeps wearing steward badges on red T-shirts tried to make him pay fifteen quid at the gate to get in, and when he said he was family they looked at him as if he were a groupie trying to get backstage at a concert. Eventually they let him through and he lurked at the back door, appalled. A terrible woman was making a speech on a little raised platform under a sage green canopy on the lawn, behind her the sea and sky and miles of filmy dove-grey waves curling at the base of cliffs on the far side of the estuary. It was like the sermon on the mount, except that there were sunbrowned arms and legs all over the place. He looked at the multitude and hated their stupid smiling faces and sincere frowns. The woman was one of those rare old people who have sharpened with time, seeming to have undergone a kind of antithesis of senile dementia. What she said, of course, was the usual self-knowledge crap, he could have cobbled it together himself given the time, but she had grace and timing and a high poetic style.

He saw faces he knew, Essie, Feargal, all that lot, James, Julia – oh Christ, Julia, he'd forgotten all about her. She mustn't see him. But as he was thinking it she turned her head as if she knew he was there and stared at him with no appearance of surprise. He couldn't smile and she just went on staring and staring at him in a fixed, unnerving way. He blushed. He saw now that one of the red T-shirts was picking its way discreetly through the massed devout to tell James he was here.

At his side appeared a grimy grinning George wearing cut-off jeans with long elaborate frays, hair tied back in a witch's broom of a pony tail. 'Hi, man. Hey, I'd get out of here if I were you. This is no place to break down, the wolves are closing in.' He laughed in much too loud and undisciplined a way so that here and there a few heads turned.

Swan Mary never faltered. She never would. Now Essie was looking at him. A pang of horror crossed her face.

'Honesty, man, it doesn't pay,' said George with his old dog smile and weeping, dancing eyes, 'you found it out, hey? Me, too. I couldn't help it either, ah, look at her, a thing for an old man to make a fool of himself over. Eh?' He laughed again and sang: '*Rambling Rose, Rambling Rose, where you wander no one knows . . .*'

Bob sank back into the house. He went into the big sitting room, which was blissfully empty, but the woman's voice followed him clearly and he realised he was listening to some form of amplification. James came in all stiff and furious, ginger hair standing on end.

'How you can be taken in by all this, I don't know,' said Bob by way of greeting.

'What the fuck do you think you're doing here?' James said very quickly and quietly.

'Nothing, nothing.' Bob waved a hand. 'It was a mistake, I see that. Just a visit, that's all. Bad timing, I can see. I won't stick around.'

'Are you mad?' James came close and looked up into his face. 'Do you know what you've done? You've fucked up a nice little Irish family. You deserve to get your head kicked in, you really do. And you're fucking things up for us, too. We have to live here, you know.'

Bob fell limply and with no grace whatsoever into a chair. He looked very tired.

'You'd better leave as soon as possible,' James said.

Bob held up his hands weakly. 'Surrender, surrender,' he said in a bored voice. 'Just give me five minutes. I'm on my way.'

'Like now. I'm not kidding.'

'Sure,' said Bob. He waved his hand at the window: 'I can't take all this.'

They looked at each other with hostility. The woman's voice said that God was a child. She said the first age was God the Mother, the second God the Father, and the third was coming, the age of God the Child. That was the true meaning of the trinity. James frowned at his watch like a man in a hurry running over Waterloo Bridge. 'You've got fifteen minutes,' he said. 'I'll return at three twenty-two and make sure that you're gone.'

'Well, go on,' said Bob, 'go back to your talk, you're missing it, aren't you?'

'I'm taping it.'

'Good, is she?'

'She's good.' James walked out.

'Bastard.' Bob reached out and picked up the phone and dialled. Of course there would be no answer because everyone was at the Fleadh. He noticed a copy of *A View In Delft* in the bookcase and smiled humourlessly. Then Marie said hello and he was thrown into confusion.

'Hello?' she said again.

'It's me. I'm at Dundreen,' he said.

There was a silence. Then she said, 'The bus broke down.'

'I'll be at the signpost in twenty minutes. Grab a few things and just come. Don't worry about what to bring, you can get stuff in Dublin. We'll go up the north road, it'll be empty. Don't worry. If you're not there I'll just drive on and that'll be that.'

Another silence.

'Twenty minutes,' he said again and put down the phone, sweating fear.

53

It was hot in the kitchen. Marie leaned against the sink. She'd been about to put a roasting tin with a shoulder of pork into the oven. Through the open door she could see Con sitting like the Sphinx in front of the TV, cup of tea on one arm of the chair, box of tissues on the other. She'd wanted to go to the Fleadh, anything was better than hanging round the house now; but instead she'd been running about after him all day long, him and his cold. Flu, he thought it was. Both of them were sulking. He muttered, blew his nose, spat. She looked at the clock. Three fifteen. The roast sat there in its tin waiting to be put in the oven. She gazed at it.

'Who was that?' he asked.

'Julia,' she said.

Con turned and knocked his cup of tea off the arm of the chair. It splashed all over the place. 'What a stupid place to leave the tea!' he said.

Marie got a cloth, sighing, went in and knelt to mop up the mess. 'But you always have your tea there, Connie,' she said.

'Well, it was waiting to happen. Why couldn't you have brought that little table over?' he said peevishly.

She got him another cup of tea then put the meat in the oven. Then she went upstairs and took the bag that she hadn't yet unpacked from yesterday, glanced around the room, took two letters from her underwear drawer and left one in Simon's room and one in Julia's.

'I'm just going down to the village,' she said to the back of Con's head when she came down. 'We need one or two things.'

He grunted. 'Don't be long.'

She looked her last at the back of his head, which still had a youthful look because of the thickness of his hair. She touched his old dogstooth jacket hanging on the back of the door.

Then she went out and walked down to the signpost. The summer meadow was full of flowers, honeysuckle bloomed in the hedge. She stood by the signpost with her bag at her feet, pretending to look in her purse so that if anyone saw her they'd think she was just checking to see how much money she'd got. She felt as if she was waiting for a bus.

After a while a car approached and she tensed up, but it was only tourists who waved gaily at her as they passed. She waved back. This is ridiculous, she thought. It'll never work. Someone will see.

Then the big familiar car appeared in the distance. She remembered what he looked like as soon as she saw him. She got in and threw her bag into the back. Her heart began pounding with fear. He squeezed her knee, scarcely glancing at her, and drove on grimly through the village as if through the valley of the shadow of death, down to the north road, where they sped away.

54

O'Leary's was a dim blue fug. Everyone was dead drunk apart from Iko's kids. In a corner, bearded men and long-haired women beat bodhrans and bashed guitars. Ger Sheehan played the spoons with practised ease.

Iko said someone had lit a fire under the back of his bus last night. 'Not much damage done, but shit, I mean, man, there was kids inside, and my missis.'

'Rednecks,' said Clyde. 'You know anything about it?' he asked Tim Pat and Mike and Ger. No one did.

Iko rolled a cigarette. 'Hosanna, they're calling her. Holy Rosanna, ha ha! Rosanna, of all people!'

'Here's to our own holy Rosanna!' Ger said, raising his glass and laughing. 'Pulled a fast one on the lot of you, she has. Gone and got herself sanctified.' He roared with laughter.

Clyde wouldn't think about that. It was just Rosanna trying to get attention as usual, any way she could. She should have been here, stupid cow, she'd have enjoyed this.

'What you doing up at that funny farm, anyway?' he asked Iko scathingly. He'd drunk so much that nothing made any difference now, and he could just go on and on and never stop because that's the way he was.

'I'm taking the waters,' said Iko, unperturbed. 'They've got nice food and music and a bouncy castle and all that for the kids. And this woman, she's interesting. No, straight up, I'm going back up there later. Anyway it's Dolly really and the girls, you know. They wanted to see her. Me, man, I don't need no crutch.' And he raised his glass and drank.

'How'd they get planning permission for all that, anyway?' asked Clyde.

Tim Pat shrugged. 'Search me.'

'Jammy beggars, they are.' Clyde lowered his voice and spoke to Iko. 'Tight as that drum. How come the Drug Squad never gives 'em a call, eh? Money talks.'

'Yeah.' Iko was no stranger to money either, Clyde thought, filthy rich parents, him and Dolly both.

'I mean, all the rest of us it's once a fucking year. I mean even those stupid cunts who think tea and coffee are drugs, even they get it in the neck but not the fucking Sawles.'

'Yeah.'

'Discrimination,' Clyde said. 'It's everywhere. We're the niggers here.'

'Hey, d'ye hear that?' said Mike excitedly.

'What?'

'Bob Sawle.'

'What?'

'Well, I didn't lay eyes on him myself . . .' someone else was saying.

'His car.'

'What time?'

'You're joking me.'

'Heading out on the Ballinaphuca road.'

It was a gift. Clyde hadn't kicked anyone for a while. He felt a little sick with excitement as he drained his pint and added the glass to the host of other foam-ringed empties. He started at once on another. Iko picked up his mandolin and started to play Carolan's Concerto beautifully.

'He's never gone to Ballinaphuca, surely?' Tim Pat said.

'No, he hasn't.' Iko did not look up from the mandolin. 'He was up at Dundreen a while ago.'

'Well, why didn't you say so, you fool?'

Iko shrugged.

'Gone up there, has he?' asked Clyde with a thin smile. His knob began to itch. He thought of the Vigo whore. 'Gone up there, up there, that stupid place? Who's coming?'

'He's a bigger fool than he looks,' said Tim Pat, reaching for his drink.

'Who's coming? Who's coming?'

But the others just went on drinking.

Clyde took his glass and went out and stood in the square. Over the road people were gathered round the bonnet of a car upon which a small big-eared boy made a tin whistle wail with the world's woes. Some thick bank clerk type and a clean toothy woman asked Clyde the way to Montsalvat. Montsalvat now, not Dundreen. What a fucking stupid name. That's what he told them and they hurried away. Clyde smiled, feeling dangerous. Good. The sun had fallen a little over the tall-masted smacks, shadows were long. Drunken people reeled about the streets. He got a hot dog dripping with slimy onions and tomato sauce from the van by the Cross, ambled down to the harbour jingling the money in his pockets. He felt like blowing the lot, he'd be all right, there was more where that came from. There was music in all the bars. He met a friend down from Clare for the Fleadh and the two of them went back to his van round the back of the church and got blown away for a couple of hours by one incredible Thai stick.

When he came round it was nearly dark and the town was buzzing. His knob still itched. Christ! From loudspeakers positioned in the corners of the square a military-sounding band played 'Roddy McCorley'. Old men in caps gathered to sing in Biddy O'Neill's bar on the quay. Someone had a fight and some glass got broken down by the chipper. The stone benches round the Cross were full of people with glasses and bottles. Clyde found Ger and the Pads and Tim Pat there with a bottle of Jameson's doing the rounds. They drank and watched the young girls, all done up in their best, going by to the Strangarvan Hotel where the dance was due to begin soon. Julia was not among them.

Con appeared suddenly, very sober and quiet and angry. Christy was with him. Con asked if anyone had seen Marie. He said when he got hold of her he was going to wring her neck slowly and put out both her eyes. He looked ill. His hair stuck up and his voice was thick with flu.

There was a little silence.

'Con,' said Clyde, 'do you know who's back?'

The same thought occurred to all of them except Con who said, 'What? Jesus!' and cleared his throat and spat. His eyes bore a permanently wounded look. Sneezing and swearing, he strode to the chipper van. He was starving. He'd fallen asleep and woken up to find the meat burned to a cinder, nothing on the stove and still no sign of Marie, and he realised she'd just sneaked off to the Fleadh without telling him. His throat was sore. Selfish bitch.

Clyde watched him, taking a slug from the whiskey bottle that Tim Pat stuck under his nose. He felt all nervy and mad, like Molly just before he loosed her after a hare. Someone, somewhere, was in for a thumping. A good one. Sometimes he wondered how far he could go, how much of a mess he could leave behind. Sometimes he thought he could go all the way. They'd be after him then, that was the trouble.

'Bob Sawle's around,' said Clyde as soon as Con returned with his sausage and chips in a paper. 'He's up at Dundreen.'

Con didn't react. The bottle came his way and he drank from it. His nose ran. The germs on that now, thought Clyde. Con sat down on the bench and ate steadily, sniffing all the time. 'Bloody hell,' he said from time to time, sucking his greasy fingers, 'bloody hell.'

'Odd, that,' Ger said.

'What is?' asked Christy, slightly belligerent.

'I dunno,' said Ger.

'Think she's gone up there?' asked Clyde, voicing it right out. 'Would she do that?'

'Oh, she wouldn't, she wouldn't surely!' said Christy.

Con still said nothing, but when the bottle came his way he tipped back his head very far and took a long and impressive drink.

Clyde stood up with a suddenness and air of decision that made everyone stand back a little in expectation. 'Let's go up there and see,' he said quietly.

Trouble quivered in the air around the bunch of them, like heat. Con drained the bottle.

'No trouble,' said Christy.

'No, no trouble,' said Mike.

'Bollocks!' roared Con in a voice that caused people on the far side of the square to turn their heads and look. 'Bollocks! Bollocks! Bollocks!' And he jumped to his feet and hurled the empty bottle of Jameson's against the old grey cross.

'Now Con, Con, Con.' Clyde and Christy restrained him, sitting him down again on the bench. 'Christ, man, do you want the guards on our necks?'

'Come on,' said Con, sober again, and he started walking. They all followed.

'Where you going?' Christy asked.

'Dundreen.'

'Yeah!' said Clyde. Ger grinned.

They went in two cars, Con's and Clyde's, all of them much too drunk to drive, but nobody cared. Rosanna should have been here, Clyde thought. She would've loved this. What the hell was she playing at? Then he remembered that Julia would be there too

273

and suddenly regretted the whole thing; but it was too late for that now, so they rocketed crazily out of town, hyping themselves up for adventure. They flew, adrenalin pumped. Tim Pat and Mike laughed in the back.

'He was up there, wasn't he? Sure, she was keeping in touch with him through that place, stands to reason.'

'Poor old Con! Poor old Con!'

They reached Dundreen and turned down the winding track towards the cliff's edge, They drove up to the front of the house and walked straight in. A Hemingway American in a lumberjack shirt was taking tickets on the door. He didn't want any trouble, he just let them walk in. 'The dancing's about to start,' he said with a smile. 'Enjoy.'

They sort of expected a ballroom but it was a big strange round room, in darkness except for a spotlit area in the middle where a small wiry man and a chunky woman were limbering up, both of them clad in purple longjohns. There seemed to be scores of people sitting cross-legged in the darkness but you couldn't see who. Then their eyes got used to the dark and they could see everyone quite clearly and everyone could see them, had been able to since they'd walked in, but no one was looking.

The man and woman walked about not looking at each other, shaking out their arms and legs. Music burst from somewhere, rattling, clicking, disjointed. They danced, slow, staccato, disjointed, totally separate. It was very quiet and you could hear the boards give softly. They were precise but not graceful, very serious. 'Lovely!' Tim Pat called when the music ended, and people turned to look at them, but more music started at once and they were off again.

Con's eyes searched and searched the crowd with mounting anger. Of course Marie and Bob Sawle weren't here. Tim Pat and Ger seemed to have forgotten why they'd come. They chortled in a smothered way like children, pretending they thought it was time to clap whenever there was a pregnant pause in the action. Everyone tried to ignore them. The performers did not falter. At last there was another lull in the music. 'Lovely!' Tim Pat called again. Con caught the eye of James who sat near the front by the side of an old lady in white. There she was, the Mighty Quinn, thought Clyde, then stiffened. Julia was there. She looked at her father and then at him, her face indifferent.

More music, this time sweeping, full of bells and strings. The dancers balanced and dipped, silent, bare feet trembling on the pine boards. Con signed to James and went out into the passage. Clyde and the others followed.

'No trouble, no trouble,' Christy said uncomfortably.

Clyde just stood back against the wall. He got out a box of matches and struck one quickly, shook it out, pinched the hot tip and stuck the clean end between his teeth, all in about thirty seconds. His lips quivered back from the match, showing his small white teeth. This was turning out to be a bitch. He thought about himself running in there with a machine gun, just opening fire, spraying it about casually. First they'd run like chickens, then they'd lie still. He felt ugly. Something shook inside him, as if an internal organ was shivering. He was scared. Then he thought, no, I'm all right, I'm all right. It was just that he'd put a lot away in the past twenty-four hours, one way and another.

James came out with a worried look on his face. 'My brother was here,' he said at once. 'Is that what you've come about?'

'I've no quarrel with you now, James,' Con said, his voice shaking a little. 'Is he not here?'

'No, he left about three.'

'Three?'

' – ish.'

Feargal came out and looked anxious and George, for Christ's sake, that stupid old fuck, and one or two other loiterers. Clyde's heart was racing horribly, he glowered at them all.

'Three,' Con said again. Such a look came on his face that everyone fell silent.

'Come into the drawing room,' said James and led the way with a gracious flourish. Jackie Bat's old dog lay fat and panting on a beautiful white rug.

'I was going to give Jackie a dog,' Con said irrelevantly as he sat down.

'As soon as he came I told him to leave,' James said wearily. 'I don't think he'll be back.'

Con laughed shortly. 'No,' he said with clipped anger, 'he

won't be back. I'm just popping down to the village, says she. She's done it. She's only gone away with him.' His eyes were red and dry.

James started apologising as if he'd done it himself. The rest of them, in some degree or another, felt a certain glee. This was first-hand scandal, a big do.

Clyde stepped forward. 'You wanna go after them, Con, I'll come with you,' he said, and he meant it, and God knows where it would end. Tim Pat said he'd come, so did Ger.

'Where?'

Con turned to James.

'I don't even have his address,' James said, putting up his hands. 'All I know is he's been living in Dublin.'

Julia came in, looking from one to the other quickly.

'Your mother's gone,' said Con.

'What?'

'Your mother's gone with his brother. Get your things now.'

'I haven't got anything. What do you mean, gone?'

'Gone.'

'What are you talking about?'

Con lost his temper and shouted at her. 'Go and get your things.'

Julia looked straight at Clyde for some reason and he saw that she was very shaken. He tried to look inscrutable and at the same time convey anger and danger and brooding and hidden depth. He wanted them all to vanish and for him to be alone with her in some dangerous place where he could rescue her from something. 'What happened?' she asked, as if she was asking him.

'Now, look, we don't really know that anything's happened,' said Christy.

'Please,' said James. 'Please, let's not spoil the entertainment.'

'Go and get in the car,' Con told Julia. 'I just want a word with James.'

'I really don't know anything at all,' James said, 'I only wish I did. I don't keep in touch with my brother these days, haven't done for quite some time. If there's anything at all that I can do ...'

'I've waited all year to see Swan Mary,' Julia said. 'Why do I have to go home? It's not going to make any difference to anything, is it?'

'In the car!'

She said nothing but went tight with anger and walked out. The others followed, thinking she'd go to the car, but instead she turned and walked back towards the circular room.

'Julia!' roared Con.

She vanished through the door. Con ran after her, then Christy, then Clyde, then all the rest.

'Oh Christ!' groaned James.

Con marched in, blinking, all the lights were now on, looked around and blundered through the crowd to where Julia sat staring at the ground stony-faced, long fingers looped about a bony brown wrist. He yanked her up and dragged her out with everyone watching, Swan Mary and all. Julia started crying with embarrassment and George, who happened to be near the door, stepped in front of them. He made a gentle, calming movement with his arms. 'Fuck off,' Con said.

Swan Mary was immobile, stern. Impossibly, a fair minority still contrived to look happy and composed in the face of all this.

'I'm sorry, everyone,' James was saying, 'I think if we could just ...'

'Oh, why are you doing this?' Julia hissed at Con, and he slapped her smartly across the face once and pushed her before him out of the room.

There was a shocked silence.

George made as if to go after them but Clyde stepped in front and thumped him in the gut hard enough to double him over and make him grunt. It all happened very fast. George raised his head with a stupid grin and giggled and Clyde nutted him hard, turned on his heel and was gone.

George's big brown wounded eyes looked for Essie, who leapt to her feet and ran over, dredging tissues from her pockets to mop up the thin red blood and yelling in a terrible voice: 'You are dead meat, Clyde, you bastard, you slimy little apology for a human being! Do you hear me? You have got away with enough around here!'

People tried to hide laughter. Some babble broke out here and there. 'Could you all just ...' James appealed, and Helen stood stiff and white. Everything was breaking up. But then Swan Mary, with perfect timing, rose to her feet and stepped forward and opened her mouth and started to sing in a rich throaty contralto, the voice of a much younger woman, so that for a moment she seemed like a lipsynced head in a film, that of a turtle or an alien. She sang over and over the same four syllables, raising her arms as if drawing support from them all. A few, mainly her own people, joined in, then everybody else.

It went on and on.

Essie took George into the kitchen and washed his nose and gave him a hug. Oh God, if they suss me, she was thinking, I'll lie, I'll just deny all knowledge of it. They can't prove a thing. The sound became a continuous ringing bell in the round room, falling and rising, on and on and on endlessly. George smothered a laugh and sang softly in counterpoint: '*Always look on the bright side of life, dee-doo, dee-doo dee-doo dee-doo ...*' and Essie laughed and joined in and they sniggered like children outside assembly, while the rest lost track of time and the hungry dark of eternity crowded the windows.

Clyde got a glimpse of Julia sitting bolt upright, furious and uncowed, in the front of Con's car. Then he had to get into his own and follow on with Tim Pat and Ger. At Con's they stopped and Julia got out and walked up the path and into the house. Christy and Mike drifted away apologetically, wishing they'd gone to the dance.

Con came and leaned on Clyde's van. 'Who's coming?' he asked, looking at no one and speaking flatly.

'Where?' asked Ger.

'I'll come,' said Clyde.

They left Clyde's car there with Molly in the back and all got in Con's, Tim Pat in the front, Ger and Clyde in the back.

'Dublin,' said Con.

'What?'

Con started to drive fast.

'Dublin?' Ger said. 'You mean we're going all the way to fucking Dublin?'

'Yeah!' Clyde leaned forward, agog. He felt like a crazy in an American road movie and wished he had his gun with him. Yeah,

Dublin, why not?

'Why Dublin?'

'Cos that's where he lives, we go there and ...'

'Yeah!' said Clyde.

'Crazy,' Ger said, 'you don't even know where.'

They flew on. It was dark. A dog ran out and bit the wheels. 'The ferryport,' said Con grimly, 'stands to reason. They won't stick around. We just wait at the ferryport till they turn up.'

But by Strangarvan they'd started to sober up a little. 'You know, they could be anywhere,' said Tim Pat sensibly. 'For all we know they've gone to Cork instead and got on a boat there.'

'Who's to say they're even getting on a boat?' Ger added.

But still they drove on. Clyde felt savage, grinning into the darkness out of the window. He whistled a slow piercing dirge that drove the others mad, but no one liked to say.

A few miles further on Con stopped the car suddenly. 'Oh, what's the point? What is the fucking point?' he said in the same flat voice, now trembling slightly. 'I don't want her back now anyway.'

'Don't give up,' said Clyde. 'Not now. Not now.'

'Con's right,' Tim Pat said.

'Yeah,' said Ger, 'we could kick his face in but that's about all.'

'Yeah? Well? What's wrong with that?' asked Clyde.

But Con turned the car around and they headed back. At Strangarvan they all tumbled out in front of O'Leary's. The place was wild, reeling. 'Fuck it,' said Con, 'I need a drop of something. I'm going to get blind drunk, blind fucking drunk.'

'Good man,' said Tim Pat, pushing open the door, and Ger patted his shoulder.

Clyde did not go with them. He just stood chewing his match, doing nothing, wondering why he felt so bad. He watched the people going past and wished there was someone he could pick a fight with. Then he remembered his car was stuck in Ballinaphuca and spat out his match.

55

Clyde tiptoed up the path without disturbing the dogs and tapped on the door. He'd checked it out. Simon was with his Aunt Therese, Con was filthy drunk in Strangarvan.

She opened the door. 'Hi, Clyde,' she said. She held a letter in her hand.

'Hi. Is Con there?'

She shook her head. 'What happened?' she asked in a bored voice. 'Did the lynch mob break up?'

'Hey listen, Julia, I tried to stop all that. Took me till past Strangarvan to get them to see sense.'

'You?' she said. 'Since when have you turned down the chance of a fight? What would you have done if you'd caught up? The same as before? That was terrible! A typically male thing to do, of course. Where did you leave my dad?'

He gazed in wonder. Who else would have the nerve to talk to him like this?

'Well?'

'Strangarvan,' he said.

She gave an exaggerated sigh.

'Hey, Julia, I had to hitch all the way back here for my van, how about a coffee? Just a quick one?'

'Oh, all right,' she said at once to his amazement, 'come in for a minute.'

He felt a quickening of excitement as he stepped in. He was terribly nervous and thought he could smell his own fear. Surely she knew. The range glowed, a pair of Marie's shoes stuck out from under a chair, her knitting lay on the settee. 'So you're not at the dance?' he asked.

'Do I look as if I am?' she said, going into the neat humming kitchen. 'Sure, I'm there having a whale of a time.'

'Want to go? I could take you in. Got the van outside.'

'You could not indeed,' she snapped, bustling about making instant coffee. He stood in the doorway watching her.

'How'll you manage now? The three of you?' he asked.

'Oh, we'll manage fine. And I'll get my own way about Montsalvat in the end, too,' she said confidently. She shoved the coffee at him then came out into the room and sniffed and started emptying the ashtrays briskly into the range. She was terribly skinny, her long brown thighs parted at the top before they ran into her shorts. He looked at the gap between them, holding his mug in one hand and drinking the coffee.

'There,' she said and looked at him. She seemed to be considering something. Then she said, 'I know where they've gone.'

'You do?' He tried to be cool.

'Yeah.' She went over to the door, felt in the pocket of a coat and brought out a scrap of old envelope. 'Well,' she said, 'what would you say? I found it in her jeans pocket when I was doing the laundry yesterday. Stuffed right down, it was.' She came over and showed him. It was a Dublin address. 'You know, she's not so clever. I had a funny feeling soon as I saw it. It's not Aunt Maura's. Who else does she know in Dublin?'

She was as tall as him now, he noticed. Clyde was just about close enough to reach out and touch her chin, so he did.

'Don't, Clyde,' she said and rushed away and sat down in the armchair. He followed, falling to his knees at the side of the chair and gazing hawkishly at her face. He wanted to lean in towards her like a drawn flame and be comforted. There was a horrible silence. Then he kissed her very firmly and passionately, getting his tongue in a little between her tightened lips. She leapt up, pushing him aside and wiping her mouth vigorously with her fingers. She might just as well have thrown up all over the carpet.

'Now stop it, Clyde!' she shouted. 'You've no cause to do that!'

He jumped up, too, horrified. 'You cruel bitch!' he shouted with tears starting into his eyes. 'You cruel bitch!'

Julia ran out of the house, down the drive and out into the lane. He just stood there listening to her frightened footsteps. What now? He blinked very rapidly and the tears retreated. He saw the scrap of paper with the Dublin address lying on the rug, picked it up and shoved it in his pocket. Then he went upstairs and searched for Julia's room, just to see it once quickly before he went. Must've drunk more than he knew or something, his head felt all light and shivery as if it was about to disintegrate. First he hit on the big bedroom with the double bed all made, everything very neat and boring. Then Simon's, full of bicycle wheels, 'Now That's What I Call Music' tapes and loud paperback books about the supernatural. Julia's was the one at the end, the dark messy lair with posters of Prince and U2 and Swan Mary, and books and crisp packets and chocolate wrappers, hundreds of them, and crap little ornaments, chipped and absurd, gathering dust. Those were her clothes discarded all over the floor in heaps, her pink and white knickers, her tights, her dirty T-shirts. That was her bed with the rumpled sheet and the yellow quilt, her pillow, her hairs on it. Clyde walked about looking at everything intently, opening drawers, inspecting underwear, sniffing things, sifting through the homework scattered on the rug, even looking under the bed.

He listened: no sound. He lay down quickly on the bed, put his head on the pillow and breathed deeply. He could smell her, all young and rank. There was something hard under the pillow. Clyde reached in and pulled out a little red book. It was her diary.

'I don't know what it was,' he read, 'he had something about him and he was round the house a lot and they always used to laugh at me and make fun of the things I said, and I knew of course he was much too old ...' There was a lot of cosmic crap and a lot of mundane stuff: got up, went out, that sort of thing, and some billowy pencil drawings of girls' faces. Then, 'What would he see in her? She's old. She's getting fat! He can't like her, he can't, he can't, he can't!!' The word *can't* was written many times over in capitals. He flicked backwards and forwards. Lots of gushy stuff. 'I love him, I love him, oh, God, why must my very first love be unrequited?' She'd drawn a picture of a heart with a dagger through it and great drops of blood pouring out. She'd really got into the shine on the drops. 'I hate her! I hate her! It's all her fault! I hate hate hate hate hate her. He's gone. I don't care what they say about him. I know he's innocent. His car's still up there. The wagon's empty. I cry every time I go past it.'

Clyde raised his eyes and gazed at the wall where rock stars pouted. 'Now you've done it,' he whispered. 'I'll kill him.'

Then he saw his own name: 'Clyde has a thing about me,' he read. 'I can tell. He's kind of creepy. I don't suppose he can help it, he's subhuman.' It was the only mention of him.

He heard the sound of a car, then voices, and ran downstairs. He was just in time. The door opened and there was this grief-sodden man with dirty hair hanging down over his face, Samson bringing down the Temple. He looked ill and worn out, or maybe it was just that the process of neglect that would possibly overtake him had already begun. He came in with Julia and Simon behind him, Simon's face all red and bleak from crying.

'Fuck off out of here and never show your face again,' Con said, his voice full of snot.

So she'd told him.

'OK OK,' said Clyde, edging past them. 'OK, OK,' and slid out into the night.

Con picked up Marie's knitting and dropped it, needles and all, into the slumbering range, which clicked its throat experimentally once or twice before flaring up. Simon started to cry again, blubberingly, his head hanging.

'Look at me, look,' said Con, falling back into his chair. 'Weak as a bloody baby, I am. Look at me.'

Julia ran about. 'Have some of this now, it'll make you feel better.' She gave him a glass of water and he sipped it absentmindedly. 'You've put something in this, Jule,' he said accusingly.

'It's all right,' she said, 'it's only a little flower essence. Just you sip it nicely now.'

Simon ran upstairs and went into his room. There was a letter lying on his pillow. He ripped it open. It was from his mother, telling him she loved him and he must come and see her whenever he could. It made him cry even harder than before, doubled over on his bed.

56

The sea boomed with a vast silent voice like a drum out on the edge of space. Clyde felt almost sober again, standing in the lane outside Con's watching Molly pee in the ditch, clear-headed under the starry sky. He got in his car and just sat there, knowing he was perfectly capable of driving. It was as if the booze had seeped out of his pores and formed a cloud outside him, one that fizzed and popped with anger, a cartoon thing with jags of lightning piercing its heart. Poor Molly crept into the front seat beside him and he fondled and squeezed her ears, sometimes twisting their bulbous roots cruelly and making her whimper with pain. Whatever happened from now on, he thought, it was not his fault. It was just that the devil got in him, making him do these things. It was his mum. It was Melanie Broadbent. It was Julia. She'd find out, she'd know it was all her fault, she'd feel guilty. So she should. He just did what he did. She'd see the diary open and know that he'd read it. He thought of a song Rosanna sang: killed the only woman I love because she would not be my bride. Oh, he thought, if only. He let go of Molly.

Something was wrong. He knew because he was half way to Strangarvan, sailing along through the kind of starry night where you find yourself looking for UFOs, and the old van was going like a dream the way it never did, and he couldn't remember leaving Con's. He was singing. He was bad Billy the Kid, special, a creature operating beyond the limits of other people. He fought the law and the law won. His eyes and lips narrowed, he seemed to implode.

A few crumpled people were still out and about when he reached town. Broken bottles lay about the square. He went to his shed in the back road, pumped up the gas, got his gun out from under the mattress and lay down with it, polishing and playing with it, smoking cigarettes and listening to a tape of country songs because he wanted to hear 'El Paso', to shoot down the handsome young stranger in the cantina, to flee, to do it all for love, to die in her arms and see her realise, too late, too late, that she had loved him all along. Shot him down down down in the cantina. Clyde played his gun like a guitar and sang along in a quavering voice. He was randy, throbbing with it, itching and twitching, so wide awake it was ridiculous and there was nothing to do, nothing at all to do. He was utterly bored, alert, crammed with something nameless that seethed and writhed like a witch's stew, dully popping bubbles of thick grey sludge into his soul. He felt as if he was suffocating. Christ! He wriggled like a kid with worms.

Kill someone, he thought. The ultimate, murder. What a word, hey? Murder most horrible, Death Row, his face in the paper, one of the greats, up there with the best, his waxwork in the chamber of horrors, magazine articles, his faded face, always the same image, brooding and strange, etched into people's brains, and then a film about him, played by ... who? Someone like, like, not Clint Eastwood, no, he's too old now, who? Me, of course, that's where I should be. There. The lone figure, the sky red. Soundtrack available.

He loaded the gun with number six shot and put it in with his fishing tackle. Then he went outside and climbed into his car and started driving north. He had the address in his pocket. It was a long shot. Ha! A long shot! That was good. He wouldn't think, he'd just do it. Why not? This time really go for it. Hadn't eaten in years, he suddenly realised, not since a hamburger last night, and his stomach was sick with hunger. He thought perhaps now it was not just the drink that was making him feel so ... what else had he had? The Thai, maybe, or what else, what else had he had? Something in all of it had formed an egg of darkness round him. And that was not his fault either. Old van's running well, he thought. Johnny Cash sang in his brain, on TV singing in San Quentin to all those rapists and murderers with ordinary faces who said that he was Mom and America and Apple Pie, or words to that effect. Johnny Cash sang:

> *Killed a man in Memphis,*
> *Just to see him die ...*

'Just to see him die,' sang Clyde.

He reached Mick Madden's as the first cocks were crowing in the darkness. A bunch of them were still up, sitting stoned out of their heads round the kitchen table. Bunches of herbs hung drying. The doors and windows were painted in bright picture-book primaries. Hundreds of battered paperbacks covered the walls. A big hare hung high from the ceiling under the stairs. The dogs, emaciated hounds with twitchy eyes and scarred noses, were used to such things and only occasionally glanced up at it with noble acceptance.

Mick lounged in front of a roaring fire, an old Irish hippy in abject dungarees and strikingly battered old homburg, doing his best to perfect the mountainy man look and succeeding. Mick sold poteen. 'Sure. How much?' he said, reaching under his vast armchair and pulling out what looked like an innocent bottle of lemonade.

'Just one,' said Clyde, discreetly drawing a note out of his breast pocket. Shit! Money lower than he'd thought. Need petrol. Turn the engine off, coast down hills, save that way. Get some more. How? Not here any more. Killybegs? Cork? 'Can I leave the dog here for a bit? I've got some business,' he said.

Mick shrugged. 'Taste it,' he said, 'go on, taste the stuff. Like swallowing golden light.' He got up and took a little pewter egg cup from a row of them that sat on a ledge above the fireplace, uncapped the bottle and poured. Clyde took it and drank and agreed that it was indeed like drinking golden light, that that was not a word of an exaggeration. His knob itched again, this time in a sudden spiteful burst; the Vigo whore came back into his mind, but he closed his eyes and drank the thought away. Then he asked for something to eat and someone brought him a plate of lukewarm vegetable stew. It was delicious and he wolfed it down, asked for more, wolfed that down, too, had another drop and was on his way, leaving Molly behind shaking with misery at his departure.

Mountains, glens, miles of fuchsia, valleys, hills, Mallow, where he filled up with petrol, Mitchelstown Creamery, Cahir: little towns going about their summer mornings. Dear old Ireland, never changing. Under the Rock of Cashel he stopped for a few moments and smoked a cigarette, took the gun out from his tackle bag and thereafter kept it brazenly beside him, thinking that he might, he really might, shoot any bastard cop that flagged him down, in the leg or something at least. His scalp felt hot and tight. From time to time he stole a mouthful of poteen as he drove. It was glorious heady stuff with a tang unlike any other spirit, and it made him proud and strong, inexorable. But no one challenged him. He was the pretty outlaw. No, he wasn't pretty, but he felt pretty, with his lips so hard and his cock so itchy, no one could catch him, he was invisible, riding the lonely boxcars, onwards, onwards, the radio playing, gliding onwards with his lonely power, the power of death. He felt like God.

He reached Dublin around ten. Somewhere in a grey suburb he stopped and stuck the gun down among the fishing rods again. The address was near the centre of town. He wasn't too sure of Dublin, just kept heading in, sweat forming on his upper lip, floating this way and that vaguely in the expected direction, here and there, round and round and − my God, my God, the traffic, the Guards, Christ, even soldiers, and millions of faces. Christ, he needed out of here − round and round and round saying, keep your head, boy, just keep your head, lips dried out, dying for another drink till suddenly after what seemed like hours he came to his senses and went into a filling station and bought a map.

It was just round the corner. He smiled and his heart began to thump. God was on his side.

It was one side of a terraced square, posh but slightly seedy. Of course there was nowhere to park, and God, my God, God was laying it all out, making everything clear, there was the big green car pulled up against some railings. That frightened him badly. He shivered in the sun. What am I doing? he thought for a moment, bewildered, why am I here? and went round and round in circles hopelessly looking for somewhere to park. After half an hour of sweating and swearing he sneaked in somewhere miles away, had a long sweet pull on the poteen, got out and shouldered his tackle bag, paid the parking meter − how long? he was thinking, how long do I need? − and walked back with his map.

It was a dusty, leafy area full of heavy traffic. Remorseless, the great lorries and buses thundered by. Clyde hated it. Couldn't live like this again, he thought. Not now. It was the kind of area where nobody lived for very long, full of multiple doorbells and obscure-looking businesses up flights of steps. He found the square, saw the green car. There it was, number seventeen. The house had steps and a red door.

The sun blazed. He stood on the steps in a state of delightful trembling. There were four bells and a heavy brass knocker like a plaited ring. The door was not locked and opened silently when he pushed it. How easy it was. Anyone could do it. Little thrills of delight ran down his scalp. It was dim and stale in the wide hall. Heavy rock music throbbed up from the basement and there was radio talk on this floor. Plenty of noise, good. Flat Four. Two. Three. Must be upstairs. He tiptoed up the creaking staircase and stood on a wide landing with no carpet and a great big mirror in which he saw himself, a small grey cruel slip of a thing, and was pleased. There was only one door up here and it had no number on.

Knock on it, go on.

He got out the gun. That felt better. He needed a shit. And if it wasn't them he'd shoot anyway, aimless and random as death itself, he'd gone this far. Just to see ... Clyde knocked but no one came. He knocked again. Still no one came. He was enraged, wanted to shoot the door, kick it down, trash whatever was inside ... but instead he knocked one more time.

The door opened and Bob Sawle stood there. He looked older, stupider, smarter and more boring, like a bank clerk or something. Clyde pushed the gun at him immediately, stepped in and closed the door behind him. His fear was like a magic wolfskin, conferring power. He had to go through with this, all choice had been taken away. They'd act out some awful disbelieving scene, they'd all play their parts. Bob just stood there looking at the gun stupidly, his expression one of profound disappointment more than anything else. Clyde pushed him with the gun, motioning for him to back up into the doorway he'd just emerged from.

'Not in there, not in there,' Bob said, never taking his eyes from the gun. But of course he had to go in. With a gun you can make anybody do anything. Marie was sitting on the end of a rumpled red bed with one foot stuck underneath her, all done up in this short skirt with ankle boots. She looked good, he supposed, nothing like Marie Mullen. Poor old Con. She looked up and saw Clyde, jumped up and stared but didn't say a word. Then she looked at Bob, still mesmerised by the gun.

'Marie,' Bob said uncertainly.

'Shut up,' said Clyde, levelling the gun.

'Clyde!' Marie shouted.

'Shut up.' He swung it on her.

She gave a kind of shudder as if someone had just thrown cold fish over her.

'Over there,' said Clyde, motioning with the gun. Bob went

over to her and they put their arms round each other quite automatically, like children, watching him with empty faces. Shoot. Shoot.

The flat was a rich mess and stank of sex. There was a fat bundle of ten pound notes and some change lying on the windowsill, just dumped there. Clyde stirred the air with the point of the gun.

'Is Con with you?' Marie asked.

'Shut up.' Shoot. Now. One. Two.

He made them sit down on the end of the bed, then he went and stood over them, gritting his teeth and trying not to laugh, pressing the muzzle of the gun into Bob's right temple so hard that the skin turned white. She made a peculiar chesty sound and drew back. 'If you move,' he said to her, 'I'll kill him, and if he moves I'll kill you.'

Nobody moved.

Marie began to cry quietly. Sawle looked as if he was going to be sick. Clyde cocked the gun. Sawle closed his eyes and drew back his lips. 'Oh God,' he said, 'oh God, oh God,' and sobbed in terror.

Clyde took the money from the windowsill on the way out.

He pulled into a layby somewhere in the midlands and thought he must sleep for a little bit or he'd crash the damn car, but as soon as his eyes closed he jerked awake, sweating.

Suddenly the cars going by were enemies. They'd be after him. He was going down. Life. Oh God, he was going down! His fingers shook as he drew the gun out of the tackle bag and he laughed guiltily. Not many could say they'd done that: wanted man, face on a poster. He laughed. Christ, he told himself, what are you making such a fuss about? You've only shot someone. People do it every day. Then he thought that his soul was damned and wondered what that meant and felt terror consume him in great fiery tongues and hardened himself to it, as he had to. Christ, he had to get his brain sorted out.

He wanted the West, the wild, wild West, the only place for a man like him. Clean his brain with that good clear air at last. He had a drink of the poteen, wiped his soaking brow with his cold hand and drove on till he found a little town, a shop, a Post Office, got out and bought a pie and some cigarettes and half a dozen bars of chocolate, whole nut. No one batted an eyelid, he could have been anyone. No one challenged him. Perhaps after all he hadn't done it. Perhaps he was safe. But everything felt somehow as if it had changed so he guessed that he must have done it. In the car he ate the food in about three minutes flat and drove on feeling sick. From time to time he glanced down at the gun lying across the passenger seat: 'Zap!' he said. 'Blam blam blam. Dadadadadadadadada ...' meandering in dreams as he drove, besieged in, in, damn these houses, useless for sieges, front and back doors ... in the beach house, only one door to cover, and he was demanding, what?

> *Was it me who shot him down in the cantina?*
> *Was it my hand that held the gun?*
> *Come, let us fly, my Magdalena,*
> *The dogs are barking and what's done is done.*

Sometime in the afternoon, wild-eyed with lack of sleep, he reached Mick Madden's. Molly and the other dogs rushed to greet him, Molly with sycophantic joy. 'What you been up to, man?' Mick Madden asked him. Clyde looked mysterious and said he'd just been about. The hanging hare was getting high. He couldn't face the poteen they offered and fell asleep in a corner of the room, sleeping for so long that when he awoke all the people had gone and he was lying alone on the rug with Molly. A black cat had sneaked in under his armpit and a blue dawn was looking in at the little window.

He sat up, raided the breadbin and finished off some old soda bread, hauled his tackle bag and went outside and stood about watching the light come up. The clear weather had gone and a warm comforter of mist covered everything. A soft day. Molly peed and shook herself, running gratefully about the yard. 'Come on,' he said, opening the car door. She dived in. 'Home!' she seemed to sigh as she sank down in the back with a grunt.

He was in Strangarvan by nine, catching the tail end of the Fleadh. The town was full of hungover people, the bars full of others who'd never gone home, who'd fallen asleep under tables and behind counters. No one looked strangely at him. One or two people said hello just as if nothing had happened. A sudden icy sweat burst out all over him like a cold shower. Getting ill. Early as it was, the loudspeakers in the square coughed into life and played 'When You and I Were Young, Maggie'. Clyde went to his shed in the back road, looked around at the narrow straw mattress, the candle wax, the single calor gas ring. It was a vagrant's room. He put one or two things into the van and stood there, leaning on the roof, thinking for a moment. The fact that they weren't after him didn't mean a thing: they just hadn't found the bodies yet.

He filled up the tank and drove out to Ballinaphuca. Perhaps he'd finish it off, he thought, wipe Ballinaphuca off the face of the earth. Bang! Bang! Bang!

The great sweep of the valley appeared, dusty with mist. Oh to be up there on the mountain with the old dog at his heels, just him and the dog and the gun and the mountain, real life. He loved this place but it had let him down. *They* had let him down. He roared into the village, come and get me, come and get me, you'll get a bullet in the head, I've already done it, I could do it again easily.

He parked outside the shop, went in and got himself a giant block of whole nut. Mrs Davy served him cheerfully, talking about the Fleadh and the weather and the new paint job they were doing on the old schoolhouse. He went out. There was Tommy tinkering with a car engine, Barney Mac in his long leather apron driving along his two stubborn red bullocks, flicking their rumps with a thin switch.

It was uncanny, you'd think nothing had ever happened. But something had. Fear came up in his throat like a stone and he couldn't get rid of it. Worse, he didn't know what he was afraid of: his heartbeat, the foghorn baying, this mist oddly descending from Rossa. It was just one of those times when he got scared, really scared, and he never knew what he might do when he got like this. His soul was smarting.

He'd go and see Rosanna. Time for an end to all this holy miracle stuff. Times like this, she always came through. They could go and hole up somewhere for a few days and get back to some kind of normal. He got back in his car and drove out past

Con's place and turned down past the Virgin Mary to Rathmeelabo, down the snakey lane to the parking place from which a little track led down to Padraic's front door.

He took his tackle bag and walked down with his shoulders hunched and his hands in his pockets, feeling like Bob Dylan on the cover of *Freewheelin'* but without the girl. A great sheaf of wild flowers stood in one of the windows of the house and a broom leaned up against the open door. Chickens pecked the cracks between the flagstones. He called but no one answered so he went round the back.

Rosanna was sitting on a kitchen chair in the doorway, sewing away at some old cloth. Her thick fingers protruded from black fingerless gloves and her hair stuck out all round her head. She was like some spectral crone sitting there in the pale mist. Clyde went to the water barrel and dipped in a hand and splashed water over his head. 'So how's it going?' he asked.

Rosanna smiled. 'Come in, come in, my old true love,' she said, never slowing in the long sweeping movements of her sewing, 'and how are you?'

'Where's Padraic?'

'There.'

He followed her eyes. Padraic was high upon the hillside with his horse and dogs, a mile or two away.

'How long is he away for? Come on, Rosanna, what's been going on? What's all this?' He indicated her hands. 'How did you work it, Rosanna? Go on, how did you work it? I know you're mad but you've really gone to town with this one.' He came and squatted down beside her, looking at the side of her face. She was homely and familiar to him, getting old now with the loose skin under her chin and the wrinkles in the corners of her eyes, but she was still rather striking in a bashed about kind of way. He reached out and started caressing her breasts roughly, squeezing and pulling at them. They were small and weak and defenceless. He didn't know why he was doing this, habit, he supposed. Rosanna pushed him gently away and the touch of her gloved hands made him shiver.

'Not any more, Clyde, my love,' she said. 'Not any more. I can't.'

He couldn't hide his desperation or revulsion, picking at her as if she were a bird he was plucking. 'Are you fucking that old man?' he asked. 'Are you that revolting?'

She turned her head and looked him square in the face. Her eyes were milky and for one horrible moment he thought she'd gone blind. 'Of course not,' she said. 'What do you think I am?'

'A nutter.'

'True,' she said. 'Take your hands off me, Clyde, I'm protected by Jesus.'

'Oh, don't be stupid!' Clyde got up jerkily, scared, and walked about. She went back to her sewing. He couldn't stand all this kind of thing, he ought to knock her about a bit, knock it all out of her. 'You stop this now, Rosanna,' he scolded, 'you just get your head back together. You'll go mad if you stay here, you're going mad now.'

She gave a stupid laugh. Madness frightened him. He started trembling again. 'I'm going up-country,' he said. 'I'm on the run. I committed armed robbery. Are you coming?'

'Armed robbery?' She looked interested.

'Oh Christ, Rosanna,' he said, making fists. 'I think I killed someone.'

'Who?'

'I don't know. Bob Sawle, I think. Maybe Marie.'

'You're dreaming.'

Of course, he was dreaming. The mist was hypnotic. 'I've got to lie low for a bit. Up-country. Come on, we can get your stuff from Anagar. Come on, Rosanna, you can't just hang around here. This has gone far enough.'

'I'm staying here.'

'For God's sake!'

'What about these?' She held up her hands and he flinched a little. 'I need looking after. It's clean here.'

'They're not real,' he said bitterly. 'You've just thought them there with your mind, that's all you've done, you can just think them away again.'

He hated the smile she had, this slavering imbecile smile. 'You'd dump me somewhere,' she said.

'So? What do you expect out of life?'

She laughed at that.

'Come on, the poor old sod's not expecting you to stay anyway. He could do without it, you know.'

But she just went on sewing, smiling that irritating smile. He came and gripped her shoulders and looked into her face. 'Are you in? Are you still in there?' He tapped on her forehead with his knuckles. 'For God's sake, listen to me. Listen. This is a nightmare. I don't know which I am. Did I or didn't I? Do you understand?'

'What's the matter, Clyde?' she asked sweetly. 'Are you getting a conscience in your old age?'

'No, but I need to know,' he said. He was in deadly earnest.

'God's watching you, Clyde,' she said. 'He's watching you now, all the time, loving you in spite of it all, Clyde.'

He couldn't take it. 'What are you talking about?' he cried. 'When are you finishing with this stupid charade? Oh, stop all this shit, I can't stand it!'

'And the devil, he's watching too, Clyde. The devil lives on Anagar. He's in the barn.'

Clyde felt his every hair stand on end. He shook her. 'Stop it, Rosanna. Stop it! You're worth more than this, you don't have to go mad like this. Come with me now before it gets any worse. Rosanna, come on, will you? Just come on.' He was furious. She was possessed and he wanted her back, but not this Rosanna. He wanted the old, stupid, pissed Rosanna. 'I don't want to go on my own this time,' he said.

'Not my choice now, you see, Clyde,' she said. It was hardly even her voice.

'You are off your tiny trolley,' he said, his eyes tragic. 'Oh God, you've gone, Rosanna, you have finally gone. This is terrible. Terrible!' He hit the wall and spun round. The chickens scattered.

'Don't frighten my chook-chooks,' she said mildly.

'You don't believe all this shit! You don't believe it!' Clyde thundered and paced and shook his fists at the ground. 'It's all fake! I hate all that stuff! It doesn't mean a thing. What are you doing? What are you doing, woman, for Christ's sake!'

She went on sewing, but her fingers trembled a little.

'Look at me. Look at me,' he said. 'I'm shaking. Here. Touch my hand. You can come with me. Come with me, Rosanna, don't you understand what I'm saying? Come back to real life, Rosanna – ' But she shook her head. 'Want to play martyr, cunt?' he asked. 'Want it for real?' He got out his gun and took aim at her face, just like in the good old days.

'I'm not playing any more, Clyde,' she said. He saw her swallow. Then she looked up at him and he saw in his sights the shine of her eyes and teeth and was suddenly in mortal fear that she'd start bleeding from the eyes, the way he'd heard some of them could. A horror vision flicked into his brain.

'I put a spell on you,' she sang slowly, 'because you're mine . . .'

Clyde turned and ran, the nape of his neck crawling.

He drove back through the village, past the strand, the unused beach house where he used to live with Rosanna, his favourite car wreck of West Cork, the few tents pitched here and there around the bay, out along the coastal lane where long flowering meadows rippled for a mile above high cruel cliffs, to Ballinaphuca Point. He used to hunt here with Molly. One more time, he thought, and left the car in a layby and walked down to the cliff's edge and stood there looking at the cormorants hunching on the needle rocks.

Molly nosed around one of her old favourite warrens. Small yellow flowers trailed about his feet. The sea was wild and a fine spray spattered him where he stood. The foghorn still bayed. His fear grew, became terror, so that he trembled as he looked back at the valley, the peaceful smoke from the chimneys, the sheep here and there, the road rising over Miley's Gap and people going about their business, putting out to sea, driving cattle, cooking food, changing babies, getting drunk. They'd left him out. All of them, everywhere, had left him out. But he could blast them all to kingdom come if he wanted to.

He was weak. His knees gave way and he sat down. Clyde wept by the sea's edge. 'I didn't do it!' he said, 'I didn't do it, I didn't do it,' and realised that he was crying with relief because he knew now beyond a doubt that he had not done it, because he remembered now their two bowed necks and that he had just turned round and walked out, taking the money, thinking that in a funny sort of way he'd just brought them closer together.

So much for that.

He walked back to the car and sat in it for a while. He'd keep the gun; it was still an option. Molly panted in the back. He was going up-country for a long, long time. He thought of all the other places he could go to, oh yes, many places, many people, on the road again, on the road. Maybe get a rabbit, gut it, light a fire somewhere, half for Molly raw, the rest on a stick, eat it. He turned the key and sat there with the engine idling for a while.

Faretheewell, sweet Ballinaphuca by the sea.

Eventually he drove off up the north road, passing Barney Mac with his black dog at his heels. Unsmiling, they saluted each other. A little further on a gang of men mixed cement in a clearing at the side of the road, something to do with a new picnic area. Every car was a mild diversion. They watched him go by, noted the direction, the time, that kind of thing. Then they looked back to their work.

'Turn it east,' said Paddy Bawn.

A Selected List of Fiction Available from Mandarin

While every effort is made to keep prices low, it is sometimes necessary to increase prices at short notice. Mandarin Paperbacks reserves the right to show new retail prices on covers which may differ from those previously advertised in the text or elsewhere.

The prices shown below were correct at the time of going to press.

☐	7493 1352 8	**The Queen and I**	Sue Townsend	£4.99
☐	7493 0540 1	**The Liar**	Stephen Fry	£4.99
☐	7493 1132 0	**Arrivals and Departures**	Lesley Thomas	£4.99
☐	7493 0381 6	**Loves and Journeys of Revolving Jones**	Leslie Thomas	£4.99
☐	7493 0942 3	**Silence of the Lambs**	Thomas Hams	£4.99
☐	7493 0946 6	**The Goldfather**	Mano Puzo	£4.99
☐	7493 9605 9	**Fear of Flying**	Erica Jong	£4.99
☐	7493 1221 1	**The Power of One**	Bryce Courtney	£4.99
☐	7493 0576 2	**Tandia**	Bryce Courtney	£5.99
☐	7493 0563 0	**Kill the Lights**	Simon Williams	£4.99
☐	7493 1319 6	**Air and Angels**	Susan Hill	£4.99
☐	7493 1477 X	**The Name of the Rose**	Umberto Eco	£4.99
☐	7493 1931 3	**The Ex-Wives**	Deborah Moggach	£4.99
☐	7493 0581 9	**Daddy's Girls**	Zoe Fairbairns	£4.99

All these books are available at your bookshop or newsagent, or can be ordered direct from the address below. Just tick the titles you want and fill in the form below.

Cash Sales Department, PO Box 5, Rushden, Northants NN10 6YX.
Fax: 0933 410321 : Phone 0933 410511.

Please send cheque, payable to 'Reed Book Services Ltd.', or postal order for purchase price quoted and allow the following for postage and packing:

£1.00 for the first book, 50p for the second; **FREE POSTAGE AND PACKING FOR THREE BOOKS OR MORE PER ORDER.**

NAME (Block letters) ....

ADDRESS ....

....

☐ I enclose my remittance for ....

☐ I wish to pay by Access/Visa Card Number ☐☐☐☐☐☐☐☐☐☐☐☐☐☐☐☐

Expiry Date ☐☐☐☐

Signature ....

Please quote our reference: MAND